The Fleur de Sel Murders

ALSO BY JEAN-LUC BANNALEC

Murder on Brittany Shores
Death in Brittany

The Fleur de Sel Murders

-->* **A BRITTANY MYSTERY** *<--

Jean-Luc Bannalec

Translated by Sorcha McDonagh

Minotaur Books
New York

THE FLEUR DE SEL MURDERS. Copyright © 2012 by Verlag Kiepenheuer & Witsch, Cologne/Germany. Translation copyright © 2017 by Sorcha McDonagh. All rights reserved. Printed in the United States of America. For information, address St. Martin's Press, 175 Fifth Avenue, New York, N.Y. 10010.

www.minotaurbooks.com

Designed by Devan Norman

The Library of Congress has cataloged the hardcover edition as follows:

Names: Bannalec, Jean-Luc, 1966– author.
Title: The Fleur de Sel murders : a Brittany mystery / Jean-Luc Bannalec.
Other titles: Bretonisches Gold. English.
Description: New York : Minotaur Books, 2018. | First published May 2014 as
    Bretonisches Gold by Verlag Kiepenheuer & Witsch, Cologne, Germany.
Identifiers: LCCN 2017045698 | ISBN 9781250071903 (hardcover) |
    ISBN 9781466883130 (ebook)
Subjects: LCSH: Murder—Investigation—Fiction. | LCGFT: Detective and
    mystery fiction.
Classification: LCC PT2662.A565 B74513 2018 | DDC 833/.92—dc23
LC record available at https://lccn.loc.gov/2017045698

ISBN 978-1-250-30837-5 (trade paperback)

Our books may be purchased in bulk for promotional, educational, or business use. Please contact your local bookseller or the Macmillan Corporate and Premium Sales Department at 1-800-221-7945, extension 5442, or by email at MacmillanSpecialMarkets@macmillan.com.

First published May 2014 as *Bretonisches Gold* by
Verlag Kiepenheuer & Witsch, Cologne, Germany

First Minotaur Books Paperback Edition: March 2019

10 9 8 7 6 5 4

à L.

To get to know someone,
you need to go through seven sacks of salt together.

—BRETON SAYING

The Fleur de Sel Murders

The First Day

The *fleur de sel* gave off a curious fragrance of violets in the days after the harvest; it mingled with the smell of rich clay and the salt and iodine in the air that people here in the middle of the White Land—the Gwenn Rann, the far-reaching salt marshes of the Guérande—smelled and tasted more strongly with every breath than anywhere else on the coast. Now, at the end of the summer, the distinctive scent filled the salt gardens. The old *paludiers*, the salt farmers, used to say that it made people faint sometimes, that it caused mirages and hallucinations.

It was a breathtaking, bizarre landscape. A landscape of the four elements needed for the alchemy of the salt: sea, sun, earth, and wind. Once a large bay, then a lagoon, a mudflat, a marsh put to good use by skilled hands, it was situated on a peninsula created by the raging Atlantic Ocean between the Loire and the Vilaine. The majestic little medieval town of Guérande, from which the area took its name, marked the northerly reaches of the salt gardens. In the south the gardens tailed off into the remaining part of the lagoon, and beyond that lay Le Croisic, with its enchanting port. You could see it from there, that impressive spectacle: with its mighty tidal rhythm, the Atlantic filled the lagoon with water, carrying it right into the delicate capillaries of the salt gardens. Especially on days when the *"grande marée"* happened, the spring tide following the full moon.

The White Land was completely flat, without a hint of a slope. For more than twelve centuries, it had been broken up into countless large, small, and very small rectangular salt ponds, laid out with mathematical precision and in turn bordered by random-looking fluid shapes made up of ground and water. An endlessly branching, elaborate system of canals, reservoir pools, preheating pools, evaporating pools, and harvesting pools. A system with just one purpose: to keep the sea moving as slowly as possible using sluice gates so that the sun and the wind made it evaporate almost entirely, until the first crystals formed. Salt was the purest essence of the sea. "Child of the sun and wind," people called it. The pools had poetic names: *vasières, cobiers, fares, adernes, oeillets*. One of the *oeillets*, the harvest pools, had been in use since Charlemagne's time. The harvest pools were sacred to the *paludiers*—everything depended on them, on their "character": the floors of the pools, the different types of clay and the various mineral compositions. Lazy, generous, cheerful, feverish, sensitive, harsh, contrary—the *paludiers* talked about them as if they were people. That's where the salt was cultivated and harvested in the open air. White gold.

Incredibly narrow, unpaved paths meandered between the pools, creating inextricable labyrinths, generally accessible only on foot. The salt marshes may have been flat, but you still couldn't see very far. Overgrown earthen walls of varying heights ran alongside the pools and pathways. Scraggy bushes, shrubs, tall grasses crooked and bleached strawlike by the sun. A gnarled tree here and there. And the *cabanes,* the salt farmers' huts made from stone or wood or metal sheeting, were scattered about.

Now that it was September, that dazzlingly bright white was all around. The white of the salt that had been piling up into impressive mounds over the summer. It lay in careful heaps, narrowing to peaks like volcanoes and sometimes two or three meters high.

Commissaire Georges Dupin from the Commissariat de Police Concarneau couldn't help smiling. This landscape was surreal. Amazing scenery. The atmosphere was heightened by the overabundance of color in the sky and the water—an extravagant display of every shade of violet, pink, orange, and red—caused by the setting sun. And as the late-summer evening slowly closed in, a refreshingly brisk breeze picked up at the end of another baking-hot day. Commissaire Dupin locked the car, one of the force's official blue, white, and red cars. The impressively old and problematically small Peugeot 106 served as the commissariat's general backup car. Dupin's own dearly beloved, equally ancient Citroën XM had been at the garage for ten days. It was the hydropneumatic suspension, for the umpteenth time.

Dupin had parked at the side of the road, half on the grass. He'd walk from here.

It was a narrow little road that meandered through the salt marshes, but at least it was paved. It had not been easy to find. Branching off the Route des Marais, it was one of only three winding roads between Le Croisic and Guérande town that cut across the Salt Land.

Dupin looked around. There was nobody in sight. He hadn't met a single car on the entire Route des Marais. In the salt marshes, it seemed the day had come to a close.

He had only a hand-drawn sketch of the place he was trying to get to. It showed a hut near one of the salt marshes, toward the open lagoon, about three hundred meters away. He would search the salt mine in question and the huts linked to it, keeping an eye out for "anything suspicious"—he had to admit it was all a bit vague.

Once he had taken a look around, he'd head straight for Le Croisic. Dupin figured this was how it would go: after a brief and likely fruitless inspection of the area, he would be in Le Grand Large a quarter of an hour from now, eating Breton sole fried a golden brown in salted butter. And over a glass of cold Quincy he would be looking out at the water, the pale sand and turquoise of the lagoon, watching the last of the light gradually disappear in the west. He had been in Le Croisic once before, last year, with his friend Henri, and had great memories of the little town (and of the sole).

Regardless of the fact that the reasons he was here were extremely vague, dubious, and downright ridiculous, Commissaire Dupin was in a decidedly good mood this evening. In fact, he had had an overwhelming urge to get outdoors again at last. He had spent five weeks—more or less every single day—in his stuffy, airless office. Five weeks! Kept busy with mind-numbing desk work, official paperwork, the usual trappings of bureaucracy—the tasks that, unlike in books and films, filled the life of a real commissaire over and over again: new patrol cars for his two inspectors were accompanied by new "Regulations for the Use of Vehicles Allocated for the Fulfillment of Police Duty," eight hundred pages long, with nine-point type and practically no line spacing, it was "extremely important," with a "number of crucial reforms" according to the prefecture; a raise for his ever-patient secretary Nolwenn (finally!)—he had been fighting for it two years and nine months; painstaking filing for two old, trivial cases. This was a record for him since he had been "relocated" from Paris to the middle of nowhere: five weeks of office work during these magical late-summer days, when September's enchanting light outshone every other month yet again. Weeks of a settled, spectacular Azores high, like something out of a picture book, not a drop of rain—*"La Bretagne fait la cure du soleil,*" Brittany is getting the sunshine treatment, the newspapers reported. Five weeks in which Dupin's bad mood had worsened on an almost daily basis. It had become unbearable for everyone.

Lilou Breval's request that he take a look round the salt marshes—although he had absolutely no connection with this area—had been a welcome excuse to really get out and about. Dupin didn't mind what excuse it was in the end. And much more important: he had owed Lilou Breval a favor for a long time now. The journalist from the *Ouest-France* stayed away from police officers on principle—not least because she came into conflict with police and legal regulations on a less than infrequent basis with her largely unorthodox methods—but somehow she had come to trust him. Dupin respected and liked her.

Lilou Breval had provided him with "certain information" from time to time. She had last "helped" him two years ago during the case of the murdered hotelier in Pont-Aven that had ended up capturing France's attention. Lilou Breval was not that involved with everyday journalistic work, specializing instead in large-scale research and stories, mostly very Breton stories. Investigative ones. Two years ago she had played quite a significant role in uncovering a colossal case of cigarette smuggling: 1.3 million cigarettes had been hidden in an enormous concrete pillar that had supposedly been built for an oil rig off the coast.

Lilou Breval had called Dupin the night before and—something she'd never done before—asked him to do something: to take a look at "a particular salt pond and a hut nearby." Look out for "suspicious barrels" there, "blue plastic barrels." Apparently she couldn't say what this was about yet, but she was "reasonably certain" that "something very fishy" was going on. She said she would drop in to the commissariat as soon as possible after he had inspected the area so that she could explain everything she knew so far. Dupin hadn't even begun to understand what this was all about, but after asking some questions that went unanswered he had eventually murmured "fine, okay" and Lilou Breval had faxed him a sketch of the paths and the area that morning. Of course Dupin knew that he was contravening every possible regulation, and on his way here he had felt a tiny bit uneasy, which was not usually his style. Officially, he wasn't even allowed to be here—he ought to have asked the local police to look into the issue. Not least because the Département Loire-Atlantique, where the salt marshes were located, was not even, from an administrative point of view, part of Brittany anymore—let alone "his patch"—ever since it had been snatched away from the Bretons "with legalized violence" during the much-maligned "Reform of Administrative Structure" in the sixties. Culturally, in daily life and in the consciousness of the French, however—and also in the rest of the world—the *département* was still Breton through and through to this day.

But his brief moment of doubt was soon forgotten.

Dupin owed Lilou Breval, and he took that very seriously. A good police officer depended on someone doing them a favor now and again.

* * *

Dupin stood next to his patrol car, towering over it with his generally sturdy build and broad shoulders. To be on the safe side, he glanced at the sketch again. Then he walked across the road and started down the grassy path. After just a few meters the first salt pools appeared to his right and left, the path falling sharply away right to the edges of the pools. A meter or a meter and a half deep, Dupin reckoned. The pools were all kinds of colors—pale beige, pale grayish, grayish blue, others were an earthy brown, reddish, all crisscrossed by narrow clay footbridges and dams. Birds strutted about round the edges, looking like they were on a silent search for food. Dupin had no idea what they were called; his ornithological knowledge was lacking.

The landscape was truly extraordinary. The White Land, it seemed, belonged to people only during the day, belonging entirely to nature again in the evening and nighttime. It was quiet, not a sound to be heard apart from an odd kind of chirping in the background, and Dupin couldn't tell whether it was coming from birds or crickets. It verged on the eerie. Every so often, a cranky gull screeched, an emissary from the nearby sea.

Perhaps coming here had been an idiotic idea after all. Even if he were to see something suspicious—which he wouldn't—he would have to let his local colleagues know immediately anyway. Dupin stopped walking. Maybe he should drive straight to Le Croisic and forget this cryptic mission. But—he had given Lilou Breval his word.

Dupin's deliberations were interrupted by his mobile ringing. It seemed even louder than usual in this meditative silence. He fished his small phone out of his pocket, his face brightening when he saw Nolwenn's number.

"Yes?"

"*Bonj*—aire.—there?" There was a small pause, then: "—air—And have—trip—kang—roo—?"

There was a terrible clicking sound on the line.

"I can't hear you, Nolwenn. I'm already at the salt marshes, I . . ."

"They—between the—I know—ly—kangar—"

Dupin could have sworn he had heard the word "kangaroo" for the second time. But he might have been mistaken. He spoke much more loudly this time.

"I—honestly—cannot—understand—a—word. I'll—call—you later."

"—just—ay—ter," and the connection seemed to drop altogether.

"Hello?"

No response.

Dupin didn't have a clue why Nolwenn was going on about an

Australian marsupial. It sounded preposterous. But he didn't agonize over it any longer. Out here in the back of beyond, Nolwenn was undoubtedly the most important person to him. And although he felt a little bit "Bretonized" by now, he would still be lost without her. In fact, Nolwenn's scheme was called "Bretonization," and came with the motto: "Brittany: Love it—or leave it!"

He thought highly of Nolwenn's practical and social intelligence as well as her inexhaustible regional and local knowledge. And her passion for oddities and "good stories." The kangaroo must be one of them.

Dupin had just started to refocus on the task at hand when his phone rang again. He answered automatically. "Can you hear me now, Nolwenn?"

For a few moments he couldn't hear anything apart from some more loud clicks.

Then suddenly there were a few reasonably comprehensible words: "I'm looking forward—morning, Georges. Really."

Claire. It was Claire. The line went bad again almost immediately.

"—aurant—ure—ning."

"I'm—I'm coming tomorrow evening. Yes, of course!"

There was a pause. Which was followed without warning by an earsplitting hiss. Tomorrow was Claire's birthday. He had booked a table in La Palette, her favorite restaurant in the Sixth Arrondissement in Paris. A great big boeuf Bourguignon with hearty bacon and young mushrooms, braised in the finest red wine for several hours, the meat so tender you could eat it with a spoon. It was meant to be a surprise, although he assumed that Claire had long since cottoned on because he had dropped far too many hints, as usual. He was going to catch a train at one o'clock and be in Paris at six.

"Did it seem—to come—betwee—! Is—ways—unclear?"

"No. No. Not at all. Nothing is unclear! I'll be there at six. I already have my ticket."

"I—barely hear—"

"Same here. I just wanted to say that I'm really looking forward to it. To tomorrow evening, I mean."

"—just—dinner."

"I've arranged everything, don't worry."

Dupin was speaking too loudly again.

"—fish—later."

This was pointless.

"I'll—call—you—later—Claire."

"—maybe—later—work—better—"

"Okay."

He hung up.

After meeting last year in those late-August days in Paris, which had been so wonderful, they began to speak on the phone every day and see a great deal of each other. It was mostly spontaneous, they just got on the TGV. Yes, they were back together. Although they hadn't said it out loud and it was still far from official. Although Dupin had made the awful mistake of mentioning it vaguely in an unguarded moment to his mother, who was immediately delighted, in a far from vague way, that she might now get to have that long-awaited daughter-in-law after all.

Claire had just been in the U.S., at a cardiac surgery training course at the famous Mayo Clinic. So they hadn't seen each other for seven weeks, although they had spoken on the phone a lot. That was definitely another reason why Dupin had been in such a bad mood recently. Claire had only been back two days now. And that was a large part of the reason for Dupin's good mood today. But he was a bit nervous. In general. He didn't want to mess up what he had with

Claire again, not like he had done the first time round. He had even bought the train ticket three weeks ago to make sure that nothing could get in the way.

He would call Claire back from Le Croisic very soon. And talk to her again about tomorrow in peace and quiet. Right after the sole.

He would be quick here.

Commissaire Dupin was pretty sure he had seen someone close to the wooden hut. Only briefly, for a split second. More of a shadow really; it had disappeared again instantly.

The commissaire slowed his pace. He scanned his surroundings. He was about twenty meters away from the hut. The path ran past it and looked like it plunged headlong into a salt pond.

Dupin came to a stop. He ran a hand roughly down the back of his head.

His instinct told him something wasn't right. He did not like this situation one bit.

He took another careful look around. Objectively, there was nothing that looked suspicious in any way. And what if it had just been a cat? Or another animal? Perhaps he had only imagined it. That was entirely possible in this atmosphere. Perhaps that beguiling scent, more intense this deep in the salt gardens, was beginning to have a hallucinatory effect.

Suddenly, out of nowhere, there was a hissing, a strange noise, metallic, high-pitched, and followed by a small, dull thud from close by. A flock of birds rose upward with loud squawks.

Dupin recognized the sound immediately. With a speed and precision that would have seemed unthinkable judging from his heavy build, he flung himself to the ground on the left, where the narrow strip of grass fell steeply away to a reservoir pool. He rolled away skillfully, turning so that he slipped into the pool legs and feetfirst, and found his footing. The water was about half a meter deep. Dupin drew his weapon—a SIG Sauer 9mm—and instinctively trained it on the hut. It was far from perfect cover, but it was better than nothing. The bullet had hit nearby, to his right. He couldn't tell exactly where it had come from, whether it was from the large hut or one of the smaller shacks nearby. He hadn't seen anything at all. Dupin's thoughts were racing. You didn't think in a normal way in a situation like this. Instead a hundred things mingled at once: bright, sharp observations, reflexes, instincts, and scraps of thought muddled together feverishly and produced what people vaguely called "intuition."

Dupin needed to work out where his assailant was. And hope that there was only one of them.

There were three sheds in his line of sight, all close together. The one closest to him was about ten meters away.

The shooter couldn't have been all that close, otherwise he wouldn't have missed his target.

Again the high-pitched noise—and another dull impact. Not far from him. And again. And once more birds took fright and rose screeching into the sky. Dupin slid lower into the pool, kneeling now with the water up to his stomach. A fourth one.

This time the bullet couldn't have missed him by more than a matter of centimeters. He felt something on his left shoulder. It felt as though the shots were all coming from one direction now. Then suddenly there was silence. Perhaps the assailant was trying to find a better position.

It was clear to Dupin that taking cover in the pool was not a solution. He had to do something. His thoughts were racing. He could only have the element of surprise on his side once. Hopefully. Just once.

He leapt out of the pool at lightning speed, pointing his gun toward where he believed the shooter was, firing again and again as quickly as the gun would allow. He stormed toward the closest hut as he did so. He had emptied the magazine by the time he got there. Fifteen shots.

Dupin took a few deep breaths. There was a deathly silence. The commissaire was curiously calm, as he always was when a situation was volatile. Still, a cold sweat had broken out on his forehead. He didn't have a second magazine with him. There was one in the glove compartment of his car, but not here. He had his mobile, but that was no use right now, although he should obviously try to file a report soon.

The hut he was now crouching behind was made from heavy-duty corrugated iron, but it was hard to tell how heavy-duty it was. And Dupin had no idea where the door was. Or whether it was unlocked. But it was probably his only chance. He was on one of the two longer sides of the hut. The most logical thing would be if the door was facing the path, which would mean it was to his left. He knew he didn't have long to think about it. And he would get exactly one attempt to make this move.

With quick, cautious steps, he moved to the corner, pressing himself right up against the iron sheeting. He paused for a moment. Seconds later he lunged around the corner with a sudden movement, saw a door, wrenched it open, flung himself inside, and slammed it shut again after him.

The whole thing took two or three seconds. Either the assailant hadn't seen Dupin or he had been caught truly off guard. The fact was, he hadn't opened fire.

It was pitch black in the hut. The last of the dim light was only coming in through gaps in the door.

Dupin gripped the door handle firmly. It was just as he had suspected: he couldn't lock the door from the inside. Dupin reached for his mobile—that was the most important thing now. Nolwenn's number was the second-to-last one on redial. The small screen lit up a surprising amount of the space in the hut. Dupin looked around swiftly. The front half of the hut was empty, and there were half a dozen large sacks and some kind of rods in the back half. He gaped at the screen again. He had no reception.

This couldn't be happening. No reception. Not a single bar. CONNECTION NOT POSSIBLE. The message on the screen was direct and unequivocal. He was used to this: here, at the end of the world, you were often cut off from the rest of the world, indeed. It was only in the large towns that you could occasionally get good reception. His radio must be in the car—next to the second magazine. In violation of every police regulation, Dupin seldom carried it on him. Perhaps he would have found a local officer on one frequency or another. He certainly could have found someone on the emergency frequency, but that didn't matter now: he didn't have it with him. And it was extremely unlikely anyone would happen to come past this secluded spot at this hour.

"Crap."

He had blurted this out far too loudly. A moment later there was a deafening, metallic sound and Dupin nearly dropped his phone. A gunshot. And another. A third. The same hellish noise each time. Dupin held his breath. He had no idea whether the iron sheeting could withstand the bullets. Especially if the shooter was clever and kept shooting at the same place. He couldn't make out any bullet holes yet. The sound of a bullet on the corrugated iron rang out again, and this time it was louder—the shooter seemed to be coming closer to the hut. Two more gunshots in quick succession. Dupin knelt down and propped one elbow on his knee, the heel of his hand wedged underneath the door handle. But even like this it would be difficult to stop someone opening the door. The leverage he had was much worse. He had to hope that the assailant would not dare to try the door for fear of an exchange of fire. All of a sudden there was a dull impact against the door. It wasn't a gunshot, but as if a massive object had slammed into the door, then a kind of loud scraping. The door handle rattled for a moment. Somebody was right outside the door, a few centimeters away from him. Dupin thought he could hear a quiet voice saying a few words but he wasn't sure. Then things went silent again.

Nothing happened for the next few minutes. It was nerve-racking. He didn't know what his assailant would do next and there was no way to find out. There wasn't a thing he could do, except hope that the person wouldn't try to storm the hut. The one thing he would surely guess was that Dupin's mobile didn't have good reception here and he wasn't able to call for help.

But it was very likely his assailant would look around and see the patrol car. Or else there was a patrol out on the road anyway and it would report the police car directly. It also depended on the scale of whatever was going on here.

Suddenly Dupin heard a car engine, not close to the hut, but not that far away either. He hadn't seen any cars on his way here. The engine was kept running for a while and nothing was happening. Then the car moved off. Dupin could hear it, muffled but unmistakable. What was happening? Was his assailant fleeing? He had achieved something. After a few more meters the car braked abruptly. Dupin waited for the sound of doors opening. But nothing happened.

Suddenly his mobile rang. Moving automatically, he reached for the device.

"Hello?" he barked, his voice low.

All he could hear was crackling and hissing.

"This is an emergency. I'm in the Guérande salt marshes. In a hut. I'm being fired on. My car is on a side road off the Route des Marais. I walked west along the gravel path from there. Hello?"

Dupin hoped that the caller would hear some of what he was saying and raise the alarm. But it was very unlikely.

"Hello? This is an emergency!" He was practically screaming now, without intending to. "I'm being shot at, I . . . ."

"—just calling to—table—eight o'clock."

Dupin didn't recognize the distorted voice. But the phrases "table" and "eight o'clock" had been oddly easy to make out. This was unbelievable. It must be La Palette calling about his reservation for tomorrow evening. Stéphane perhaps, the headwaiter, who knew it was always best to remind Dupin of his exact booking.

"A police emergency—please call the Commissariat Concarneau—Hello, Stéphane?"

The caller obviously hadn't understood a word. But Dupin had to make use of this phone reception, no matter how bad it was. For as long as it was still there at all. There was just one solitary bar. He quickly pressed the red button and then immediately hit redial for Nolwenn's mobile number. It was ringing. Dupin could hear it clearly. Once. Then the connection dropped. He tried again. No luck. He stared at the screen in disbelief: the solitary bar had vanished.

A moment later, he heard the car, whose engine had been running the whole time, driving away at speed.

Dupin put his mobile back on the ground. He had to keep an eye on the screen. But nothing happened.

The car was out of earshot now. It had left the salt marshes. Had there been just one assailant or were there two or perhaps more? If there had been more than one, had one stayed behind? And were they now simply waiting for Dupin to leave the hut? Were they laying a trap for him?

It would be too risky to leave now. He would have to stay put. He would have to keep on waiting in this stuffy hut, unable to do anything. The situation wasn't over yet.

* * *

It was a little after ten. Nothing at all had happened in the last half hour—it felt like it had gone on forever. Dupin had stayed in this unbelievable position, sweating more and more, switching between his left and right arms every two or three minutes to block the door handle. It wasn't long before everything hurt, then gradually he had lost all feeling in his hands, arms, and legs, and at some point he went numb throughout his body. All he could feel was the occasional sharp pain in a spot on his left shoulder. He reckoned the temperature inside the hut was over eighty-five degrees, and almost all of the oxygen seemed to have been used up.

He needed to get out of the hut. And there wasn't a single bar of reception on his mobile screen. He had to risk it. He had a plan.

Cautiously, he tried to press the door handle downward.

To no avail. It wouldn't budge. Not one millimeter. His assailant had jammed the door handle. So that was what those strange noises had been when someone was fiddling with the door. Something was wedged underneath the handle on the outside. Dupin shook the handle as hard as he could. Nothing moved.

It was stuck fast. And his assailant was probably miles away.

Dupin sank into a heap. He crawled slightly to the right and stretched himself out on the floor of the hut. He was upset about what was happening but also, he could sense now, relieved that the immediate threat seemed to be over.

He had lain there for perhaps a minute, trying to get some life back into his arms and legs, which had gone to sleep, and thinking about what to do next, when he heard a crack. Quite loud. Distinct. He was certain it hadn't been an animal.

Someone was out there. In a flash, Dupin moved back into his earlier position, securing the door. He heard a soft murmuring. He pressed an ear to the iron sheeting, straining extremely hard to hear what was happening outside.

For a minute or two, everything remained quiet. Then suddenly—

Dupin flinched—a loud, echoing sound cut through the night air: "This is the police. We've got the area surrounded. You must surrender immediately. We will not hesitate to make use of our firearms."

Dupin leapt to his feet. And almost fell over.

"I'm here. In this hut." He screamed and hammered on the door. "Commissaire Georges Dupin—Commissariat de Police Concarneau. I'm in this hut. Alone. The threat is over."

Dupin was about to call out again when he paused. What if this was a trick? Who could have alerted the police, anyway? A megaphone didn't prove anything. Why hadn't anyone responded to him? On the other hand, if it really was the police, his colleagues had to establish what the situation was first. They had to make sure that the danger had definitely passed.

A moment later the door handle gave a jerk.

"We've unblocked the door. Come out with your hands up and fully open. I want to see the palms of your hands. Nice and slow."

The tinny voice had come from some distance away at the same time as the door handle was being rattled, so there had to be at least two people.

Dupin thought for a moment, then called out: "Identify yourself. I need to be sure that you're really with the police."

The answer came right away. "I will do nothing of the kind. Come out now."

This response was probably the best proof possible.

"Okay, I'm coming."

"As I said: hands in the air and very, very slow."

"I'm Commissaire Georges Dupin, Commissariat Concarneau."

"Come on, then." The tone of voice was steely.

Dupin opened the door. A bright, clean-edged cone of light fell into the hut; it must have been one of those new high-power LED torches. He stayed where he was for a few moments to make sure he had got his balance back. A moment later he stepped calmly out of the hut, his right hand in front of his eyes, his mobile in his left.

"I need a working phone. I have to make a call immediately." He had to speak to Lilou Breval. Straightaway.

"I said, hands in the air. I—" The voice broke off. And then a person was coming toward him from the right.

"What are you doing here? What the hell is going on?" It was a woman's voice, somewhat rasping. Aggressive, but composed and not even very loud. "What happened here?"

Someone switched the torch beam from focused to diffuse and Dupin was able to take his hand away from his eyes.

An attractive woman was standing in front of him, tall, with shoulder-length, wavy dark hair and wearing a light gray pantsuit, a dark blouse, and elegant dark ankle boots with rather high heels. A half-drawn SIG Sauer in her right hand.

"Commissaire Sylvaine Rose. Commissariat de Police Guérande." She paused briefly, then said, emphasizing every syllable: "Département Loire-Atlantique."

"I have to make a call. Do you have a satellite phone?"

"Unlike the Commissariat Concarneau, we carry the necessary equipment when we're on duty. What are you doing here? What kind of unprofessional operation was this?"

Dupin checked himself at the last minute, just before he might have blurted out something gruff.

"I . . . Who informed you that I"—he broke off briefly—"that I'm here?"

"You have a waiter from Paris to thank for your rescue. The one who called you about your reservation tomorrow evening. He might not have been able to understand you, but thought he heard the word 'shot,' and as a *precaution* called the police in the sixth. And as a *pre-*

caution they called us. Apparently you're still remembered there; your departure must have been spectacular. And then as a *precaution* we stopped by." Suddenly, her tone of voice changed: "What are you doing in the salt marshes? How did you end up in this hut? What's going on? You are going to explain everything to me, right down to the last detail. You won't be making any calls beforehand. You won't be doing anything at all beforehand."

Dupin would have been impressed if a burning rage had not bubbled up within him in the previous hour, a rage that had eclipsed all other feelings, including the feeling of powerlessness, and the pain in his arms and legs and shoulder. He was furious—at his assailant, at the whole situation, but mostly at himself. He knew he had been an incredible idiot. He wanted to know who had shot at him! And what on earth was going on! He had the same questions as Commissaire Rose. But, apart from telling her what he'd seen, he would not be able to give any kind of answers. He needed to find out what Lilou Breval knew right now, whatever it was she hadn't told him yesterday.

"Give me the satellite telephone," he hissed.

"I will do nothing until you've told me everything." She could not have said this more calmly.

"I—" Dupin broke off. He understood where his colleague was coming from. He wouldn't have behaved any differently, but he didn't have time for all this. "What are you going to do, arrest me here?"

"I can't do that, unfortunately. But I will drive you to the hospital in Guérande right now. And not budge a millimeter from your side until I know everything. I'm not fond of shootings on my watch. We've seen a huge number of cartridges; it must have been quite the operation. I hope you're not making up your mind to slow down my investigation. The brass are going to love you as it is."

By now a dozen police officers had come into view, each armed with a heavy torch. It had been pitch dark for some time now. Two police cars had come down the path in quick succession and were almost at the hut. The scene was dazzlingly lit up by their headlights on full beam.

Dupin thought it over. Perhaps he should cooperate. This was not his jurisdiction. Nobody was listening to him. He couldn't achieve anything here by himself; he was dependent on this commissaire, for a start. No matter how difficult he found that.

"It was because of suspicious barrels here in the salt marshes. I was following up a tip from a journalist. Lilou Breval from the *Ouest-France*. When I arrived, somebody opened fire. I couldn't make anyone out; I don't know how many people there were or whether it was more than one person. I was able to take refuge in this hut. The assailant or assailants probably left the scene around nine thirty-five."

"What kind of barrels?"

"I don't know. Blue plastic barrels. That's why I need to speak to this journalist right now, only she can tell us—"

"You don't know? You got yourself into this grossly negligent situation because somebody told you to check out these barrels? Without having a clue what it might be about? In a *département* you have no business being in?"

"I have to use the phone."

"You have to go to the hospital."

"Why do you keep going on about a hospital?" Dupin's anger was returning.

Commissaire Rose looked doubtfully at him for a second, then turned aside and called in the direction of a policewoman who was just about to tackle the hut: "Chadron. Put out a search: one person. Maybe more. No clues as to their identity. We don't know what car they're in either. The only thing we know is this: a car drove away from the salt marshes around nine thirty-five P.M., direction and destination unknown. Pointless really, but put out the message anyway."

The policewoman pulled out a radio and the commissaire turned back to Dupin, clearly annoyed. "Let's go. Personally, I dislike circumventing important service regulations. You've been shot and I'm going to make sure you see a doctor. Due diligence."

"Shot?"

"Your left shoulder is bleeding."

Dupin held his left side and turned his head. His polo shirt was wet with sweat and water from the salt ponds. It wasn't easy to make it out in the light from the headlamps, but when you looked carefully, you could see it: the left side was a much darker color than the right. And he had occasionally—only occasionally, the adrenaline had acted as a powerful stimulant—felt that sharp pain. He hadn't thought about it any more than that and had put it down to his cramped position. He could see that the polo shirt between his forearm and shoulder was ruined. He grasped his arm there. Suddenly the pain got much worse. Sharp.

"Absurd," he said with conviction. The commissaire smiled at him for a moment and Dupin could not interpret what she meant. She spoke very softly and calmly, while looking him directly in the eye.

"You're in my world here, Monsieur le Commissaire. And here you are either someone who makes my life easier or someone who makes it harder. And I can assure you, you do not want to be someone who makes it harder."

She continued at a normal volume: "Come on."

Dupin wanted to protest.

Commissaire Rose looked to the sky, murmured "Should work," and turned to her colleague from earlier:

"I need a satellite phone. You take over here while I'm gone. I'm accompanying Commissaire Dupin to the hospital. Get in touch every time there's any news. No matter what it is. I want to know everything. Everything."

Dupin rubbed his right temple. Those last few sentences had sounded disconcertingly like the kind of thing he would have said.

Commissaire Rose was walking toward the farther car. "Let's go." She had shoved her left hand into her jacket pocket, leaving only the thumb peeking out.

Inspector Chadron brought over a phone that looked, with its enormous antenna in plastic casing, like a mobile from fifteen years ago, and held it out to him.

"Speak to your journalist on the way and then go over it all again, in detail," Commissaire Rose instructed him. Dupin got into the car after her. The salt marshes beneath the clear blue-black sky; the mounds of salt illuminated by the police cars' headlights; the flashing cones of light as the police officers walked around—it made a surreal scene.

A lot had happened since he had arrived. And nothing had come of that sole he'd wanted.

* * *

"I need a coffee. Double shot. And a phone. And you have to let my inspector in to see me."

"Ninety-seven over sixty-two. Your blood pressure is still very low. But your pulse is holding steady at around one forty. Symptoms of shock. And results of blood loss. Not a life-threatening condition, but we've got to—"

"I'm not in shock. I have low blood pressure generally. Inherited it from my father. I just need caffeine and everything will be okay again. Is the wound bandaged in a way that allows me to move around freely?"

"You shouldn't be moving at all for now."

The young, clearly not very sympathetic doctor whom Dupin had just spoken to for the second time had examined him when they arrived, after an inconvenient wait of more than twenty minutes in the ambulance. Commissaire Rose had stayed outside to make some calls.

At some point, another doctor had turned up who seemed to Dupin even younger and no less indifferent. She was given the vital information and brought him into a small room a few corridors away. It was a graze wound and it had nicked the muscle in a superficial way—harmless in itself, but he had lost a lot of blood. The doctor had given him a local anesthetic—he had vehemently refused a sedative—then thoroughly disinfected the wound, put in five stitches, and bandaged it up.

It was now midnight. He had used the satellite phone on the way to the hospital, trying to get through to Lilou Breval, but he was put through to voicemail each time, on both the landline and her mobile. He hated satellite phones. The antenna had to point directly upward when it was extended, which meant that he had had to sit in an unnaturally cramped position at the beginning of the trip, and the commissaire drove eye-wateringly fast. She made sure to emphasize that she was driving carefully because of his injury. And you also had to dial any number of prefixes first (he always forgot which ones), and quite apart from which, the sky couldn't be cloudy. Between frequent bouts of cursing about satellite phones and voicemail, he had eventually told Commissaire Rose everything he knew. Which amounted to nothing at all. She made no secret of the fact that she still didn't trust Dupin as far as she could throw him. And she still seemed to believe he was holding back some information. His whole story sounded, to put it mildly, not all that plausible.

Inspector Riwal, one of his two inspectors, had set out from Concarneau as soon as he'd heard what had happened. Dupin liked him a lot, even if he had odd moods every now and then. Riwal had made his arrival known to Dupin via an obliging nurse. The doctor had brusquely instructed the nurse, with reference to "clear and strict rules," not to let the inspector in to see the "injured man" under any circumstances, especially not during the "medical history."

"After the shock and the blood loss you should drink plenty of fluids. Water or herbal tea are best. No coffee or alcohol."

Dupin's feelings vacillated between despair and fits of rage.

"But I'm telling you, everything is fine. Let the inspector in to see me. It's about important police matters. I . . ."

From the corridor outside the treatment room came an aggressive voice. "That's enough! He's my only witness. He has been treated, his injuries aren't life-threatening, he's conscious. I'm going to see him now."

The door flew open and Commissaire Rose walked in with a nurse frowning in resignation behind her. The commissaire stopped in the middle of the room. "We've searched the whole salt marsh area. And we didn't find any barrels. No blue ones, yellow ones, or red ones. Not a single one. Not outdoors, not in the hut, not in the sheds. We didn't find anything suspicious at all. The forensics team is looking for any traces that the larger barrels might have been left behind. And for footprints, tire marks, and so on. I tried that journalist of yours again, but couldn't get through. She probably just went to bed hours ago."

Dupin was about to protest. He absolutely had to speak to Lilou. They needed to get hold of her as soon as possible. Commissaire Rose beat him to it, speaking as if he wasn't in the room:

"We still don't have the faintest bloody idea what's going on here. No matter how carelessly self-inflicted it might have been—a police officer came within an inch of being shot dead. In the middle of our salt marshes." Suddenly she looked fiercely at him. "Surely you must know or suspect something! You don't just go and risk serious disciplinary proceedings because some friend of yours found something suspicious somewhere. I don't buy it!"

It was impossible to tell whether Commissaire Rose had spoken angrily. But she spoke rapidly and very firmly.

"There must be something major going on." Dupin said this broodingly to himself, realizing that it wasn't a proper answer.

"Whatever it is, I'm not going to tolerate it. Not on my beat. An innocent person could have been caught up in it too."

Dupin was about to protest this time—very sharply—but at the last second he decided against it. And he was glad he had. He understood the commissaire. All too well.

Besides, he felt rather awkward with his upper body bare, sitting dirty and sticky on a hospital bed, with a bandage on his left shoulder and the cuff from the blood pressure monitor still around his upper arm.

"Do we know yet who owns the salt marsh?" Dupin had made an effort to strike a cooperative tone, and this seemed to have something of an effect.

"Of course we found out ages ago who owns the salt marsh where your exciting adventure played out. My colleagues are trying to get through to the owners and speak to the head of one of the cooperatives in the salt marshes—the salt marshes right next door belong to him. The same goes for the director of the Centre du Sel. She knows every single *paludier*. And every pool."

Dupin had just noticed, and this was really neither here nor there, but the commissaire's hair was in constant motion, even when she was standing still. And although it was difficult to imagine right now, deep laughter lines betrayed the fact that she could really laugh—and that, in theory, she must do it a lot.

"You let the commissaire in to see him; I'm going in too."

There was more hubbub from the corridor. Dupin recognized Riwal's voice. He had sounded very forceful.

"I haven't let anybody in to see the patient, that woman just stormed in earlier," whimpered a crestfallen voice. A moment later, Riwal was standing in the room too. A plastic cup in his right hand.

"I brought you a coffee, boss. Double shot. That's what it said on the button anyway. There's a vending machine in the waiting room."

Dupin wanted to hug his inspector, something he would never

actually have done, of course. He was just that happy to see him. And the coffee cup. It was a ray of light.

"Well done, Riwal."

Riwal came over and handed Dupin the cup with an almost ceremonial flourish.

Commissaire Rose acknowledged Riwal with a movement of her head. It was minimal but it was friendly and collegial.

"Inspector Riwal, Commissariat de Police Concarneau. This is a worrying incident."

Riwal had spoken with uncharacteristic calmness. It must have been the commissaire's influence.

"Absolutely. You can't shed any light on it either, I take it?"

"No. We just heard that our commissaire was involved in a shooting and had been wounded."

Dupin took a mouthful of the lukewarm coffee. It tasted horrible. And like plastic too. Not that it mattered. He was feeling better now. After arriving at the hospital, he had started to feel the strain of the previous few hours, a profound fatigue deep within his bones. Even though he was fighting it valiantly, he felt shattered—which he would never admit. He had been through shootings before, of course, in Paris, and a much crazier one at that—underneath a bridge outside the city, a large-scale car theft. And he had been shot once before during a hostage situation at the Gare du Nord, worse than today, in his forearm, but this was still tough.

"Do you know Madame Breval's home address, do you know where she lives?" Commissaire Rose put her right hand on her hip and her left back into the pocket of her jacket.

"Yes, I know where Lilou Breval lives. At the gulf. Near Sarzeau."

He had visited her there once during the case of the murdered hotelier.

Dupin drank the last mouthful of coffee, took off the blood pressure cuff, and stood up. At first he was dizzy, the world swaying around him, despite the coffee. He picked up the hospital-issue white doctor's T-shirt that the nurse had left out for him. His shoulder made putting it on very difficult, and the anesthetic seemed to be wearing off. The T-shirt was at least two sizes too big and Dupin was aware that he must look ridiculous. Even his jeans looked terrible, covered in dirt and bloodstains, but it didn't matter.

"About an hour from here. Let's go. Now that you've got something on." Commissaire Rose couldn't resist a smirk.

"Riwal. Could you get me something to eat from the vending machine? Anything—cookies, a chocolate bar, it doesn't matter what," Dupin said.

"All right, boss."

Dupin hadn't had anything to eat since lunchtime. His blood sugar was very low.

"And another coffee. Let's meet at Commissaire Rose's car."

Riwal was already out the door by the time Dupin finished speaking.

"Do you know where Lilou Breval works? Which of the editorial offices?" As before, there was a forcefulness to Commissaire Rose's questions and words.

"Officially speaking, she's with the editorial office in Vannes. But she mostly works from home, I think."

The *Ouest-France* was the largest daily paper in France—and together with *Le Télégramme* and *Le Monde*, constituted Dupin's routine daily reading. In fact, the *Ouest-France* was the Atlantic newspaper par excellence; it was published along the entire coast from La Rochelle upward, throughout Brittany, the Pays de la Loire, and also in Normandy. And it was available via local editorial offices in every big city.

"Perhaps one of her colleagues will know what story their friend is working on." Commissaire Rose had deliberately said "friend" with meaningful emphasis.

"I think that's unlikely."

Lilou was not the kind of person to do research in a team.

"You've got to sign here for me that you're leaving the hospital at your own risk." The indifferent doctor had been lingering in the background for the last few minutes, filling out various forms. "The standard treatment involves painkillers and then antibiotics for prophylaxis." He held out two packets to Dupin. "The painkillers will make you feel slightly woozy. So no alcohol."

Dupin took both packets, stuffed them into the pocket of his jeans, and left the room moments later. Commissaire Rose followed suit.

In no time, she had overtaken Dupin in the long corridor and was striding purposefully toward the exit. She had parked right in front of the emergency-room entrance.

Dupin stood still for a moment and breathed the mild summer night air in and out a few times. The hospital was on a slight hill right outside the town and he had a perfect view of the medieval, atmospheric Guérande from here—the contrast with the hospital's sterile, harsh lighting and functional new-build architecture could not have been more stark. Dupin found himself reminded of the Ville Close in Concarneau. There was something comforting about the way the colossal city walls and towers shone in the warm light.

Commissaire Rose was already at her car. A large, new, dark blue Renault Laguna. Dupin walked around to the passenger door.

"This was the only decent thing in the vending machine." Riwal had materialized next to Commissaire Rose's car and was holding out a packet of *bonbons caramel à la fleur de sel* and plastic cup to Dupin.

Dupin took them both gratefully. Salted caramel candy was not what he would have expected in a hospital, but obviously the local affinity for the Salt Land was huge. And he had to admit he loved those caramel candies, that bittersweetness with the flakes of salt.

"It's no sole, but still," he said.

Riwal looked at Dupin; his brow was furrowed and almost concerned. Commissaire Rose was already in the driver's seat, watching them impatiently. The air was doing Dupin good, as was the prospect of more caffeine.

"Riwal, you try the editorial offices in Vannes. And her colleagues at home, to be on the safe side. You'll still be able to get hold of newspaper staff." Even delegating tasks was helping, Dupin noticed. Everything was feeling a bit more normal now. "Have them give you the names and numbers of colleagues Lilou Breval worked with. And the editor in chief. Call everyone straightaway. And contact Kadeg, he's to come tomorrow morning and"—Dupin pondered for a moment—"he'll have to drive past our office first. There's a blue bag next to my desk. Tell him to bring it here."

Riwal knew the commissaire too well to ask questions when faced with these kinds of instructions. As Dupin briskly gave his orders, he climbed somewhat awkwardly—due to the shoulder injury and the coffee in his hand—into the car.

Once he was seated, Commissaire Rose leaned right over to him, as far as she could go, and said: "We're going to have the conversation with that journalist now, as soon as possible. You're going to be present for that, and after that—after that, you're out. Do you hear me? Then you're a witness on *my* case. And nothing more. I am the only person investigating. I mean that in a friendly and collaborative way, of course."

She spoke with perfect irony, sweetly, but she was not being sarcastic. It infuriated Dupin. But, objectively speaking, she did have everything on her side on this point, the police regulations and the law.

The smart thing was to stay silent.

In one fluid movement, Commissaire Rose started the engine and put her foot down hard on the gas.

* * *

It had taken them forty minutes, with flashing lights and sirens and speeding above every limit inside and outside residential areas, even on the smallest country roads. To Dupin's relief, they hadn't spoken much. The effects of the anesthetic were wearing off and the pain in his shoulder was getting worse. Dupin had taken one of the painkillers—he couldn't afford any weakness. And he'd eaten five of the salted caramels, which had done him a lot of good.

During the journey he had tried to get through to Lilou Breval numerous times; he was back on his mobile again—it finally had reception on this road. No luck. Commissaire Rose had looked strangely worried a few times, much more so than in the salt marshes earlier. Lilou Breval lived near Brillac, a few kilometers away from Sarzeau, right on the Gulf of Morbihan, one of the most enchanting parts of Brittany. Without any of the usual Breton exaggeration, Dupin truly thought it a wonder of nature. *Mor bihan* meant "small sea" in Breton: an inland sea linked to the "large sea"—the *mor braz*—by nothing more than a narrow passage through which the ocean surged in and out every day. It was dotted with hundreds of islands and islets—depending on the state of the tide—in the most fantastical shapes, just twenty of them inhabited. A calm sea, a few meters deep at high tide. At low tide, large parts of it were just centimeters deep or gone entirely. That's when the sea revealed kilometers of sandy, silty, or stony seafloor, with big tidal creeks and smaller ones, long dazzlingly white sandbanks as well as oyster and mussel beds. At high tide it looked as though the countless flat, thickly forested islands were floating on the sea, as though someone had launched them onto the water as carefully as boats. Romantic little woods with romantic names: The Wood of Sighs, of Lovers, of Sorrow, of Longing. A charming mixture of every shade of green and the blue of the tides and the sky in just as many shades.

Dupin's friend Henri, also a "Parisian in exile"—but who had at least married a Breton woman—owned a house on the Gulf of Morbihan, near the Port Saint-Goustan. Dupin had visited him there in June last year. He had stayed for seven days, his first days off in a long time, and he had loved it. And from there they had driven to Le Croisic too. The gulf was a world unto itself. Here, the Atlantic relinquished its terror, all of its roughness, tumultuousness, and violence, and became instead a tranquil still life. The gentle land that embraced it seemed to soothe it. But the sea was fully there. And determined everything. A particular climate dominated, which the Bretons proudly called "Mediterranean" or "subtropical." A lot of sunshine, luxuriant flora and fauna, mild, fertile. Dupin had been especially taken by the fact that there was a large reservoir for seahorses (he worshiped them almost as much as he worshiped penguins); the seahorse was also the logo of the national parks and bioreserves, because the gulf seahorse had been a protected species for years.

One of the first Breton lessons Nolwenn had taught Dupin went like this: "*La* Bretagne does not exist! There are many Bretagnes." The Breton landscape was so diverse and the differences, contrasts, peculiarities, and contradictions so great. And Dupin had realized she was right. That phrase contained perhaps the last and greatest of Brittany's secrets. And the gulf, for him, was the Brittany of summer sun, nonchalance, magnificent regattas, delightful bathing, and a leisure even the sea itself indulged in. The gulf was lovingly called the "kingdom of leisure."

During the drive, Dupin was reminded of the tragic legends about the birth of the gulf that Henri had regaled him with. The holy Forest of Rhuys had once stood on this spot—much like the rest of Brittany, it had been crisscrossed with holy forests—and this forest was home to the most wondrous fairy folk, from whom dozens of names and stories were still handed down to this day. Like villains, people began to clear the magical wood, to destroy the unique magical land, and thus drive away the fairies. They took off into the air. They cried bitterly. Their tears fell endlessly, drowning everything. In the depths of their grief, the fairies threw away their headdresses and from these, strewn with golden dust, came the beautiful islands. There were so many that there was one for every day of the year. The gulf was a sea of tears.

Lilou Breval's house—a remarkably narrow, old, beautifully renovated stone house—was in darkness, not a single light visible. It stood forlornly on a small promontory, the Pointe de l'Ours, the "Headland of the Bear." The sandy path ended here and then a few meters farther along, at the edge of the garden, the "small sea" began. So close. Lilou Breval lived alone, or it looked that way at least. Dupin had heard from Nolwenn that she used to be married, but she had been separated for years. Dupin had never heard of any new man. But that didn't mean anything, of course.

Commissaire Rose stopped right in front of the house. Dupin had undone his seat belt and opened the car door before she had even turned off the engine. Despite his injured shoulder—and with stabbing pains—he got himself out of the Renault in one smooth movement.

The first thing he was looking for was a car. He couldn't see one. Coming here had probably been all for nothing; it didn't look like Lilou was here.

"Let's ring the bell anyway. And: take this."

Commissaire Rose was standing directly behind him, he hadn't even noticed her. He turned around. She was holding out a magazine for the SIG Sauer. "In case of emergency only."

Dupin hesitated for a moment. Then he reached for his gun, took the magazine, inserted it skillfully, and put the gun away again.

The wooden gate was ajar. Dupin opened it, walked into the garden, and approached the front door.

This was where he and Lilou Breval had sat when he came over. They had sat together long into the night. The garden was a paradise. At high tide it was bordered by water, a truly wild garden with trees growing in rampant chaos, shrubs, ferns. Magnolias, camellias, rhododendrons, laurel, sea buckthorn, and Dupin was particularly struck by the lemon tree and a tall orange tree. An enchanted garden. Not of this world.

Dupin rang the bell.

"It doesn't look like anyone is in."

Commissaire Rose was again standing right behind him. Dupin rang one more time. The bell trilled through the night air.

Nothing. Dupin moved off and started to walk around the house.

"Hello? Lilou? It's Georges Dupin!" he shouted very loudly. And shouted it again.

"She isn't here," said Commissaire Rose firmly.

She came round the corner of the house now too; Dupin could see her clearly. The moon was out. Full moon had been three days ago and it was waning again already, but it was still quite bright.

"We ought—"

Dupin's phone rang. He whipped it out of his jeans pocket straightaway. It might be Lilou. Or Riwal with some news.

It was Claire. In the car earlier he had seen that she had tried to call him twice while he was being treated in the hospital. Two calls had also come through from private numbers during this time. If Dupin didn't answer, calls were forwarded to Nolwenn's office line. He really ought to answer. Claire would definitely be annoyed that he hadn't called back. She still didn't know that he was now on an investigation, of course. She would think that he might not want to come tomorrow and was afraid of admitting it to her. But what should he say now?

"Who is it?"

"It's from a withheld number."

The ringing stopped.

Dupin took a few steps to one side. Ostentatiously. And dialed.

"Hello, Riwal?" he said in a strained voice.

"Boss?"

"Have you found out anything? Have you got through to anyone?"

"Yes, I have. Were you able to speak to Lilou Breval? Is she at home?"

"No. Tell me what you know."

"There was an editor on call. He couldn't help; he didn't have much to do with Lilou Breval. But I've got numbers for two of the Vannes colleagues Lilou Breval seems to have been friends with and who might know where she is right now. And the editor in chief from Vannes. I've just spoken to him. He thinks she's crazy."

"He thinks she's *crazy?*"

"He said she works on, quote, 'insane projects' all the time and hunts down phantoms. Apparently it's getting worse and worse. He thinks she is, and I quote, 'paranoid.' He didn't know of anything specific, or anything that might have to do with barrels or the salt marshes. But he says, and I'm quoting again, 'nothing would surprise' him. He only became the editor in chief nine months ago, and sees her at most once a week. In fact he never knows what she's working on at any given time."

There was anger bubbling up inside Dupin. This was absolutely ludicrous.

"He sounds like a complete idiot. It's remarkable that she puts up with him even once a week. And he has no idea where she might be?"

"No. He hasn't seen or spoken to her since last week. He just knew where she lived. He didn't know anything about her private life."

"And her other two colleagues?" Dupin had been wandering around the garden during their conversation.

"They weren't answering, it's the middle of the night. I left messages on their answering machines."

"Fine. Keep trying. We need information."

Dupin hung up and turned around. "My colleague . . ." He stopped. Commissaire Rose was nowhere to be seen.

"Hello?"

No answer. She was probably back at the car already. She was right. There was nothing they could do here.

Dupin had just decided to head back to the car too when a light suddenly went on inside the house. The light from the ground-floor window cast clean, bright stripes across the garden.

"Hello? Lilou?"

Dupin hurried back to the front door. It was wide open. A moment later Dupin was in the large space that took up almost the entirety of the ground floor—a living room, dining room, and kitchen rolled into one. Commissaire Rose was standing by a wooden table piled high with books and journals, foreign magazines, the latest editions of *Time* and *The New Yorker*.

No sign of the house's inhabitant.

"Damn it, what are you doing?" Dupin said.

"I'm seeing if we can find any clues about where the journalist might be and what she's working on right now."

"How did you get in?"

"The door wasn't locked."

Of course. Dupin didn't know anyone in Brittany who locked their doors, apart from in the cities and at holiday resorts.

"This is trespassing, unauthorized entry to—" He didn't finish the sentence. He was aware it was strange that he of all people should be referring to regulations and laws today. Still, this was Lilou's private space. They needed to speak to her urgently, but they couldn't just walk into her house.

"We have no choice. Aren't you worried about your friend?"

For the first time this evening, there was no sarcastic undertone or any edge to what Commissaire Rose was saying. She sounded deadly serious.

"A journalist, by her own account, is working on an explosive story. She gives a police officer a tip and he is then almost shot dead during his preliminary investigations—and the journalist suddenly vanishes."

It sounded grim. Dupin had felt a certain unease, but he hadn't thought of it this way before. Or perhaps he just hadn't wanted to think of it this way, if he were honest. He realized that Commissaire Rose's words had had a significant impact.

"She hasn't disappeared. We just haven't gotten hold of her yet. She could be anywhere, at a friend or family member's house—at a boyfriend's house. Just because she can't be contacted between ten P.M. and two A.M. and isn't at home on a weeknight, it's by no means clear she's disappeared."

Dupin was trying to sound as convincing as possible and drown out his own unease. He wasn't doing very well.

"Weigh the facts as you see fit. As long as we haven't found her, she is, from a police perspective, *missing*. I can't take responsibility for any other view. In the interests of the person herself," Commissaire Rose said, walking through the room, looking carefully around her, and taking a slightly closer look at things here and there. She turned abruptly toward the stairs to the second floor.

"What are you planning?" Dupin asked.

"I'm going to search her study."

An absurd thought occurred to Dupin: Might Commissaire Rose

suspect Lilou Breval? Perhaps this wasn't about Lilou's disappearance at all? That would be—objectively—a possible interpretation: that for some reason a trap had been laid for him and Lilou had been involved in it. Although it might be possible theoretically, it was, objectively speaking, still complete nonsense.

Uncertain, Dupin followed Commissaire Rose upstairs.

To the right of the stairs was a bedroom with the door open. A fairly neatly made bed with a large, colorful bedspread and a narrow door in the wall behind it. Commissaire Rose was coming toward him through this door.

"A small bathroom. None of her things are there. Toothbrush, makeup, moisturizer. See, she's gone away for a few days."

Lilou hadn't mentioned anything to Dupin about wanting to go away. And if he were honest, it hadn't sounded that way either. She had actually said she was going to drop by straightaway once he had gone to the salt marshes.

"Maybe she's got a second home?" he suggested.

"A second home, but not a second toothbrush?"

"Maybe she's just visiting someone."

Commissaire Rose rolled her eyes.

She marched past Dupin and into the room on the other side of the staircase.

It was a study with large recessed windows on either wall. The room was dominated by an imposing old wooden table, an exact replica of the one on the ground floor. It was ludicrously laden down too. But here there were countless newspapers, papers, and documents piled into precarious towers. The only free space was a relatively large area directly in front of the contemporary desk chair.

"Her laptop is missing too."

"Astonishing—a portable device." It sounded more sarcastic than he had intended.

Without responding to Dupin—even he was embarrassed by his childish retort—Commissaire Rose lost no time starting to work her way through the first pile of papers. Dupin stood next to her and, after a brief hesitation, began to go through the documents too.

They were standing almost shoulder to shoulder in silence. Old copies of the *Ouest-France*, or sometimes just single pages; other newspapers, *Le Télégramme, Libération;* printouts of online articles, printouts of her own articles. By and large it seemed like a kind of chronological filing system, within each pile, and pile by pile. Not strictly chronological, but largely so. In fact, the most recent documents were in the smallest pile, which Dupin was going through now. The filing system ended six weeks ago, however, with just a few unread-looking current editions of the *Ouest-France* lying on top. Scattered among the piles were empty cups in garish colors, at least half a dozen of them. And three used wineglasses. It looked like hard work. Like all-nighters.

Dupin took a look at Lilou's own articles. They were on the most eclectic topics, a jumbled chaos, on issues major and minor. An angry objection to the deregulation of commercial fishing of *praires*—clams—in Concarneau from the beginning of March, which Dupin already knew about; he liked them even more than he liked any other clams, so he was inwardly torn between the understandably vital eco-logical consciousness and his gastronomic passion, because the deregu-lation meant for a start that you got to eat the mussels more often. Next he found an article from July about the Breton food industry's re-sistance in the face of an "invasion" by large brands. Dupin found quite a few notes from conversations about this. And the second large arti-cle on this topic: about the "cola war." The whole world drank Coke . . . The whole world? No. Those obstinate Gauls, the Bretons, created their own cola, "Breizh cola," in 2002, and by now a significant proportion of Brittany's 4.5 million people happily drank the caffeinated Gallic fizzy drink, even Dupin. Because it tasted better, of course, but also because it was a protest, a symbol. So many people drank it that a historic event took place: Coca-Cola, the empire, felt threatened and designed a special regional campaign with its own logo to break the wayward Gallic region's resistance. It had the opposite effect, of course, and solidarity with "Breizh cola" grew and grew. Dupin couldn't help laughing. It was a typically Breton story that was taken very seriously. And it was also a typical Lilou story.

"She certainly didn't endear herself to powerful people. One or two people would have cursed her to hell. Bravo, I say. Hats off to her," Commissaire Rose said casually as she sifted through more papers. But the words resonated with profound admiration.

"Everything from the last six weeks is missing." Dupin had double-checked very carefully.

"Odd." Commissaire Rose looked up for a moment, then set to work systematically on the next pile. A gesture that seemed like an order to be disciplined and keep working. For the first time ever, Dupin felt like he was twenty years old again and a rookie with the Paris police, assisting the senior inspectors and commissaires. His brow furrowed as he thought about it, shook his head—and then concentrated on the papers.

"The thirty-six dead wild boar," murmured Commissaire Rose.

The sentence sounded so odd and out of context that Dupin almost laughed. He recalled that the story had caused waves last year in the middle of his case on the Glénan islands, a case he had inwardly been preoccupied with for a long time. It wasn't as odd as it sounded, on the contrary: thirty-six wild boar—deemed sacred by Bretons—died from poisonous gases released during the decomposition of masses of green algae that had washed up on the shore. For Lilou, and this was the serious background to the article, it was about the causes of the *marées vertes* or the "green tides." Too many nitrates from overly intensive conventional farming found their way into the sea and stimulated the growth there of green algae and became a dangerous problem. The algae was harmless in itself, even edible, but on land, in the sun and in enormous quantities, it gave off toxic gases. A huge issue, with enormous economic consequences, and not just in Brittany.

"Here. An article about salt. From last year," Rose said.

The newspaper was extremely yellowed, covered in several places with wavy, round stains. Commissaire Rose positioned the newspaper so that she and Dupin could read it at the same time. The hook for the piece was that *"fleur de sel"* had finally become a protected designation. In future, only the handmade "flower of salt" from the Atlantic salt marshes could claim the name—salt from the Guérande, the Île Noirmoutier, and the Île de Ré. For centuries, the Atlantic's salt farmers had neglected this issue and *fleur de sel* from India and China had sprung up, one of the countless ridiculous consequences of globalization. The article was about the impressive comeback by the Guérande in the preceding decades, and by the Breton salt marshes, which had been teetering on the brink of collapse in the late sixties. And about the 270 *paludiers* who were back again too, and the twelve thousand tons of salt harvested there each year. And about the three different kinds of salt producers—the "independents," the cooperatives, and the French and European large manufacturers specializing in salt. A whole paragraph was devoted to a manufacturer originally based in the South of France, Le Sel, which even Dupin had heard of. Everyone knew it.

Dupin read the paragraph about the "Salt War" particularly closely—the war was between Atlantic and Mediterranean salt, and the Mediterranean had long since won by streamlining manufacturing and continually lowering prices. Although Atlantic salt had always had the larger share of the market up until the end of the nineteenth century, this *sel artisinal* now made up just 5 percent of French salt production. From a global standpoint, the competition around salt was fierce: fully industrialized table salt production from other European countries and from Algeria, Russia, and South America meant that the salt from the White Land was becoming a rare luxury. Apparently the outlook was tough, the passionate Breton *paludiers* were not starving—thanks in part to certain subsidies—but they weren't in an easy profession. There were some typical Lilou Breval–style barbs aimed at the large manufacturers from the South of France. Overall it was a very emotional article, however, that proudly celebrated the "marvelous ancient art of creating white gold" and demanded people banish all other kinds of salt from truly Breton kitchens. Two *paludiers* were quoted, the head of the largest cooperative, and the manager of the Centre du Sel. It occurred to Dupin that his notebook was still in his car—the replacement car—in the glove compartment (along with quite a lot of other stuff). It was one of the little red Clairefontaine notebooks that he had used since his training days for his extremely idiosyncratic "scribbles." The notebook and the notes were indispensable to him during cases. It wasn't just because of his sometimes terrible, or, rather, "selective" memory; this was his method. Or at least a sort of method. He would never have used that word. Commissaire Rose, on the other hand, didn't seem to need to make any notes.

"Guy Jaffrezic, Juliette Bourgiot." Dupin recited the names quoted in the article out loud to himself, committing them to memory. "An informative article," he added.

"At least we now know for sure that your friend was involved with the salt marshes."

"That was a year ago."

"And we know who she was in touch with in Gwenn Rann. These two people at least. Perhaps we'll find a more recent article about the salt marshes."

Commissaire Rose turned back to the piles. As devastating as it was and as vague as it all seemed, these were their very first leads.

* * *

Commissaire Rose pulled the car door shut with some force. It was a quarter to three. They had stayed in Lilou Breval's house for an hour, taking a look at the rest of the papers in the study before finishing by walking through all of the rooms again.

They hadn't found anything else relevant. Or any more articles about the salt marshes. There seemed to be only one. And as far as they could tell, there were no links to the salt marshes or anything to do with salt in the other articles.

They hadn't found any clues to support any theory other than that Lilou Breval was planning to spend the night elsewhere. Yet Dupin was becoming more and more concerned, albeit in a general way. He had tried Lilou's mobile a few more times, but there was no answer.

Commissaire Rose had gone into the garden three times and made some calls too. Dupin called Riwal but he didn't have anything new to say apart from asking whether the commissaire would mind if he drove to a second cousin's house in Bono and got some sleep there. Dupin didn't have much interest in sleep during a case. Or even in general. But he couldn't think what else they could do at this point.

"We've got three hours," Commissaire Rose said as she groped around on the side of her seat and tilted the chair back a bit. She looked like she was making herself comfortable.

"Let's rest a little. Then drive back to the salt marshes. It starts to get brighter around half past six so I want to be there then. I'll drop you off back at your car and then I'm going to open my investigation."

She looked at Dupin in a friendly way; always, or so it seemed to him, with the message: it's nothing personal. This time—although he tried with all his strength—he couldn't hold back.

"I was *almost* shot dead, I'm personally involved, I can't just watch from the sidelines, it's out of the question, I want . . ." Dupin faltered. "I mean: you know it would be better if I did the interview with Lilou Breval. She trusts me. She'll tell me everything she knows."

"You think she will withhold important information from the police if you're not present?"

Dupin didn't answer. There was quite a long pause, Commissaire Rose calmly fiddling around with her seat lever again. She let the seat back farther.

"Have you got through to anyone yet? From the salt marshes?" Dupin said in a pointedly friendly way.

"The head of the cooperative. He'll be there from seven onward."

"Does he have any idea what might have happened?"

"Not in the slightest, he says."

It was almost maddening how willingly Commissaire Rose was giving away information. It made Dupin instinctively suspicious.

"And the owner of the salt marshes?"

"Monsieur Daeron."

"You know him?"

"No."

"But you've already spoken to him?"

"Yes. He lives in La Roche-Bernard, on the Vilaine. Around twenty-five minutes from the salt marshes. That's where we got hold of him."

"And he didn't know anything either?"

"Not a thing."

"What about the barrels?"

"There are no barrels in the salt marshes, according to him. We haven't been able to get through to the head of the Centre du Sel yet. The day starts early at the salt marshes during the summer months, before the sun even comes up. With the first of the morning light."

She sounded almost poetic for a moment. "I'll speak to everyone face-to-face on site."

Dupin thought there was something smug about the suddenly very detailed information about operations he was no longer allowed to be a part of.

"Now let's get some sleep." She was absolutely serious about this. Dupin hadn't given it any thought because he had assumed she was joking.

"You want to *sleep* here? In the car?"

"By the time I'd have booked you into a hotel and dropped you off there, it would be four o'clock. This isn't Paris. So I would have had to pick you up again more or less right away."

That may well have been true. But it was still odd.

"You ought to get some sleep too. There's absolutely nothing we can do for the next three hours. You've been shot. Some sleep will do you good. Have you never spent a night in a car while you're on duty?"

With some effort, Dupin bit his tongue.

There really was nothing they could do for now. And it would be sensible to rest a little to regain some strength. But he was reluctant. Not just because he was a terrible sleeper anyway—even under normal circumstances he lay awake all night sometimes—but now, with all of the pressing thoughts and questions in his head, it would be virtually impossible to sleep. It was a ridiculous notion. Especially with the pains in his shoulder that, despite the painkillers, he noticed again as soon as he wasn't otherwise occupied. And above all: there was a stranger fifty centimeters away from him.

Dupin decided to take a walk in the fresh night air. It always helped. To marshal his thoughts. To reflect on what had happened. And to relax properly.

"I'm going to go for a little walk," Dupin said very quietly.

He had just finished speaking when his phone rang. The laborious process of getting it out of his pants pocket took a while. It was Claire. It had occurred to him that she would probably call again. He let it ring. He would call her back very soon. And then he could take his time telling her what had happened.

He opened the car door and got ready to climb out of the seat. He'd had five stitches and he was starting to feel it now. He would need to take another tablet. Dupin leaned back, waited for a moment, and started again.

"Watch out for the kangaroo. It's wild."

"What are you—"

Dupin had distinctly heard the word "kangaroo"—but another powerful, sharp pain intervened and he had to stop speaking. He felt an ache all down his left side to his foot and into each toe. He slid back into the seat. Tried to relax. He just had to be patient for a moment. It would get better soon. He breathed deeply in and out.

The car door was wide open. The air was still wonderfully mild. A perfect summer night without a hint of the season's impending end. Despite the moonlight, the Milky Way shone like a bright ribbon across the sky, flickering and pulsating wildly. Dupin had never seen a more beautiful starry sky than here, in the middle of nowhere, on certain summer nights. Above the vast Atlantic. A billion stars were visible to the naked eye, endless galaxies. It was like looking into the universe's core. Dupin realized his mind was wandering. It had been a stressful evening. Ludicrous. He would rest now for a minute or two and then take a walk through the night air. He would call Claire, perhaps Riwal again too, to discuss how to proceed tomorrow, he had forgotten earlier, he needed to . . . He would keep thinking it through now. He . . .

Dupin had fallen asleep.

It had taken less than two minutes.

The Second Day

"A nother espresso, please. And a *pain au chocolat*."
Dupin was hungry, of course, and had already eaten two croissants, so—by his reckoning—he had laid a good, neutral base in his sensitive stomach so that it could handle some chocolate along with the third coffee (very wisely he had never asked his GP, Docteur Garreg, whether these were valid theories: the idea of croissants as a base). He placed his mobile on the table, having tried Lilou over and over again. No answer.

The first ray of morning light fell on Dupin's face, gentle and soft, but still palpable. He was sitting—in his white, extremely baggy hospital T-shirt, unshaven, dirty, rumpled—on the wooden terrace of the Le Grand Large at the lovely quay in Le Croisic with its neat houses of varying heights. Near the Place Donatien Lepré, in the very place he had wanted to eat his sole the evening before. Sole was among the specialties of the superb fishermen from Le Croisic, along with langoustines, prawns, scallops, delicious sea bass, and squid.

It was almost low tide, and the motorboats were lying languor-
ously in the last of the dark green algae-infested water in the old dock
made of heavy, moss-covered stone; the sailboats stood tall, towering
up on their centerboards like unshakable monuments of the sea. It
was all directly in front of Dupin, but four or five meters lower down,
so he could mainly see a swarm of masts and steel cables. At high
tide—and Dupin was very fond of this too—the boats bobbed on the
same level as the pedestrians and café customers. The turquoise sea of
the lagoon beyond the dock with its white sandbanks that looked
like whales' backs was smooth as glass, still sleepy from the night
before. The sky was high and vast, a radiant blue. A crystal blue today.
Dupin had always planned to buy a book about shades of blue—Bretons
distinguished between dozens of different kinds. It hadn't cooled much
since yesterday, but the unique Atlantic briskness that Dupin loved so
much was still there. And it tasted just like it did in Concarneau: raw,
pungent. Across the lagoons you could see the lush green floodplains
inland as clear as day, and a good way into the salt marshes. Somewhere
out there, someone had shot at him yesterday. This morning, in this
marvelous place, it almost seemed like a strange, dark dream.

He had been feeling a little better in the last few minutes. The
caffeine. Although his shoulder still hurt. And he had just taken another painkiller. After a brief argument, Commissaire Rose had dropped
him off here in Le Croisic at his request. She wanted to drop him off at
his car. And nowhere else. She thought Riwal should have met Dupin
there and driven him straight back to Concarneau. She was oblivious
to the fact that Dupin had asked his other inspector, Kadeg, to come
here too. Dupin had made a medical argument in the end: he said his
blood sugar levels and blood pressure were critical. That he urgently
needed to fortify himself. And that it would take Riwal awhile to get
there anyway. He was genuinely surprised when she gave in, but she
insisted on listening in while Dupin called his inspector to duly give

him the instructions to pick him up in Le Croisic and drive him to his car.

Of course Dupin would not just drive back to Concarneau now and hand over *his* case to Commissaire Rose. That was out of the question. But yesterday evening he simply couldn't think how to get himself included in the investigation. And it was starting to get critical. Even this morning, on the journey from the gulf back to the Guérande—her driving style the same as yesterday, albeit without the flashing lights, and a little more out of control, in Dupin's opinion—the brainwave still hadn't come to him.

Stupidly, he had ended up falling asleep in the car outside Lilou Breval's house during the night, without meaning to. He was annoyed and it was vaguely embarrassing, all the more so because he had slept deeply and soundly in a way that was rare in his own bed, for two and a half hours straight. Having a walk around would have been the perfect strategy; an idea might have occurred to him. He really ought to have called Claire. Today was her birthday. Last night had been terrible. He would do it right now. Without caffeine, he hadn't felt capable of recounting the complex events to her. On the drive, with Commissaire Rose in the car, it would definitely not have been possible.

Dupin dialed her number and pressed the phone to his ear. It rang for a long time before she answered.

"Happy birthday, Claire. I . . . Claire, I'm sorry. I wanted to call you yesterday, I . . ."

"But you're coming tonight, aren't you?" she asked affectionately. He was relieved, but also slightly panicked. It was a complicated question. The best thing to do would be to tell her exactly what had happened the night before. From start to finish.

"When you called yesterday, I was at a salt pond—checking up on something. On the Guérande peninsula. Where the *fleur de sel* comes from"—she knew it of course—"the real stuff, from Brittany. It was a very vague tip-off. From a journalist I know. Then out of no-where, somebody"—even as a straightforward report this was hard to say—"somebody shot at me, but I'm okay, it was just a graze wound." Dupin waited to see if Claire would say something, but there was si-lence on the other end of the line. He would just finish his story quickly.

"I was treated in a hospital. A very good doctor. You would have thought so too. Then I drove with a commissaire—a madame com-missaire—to the journalist's house. We need all of the information we can get; we have no idea what was going on in the salt marshes. But the journalist wasn't there. And I can't get through to her on the phone. I'm in Le Croisic now. In a café."

There was a series of omissions in his story.

"Was it really just a graze wound? Did it bleed a lot?"

Luckily Claire sounded sympathetic.

"No. Not bad at all. On my left shoulder. I can't even feel it any-more," Dupin lied.

"And you're sitting in a café right now?"

"I needed caffeine—you know it's medicinal for me. And the doctor said I should eat something. And drink water." He was look-ing round for the waiter. He'd order the water straightaway. "I haven't eaten anything since lunch yesterday, apart from salted caramels. I couldn't call you back earlier. I've only just got here. And in the car—I mean, I don't have my car right now, it's at the garage. It wasn't my car."

"And where did you sleep?"

This conversation was veering in a tricky direction. Even though there wasn't anything awkward to tell from his night, sometimes something sounded awkward purely because you said it all in one go. Even more so if you deliberately tried to make sure it didn't sound awkward.

"I only slept briefly."

"Where?"

"In the car. In front of the journalist's house. We didn't have time to find a hotel."

"Shouldn't you take it easy? And drive home? I mean, this isn't even your case. In the Guérande. You can go home, can't you? And come here this evening?"

"I . . ." Dupin ultimately did not know how to continue. "No, it's not my case, and the plan is for me to drive to Concarneau soon."

"And where did this commissaire sleep? Who is she?"

This was not good either.

"I— Also in the car. Also not for long."

This was all total nonsense. This wasn't working.

"I want to know what happened here, Claire. Who shot at me and why. I want to catch the person, whoever it is. Do you understand? I don't want to leave it to anyone else. I want to investigate it myself."

There was a long pause.

"I understand, Georges. Yes." She sounded genuine, but crestfallen too, as she so often had before. "I need to go into the OR now. I'll call you again later. Speak to you soon."

"Speak to you soon."

Claire hung up. Dupin leaned back. He was crestfallen himself now.

Suddenly there was some loud beeping. Two beeps. Dupin saw two police cars coming down the long quay. Kadeg was in the first one, of course, making an ostentatious, unnecessary gesture with his hand to show that he had seen Dupin, and Riwal was in the second one. This was a rare feeling: Dupin was glad to see them both. Even the baby-faced, overeager Inspector Kadeg, whom he couldn't stand

and who had done barely anything but irritate him since their first day together.

With great self-importance, Kadeg parked the official police car as close to Dupin's chair as possible, while Riwal parked his car a few meters away. Other cars would only just get by. No surprise that it was Kadeg who was standing at the table first. With a surly expression on his face, he held out a large Armor Luxe bag, the sight of which, truth be told, cheered Dupin up just as much as seeing his two inspectors. He'd get changed quickly. At some point, Dupin had discovered these polo shirts by the Breton brand, renowned worldwide for its striped sweaters, though luckily most of their collections didn't have stripes. Twice a year, he drove to the big shop in Quimper and stocked up on new shirts: his usual uniform on duty and off. He had been there only on Monday and the bag had still been in his office.

"Have you officially clarified what our role in the investigation will be?" Kadeg blurted out, staccato, without saying hello, and Dupin's spark of joy vanished in a flash.

Kadeg continued: "You know that we have no authority of any kind to carry out investigative activities. I assume everything has been clarified, or else you definitely wouldn't have had me come here."

It was on the tip of Dupin's tongue to answer that first and foremost he had ordered him to come here because of the polo shirts. There he went again: this was Kadeg all over. Even after his wedding, which had taken place shortly after Riwal's wedding last year—as if he absolutely had to keep up with his colleague—he still hadn't changed. Which was understandable once you'd met his wife: a stocky martial arts teacher at the police school in Rennes whose terrierlike charm was even more irritating than Kadeg's.

Dupin had, of course, no reply for his inspector. Even this meeting here would, if it were to come out, spell trouble. How would he explain it?

He stood up abruptly. "I'll be right back."

First, he was going to get changed.

"I spoke to one of Lilou Breval's colleagues a few minutes ago. I had left a message for her earlier." Riwal had hung back discreetly before coming out with this interesting piece of news.

"And?"

"She says Lilou Breval is still involved with the Coca-Cola thing. And also the salt marshes, although the colleague had no idea what still interested her specifically. Lilou Breval called this woman briefly the day before yesterday to tell her she was coming into the editorial offices on Thursday afternoon—that's today—to get a few things done. And that she wanted to speak to her. But she didn't say what it was about. She sounded totally normal, the colleague says. The two of them spoke about once or twice a week. She doesn't know where Madame Breval is right now either, but she did know that she had driven to her parents' house a few times recently. They died several years ago. It's also at the gulf, but on the other side, right by the passage, at the Pointe de Kerpenhir."

Dupin recalled being at the Pointe de Kerpenhir with Henri. A fantastic place. To the right you could see the open Atlantic, to the left the gulf, and opposite was the pretty Port Navalo. The current was fierce there, up to twenty kilometers an hour, tremendous amounts of water, two hundred million cubic meters of it flowing in and out.

"But she doesn't have a landline number for her there. And we haven't been able to find one either. In any of the directories. Should we send someone to check if she's there?"

"Definitely. Right away."

"We have to let Commissaire Rose know. *We* can't do it," Kadeg interjected.

Dupin felt anger rising up inside him now. Without saying a word, he turned toward the door to the café and disappeared before they could get into an argument.

The bathroom was extremely cramped. It smelled so strongly of lavender it was as if he were standing in a field of lavender in the middle of Haute-Provence—there was one of those air fresheners designed for much larger rooms. With his bandaged shoulder this task was bound to be a fun one. Dupin put the bag down on the tiny sink. Then his mobile rang. Private number. He answered. Anything could be important right now.

"It is absolutely out of the question. It is utterly impossible," somebody yelled at him.

Unfortunately, Dupin recognized the voice immediately. It was the prefect. Locmariaquer, a name he could not even begin to pronounce in his fifth year of service in Brittany. And yet the name was only half as bad as the person himself. Although Dupin on principle maintained a fraught relationship with official authority figures, which had sealed his fate in the Parisian police and constantly caused serious conflict, in Locmariaquer's case there was also a genuine, profound, personal antipathy there. Of course the prefect had been informed. Someone would have told him about Dupin's "inappropriate behavior" in detail.

"I don't intend to tolerate this."

He was familiar with his superior's tirades. They were monologues. Long, heated monologues. You had to hold the phone far away from your ear and wait for the volume to reduce.

"You are going to stay with it. You are going to be equally involved in the investigation. By Commissaire Rose's side, with equal authority. I have personally seen to it. I won't be bested in this."

Dupin wasn't sure if he had heard the prefect correctly.

"But for now you'll have to do without your two inspectors."

Dupin still couldn't believe his ears.

"Hello? Dupin? Are you still there? Did you hear what I said?"

"You're saying I'm on the case?"

"Of course *mon commissaire* is on it. I'm not prepared to put up with Edouard Trottet's impertinence anymore. He has been behaving badly for decades. It's unbelievable that he hasn't been fired yet. A disgrace to every prefecture in France."

Dupin felt like the lavender was clouding his senses. "Commissaire Rose and I are investigating on an equal footing?"

"Absolutely. I've personally . . ."

Dupin did not need to know any more right now, even though he would have been all too pleased to find out precisely why the prefect had intervened and pulled off this small miracle. But it would turn into a long story; he had made that mistake before. And he was in a hurry now. Commissaire Rose had left for the salt marshes a while ago. He interrupted the prefect.

"I— Hello? I can't hear you anymore, Monsieur le Préfet."

He said this quickly and mechanically, without making the slightest effort to imitate a bad line the way, for the sake of politeness, he ordinarily at least tried to do. And then he hung up. This was unbelievable. For a moment he wasn't sure whether that had been a smart move: maybe the prefect had had more to say that he ought to know. But if so he would find out soon enough.

Dupin stuffed his mobile into his pocket, slipped on one of the new dark blue polo shirts (he had bought five of the same), picked up his bag, and left the bathroom a moment later.

He was ready for action. And what's more: he could feel it.

Riwal and Kadeg had ordered coffee. They were drinking in silence, looking—understandably—exhausted. Kadeg was still scowling.

"I've worked it all out with our prefect. The commissaires are investigating equally."

Both heads whipped round to look at Dupin.

"And what about us?" Kadeg asked. His face could sometimes look genuinely childlike. Like a small, sullen boy who was always missing out.

"You wait here and be prepared. There will be plenty to do." Le Grand Large ought to be safe, Dupin thought.

He hurried to keep speaking so that Kadeg could not say or ask anything more before he left the terrace. He was already on the point of leaving.

"Riwal, you drive me to the salt marshes. Right now. We'll discuss everything in the car."

Dupin heard the rumblings of Kadeg's protest, but he was only half listening.

* * *

Even at a distance, he could pick out Commissaire Rose. She was standing next to the little hut he had been trapped inside. There was quite a large group of police officers again. The forensics team was also there again, this time by daylight. And Inspector Chadron from the night before was there too, a redhead with a long plait and sparkling eyes. Dupin had spotted four cars on the small road, one of which was the commissaire's brand-new Laguna. It was all extensively cordoned off. Commissaire Rose had done a good job. He would have done the same thing. In exactly the same way.

He was just passing the place where he had knelt in the pool to the right. Where he had taken cover. That was probably where the bullet had grazed him. Dupin was surprised by how odd it felt to be back. He was furious, and at the same time he felt a kind of indignation and a deep-rooted unwillingness to accept what had happened.

Dupin had been lost in his thoughts for a little while. Commissaire Rose had obviously come over to him; she was almost standing in front of him now.

"I'm doing this against my wishes. You need to know that," she said.

As she had done the day before, she managed to strike a jovial tone of voice suited to a more well-intentioned message, in stark contrast to what she was actually saying.

"I do."

Dupin made an effort to give the most neutral answer possible. And he left it at that. It would clearly be unwise to begin their "official collaboration" by saying something controversial.

"We've taken another look at everything here. Especially the *tas de sel*. There were no prints on the patch of withered grass over there."

Dupin gave her a blank look.

"The *tas de sel* is the area next to the salt ponds, around the huts, where the salt is harvested."

"And the pools?"

"It's extremely dry there too; the clay is cracked. Relatively high numbers of partial prints from a relatively high number of different shoes. Mostly men's sizes, an eight or a nine. *Potentially* even smaller. *Potentially* sneakers. They could be partial prints from any point over the last few weeks; they could be Monsieur Daeron's or any number of his colleagues'. So far, there have been no usable fingerprints; they've tried the sheds and huts. We have the bullets fired by you and your assailant. They also used a nine-millimeter, but different bullets. RUAG ones, very common. Provisional ballistic examinations indicate the assailant—or assailants—had one gun."

Dupin's face darkened at the word "assailant." Commissaire Rose didn't seem to notice; her gaze had swept about during her report, as if she wanted to use the time to have a good look round, but she didn't sound distracted. "The same goes for the tire marks as for the shoe prints—difficult on this ground. Nothing significant so far. And above all, there are no traces of any kind that indicate the possible presence of heavy round objects. No signs of barrels. Essentially, we don't know any more than we did last night.

"A colleague of Lilou Breval's knows that she stays in her parents' house occasionally. At the gulf, near Sarzeau. My inspector has the address."

Dupin saw Commissaire Rose screw up her face slightly.

"You should ask the police there to send someone over to check it out right away. I haven't done anything, of course. We don't have a landline number," he added quickly. "Unfortunately, this colleague didn't know exactly what stories Lilou Breval is working on at the moment."

Now they were even. They had shared all of the information they had. Or at least he hoped so.

"I . . ."

Dupin was grateful for the interruption of someone honking their horn.

Commissaire Rose turned and walked straight toward the road. Without turning back, she called out: "The owner of the salt pond. Maxime Daeron. He just called again."

Dupin stopped, hesitated for a moment, and then got out his phone. He dialed and spoke as softly as he could. "Riwal, is everything okay?"

"Boss?"

"Have you talked to the police at the gulf yet?"

"I can barely hear what you're saying. No, not yet. Nolwenn rang just now. I was just about to call you. Maybe this isn't a good idea. Kadeg is right. I—"

"Let's leave it. Commissaire Rose is doing it."

Dupin hung up before Riwal could reply. He put his phone away quickly and looked round for Rose. She was standing less than ten meters away, also with her phone to her ear. She must have been delegating tasks of her own. Her style looked just as abrupt as his, because a moment later she put her phone back in her jacket pocket and walked to the road. Dupin followed. He still had a nasty feeling sometimes that he was here as nothing more than an assistant.

* * *

Right in front of Dupin's car—the replacement car—there was a dark green Citroën Crosser, and two men standing next to it. One of the two police officers Dupin had just seen at the cordon was headed toward them.

"Thank you, I'll be taking over from here." Commissaire Rose had beaten him to it.

She looked so elegant and stylish as she walked, her left hand in her pants pocket this time, and Dupin was struggling to keep up. One of the two men came toward her.

"This is very worrying. What exactly has happened in my salt marsh, Madame la Commissaire?"

The man, who by the sound of it must have been Maxime Daeron, was tall—almost two meters. He was wearing beige cargo pants with large pockets and a casual black linen shirt with the top three buttons undone. He had an unusual chin—narrowly tapering, pointy—fleshy lips, a high, broad forehead, quite long black hair shot through with gray strands, and bushy black eyebrows above dark eyes that seemed to consist entirely of pupil. Dupin put him in his early fifties.

"Can you say anything at this stage?" His voice was low, sonorous. Without waiting for an answer, he turned briefly to the other man, who had also come over. "This is my brother. Paul Daeron. The co-owner of the salt marshes."

Paul Daeron looked to be the older of the two brothers, but he didn't resemble Maxime Daeron at all. He was a head shorter, had a round, good-natured face, and was noticeably fatter, with short, bristle-like hair that stuck straight up. His fine facial features didn't seem to suit his overall appearance.

"Silent partner. I don't have anything to do with salt." His voice was a bit higher-pitched than his brother's and sounded more upset than the general impression he was giving off. "I breed pigs. We don't want any hassle here. We hope you'll sort this issue out quickly. We'll help you do that as best we can."

It sounded as though he'd had to force himself to say this.

"Salt marsh*es*? You referred to multiple salt marshes just now?" Commissaire Rose directed her question at Maxime Daeron.

"We own five salt marshes. But we've only got one here. The others are a bit farther south, toward Kervalet."

"Unfortunately we don't yet know what exactly happened here. But we know some suspicious blue plastic barrels were apparently here in your saltworks. During the on-scene police investigation, an attempt was made to shoot the investigating officer dead." Rose paused for a moment and nodded in Dupin's direction. "Commissaire Georges Dupin from the Commissariat de Police Concarneau, he is now on the case with us. We assumed you could be of assistance to us—it's your saltworks, after all."

Dupin was impressed in spite of himself. No maybes, nothing vague, all plain-speaking and on the offensive. The way he would have put it. Except he was just standing there mutely. An unfamiliar situation.

"We harvested the *oeillets* in this salt marsh three days ago. The *gros sel* in the morning and the *fleur de sel* in the afternoon. As we always do. Then the day before yesterday I had fresh water poured in. For the last harvest of the year. After that it'll be over. The weather is going to turn soon," Daeron said as he glanced up into the sky. "I haven't been here since, and neither have my colleagues. When there's such constant sun and constant wind, we don't intervene. There's no need to correct the water level." They were standing in the middle of the small road that didn't seem to be used much, even during the daytime. "We don't use any barrels in our saltworks. Not even for storage. But it occurs to me that some producers in the cooperative have worked with barrels recently. But you'd have to ask over there." There was contempt in this last sentence and Daeron made no attempt to disguise it. "High-quality salt must not be stored in an air-tight container; it still contains vital residual moisture that would immediately settle at the bottom of a barrel as water. Especially in a plastic barrel. If there was a barrel in my saltworks, then somebody must have trespassed onto them. Have you done a thorough search?"

Maxime Daeron's voice was commanding without being overbearing, his facial expression serious, frank, focused. His head tilted to one side as he spoke.

"When exactly was the last time you or an employee of yours was here? In this saltworks." Commissaire Rose had both hands in her pants pockets now.

"Just the day before yesterday, in the morning. I was alone. From half past six till eight o'clock. I came to let in and regulate fresh water from the reservoir pool."

"And you can definitely rule out that one of your employees has been in the saltworks since?"

"There wouldn't have been any reason to be here. But of course I'll ask." Maxime Daeron seemed perfectly calm.

"How many employees do you have?"

Dupin was finding Rose's interview method somewhat unimaginative at this point.

"Six altogether. In the salt marshes themselves, there are two men and a woman, along with myself."

"Might there be some reason why someone apart from you and your staff had been in these salt marshes? Does somebody come to collect the salt?"

"No. Just us. I'm an independent. I take care of everything myself:

production, transport, storage, packing, marketing, sales. Everything relies on us."

"Where does this salt marsh end?"

Rose was asking her questions at a speed that made it impossible for Dupin to ask a question himself without barging in. Paul Daeron nodded from time to time to underscore some of his brother's words, but didn't seem to want to be any more involved in the conversation.

"We're almost at the very edge. Up there"—Maxime Daeron pointed vaguely toward the Route de Marais—"is where it borders on Guy Jaffrezic's salt marsh. He's a salt farmer in the cooperative. That's about a hundred meters."

Dupin thought back to the night before. Jaffrezic was one of the *paludiers* Lilou Breval had quoted in her article. Not Maxime Daeron, but Jaffrezic. It was an interesting coincidence that his saltworks bordered the one where everything had taken place.

"Do you know him well?" Rose kept the questions coming fast.

"Everyone is self-employed here. And as I said: he's a member of one of the cooperatives. He's even been the head of it for a few years now. Head of the cooperative and a huge number of other societies here in Gwenn Rann."

Dupin had been in such a hurry to get to the salt marshes that he had, to his annoyance, forgotten to get his notebook out of the car again.

"So you have no idea who might have been here yesterday evening? Or what might have been going on with the barrels in your saltworks—or what illegal substance they might have contained?"

Rose's final question was clearly pointed. This prompted Paul Daeron to step in.

"How is my brother supposed to know that? He obviously has no idea. He called me during the night. Right after the police called." His voice was much softer than before. Protective.

"We don't use any additives in the Guérande. No chemicals,"

Maxime Daeron said, "nothing at all. If that's what you mean. There are no machines either, no computers, no technology. Everything is done by hand, with old tools. It's all about the *paludier* understanding his craft. It's about the sea, the sun, the wind, the soil." He said this in a very matter-of-fact way.

"And in relation to the barrels, the only thing that occurs to you is the cooperative?"

"Yes."

"What does the cooperative use barrels for?"

"Well, I think they're for transport. I don't know." He hesitated for a moment. He seemed uncertain for the first time, which was in stark contrast to his manner up to this point.

"Last year"—he broke off—"last summer we got the impression a few times that water might have been added to the saltworks overnight. Fresh water. The water levels looked like they'd been adjusted. Only slightly. And the concentration of salt too. We lost the harvest in a few of the pools several times."

"What does that mean?" Dupin was irritated that his interjection sounded so foolish.

"Everything depends on the concentration of salt in the harvest pool. If it's too high or too low, everything is ruined. It has to be around two hundred and eighty grams per liter of water, that's when the salt crystallizes. But we weren't able to say for sure. The water level thing—it's difficult to pin down. It's pure speculation, really. I'm only saying it because you're asking." Even now, Daeron wasn't speaking rhetorically.

"You don't want to believe something like that, but I know the business world. Those kinds of people do exist." It was clear that this was important to the elder brother. "You can't deny it. These things happen."

"You think someone might have brought fresh water into the

saltworks in barrels to dilute the concentration of salt and sabotage the harvest?"

It sounded preposterous, but for the first time Dupin saw the possibility of a theoretical link between salt marshes, salt production, barrels, and crime—a small amount of crime at least. "Couldn't someone just open the sluice gates to the reservoir pools and let in extra water that way?"

"That would be much too obvious. You would see the change in the water level right away. If it's fresh water, you don't have to add half as much."

"The barrels," Dupin said, his brow furrowed. "They could have had any substances inside them, right?"

Daeron looked at him, puzzled.

"I mean substances that render salt, let's say, useless. Inedible."

That would be another possibility for sabotage. Dupin didn't think the idea too far-fetched.

"Our salt is constantly and stringently checked." There was a note of indignation in Daeron's voice. "Every single harvest from every single salt marsh. By an independent lab. Twice. The system has multiple safeguards. Throughout the Guérande."

Dupin had not meant it like that. Rose came to his rescue: "We'll examine the water in this saltworks very carefully. We've already started."

This thought didn't seem to interest Daeron. He looked across his salt marsh. "So where are these barrels supposed to have been, which pools were they next to?"

"Possibly at the large wooden hut," Dupin answered as quickly as a schoolchild who finally knew something for sure.

"That's where the harvest pools are. Right in front of it." Daeron's brow furrowed.

"And there would be no point in adding fresh water to the other pools? If somebody wanted to manipulate something, I mean." Dupin had no idea how a salt marsh worked. It seemed complicated.

"No. You could easily compensate for that; the different kinds of pools are separated from each other by sluice gates." Daeron thought for a moment, then continued, clearly trying hard to be precise. "Due to high and low tides this whole area is supplied with seawater via an extensive system of canals. We fill the first reservoir pools from the large canals, the *étiers*, and after that several intermediate reservoir pools arranged in a row. From there we run water into the first salt pools every fortnight. Into the front pools."

"That's what you did on Tuesday morning? Here, I mean, in this salt marsh?"

Dupin really ought to have got his notebook quickly. This was confusing. Too many pools. Too much—potentially—important information.

"Exactly. From these pools the water runs through various other pools to the center of the saltworks, the harvest pools. The water gets more and more shallow and warm, up to a temperature of a hundred degrees Fahrenheit. There's a slight slope, which makes the water flow, meanwhile the wind and sun ensure there's continuous evaporation. So the water gets more and more salty. Until it crystallizes in the *oeillets*."

"And that's where a few barrels of fresh water would ruin everything?"

Dupin knew they had been over this point before. But he was gradually coming to understand.

"Absolutely. Everything hangs in the balance here every day. A night of heavy rain and everything is over, weeks of work. Or if there isn't enough sun and wind. Or if you make a mistake with the water quantities. Then the harvest fails. Last year the season was over by mid-August, it just rained and rained. We missed out on six weeks. A third of the usual harvesting period. It was a disaster."

"We'll check the salt concentration very carefully too," Rose said, her tone making it clear that this point had now been sufficiently dealt with and Daeron could be sure that they would follow up even the smallest leads. She went on smoothly: "Who might have an interest in destroying your harvest, Monsieur Daeron?"

Daeron drew his eyebrows together. Then shook his head. "No one. Truly, no one. I actually can't even imagine a thing like that."

"You have no idea? Think about it."

"No. I have no idea."

"Do you own a gun, Monsieur Daeron? A nine millimeter?"

"I've never owned a gun."

"And where were you yesterday evening between half past eight and ten o'clock?" Rose looked Daeron right in the eye the whole time.

"I was harvesting until eight, in one of the other saltworks, then I drove home. We live right by La Roche-Bernard. My wife was at home, we ate dinner, and then I got some paperwork done. When your inspector called me I had only just gone to bed."

Dupin had been expecting more close questioning from Rose, and also that she would speak to Daeron about Lilou Breval, but for some reason she finished with him abruptly.

"And you, *monsieur,* where were you then?" Commissaire Rose turned abruptly to Paul Daeron, making him jump. He clearly hadn't been expecting this question.

"I . . . I was in Vannes. At my company. Near Vannes. We had a few guests. Wining and dining. Big clients—we do it frequently. It went on late. Till midnight."

"And the guests will confirm that?"

Again, Paul Daeron looked surprised. "Of course."

"Inspector Chadron will ask you for the names of everyone who can corroborate your statements about yesterday evening."

Maxime Daeron suddenly looked nervous. "Could I take a look at my salt marshes? Where everything happened?"

Dupin almost looked to Rose first, but he hurried to reply before she could: "I'll go with you. Tell us if anything strikes you as strange. No matter what, even if it seems like a tiny, insignificant detail."

Dupin wisely did not look at Rose now. She contradicted him anyway.

"That is a sealed-off crime scene, I—"

Right in the middle of her sentence, Dupin's mobile rang.

Nolwenn. He had tried to get through to her several times earlier on the journey from Le Croisic to the saltworks, but her line had been busy every time. Dupin thought about it, then took a few steps to one side and answered. The reception in the White Land was flawless this morning, or at least it was on this road.

"We've absolutely got to find Lilou Breval. This is all absurd. I want you to try her every five minutes, Nolwenn. Surely she'll be reachable again at some point. Somebody must know where she is."

While they were speaking, Dupin started to walk along the road toward the Route des Marais. The morning sun made the large and small pools to the right and left flash brightly, and it was clear that the fresh breeze that had sprung up the evening before would give way to another scorchingly hot day. Although the scenery and its beauty looked much more real today, Dupin still felt like a stranger in the White Land, oddly dazed as if this bizarre world only put up with visitors reluctantly.

"If Lilou didn't pluck the idea out of thin air, then there were barrels in the saltworks that didn't belong there. With something inside them that didn't belong there. So the barrels weren't here by chance. So the saltworks weren't a random location. There are more secluded spots than the saltworks for hiding illegal activity," he said, and ran a hand through his hair. "Although they are very secluded at night."

It was not uncommon for Dupin's conversations with Nolwenn to be a chance to describe confusing events in a different, more succinct way the second time round. The new narrative style sometimes made things clearer for him. But it didn't even vaguely work this time.

"I only know her articles, but I consider Lilou Breval a highly credible person who does conscientious research," Nolwenn said emphatically, "and she's not afraid of anything or anyone. Examine everything in the saltworks very carefully. There'll be something to it."

"We don't even know if she ever saw a barrel here herself, or just heard about it or suspected it."

Suddenly a van rumbled past him, clearly going too fast, sending small stones flying meters into the air and hitting Dupin in the leg and hip.

He hesitated for a moment, but then he asked what he had been meaning to ask. "So—the thing with the prefect. Do you know what . . ."

"There's a longstanding and painstakingly nursed enmity between the messieurs. I thought it was crucial to make the prefect aware that Préfet Trottet would, as a matter of principle, stop at nothing to exclude you and the Finistère area from the investigations. And therefore him in particular, too."

Dupin had been thinking that this miracle must have something to do with Nolwenn. Who else?

"Thanks, Nolwenn."

"Collar the culprit, *mon Commissaire*. It's unacceptable. Nobody shoots at a commissaire from Concarneau."

The disgust came from deep down inside; Nolwenn's entire being resonated with these words. He loved her for it.

"You're not forgetting that you wanted to go to Paris today? Her birthday. She's tried to call you several times, but she hasn't left a message." Nolwenn sounded sympathetic.

"I know. I . . ."

Dupin changed the subject.

"There's something else I need to know. Lilou Breval wrote a long article about the saltworks in June of last year. Could you check if she has published other articles about the Guérande? About salt or the salt farmers? The competition between Mediterranean and Atlantic salt? And any of her other articles that touch on the saltworks? It doesn't matter what aspect of them it is. And I'll need every article from the *Ouest-France* about the saltworks, not just her articles. Everything from the last few years. And from the *Télégramme* too."

"I'm on it."

Nolwenn had hung up (nobody hung up more quickly than Dupin, apart from Nolwenn).

Dupin turned round. He had walked a good half kilometer and at some point had turned onto one of the paths that branched off the road. It all looked exactly the same as Daeron's saltworks. His brow furrowed, he trudged back the way he'd come.

The Daerons and Commissaire Rose were nowhere to be seen. The only people around were the two police officers dutifully standing by the cordon.

Dupin took the turn for Daeron's saltworks. Inspector Chadron was standing halfway to the hut, and she seemed to be waiting for him.

"Commissaire Rose asked me to tell you a few things," she said. Her facial expression was neutral. As was her tone of voice. As though she was even picking up facial expressions and tones of voice from Rose.

"She said she didn't want to disturb you during your private conversations. But that she thought it appropriate to proceed with the investigation."

Dupin was too taken aback to answer.

"She has driven on ahead to see Monsieur Jaffrezic. You're to meet her at the cooperative headquarters. Near the warehouses. If you drive along the Route des Marais toward Guérande town, there are signs for it. It's about two kilometers away."

Unbelievable. So she must have driven down the road just now. There was no other route.

"We've already clarified whether Maxime Daeron's employees were in this salt marsh after Tuesday morning and the answer is: apparently not. At least not according to the statements from the people questioned, which we will of course verify. Above all," she continued, still in that same neutral tone of voice, "Commissaire Rose said you ought to know that a neighbor saw Lilou Breval last night near her parents' house on the gulf. Around eleven o'clock. Some of our officers were there. The report just came through. They haven't come across Madame Breval this morning, but she was there last night, anyway. The neighbor didn't notice anything unusual. She said Madame Breval was alone. Commissaire Rose says you should stop worrying."

Now Dupin wasn't sure there hadn't been a certain undertone to Chadron's final words after all. But it had been Rose who had been worked up—or more worked up than he was, anyway. But if Dupin were honest, even he felt relief now. A great sense of relief.

He turned round without a word and walked quickly back up the path. He took out his phone as he walked, called Riwal—who had dropped him off and driven straight back to Kadeg at Le Grand Large—and in just a few brief words gave him some tasks to do. Rose would be kept in the dark for now.

A minute later he was standing by his car. He had no idea how he was supposed to drive with his injured shoulder, or even get into the dwarf-sized car at all, but it would work out somehow, he reasoned with himself. In a foul mood, he crawled into the Peugeot. Although he was now officially a part of the investigation, he was not pleased about this. Any of this. He had felt like a shadow of himself in the conversation with the Daerons. And this wasn't his turf either. Dupin did not take well to strangers.

* * *

"Ah, Monsieur le Commissaire, Monsieur Jaffrezic was just about to show us the barrels they use in the cooperative. *Blue plastic barrels.*"

Rose barely glanced at Dupin.

"*Bonjour, monsieur,*" muttered Dupin. He rubbed the spot where he had bumped his head yet again while getting out of his car.

"Come with me. Take a look at everything, if you think it's necessary. Believe me, our barrels were not involved in that mad shoot-out."

Of course everyone knew about it. Radio stations and Web sites were already reporting on the "mysterious criminal activity" and "hours of fierce exchange of fire" in the salt gardens, in which "the well-known commissaire Georges Dupin came within an inch of being shot dead." Unsurprisingly, his presence there was commented on: "The reason why the commissaire was in the Guérande salt gardens, outside of his jurisdiction, is thus far unexplained."

With a cheerful "Come on!" Guy Jaffrezic set off and was now walking across the broad gravel path that led away from the parking lot, past one of the cooperative's ten imposing, long warehouses. Jaffrezic, whom Dupin would have put in his early sixties, was short and very plump, with darting eyes and equally darting hands that were constantly gesticulating. This was in odd contrast to the physical calm he radiated, as if his eyes and hands belonged to a different body. Dupin only just stopped himself from smiling.

"We only started using the barrels recently, this season. For the dried salt. The salt for the salt mills. We've been producing it for two years. People love it. A bestseller. The *gros sel spécial moulin.* I don't know if you're familiar with it."

He turned to Dupin, seeming to assume that Rose was already familiar with it. He was correct on both fronts.

Dupin sighed. Up until a few years ago, salt had simply been salt to him (and he still thought this a reasonable attitude). During their Breton lessons, Nolwenn had given him a few preliminary briefings. He hadn't listened properly on this topic, he had to admit.

"Commissaire Rose said you're the commissaire from Paris. People have heard of you."

After more than five years in Brittany, Dupin didn't even respond when he heard this kind of thing.

"You won't have a clue about salt."

Jaffrezic's sentence was resonant with a profound sadness. And worry. And sympathy.

"Without salt, people die. You must never forget that."

Dupin almost blurted out: "They die with salt too."

"I'll show you everything and explain everything you need to know, sun and wind permitting."

This was—just like his comments about the *sel moulin* earlier—expressed in an unmistakably pedagogical tone of voice. Like the prelude to a guided tour.

"This is a police investigation. There was an attempted murder," Rose interrupted in a friendly but firm manner.

Jaffrezic remained utterly unfazed, continuing in the style of a saltworks tour guide. "We leave the *gros sel moulin* to dry in the sun for forty-eight hours after harvesting it, sometimes even seventy-two hours, at least a day longer than normal *gros sel*. Then it goes into the barrels. But only to transport it to these warehouses. The most significant difference is between *gros sel* and *fleur de sel*. Those are the two basic kinds of salt."

Jaffrezic left the gravel path, took a sharp left, and walked down a small grassy path that led right into a salt marsh. Beyond a large reservoir pool, the rectangular pools began, and through the water that was now just ten centimeters deep, the blue-gray floor shimmered. The warm air was close and there was a strong smell of salt, of rich earth. Brackish water.

"The 'flower of salt' is the finest and most refined of any salt in the world, and also the most rare. Did you know that up until the eighties it was used for preserving sardines and was generally considered inferior?"

Dupin had never known that.

"Right after harvesting it has a violet fragrance and a slight rosy shimmer. After drying, it's dazzlingly white! It makes up just four percent of our output." Jaffrezic's voice and facial expression became dramatic now. "It only forms under perfect weather conditions. It's alchemy. Lots of sun, not much humidity, and a constant wind that must be neither too strong nor too weak. It's much too weak today. The easterly winds are the best!" Jaffrezic's eyes sparkled knowingly. "A mild wind blows the fine salt crystals floating near the surface together, which produces an ice-like layer. *Fleur de sel* floats on the water! Small, moving islands, did you know that?"

This was news to Dupin too.

"If the wind is too strong or the water in the harvest pools is moved carelessly, the *fleur de sel* sinks to the ground and is lost."

"Are we nearly there yet?" Rose asked bluntly, making it clear that she wanted to get down to business. The mud footbridges were getting more and more narrow and they had already taken several turns. Commissaire Rose was walking two or three meters behind Dupin. Jaffrezic blithely ignored her question.

"Ordinary salt, so-called table salt, consists of up to ninety-nine percent sodium chloride. It's outrageous! Our salts are only ninety-one percent sodium chloride; the rest is residual moisture, which is pure seawater—we call it the 'mother of salt'—and numerous essential minerals and trace elements. Magnesium, calcium"—the head of the cooperative couldn't help getting more and more excited—"manganese, iodine, of course. Sixty different ones! Iron, zinc. And selenium! Bromine, sulfur."

It sounded absurd. Dupin was particularly unconvinced by the potential advertising power of sulfur and bromine. But there was pride on Jaffrezic's face.

"That's what gives it its unique flavor! It's much milder, yet tastier, more aromatic and full-bodied than crude salt. Without any bitter notes. The only salt with a bouquet!" He had now lapsed completely into a script that had been trotted out a hundred times before. "Connoisseurs from all over the world worship our Breton *fleur de sel*. A part of mankind's culinary heritage."

Dupin couldn't help grinning. In Brittany, salt was clearly not just salt.

"The consistency and oil content set it apart from every other salt too: the fine crystalline structure falls apart like a breath on the tongue!"

"And also on tender salt lamb from the meadows of Mont Saint-Michel, once it's been in the oven at a hundred and eighty degrees for seven hours. With garlic, rosemary, and shallots, basted with white wine at regular intervals," Rose said.

At first Dupin wasn't sure he'd heard right. He turned around and saw, for a moment, a pretty, unguarded smile spreading across her face. She really had said it. Before he could reply—he would have liked to have said something nice in response—the smile had vanished once more.

"Watch out!"

Jaffrezic had made a sharp left turn onto an incredibly narrow dam that ran between two pools toward a mud wall. Dupin nearly walked straight into the pool. Deftly, and without slowing his pace, the corpulent Jaffrezic strode along the dam toward a gap in the wall.

"You've got to imagine us going along these narrow dams and footbridges even with full wheelbarrows."

A moment later they were looking at a row of huge salt mounds on green tarpaulins laid out on a broad strip of grass between two salt marshes and, next to them, also arranged in a row, some blue plastic barrels. Dupin guessed they were about an arm's length across.

"Your mysterious barrels. *Voilà!* Look, that's our normal *gros sel*. That will become our *sel moulin*. It forms in a different way from the *fleur de sel*; the salt crystals settle on the clay floors of the harvest pools, wind and sun permitting! The clay gives the salt that distinctive pale gray color."

Dupin was standing at the barrels, looking them over. Rose joined him.

The barrels were empty, standing neatly in single file. So they really did exist. Blue barrels in the saltworks. After all. The salt farmer didn't seem worried that the commissaires weren't listening.

"Anyway. It's brought to the edge of the saltworks in a wheelbarrow. After two days' drying time, it's poured into these barrels. Then the salt is stored in the barrels in the sheds. Until it's packaged up. And that's the sum total of the mystery of the blue barrels."

Rose and Dupin were listening closely again now.

"That's all you use the barrels for?" Dupin cut in.

"Absolutely."

"And they're only used in your cooperative?"

"We're talking sixty-seven *paludiers*!"

Dupin had whipped out his Clairefontaine. At last. He had almost forgotten it again when he was getting out of the car just now (which was not a good sign), but had remembered it at the last second. He began to make notes on certain things. Based on the simple principle of whatever seemed important to him. Instinctively. This was actually quite an intricate system.

"And how might some of these barrels have ended up in Monsieur Daeron's saltworks?"

"It's not possible."

"But it happened."

"What do you think happened over there, Monsieur Jaffrezic?" Rose interjected.

"Did you actually see the barrels there? As I said, I consider it out of the question. Not our barrels!"

Dupin and Rose were silent.

"Perhaps," Jaffrezic left a dramatic pause, "it was Mikaël's crazy dwarves. From Pradel. Who knows?"

Dupin had lost count of how many times he had been told Celtic legends and myths during investigations. As a distraction, for fun, or, and this was not uncommon, in all seriousness.

"As soon as the last *paludier* leaves the saltworks of an evening, the saltworks no longer belong to us humans. They notice immediately. There's something odd about it." Jaffrezic was doing this very skillfully (and he was also giving a good description of how Dupin felt yesterday). "That's when the saltworks belong to them, and the dwarves come out: ten of them or a hundred or a thousand. With blue wheelbarrows— blue like your barrels. They used to work Mikaël's saltworks at night, until they found it too much work, and one night they heaped up a gigantic mountain of salt, and all the saltworks were buried underneath fifty meters of the purest salt."

Jaffrezic looked at them dramatically. "Diabolical little creatures. They're still up to no good nowadays. And it's not just them!" He let out a brief, loud laugh.

"Monsieur Jaffrezic, do you know of anyone who would have had motive to sabotage Maxime Daeron's harvest?" Rose asked. The funny myth clearly left the commissaire cold. Dupin was reminded of Riwal. He'd definitely know the myth.

Jaffrezic became more helpful all of a sudden. "We've been trying to get Maxime Daeron to join the cooperative for years. It's no secret. If that's what you mean. Apparently he doesn't need it." His eyes were darting around even more quickly now.

"And so you or someone from the cooperative put pressure on him by destroying parts of his harvest? Did you want to use that to force him to become a member of the cooperative?"

Rose was unbelievable. She phrased these accusations without making them sound like accusations at all.

"You cannot, thank God, be serious."

"How does it work—the cooperative?" Dupin asked.

"Members are obliged to hand over their whole harvest. And we store it. In these warehouses here. At a specific price per kilo, which everyone determines collectively every year."

Jaffrezic seemed pleased by Dupin's interest. And this time he was making a clear effort not to speak with so much of an emphasis on salt tourism.

"Look, the harvest can fail in all kinds of ways. If there's a rainy summer, that could cost an independent *paludier* his livelihood. That's the crux of the cooperative idea: we've built up a quantity of stock to last two or three years, so we can compensate for the failure of an entire season and still keep up a steady supply. We thus guarantee a calculable income for all of the *paludiers*, proportional to the amount of salt handed over. Of course you don't get rich in the cooperative, but you won't be poor either. Not joining is antisocial, that's how we see it. Daeron wants to go it alone. *We* accept that, but the big corporation doesn't."

"Really?" Rose sounded openly impatient now.

"Le Sel has been trying to buy up everything for years."

"What do you mean—"

Dupin's phone interrupted Rose. He quickly took it out of his jeans pocket.

"Nolwenn, I can't ta—"

She didn't let him finish: "Lilou Breval tried to call you. I think I saw her number on the screen on your landline. You ought to be able to see it on your mobile too. The call was transferred to my extension, which was busy. Then it started to record but she didn't leave a message. She must have called when you and I were talking to each other. I called her back straightaway, multiple times. She's not picking up. Or she's got no reception. That can be an issue at the gulf."

"Shit."

Rose and Jaffrezic looked quizzically at him.

Dupin glanced at his mobile and saw Lilou's number. He had missed Lilou's call! And she was the only one who could shed some light on this situation. They were depending on her, everything depended on her—and he had missed her call.

"Keep trying, Nolwenn. This is turning into a farce."

Dupin hung up. The way Rose had positioned herself near him made it clear she was expecting an immediate update.

"Lilou Breval just tried to call me," Dupin said softly, hesitant, "but now we can't get through to her again."

"I suppose your line was busy?" Rose turned away from Dupin, her tone coolly implying: *This is all absurd.*

A moment later, she turned back to Jaffrezic. "Le Sel. We were talking about Le Sel, *monsieur.*"

"Ah yes. It's a big corporation. From the south. They're destroying everything. They've bought up more and more salt marshes over the last decade, at highly inflated prices. They're constantly making us all offers, Daeron included. Have you not met Madame Ségolène Laurent yet?"

The world of "pure sea salt" might have been a wonderful world in culinary terms, but it was clear that as an industry it was in fact an extremely complicated world. A tough world. And thus a very human one, thought Dupin.

"No."

"The 'empress,' an attractive cross between Marie Antoinette and a barracuda," said Jaffrezic earnestly. "She's always trying to exploit the Centre du Sel and Juliette Bourgiot, who is the head of it."

If Dupin recalled correctly, Juliette Bourgiot was the second person from the salt marshes to be quoted by Lilou Breval in her article.

"What do you mean by 'exploit'?" Rose was sounding more and more irritable.

"The Centre du Sel is a real institution in this community and this region. It used to be overwhelmingly financed by tax money—like a lot of things in the White Land it was subsidized by the state in one way or another. But the Centre's stylish new building was largely financed by Le Sel two years ago. That creates certain 'obligations,' whether people like it or not."

Dupin had made note of all of these names. Very legibly. On difficult cases, particularly since his police work had started to involve Breton names, which were quite often unpronounceable, he occasionally made an actual cast list on the last page of his notebook, as one would for a play. Juliette Bourgiot: head of the Centre du Sel, Ségolène Laurent: director of Le Sel, etc.

"Is the Centre du Sel the large wooden building on the right-hand side on the way here?" Dupin tried to get back into the conversation, still kicking himself about the missed call.

"No. That's *our* center. The cooperative's. The Maison du Sel!"

"What happens there?"

"We show people the world of salt. They're guided round, they can do some harvesting themselves, they have the cooperative explained to them, they get to look at a little exhibition—not as in-depth as in the new Centre, of course. And we sell our salt there. There's quite a lot of direct selling at this stage, even via our online store."

"I take it the Centre du Sel does something similar?"

"As well as the lobbying work for Madame Laurent."

"And who's in charge of the Maison du Sel?" Dupin was filling out the table in his notebook.

"Me. The head of the cooperative."

"And what does—"

Dupin's phone shrieked again, right in the middle of another of Rose's questions. Dupin answered. It was Riwal.

"Riwal, this really isn't a good—"

"A woman's body. In the gulf. In the Locmiquel and Larmor-Baden oyster beds. Right opposite the passage—across from Kerpenhir and Locmariaquer!"

Dupin froze. "What?"

"We were listening to the police radio. Two minutes ago there was a phone call to the police in Auray. Oyster fishermen found a woman's body in their beds, it's low tide." Riwal fell silent briefly. "She's around forty years old, they estimate. Short hair. Sweater and jeans. Identity as yet unknown. She hadn't been in there long. We don't know any more at this point. We—"

That was enough. Dupin hung up. He felt his muscles cramping. His shoulder was terribly painful. He was nauseous.

Surely it couldn't be true. She had tried to call him a quarter of an hour ago. How could that be? But: everything fit. The place. The short hair. The age. And, worst of all, he had—if he were honest—a funny feeling deep down this whole time. It would be too much of a coincidence.

Jaffrezic and Rose were staring at him, both of them seeming to know that something had happened. Dupin stood almost paralyzed for a moment, then abruptly snapped out of it. But before he could even say anything, Rose's mobile rang. An almost old-fashioned, high-pitched, very loud ring. She reached blindly into her jacket pocket, whipped it out, and held it straight to her ear.

Dupin knew what was coming. He wasn't going to wait. Without looking around, he walked back up the path they'd just come down. Back to his car.

* * *

There was an extreme brutality to it. The dead body in this utterly peaceful scene. They were standing on the ocean floor of a wide bay, in the middle of the Anse de Locmiquel, hundreds of meters of coarse sand with huge numbers of oyster and mussel beds nestled in it. In a few hours, perch would be swimming here again, giltheads, barbs, pollack. The sky was blue, adorned with a few scattered fair-weather clouds like balls of cotton, and the inky blue Morbihan shimmered in the distance, a few hundred meters farther south. Beyond the clearly discernible passage, the open Atlantic flashed, silvery and restless.

It was Lilou Breval. Dupin recognized her from meters away. It looked as though her head had got caught between two wooden struts of the long, wooden oyster beds. It was stuck fast. Perhaps that had been the only thing stopping the body from getting pushed farther through the gulf by the currents. It was a macabre scene. The journalist's closed eyelids looked oddly peaceful, but she had a tortured expression on her face. On the left-hand side of her face, there was a large wound at her temple, and it was terribly swollen. Otherwise her body looked unscathed. Her hair and clothes were already dry again. Not far from the body, three large aluminum cases lay in the middle of the seabed: the pathology and forensics teams' equipment.

Dupin was standing next to the dead body, very close to it. Motionless. Stony-faced. His gaze was riveted on Lilou, eyes narrowed, facial muscles tense.

Having arrived just before Dupin, Rose had—very authoritatively—"requested" that the pathologist and both members of the forensic team from Vannes, as well as the two local police officers, give her and Dupin a few moments alone. Already absorbed in the task at hand, they had been grumpy as they obeyed this order.

"We're going to get the perpetrator," Rose said coldly, low-pitched, without emotion, but with great determination. "Even the smartest perpetrators commit their deeds in the real world—and in the real world, everything leaves a trace."

Dupin closed his eyes, took a deep breath, and lifted his head, his chin jutting forward.

"Yeah. We'll get him."

"Soon we'll know whether that wound was the cause of death. It looks like it. She was at the very least severely injured. And undoubtedly unconscious."

Dupin opened his eyes again and ran one hand roughly through his hair. It was a while before he responded.

"Yeah."

"So the call today wasn't even from her—it was just from her phone. We'll try to locate it. That could have been the perpetrator calling you."

Suddenly the call seemed creepy to Dupin. Malicious. Did a stranger dial his number from Lilou's phone? But why? And Rose was right, it could have been the perpetrator.

"The lowest point of the low tide was at half past eight. I think the water had retreated from the bay by half past five. So the body has lain here since at least then. Soon we'll find out whether she was already dead."

"Put out a search for her car immediately," Dupin said mechanically.

"They're already on it. We've got support from Vannes and Auray. I've sorted everything. Lilou Breval probably didn't get very far during the night. After she got to her parents' house. Either she drove on to wherever the murderer was lying in wait for her, or she had arranged to meet them. In any case, it was most likely not far from the gulf."

"Or perhaps she wasn't the one doing the driving by that point. And"—the car wasn't at her parents' house after all—"the murderer placed Lilou's body in the car and drove it away."

"If so, she was probably murdered at their house."

At this stage, these were all hypotheses, free association really. But it did Dupin good, it grounded him, giving him a little something to hold on to in this horrific situation. He knew what he was like; he had to take action and keep busy. He had to throw himself into the case with double or triple the energy he usually did. His emotions would haunt him later.

"The murderer—or murderers." Rose's expression was grave.

Both of them were silent for some time.

"How well did you know each other?" Rose asked eventually, her voice sympathetic.

"I . . . . just a little. We . . . ." Dupin broke off.

They hadn't really been friends; they had only seen each other a handful of times over the past few years, and then only briefly—they had spent a longer time together just that one evening in her garden—and they had spoken on the phone occasionally. But that didn't matter, there were people with whom you had a connection from the very beginning and it was clear that you understood one another. And that didn't happen all that often. They could have become friends; they had both been aware of that and taken great pleasure in it.

A tall, heavyset man peeled away from the group huddled together about twenty meters away—Dupin had completely forgotten about them—and came over to the two commissaires somewhat hesitantly. It was the pathologist.

Dupin ran a hand through his hair again. He wouldn't be able to stand a work-related conversation. Not now. Pathologists were a strange species. Not his cup of tea.

"I'll drive over to the parents' house," he said quickly.

Rose understood. She nodded. "I'll have a quick word with everyone and then I'll follow you."

"We've got to tackle these salt world people. Pick up our conversation with the head of the cooperative, find out what else Lilou was interested in at the salt gardens, apart from what was in the article. Meet with the director of Le Sel. Find out who Lilou spoke to, who she knew in the salt marshes. And we've got to search her house again. Take a look at her online accounts, her call records, everything. And pay more attention to the blue barrels."

This was an overexcited flood of words. Dupin knew that he had just been stating the obvious. And yet it helped him compose himself. He needed to be meticulous with the few leads they had. Immerse himself in them, sink his teeth into them. Persevere. And hope to come across something that would help them make progress. Lilou Breval was really dead. Murdered. She had probably already been dead last night when they were in her house.

"We'll do it. *All* of it." Rose's words were a declaration of war.

The pathologist had pointedly gone over to his case to take something out. He wanted to continue his work.

Dupin turned away.

He walked along the oyster beds part of the way, making a detour just big enough to avoid encountering the rest of the group, which was starting to move as well.

* * *

Dupin had some trouble finding the house. The old Peugeot did not, of course, come equipped with a navigation system. Rose, who was probably a matter of minutes behind him, had described the route to him as best she could on the phone: The "Route du soleil," a small road that led to the sun-drenched headland, past the ruins of the fairy stone, the Men-er-Hroec'h—originally a twenty-five-meter-high menhir and the largest in the world until it broke into four pieces at some point thousands of years ago.

The house was in a small wood at the gulf, a little outside Kerpenhir, on a narrow outcrop of land crisscrossed by tiny unnamed tracks and paths.

Dupin eventually arrived at four almost identical-looking old stone houses standing close together. The Brevals' house was the last one in the row. The neighbor who was likely the last person to have seen Lilou Breval alive also lived in one of these houses.

It all felt quiet and peaceful. The glittering sun was almost at its peak, a merciless sun that beat down, making people flee and lending a melancholy to the shadows of the dense little wood next to the houses. In certain places, blurry glimpses of the bright gulf shimmered between the dark trunks of the stone pines. The investigators would arrive in their cars any minute now, and that's when professional chaos would break out. Dupin was glad to be on his own a little longer. He parked his car a good distance from the house; the forensics people would examine everything on the street in front of the house too. Lilou's car must have been parked here, and a second car must have been somewhere round here too. Dupin was standing right outside the house when his phone rang. It was Commissaire Rose.

"My team have found four blue barrels. Judging by the description they're the same as the ones in the cooperative. In a fallow salt pool. At the edge of the salt marshes, near Pradel. I had ordered the whole area to be searched systematically. The barrels are open and empty. We're having them examined for residue."

"Whom does the salt pool belong to?"

"We don't know yet. But we're working on it. In theory they could just be a few harmless barrels belonging to the cooperative that somehow ended up there. But it would be too much of a coincidence."

"Why were they in those salt marshes? In that spot?"

Dupin knew Rose couldn't answer these questions, of course. "Why these damned barrels again?" He sounded aggressive, speaking as if to himself.

"I'll be right with you. Wait for me."

Rose had hung up on her last syllable.

It had all started with those damn barrels. They needed to know what had been inside them. That could make a lot of things clearer.

The Brevals' house had just two small windows facing the street; it was all oriented backward, toward the wood and the gulf. A narrow path led to the side, where the main door was.

The silence was almost eerie, apart from the birdsong typical throughout the gulf. Henri could distinguish between birds effortlessly; the gulf was one of the most significant bird habitats in Europe, as were the salt gardens. Without even thinking about it, Dupin drew his gun. The door was closed and looked fully intact. Like at Lilou's house, the narrow path carried on past the front door and along the side of the house.

Dupin moved slowly, avoiding any unnecessary sound on the gravel. He stopped at the corner of the house. He scrutinized his surroundings. He knew it was unlikely that anyone was still here, least of all Lilou Breval's murderer. But he suddenly felt a little like he had the evening before. In the salt marshes. This was crazy. He shook himself. Then he stepped—the gun still firmly in his grasp—around the corner of the house and found himself in the garden.

There was nobody to be seen. A stone patio, a small table, three chairs, a turquoise lounger on the lawn. It was a modest garden and merged into the little wood without a fence or any other markings. The patio door stood wide open. Dupin knew he ought to wait for Rose.

He went inside. The overhead light was on. The room was cramped with little light from outside—there were only two windows on this side too, although they were bigger than the ones on the other side. It was pleasantly cool.

On first impression, there was nothing unusual about the house. The furnishings were very simple, modest, almost spartan; everything seemed on the old side. There was a kitchenette to the left; next to that was a small corridor leading to the front door and another, closed door; opposite that, a narrow staircase to the floor above; to the right was the living room with a white painted wooden table and four chairs, against the wall behind that was a worn-out sofa; and next to it, in the right-hand corner, was a new sofa. Dupin moved slowly through the room.

"Hello, is anyone there? This is the police."

"Whom are you expecting?"

Commissaire Rose had suddenly entered the house behind him.

"You were going to wait for me," she said. Surprisingly, this sounded almost friendly. Her eyes darted around the room.

She walked over to the door next to the corridor as though she had been coming in and out of the house for years. As she did so she took a thin silicone glove out of the pocket of her coat and slipped it on. She opened the door in one fluid movement. There was a small toilet on the other side.

"The fallow salt pool belongs to Le Sel. It hasn't been used for two years. No more good clay in it. The barrels are actually identical to the ones at the cooperative. 'Super wide-necked barrels.' Eighty centimeters high, fifty in diameter. Drop handles on the sides. The manufacturer is called Fasco, they're based in the South of France. The barrels were in a harvest pool."

She glanced into the corridor, then began to climb the stairs.

Dupin had to take a moment to compose himself. The scene reminded him too much of being in Lilou's house the night before.

"Why are we finding the barrels in one of the Le Sel salt pools now? What does that mean?"

"We'll ask Madame Laurent. If she and Le Sel were in on it together, it would be extremely stupid to take the barrels to your own salt marshes, of all places."

She was right, of course. But perhaps this trick was part of a staged scene?

"Where can you buy these barrels? In special shops?"

They had reached the second floor. Dupin was hard on Rose's heels.

"We don't know yet. Lilou Breval's mobile can't be traced. It seems to be switched off. Or destroyed. We've applied for the call records, and for the landline too." Rose seemed to be telling him all of this in an offhand way. "We have the results from testing the salt concentration in Daeron's harvest pools. Annoyingly, they're not clear-cut. Apparently the values are slightly below what they should be. But it's not that easy to tell, because in nature, evaporation levels and speed vary. You never know exactly what given value should be reached on a given day. The experts aren't ruling out freshwater having been added, though. Apparently it would have to have been done very subtly, very expertly. But, as I said, they couldn't establish anything definitive."

Dupin sighed. It would have been too perfect.

Strangely, the second floor seemed much more spacious than the floor below. Two generous-size rooms and a bathroom that must have been there since the eighties, like the kitchen below. The first room was almost empty; it looked sad, two old chairs in a corner. They had only glanced inside.

They were in the second room, a bedroom with a narrow double bed.

Rose was looking at everything very carefully. "Nothing to indicate a struggle, a dispute, or that someone was overpowered," she said.

There was a dark brown oiled leather suitcase lying open on a simple chest of drawers. Rose set to work on it.

"Moisturizer, two eyeglass cases, a toothbrush, a charger. She was planning to stay the night here. When she got here, everything was probably still okay."

"Somebody must have known that she intended to come here, to spend the night here," Dupin said, lost in thought.

Rose was already on her way back to the stairs.

"I've instructed Inspector Chadron to include both of your inspectors in the investigation. We could do with every police officer available. So they don't have to stay hidden anymore, as nice as it might be in Le Grand Large."

Rose's face was impassive as she said this. Dupin struggled to remain equally impassive. He had no idea how she had got wind of Kadeg and Riwal, of the fact that Riwal hadn't driven back to Concarneau at all. And where the two of them were. She had probably known this the whole time.

Rose was downstairs again and making her way toward the white table in the living room. A plate, a torn-off piece of baguette, a bit of paté. An open bottle of Madiran, the glass unused. The bottle opener with the cork next to the glass. As though Lilou had been sitting there just minutes before and had simply gone into the garden for a moment. A sad sight. Dupin could feel his stomach tightening.

"She had just sat down to dinner, and then something must have happened. She was interrupted. Before she could even pour herself a glass of wine," Rose said, more to herself than to Dupin.

"The laptop is missing. The rest of her things are all there, but no laptop." Dupin had been keeping an eye out for it upstairs but hadn't seen it. He had also looked for work documents, including some from recent weeks.

"The murderer must have been in this house. And they'll have removed anything they didn't want to fall into our hands. Even if they didn't have much time."

Although there was always an element of speculation in these kinds of conclusions, Rose's mind was razor-sharp, always moving forward, pushing for specific scenarios. Dupin had a feeling her assumptions were correct, despite there not being any evidence to support them yet.

"We ought to—"

Midway through his sentence, both of their phones rang. Dupin automatically went outdoors and answered.

"Monsieur le Commissaire?"

It made Dupin mad when Kadeg asked if it was him on the phone, when Kadeg himself had just dialed Dupin's number. This had always been an idiosyncrasy of his inspector's. This time, Kadeg carried straight on in his eager staccato voice, which was a sign he had uncovered something.

"We're in the salt marshes, near Pradel. Inspector Chadron requested us." He sounded pleased. "I know the barrels from Fasco. They're normal trade barrels. You can get them in any good DIY store. I Googled them on my smartphone just now." Kadeg paused, as though he wanted to pass his miracle device to the commissaire down the phone line. "They're made from food-grade, low-density polyethylene. Particularly good for paste-like substances with high viscosity. Smooth inner walls, extremely easy to clean, don't retain residue.

Particularly large opening for pouring in substances, with air- and watertight screw-on lid. Rubber seal. Temperature resistant between negative four and one hundred seventy-five degrees Fahrenheit. EU license for durability when used with solid substances, pastes, most acids, and lyes."

As much as he wasn't in the mood, Dupin almost burst out laughing. He hoped that Kadeg had read all that aloud, but maybe Kadeg was just an expert in low-density polyethylene barrels. Dupin wouldn't put any absurd passion past Kadeg. But much more important: as depressing as it was that anyone could have bought these barrels anywhere, Dupin was very interested in the question of the barrels' specific uses. It sounded very technical.

"What do people use them for?"

"I did just go over that: they're more or less universally useful, that's the great advantage of these barrels. I use them at home myself. In the garden. To store apples, for instance. As I said, they're fully food-safe."

"But you could keep dangerous substances in these exact barrels?"

"It's due to the fantastic molecular qualities of the—"

Kadeg was gradually becoming unbearable, so Dupin interrupted him.

"Understood—and if they were lying underwater in a pool for a few hours, you wouldn't find any of what they had contained on their perfectly smooth inner walls."

"No, the residues would only be traceable in the water of the pool."

"In extremely low concentrations that would be hard to detect, I imagine."

"That depends on the substance, according to the chemist on the forensics team. He has carried out some toxicological rapid tests. All normal so far."

"Brilliant." Dupin groaned. "Anything else, Kadeg?"

"The government's food chemist responsible for the salt marshes got in touch. She'd like to speak to you and Commissaire Rose face-to-face. She's deeply concerned, of course. She's asking whether we have any theories yet. Whether we fear that the quality of the salt output from any salt pond could be compromised. There are very strict requirements in place. And the salt marshes are a priority conservation area. She'd like to know what's going on with the barrels. She—"

"Is that it, Kadeg?"

"She's insisting that—"

Dupin hung up. He looked around. During their conversation he had walked through the garden and a little way into the stone pine wood. The garden and this section of the wood weren't visible from any of the other houses due to high laurel bushes and fig trees forming a solid wall. The gulf was even closer than it had looked earlier. It was particularly dark in the little wood and pleasantly cool, a stark contrast to the harsh brightness of the day. If Lilou Breval had been killed in her parents' house, had the murderer disposed of her body right here in the gulf? At first glance, there were no signs of that. Dupin walked across the soft ground toward the shore.

He was not an expert at estimating tides—to his own regret—but depending on when it happened, there might not even have been enough water. Even now, midway between high tides, there were a hundred meters between the shore and the waterline. It smelled of mud flats, silt, and seaweed.

"Commissaire?"

It was Rose. She was standing at the edge of the little wood, calling to him at the top of her voice. But astonishingly gently.

"They've found Breval's Peugeot. A minute away from here. Right at the passage, on a small path that leads to the sea."

That was quick. And crucial.

"I'm coming."

Dupin would have liked to keep looking around, as he usually did. But perhaps the car would shed some light on the case.

* * *

Dupin was standing on a narrow strip of sandy beach dotted with dark, pointed rocks; beyond them were marram grass, tall pines, and stone pines. There were stone pines everywhere, and Dupin loved them. This was the tip of the narrow headland on the western side of the gulf and it looked like it was reaching out toward the opposite side in despair. The Pointe de Kerpenhir, or "gateway to the gulf," lay in front of him, the incredible passage offering up a terrifying spectacle today: the great Atlantic—to the right—lay smooth as glass in front of him, just like the small sea—to the left. Both were perfectly calm but between them the water rippled hard, white crests of foam dancing wildly about. You could see it: the violence, the pressure from the bodies of water flowing inward, the impact of the chaotic currents of up to twenty kilometers an hour. Three hundred million cubic meters of ocean flowed in or out every time the tide turned.

"Yes, two longer interviews. The one with Maxime Daeron came out three weeks after the long article, so about a year ago. The second one, the interview with Ségolène Laurent, only came out two months ago. In July."

Nolwenn had been quick. As always.

"I want to read them both."

"I'll send them to a police station near you, then they can print them out and bring them to you. It would all be easier with a smart-phone; you really should consider using the one in your desk drawer. It would be really useful."

He had been having this discussion about smartphones with Nolwenn for a long time and Dupin had no illusions about it: he would lose eventually. In January the commissariat had been kitted out with the latest generation of stylish smartphones that could "do anything" and his two inspectors had been very pleased with them, especially Kadeg; Dupin had refused to use one so far. He could just imagine getting that notification in a dicey situation: "System failure." You needed a diploma to use the phone he already had. But now was not the time to continue this discussion. Besides, he had Nolwenn, what did he need a smartphone for?

"Send it to the commissariat in Guérande town. To Riwal. I don't know how much longer we'll be at the gulf."

"There were also two shorter articles in the *Ouest-France* relating to the salt marshes. But not by Lilou Breval. One about the new salt. The *sel moulin*. A silly fad, if you ask me. And one about the extension to the Centre du Sel building. But that was also just a few lines long."

"Send me those articles too."

"Okay."

"And look up whether there were any reports generally, not just in the Guérande, on illegal schemes relating to salt farming. Forbidden or controversial additives, manufacturing processes, whatever."

"No problem."

"And," Dupin took out his notebook, "look out for anything interesting on 'super wide-necked barrels.' Whether they come up in relation to any criminal activities somewhere. Made by Fasco. Or other companies too. Large barrels."

Dupin was aware that this task was extremely vague. However, if there were anything to be found, Nolwenn would find it.

"You're not letting up on the barrels. And a good thing too!" Nolwenn's tone changed. *"Monsieur le Commissaire?"*

"Yes?"

"Claire just tried to get through to you again. I told her the case has changed dramatically and that it's a murder case now—and also that the préfet officially instructed you to lead the investigation for Finistère, as it's equally affected. And how upset you are that this happened today of all days. How unlucky it is. But all the same: you should call her."

Dupin didn't yet know when or how, but yes—he needed to call Claire. He wanted to call her, of course, and do everything in his power to make it to Paris that evening.

"I will. And . . . thank you, Nolwenn."

"It's a great loss for Brittany. For Breton journalism. She's irreplaceable! It's horrific."

Dupin was confused for a moment. Nolwenn had abruptly returned to Lilou Breval. He had still been thinking about Claire.

"Yes—yes, it is."

Dupin hung up. The sun beat down even more harshly than before; it was almost unbearable. Everything around him was sparkling brightly. A cap would have been useful; he had a couple of them but never wore them.

In front of him, the saddest memorial Dupin had ever seen rose up into the sky. It was a well-known story. Hammered into pale gray granite, overgrown with yellow-and-orange lichens and moss, a fisherman's wife with a child in her arms keeps watch for a husband, never to return. It's clear she knows he's not coming back but also that, for all eternity, there is only one thing she can do—or wants to do: keep watch for him, day after day. It stood on a high, round pedestal made of granite, on a small island of black stone, just short of the tip of the headland. You could get there with your feet dry if the tide was very low, while water washed right over it when the tide was coming in. And the woman and child stood amidst the raging sea.

Dupin turned round. He could see Commissaire Rose through the trees as she bent over the backseat in Lilou Breval's car fifty meters away. Her Peugeot was on a small, sandy path leading into the patch of woodland. That's where the perpetrator had parked it. It had been just two minutes' drive from the Brevals' house after all.

It would definitely take a while for a third team from forensics to be on the scene; two teams had already been deployed.

Rose and Dupin had been doing an initial inspection of the Peugeot when Nolwenn called. The car doors were open when they got there and the car key was missing.

On first impression, without technical support, there was nothing suspicious about it, nothing at all. It was maddening: so far there were no leads.

Dupin knew this was a deeply ingrained idiosyncrasy, but on principle he couldn't stand people listening while he was on the phone, no matter what he was talking about. It was even worse during a case and in this specific situation. So he had walked some distance away and left Rose to examine the rest of the car.

He walked back slowly. Commissaire Rose was crouched down, still preoccupied by the backseat. To the naked eye, there was nothing unusual so far.

"Any news?" He heard the words coming to him from the car.

She hadn't turned around and Dupin was still a few meters away. Baffling. He thought for a moment, then briefly summarized the phone call with Nolwenn. Rose listened without commenting, as though she wanted to make sure he was reporting everything.

"We didn't find any of those interviews at Lilou's house. Or at her parents' either," Dupin concluded his short report.

"What we do know is this: Lilou Breval was still interested in the White Land recently. Also, we have two more people we know she knew in the salt gardens—and that she had spoken to them. That makes four already. And there was definitely more material than what eventually went to print. There will have been initial drafts, transcripts of the recorded interviews that have more in them," reasoned Rose, "on her laptop and maybe printed out too. But we haven't found any of that yet."

"The murderer doesn't know what we know," Dupin said thoughtfully, but urgently. "There's no way for them to be sure what leads we've actually got and what we think is relevant. They'll get rid of anything they consider a potential clue."

"We'll do some more digging at the editorial offices. And look at her email account. She might have sent in earlier drafts." Commissaire Rose turned to the backseat. "So far it's impossible to say whether she drove herself here or was brought here. Defenseless. Perhaps already severely injured, or even dead. I haven't found anything that gets us anywhere."

The inside of the car looked a little bit like Lilou Breval's house. On the passenger seat and the backseat there were magazines strewn wildly about, a few books, newspapers, the *Ouest-France,* and particularly editions of *Le Monde diplomatique* and *Libération.* Several glossy journals about garden design. All of this had been Lilou's life; now it was a meaningless mess.

Rose was wearing skin-colored silicone gloves again. On her, they almost looked like a fashion accessory. There was no sign of the stresses of the previous night about her clothes or about herself.

"Virtually sterile." Dupin was standing in front of the empty trunk.

"I never use mine either." Rose shrugged. "There's always the backseat."

Dupin had his Clairefontaine out. Open at his list of people. Each name was circled. Underneath, beside, and above them were key words about the people, a technique that swiftly made the double-page spread confusing. Some names were, for reasons known only to him, circled twice, with wildly scribbled symbols added: exclamation marks, question marks, plus signs, and even things crossed out.

"I'd like to speak to this food chemist who wants to see us so urgently." It occurred to Dupin that Kadeg hadn't even mentioned her name. "We need an expert. I want to know her general thoughts on the barrels in the salt marshes. And what illegal schemes you might have if you were producing salt."

Dupin could feel the feverishness he experienced whenever he was caught up in a complicated case. It was an odd state. In a way, he stepped away from the world every time. He forgot everyday life. So there was nothing but the case and all of his questions, which was a sore point in his relationship with Claire. But at the same time, this was when he was absolutely in the real world, more precisely and clearly than at any other time. Doing just one thing: solving the case.

"We'll do that. But first we should talk to the director of Le Sel, Madame Laurent. She lives at the gulf too," Rose said offhandedly.

"She lives at the gulf too?"

"We don't know yet if it's her home or a *résidence secondaire*. A huge number of Bretons have 'a house at the gulf.' Not just the wealthy. Many from the Guérande too. It's nothing unusual."

Dupin almost asked whether she was one of them. It had sounded a little that way. Some Concarnese had a house at the gulf too, Dupin knew that. Henri, of course. One of Nolwenn's brothers and also a sister. The gulf was big—twenty kilometers long from east to west, and fifteen kilometers from the sea to Vannes—and a favorite spot amongst Bretons. They considered the gulf, Dupin had come to understand, as *their* Mediterranean or, more accurately, their form of Mediterranean; the Mediterranean atmosphere, only better, Atlantic. Or rather, Breton. Also part of the gulf was the beloved Presqu'île de Quiberon, which bordered it on the west side, as did the megalithic menhir-mecca Carnac and the Hoedic Islands off the coast and the "South Sea beauty" Île d'Houat with the "Treac'h ar Goured," said to be the most spectacular beach in Brittany and, above all of course: the legendary Belle-Île.

"We should also speak to the head of the Centre du Sel as soon as possible, Madame Bourgiot. And step up our conversation with the director of the cooperative."

Rose sounded sinister when she said "step up." Her "we should" sentences were firm guidelines with no room for discussion. This was how they would proceed, with interviews in this order.

"Where do you think Lilou Breval was thrown into the water?" Dupin had walked a few meters away from the car.

Rose straightened up abruptly, took the gloves off, and walked, without saying a word, between the tall stone pines toward the farthest outcrop of the headland. Someone had put up a circular viewing platform here, only slightly raised. It was about thirty meters from the car. Rose didn't stop until she'd reached the end where there was a low, flat stone wall that was more of a trip hazard than a protective measure. She put her right foot on it, hands in her pants pockets. The water roared right past the outcrop, directly beneath them. Dupin stood next to her, gazing into the gurgling current.

They remained like this for some time. Then Rose broke the silence, her eyes fixed steadily on the water.

"Here in the passage there are dips and shallows of up to forty meters. All along the main channel where the water comes in and out. The body could have disappeared forever here. It was highly likely to do so, in fact—and once the low tide had come, it would have dragged it into the Atlantic forever anyway. The currents go out into the open sea for kilometers." Rose spoke more and more darkly as she went on. "But surely the murderer couldn't wait for the tide to change."

It would have been the perfect spot to choose, as macabre as it sounded: perfect and practical in every way. There was nobody here at night; the closest houses, including Lilou's parents' house, were half a kilometer away, small patches of woodland all around.

Dupin felt dizzy all of a sudden. His gaze was submerged in the eddies. The word "shallows" had always frightened him as a child; it sounded like "shadows" to his ears. Dark, shapeless creatures that pulled you away into the depths. His anxieties about boats had probably started there.

"Let's go. The forensics team will be here soon."

He desperately needed a coffee. He would pass a place where he could stop off briefly along the way. And he'd be able to take a pill too—the pains in his shoulder had gotten worse again. Maybe there would even be a ham and cheese sandwich.

* * *

The compromise had been to pass by the salt marshes where the barrels had been found, not far from Pradel, and meet the food chemist there "briefly." Dupin had wanted it this way round—Rose the other way. And then they would speak to Madame Laurent, who was having a meeting with Madame Bourgiot anyway, so they had decided to meet them both together. Dupin wondered if he would have to pay later for his mini-victory on the order of business. The very idea of having to investigate with someone had never sat right with Dupin—in practice it was even worse, as he had been forced to realize. Even on the issue of what to do next, or rather, first. An issue—and it was simply one of many—that was always essential in an investigation. Sometimes crucial. Dupin couldn't simply walk away or drive off like he usually tended to do and follow a hunch—a hunch so deep down inside that even he was barely conscious of it—whenever he felt like it. A hunch he didn't even have on this case yet. That morning he had been thinking of suggesting to Rose that they split up. He didn't fully trust her—and on her turf, with her team, she had serious advantages that would leave him in a poor position.

They had parked their cars on the Route des Marais and walked. Dupin had parked right behind Rose. There had been another Renault in front of Rose's Renault, the same car, but in jet black.

"I've had Daeron's salt marshes banned from producing salt until further notice. And this one too, of course, although it's not being cultivated at the moment. Until there's no shadow of a doubt that those four barrels and what they contained are completely innocuous."

Céline Cordier was standing in front of them, her stance relaxed, in stark contrast to her resolute words. Dupin had a different image in his mind of a state-appointed food chemist. More like a scientist. In a white coat perhaps. Céline Cordier looked like a graphic designer from a trendy agency. A plain blue T-shirt with a bright red circle printed on it, tight faded jeans that made her hip bones stick out, and a pair of dark blue Converse sneakers. Rangy, almost as tall as him, a little lanky—nicely lanky—shoulder-length, layered black hair, amber eyes. Around midthirties.

"Whatever is going on," she continued, "it's clear there is considerable criminal intent at work. A shooting, the murder of a journalist who appears to be linked to it."

So the news had already spread. This was to be expected, of course. It had happened in next to no time. The oyster fishermen had found the corpse, someone in the editorial office had been asked about relatives, and so on. And this was a well-known journalist, after all. A murder. And naturally people would draw a link to the shooting yesterday, on the basis alone that he himself had turned up in both places. It was on the radio and in the online editions of the newspapers, it would be in print tomorrow.

Dupin basically understood the food chemist's frightened attitude.

But her arrogant, demanding manner annoyed him. Clearly it annoyed Rose too.

"We have not yet been able to confirm the presence of any substance that does not belong here. Our forensic chemists have taken various samples. From different pools. In particular, from the harvest pools."

Rose had taken up her usual stance—her right hand in her jacket, the thumb poking out—and was speaking firmly. She had calmly pretended not to hear Cordier's implicit question as to whether there were any link.

They were standing on one of the wider footbridges amidst the salt ponds where the barrels had been found. It was clear the harvest pool was not being cultivated; the water was full of algae and easily twenty centimeters deep. Dupin noted with relief that a light breeze had started up again in the White Land, as it often did when the tide was on its way in, clearing the air and making the blue of the sky and every other color more vibrant: the green and flaxen yellow of the grasses and ferns, the colors of the shimmering salt pools on their way here; shades of silver, blue, green, as well as red and pink. But above all it touched the intense blue of the four barrels that lay on their sides around the edges of the pool like strange sculptures and made it more dazzling. There was no sign of the seals or any kind of lid. There they were: the mysterious objects Lilou was interested in—they existed, they were real. And yet they remained, for now at least, just as mysterious as before.

"The situation is too unpredictable for my liking. We're already running tests in neighboring salt marshes. And we also don't want to lose any time in—"

"You're running *what*?" Commissaire Rose cut her off sharply.

"Our own tests. We've got to decide whether, over and above the measures taken, all salt marshes are to be shut down, until you or we know something."

"All of them? And who is *we?*"

"I head up the scientific department in the institute, and my colleague is in charge of the administrative section. In the end, I decide. There are strict regulations about this and I'm staying in touch with Paris, which could make any decision at any time and will abide by my expert report. This is an extremely sensitive food manufacturing center, which, unlike indoor factories, is largely unprotected and left at anyone's mercy. Tens of thousands of people will consume the salt that is being produced in these salt marshes over the course of just a few weeks."

Unimpressed, Rose sighed loudly during Cordier's explanation. Dupin wanted to get to the point uppermost in his mind at last.

"So what do you think might have happened, Madame Cordier? Here in the Salt Land? What dodgy, illegal things could have been going on? What might the barrels have contained?"

"Illegal schemes, acts of revenge, sabotage, outstanding payments, competition. I don't know. I don't know these people. I'm the wrong person to speculate."

"I specifically mean the salt itself—what are you afraid is wrong with it?"

"You could add substances that would make the salt unusable, even if the substance itself were harmless. The entire harvest. Dyes, for example. Or substances that would damage the floors of the salt marshes. Potentially for years to come. Or even worse, toxic substances. They wouldn't just destroy one harvest, but the reputation of the salt marshes for years and years in all of the Guérande."

Of course. Lilou had written about the "salt war." Dupin remembered the article well. Somebody might have it in for the whole place. The salt gardens of the Guérande. But if you wanted to damage the entire White Land, you would probably go about it differently. And if Dupin understood correctly, the Guérande didn't put up stiff competition anymore anyway.

"We're not working on that assumption at the moment. But we're checking everything, of course," Rose said calmly.

"And from our point of view, we still need to rule out the tiniest potential risk," Cordier said in a tone that brooked no disagreement.

Dupin thought hard. It was conceivable, this possibility had come up this morning, after all: somebody here wanted to harm someone else. Wanted to harm Daeron. An individual, a group, a cooperative, a business. Different forms and levels of sabotage were possible.

"So how would you go about sabotaging someone else's salt harvest?"

Dupin was very interested in this. They needed to think outside the box.

"There would be many different substances for that. But you'd be able to detect those. The most malicious thing would be to add water during critical stages; that could never be detected, it—"

"Fresh water?"

Maxime Daeron had mentioned this very thing to them earlier.

The food chemist looked at Dupin in surprise. Only now did he notice that her lips were made up in the exact same shade of red as the circle on her T-shirt.

"Harvests and hence incomes can be sabotaged by fresh water. But as I said: if you try to shoot a police officer dead to stop him finding out what you're doing, there might be something more controversial going on. Not involving four barrels of drinking water."

That was in fact what Rose and Dupin would have said. This was exactly what was bothering them too. Or it did Dupin, anyway.

"So we do have cause for grave concern," Cordier concluded.

"And we have—"

Dupin was interrupted by Rose's mobile. She stepped aside and picked up. You could just hear her saying, "Okay, Chadron," before lowering her voice.

Céline Cordier didn't seem in the least impressed by the interruption, carefully taking her own phone out of her jeans pocket and starting to type something.

Dupin had begun to balance his way across the ridiculously narrow footbridge to the pool in front of them, where the barrels lay. There probably wouldn't be anything more to see close-up. The experts had done an initial examination and hadn't spotted anything. After a few steps he realized that someone was behind him. He looked round. It was Rose.

"Chadron. The forensics team have found fingerprints in Lilou's parents' house, on the door to the garden, and they're not hers. We're collecting prints from everyone we've already come across—here in Gwenn Rann."

Before Dupin could say anything, Rose carried on—returning to their earlier topic so abruptly it was as though the interruption of the phone call had never happened:

"Uncovering sabotage carried out by independent *paludiers* or ones belonging to the cooperative could damage the reputation of a large business and its director who had been aware of it, or even ordered it, to such an extent that whole careers would be destroyed—and, even worse, some big plans. That would be enough of a motive."

Her voice was low, but extremely firm. It was on the tip of Dupin's tongue to come back to the fingerprints again, just to make a point. It was potentially not insignificant news, but they would just have to wait. And what Rose said was correct.

Dupin had reached the end of the footbridge. There was nothing more to see close-up. He knelt down and Rose continued:

"It would be the end for the cooperative too, or an individual independent. In any case, to do something like this, you would have to be desperate or cold-blooded, and once you'd started, well then—"

She broke off. Dupin knew what she meant. He had witnessed

dozens of stories like that. Oddly, setting foot over a line that was not too serious in itself was sometimes enough to produce the psychological willingness required to do worse things and, interestingly, these things no longer seemed so bad. More like "necessary adjustments." Yes, they probably ought to seriously consider the sabotage of the salt harvests—regardless of motive it was potentially a systematic scheme and Lilou Breval had stumbled across it. But Dupin also felt they needed to keep looking for other potential theories.

He turned round, a signal to Rose on the narrow footbridge that it was time to do likewise and pick their way back the way they had come.

A few moments later they were standing with Céline Cordier again, who casually finished what she was typing before putting the smartphone into the back pocket of her jeans again.

Dupin still had some questions that were bothering him.

"Are there substances or chemicals that could be added during the manufacture of salt to increase the amounts produced or the quality of the salt? Half-legal, half-illegal means?"

"No. Not with sea salt. It's not created, it's extracted. Just released, you could say. Natural evaporation works perfectly efficiently and can't be increased in any way. And certainly not by adding chemicals. The composition of the salt is perfect here—there's nothing you could add to improve it."

Cordier was almost speaking in a normal tone of voice now; the aggression had vanished.

"What about any methods used outside France or Europe? Is there anything out there that someone here might illegally add to keep up with them?"

"I don't know the answer to that. But they mine salt deposits from the earth. That's irrelevant in cultivating sea salt."

"Are there any organic threats to the salt marshes that need to be kept in check? Bacteria? Like with mussels and oysters?"

Rose was right, you could approach it from this angle too.

"No. Apart from salt-loving or 'halophilic' bacteria—which are harmless and sometimes responsible, along with the clay, for the pools' intense red, pink, or purple coloring—bacteria have no chance. Salt is biochemically resistant."

There was a perplexed pause.

"Listen, we're looking into the complete suspension of production," Cordier said with bureaucratic frigidity. "The existing stock would only be released for sale following thorough testing." Her afterthought sounded surprisingly empathetic: "I'm aware that even a temporary closure of the salt marshes would really affect the *paludiers*. But this is about protecting the consumers. And that takes priority."

"There's always someone who profits from a catastrophe. Someone who has an interest in such things," Rose said pensively. Which made it sound dramatic. A moment later she was looking at her watch: "We've got to go."

They had an appointment.

* * *

The newly built Centre du Sel was impressive. And tasteful. Made entirely from natural materials. Untreated oak, pale granite, glass. Angular, nesting structures but not outrageously overdone. An exhibition entitled "The Magic World of Salt" was on display in the large hall. One of the things they'd done was to re-create a whole harvesting pool, as well as a miniature salt marsh. There were also "experience rooms" and display boards ("The History of Salt," "Salt for Gourmets"), a café, and the "*boutique de sel.*" Along with the various salts and salt products (mustard with *fleur de sel*, chocolate with *fleur de sel*, relaxing baths with *fleur de sel* . . .) there were also books, posters, DVDs, and magazines in the boutique. There was no sign of the salt world's "modest" financial conditions in the Centre du Sel.

A staff member had led the two commissaires into a conference room, not far from the "experience rooms." Madame Laurent and Madame Bourgiot were sitting at a pale oak table that was really too big for the not-very-big room.

"Where were you last night—both of you? From eight o'clock onward? And during the night?"

Never in his entire police career had Dupin ever begun an investigative interview with this sentence. Rose had done it, in her pleasant way, which made two things clear: this is a routine question and does not mean that we suspect you—and in the event we do in fact suspect you, you'd better brace yourself.

"And tell us who can confirm it."

Madame Laurent slowly brushed her hair—chin-length, dark blond with golden blond highlights, straight but with impressive volume—away from her tanned face with her right hand and settled it elegantly behind her ear. On the left-hand side, her hair kept falling across her face, no doubt the whole point of this asymmetric hairstyle. She was probably in her early fifties, an attractive woman wearing a dark pantsuit very similar to Rose's. Unlike Rose, she was not wearing a blouse, but a silk top with a deep V-neck, a pale lilac shade that suited her.

"I had things to do in Vannes until around twenty past seven, a meeting with a sausage producer—Monsieur Alain Doncieux, he owns the company—and then I drove home. I live at the gulf. On the Île d'Arz. I sat in the garden and then read in a lounge chair, drank wine, and looked happily out over the gulf from time to time. Until almost midnight. With this wonderful weather we're having."

An accurate answer, given very competently. Madame Laurent beamed at Rose. And added: "Do you believe there's a link between the death of the journalist and the shooting at the salt marshes last night? There's talk of murder in the media and that they're presumably related."

As she so often did, Rose didn't seem to realize that someone had asked her a question, which Dupin had long since recognized as a tactic.

"Was anyone at your house? Did you happen to send emails from a computer connected to the landline? So that electronic protocols could prove that you were there? Did you make or receive calls on the landline?"

The same old spiel. Perfectly friendly, nothing seemed to be for the sake of rhetoric, or even aggressive.

"As I said: I was reading. Pierre Lemaitre, the winner of the Goncourt Prize. Simply wonderful. And looking out over the water. No emails, no visitors, no phone calls all evening." She cast a serious glance at Dupin's bandage, peeping out from underneath his polo shirt. "I got something to eat in the kitchen at one point." She laughed. "I don't have an alibi. No witnesses whatsoever. And no neighbors can see me in my garden either. And I live alone."

Again she smiled, without a trace of smugness—and hence the highest form of smugness, which actually commanded some respect from Dupin. Madame Bourgiot, on the other hand, was looking over at the head of Le Sel a little nervously. She scooted back and forth on her chair, and it became clear that she was trying not to. The director of the Centre du Sel was young, perhaps early thirties, dark curly hair tied back, heavily made up, wearing a pair of those thick, dark, expensive eyeglass frames. She was wearing a dark suit and excessively high-heeled pumps. Yet she seemed pale next to Madame Laurent. One thing was clear: Madame Laurent was the real boss here.

"And you, Madame Bourgiot?"

"I was here. Until maybe quarter past eight, half past. With a

JEAN-LUC BANNALEC

colleague—she's in the bistro today. Since the beginning of September, we've only been open till seven. Then I drove home and had dinner with my husband. We live in Le Croisic." She hesitated for a moment. "Rue de Goélands, near the Mont Esprit."

She looked at Dupin now, who still hadn't said a word, with an uncertain, expectant look.

Of course he knew the Mont Esprit. It was one of the two "hills"—that's really what they were called—that had continued forming right up into the nineteenth century. They were due to the gradual buildup of ballast jettisoned by large salt ships in the harbor of Le Croisic so that the ships could then load up the white gold. Henri had told him people were very proud of these hills.

Rose continued, unperturbed. "Apart from your husband, did anyone see you or speak to you when you came home? Or did you make any phone calls?"

Madame Bourgiot tried to make eye contact with Madame Laurent, but then she seemed to feel that was inappropriate. She looked at Rose again. Dupin had got his notebook out and was leafing through it distractedly. In the end he hadn't got a coffee on his way back from the gulf to the White Land. He hadn't seen anywhere on the journey where he could have stopped quickly without making a fuss. Besides, Rose had been driving close behind him in her big Renault, almost without leaving a gap—he had wondered why she didn't just overtake him and drive on.

He had tried Claire's number four times during the journey—but kept getting her voicemail. That wasn't good.

"I spoke to Monsieur Jaffrezic from the cooperative briefly one more time. On my mobile. It was about things for the boutique," Madame Bourgiot finally said, still looking nervous and unsure.

"What 'things'?" Dupin asked brusquely.

"We've sold out of some of the cooperative's products and urgently need more stock. Quantities in the hundreds. The blends of *fleur de sel* with various herbs, especially *piment d'Espelette*." She suddenly seemed in her element now. "But also the one with lemon and dill. We had placed the orders a full two days before. I hadn't been able to get hold of him all day. He was expecting my call. During the season, there are often things to deal with in the evenings too. That's totally normal."

Her nervousness seemed to have lessened as she answered, and she was calming down.

"But the cooperative has its own Centre du Sel, of course, where they sell products. Monsieur Jaffrezic runs it himself." Dupin noticed his voice sounded a little hoarse. He urgently needed caffeine.

"Maison du Sel. The cooperative's one is called Maison du Sel," the director of the Centre du Sel corrected him. "They sell their salt directly there, that's true. But this one is the public center, the community one; we sell all of the *paludiers'* salt here." She nodded toward the boutique. "The independents' salt and the cooperative's. And of course Le Sel's. The center is dedicated to the entire salt gardens, it belongs to everyone."

"I . . . excuse me a moment." Dupin stood up midsentence and walked toward the glass door with all three women's eyes fixed curiously on him.

"I'll be right back." He left the room, gently closing the glass door behind him and heading straight for the boutique counter and the young woman standing behind it. Dark brown ponytail, a dark blue T-shirt with CENTRE DU SEL printed discreetly on it. Dupin hadn't realized the three women would clearly see him here. But that didn't matter now. He wasn't at his best, his mind wasn't working properly and he needed it very urgently now. A fully intact mind.

"Two espressos, please."

In fact, he desperately needed to eat something too; he had wondered on the journey whether Rose ever ate at all; perhaps she had stealthily eaten this morning after dropping him off. There was a display cabinet of delicious-looking quiches: tomato and sardine, fresh salmon, baby artichoke, all with a generous sprinkling of *fleur de sel*—but that might be a little inappropriate in this situation. Without thinking much about it, Dupin reached for the *bonbons caramel à la fleur de sel*. With less enthusiasm than yesterday, but still: they were seriously handy on the move, real blood sugar boosts and you could eat them discreetly.

With practiced movements and at impressive speed, the young girl had prepared the two coffees.

"Tell me, do you see Monsieur Jaffrezic here often? The head of the cooperative?"

"I know him." Her voice was confident, determined, an amusing contrast to her fragile appearance. "He comes pretty regularly. Once or twice a week."

Dupin took a step to one side and began to drink the first coffee in expert sips. It was perfect, absolutely perfect. And not too hot. So he drank the second one immediately.

"Excellent coffee. And when did Madame Bourgiot leave last night?"

"Sometime around half past eight. Maybe a bit earlier."

Dupin fished a ten-euro note out of his pants pocket, murmured "thanks," and on his way back to the conference room he opened the packet of candy (a long tube of ten this time, even handier). As he entered the room, he popped one in his mouth and slipped the packet back into his pocket.

Madame Bourgiot had just finished saying something. She looked at him in bemusement, at Madame Laurent in amusement, and Commissaire Rose didn't look at him at all.

"Fine, as discussed, we'll speak to Monsieur Jaffrezic. I—"

"In the interview that Lilou Breval conducted with you, one of the things discussed was the conflicting interests and disagreements in the White Land. The battles over the salt marshes, correct? Tell us about them," Dupin butted in, and surprisingly Rose didn't stop him. He was back in the zone now, feeling much better. Whether the effect of the caffeine on him was physical or even mainly psychological by now—which was what Nolwenn suspected—it didn't matter: it was always prompt.

"It was a long, very good conversation. About the changes we're seeing everywhere. The White Land hasn't been spared. An intelligent and committed journalist."

Her answer wasn't bitter. It was relaxed. When they had arrived earlier, Riwal had handed him the interviews and articles that Nolwenn had faxed over and they had skimmed them in the car. There were a few interesting points, although nothing of substance.

"More specific. We need you to be more specific. You've openly stated your intention to take over the salt gardens more or less in their entirety. And that what you'd like best of all is to buy up everything. You already have twenty-five percent. Did Lilou ask about your specific plans? What do they look like?"

That had just been one part of the interview, expressed with a forthrightness typical of Lilou; there had been talk of a "Battle for the White Land," of a "silent occupation," although Lilou didn't keep insisting on this, she hadn't taken it to extremes.

"As I said, it was an extensive, constructive conversation about—"

"That's enough." Rose's voice was getting loud, very loud, furious, but controlled. "We want to know what's going on here. What is happening in these salt marshes? Whatever it is—it led to a murder, almost two."

Dupin had no idea whether Rose's temper was genuine or just very convincingly acted.

"Of course it's a 'battle,' but it's not about the individuals in the salt gardens. It's a battle for the future of the Guérande, over the issue of whether it can survive at all."

Madame Laurent was raising her voice now too, but was still composed. "Yes, we think that Le Sel ought to be the future of the salt marshes, we make no secret of that. To protect them! And yes, of course it's also because we see great economic prospects for the salt. A good business." She lowered her voice again finally. "Premium gastronomic products are on the rise everywhere, thank God, and pure sea salt is one of them. *Fleur de sel* needs to be like Champagne, Bordeaux, foie gras. A luxury delicacy. And that very potential is being squandered here; it could all be set up so differently. In production, marketing, sales. Look at this building. Of course Le Sel made a big contribution here. The local authority is not in any kind of position to do that. You only have to compare it to the shack in front of it to see. And this is all for the good of the salt gardens. It could all be improved significantly without us having to touch the traditions at the heart of it. Everyone would benefit from it. Especially the *paludiers*. We would keep employing them in their salt marshes if they sold up. And give them better salaries."

It had turned into just as much of a business-focused speech as a personal one; she had done it perfectly. It had included all of the flowery phrases that usually set Dupin's teeth grinding, but strangely this hadn't happened. He had even sneaked another caramel candy into his mouth during it. Madame Laurent was truly good. Madame Bourgiot remained motionless throughout the little speech, not giving even a hint of a reaction.

The Le Sel chief went on: "Yes, we would ideally like to see the entire White Land in Le Sel's hands. But do you think in all seriousness that we would shoot police officers and murder journalists because of that?"

"If ambitious careers and everything that someone has built up are suddenly endangered, people do all sorts of things," Rose said quietly, and Madame Laurent threw her a cool glance, "and the repeated failure of a harvest would be an emergency for a self-employed person. And he might need to sell. One could arrange for the repeated failure of harvests."

This time Ségolène Laurent tried a different tactic. She leaned forward challengingly and answered icily.

"Yes, we make offers, high and even excessive offers. Yes, there are significant disputes here in the salt gardens, like I said, about specific economic interests that lead to conflicts. But no, we're not sabotaging any harvests, we are not committing any criminal acts."

Her display of frankness was a tried and tested rhetorical weapon.

"You've spoken out against public subsidies of the salt gardens in the *département* and also at the ministry in Paris," Dupin weighed in again.

The salt-garden subsidies had been another point of interest in both of the interviews.

"I did. It's an artificial, always inappropriate, and not to mention unfair measure."

"You yourself carry out powerful, targeted lobbying."

"Of course." Madame Laurent raised one eyebrow almost imperceptibly. "That's what I'm paid to do."

Madame Bourgiot cleared her throat. "So you really do see a direct link between the shooting, the murder, and the Salt Land? You believe there are criminal elements at work who have direct connections to the salt?"

Bourgiot's question sounded, after everything they had just discussed, almost quaint, yet her tone of voice was far from naïve. And what was more, she had hit the nail on the head. So far, this had been their exact problem. They had no idea if there was a direct link at all. And if so, what it was.

"We know there's a link," Rose claimed confidently. "Tell us why we found the blue barrels that Commissaire Dupin went to see in Maxime Daeron's salt marshes in *your* salt marshes?"

"I don't have the faintest idea."

The most likely reason, of course, was that someone had simply dumped the barrels anywhere after the incident. In the salt marshes that weren't in use. It was also far from clear whether the perpetrator knew that Lilou had given someone a tip about the barrels. Perhaps someone had wanted to incriminate Le Sel specifically. Anything was possible at this stage.

"Does Le Sel use barrels like that for anything?"

"No."

"And the dried salt for the mills? How do you transport that? How do you store it?" Jaffrezic's lectures had been useful to Dupin.

"In sacks, like the other salt. The insides are coated with silicone."

Dupin moved on to his favorite point: "What do you think might be going on with the blue barrels?"

"I really don't know."

"And you, Madame Bourgiot, do you have any idea what the barrels might have contained?"

"I hope they didn't contain anything that doesn't belong here. Céline Cordier has been breathing down our necks since this morning, threatening to have all of the salt marshes shut down. I can't make any sense of what it might be. And I don't know anyone round here who would be so irresponsible as to tamper with such delicate things. Let alone someone who would commit a murder."

It was incredible how she had changed during the conversation. Her voice was piercing now, almost firm. Earlier she had been unsure, even nervous. Almost as if she had been putting on an act.

"What was Lilou most interested in when you spoke a year ago, Madame Bourgiot?"

"Very general information. She dealt with the salt and the

Guérande in a more comprehensive way the first time. We compiled detailed information for her. She dropped in to see us twice. It was a really good article for us. It wasn't about anything . . . controversial. She concentrated on the salt farmers' rather difficult economic position," she said, adding quickly, "which is stable overall, of course. Not a cause for concern in any way."

Commissaire Rose cleared her throat. "Whatever happened here, whatever is going on here—we will find out. So if you have anything to tell us, you're better off telling us now."

Rose seemed to have got her teeth into something. Or she was following a lead that Dupin didn't know about yet.

Dupin saw Riwal suddenly standing outside the glass door and almost jumped. His inspector was making some elaborate gestures. It looked hilarious. Riwal was trying, in vain, not to be too obvious about it; quite a large group of tourists were walking right past him. Kadeg was standing diagonally behind him. Riwal's hand gestures were getting more extreme. Dupin shook his head; he didn't want to interrupt the conversation right now.

Riwal shrugged his shoulders apologetically and gesticulated all the more wildly.

"I . . . Excuse me."

Dupin stood up. A moment later he was at the door and then out of the room. He'd be quick. The three women hadn't noticed Riwal yet.

"Sorry, boss."

"What is it, Riwal?"

"Maxime Daeron wants to speak to you. Immediately. He said it was very urgent. Face-to-face, with you."

"Just me?"

"Just you."

"Where is he?"

"In his house at the gulf."

"In his house at the gulf?"

"In his house at the gulf."

Dupin hoped nobody had heard this absurd exchange.

"He says he can meet you wherever you want."

Dupin reflected. He'd finish this interview at least. "Fine, tell him to come here."

"All right, boss. I'll let him know."

Riwal had already turned away and pulled out his phone.

"Wait. I . . . In fact it would be better to meet at his salt marsh. Where everything happened."

Dupin would have liked to walk through the salt marshes again this morning.

"All right." Riwal turned around and walked toward the exit.

"Riwal?"

His inspector turned around again without a trace of irritation. He had been working with Dupin too long for something like this to bother him in the slightest.

"Boss?"

"I . . . Tell him I'll come to him."

"Okay."

"I thought Daeron lived in La Roche-Bernard."

"Maybe his house at the gulf is just a *résidence secondaire,* lots of people here have—"

"I know, Riwal. So does he spend time at the gulf during the week too?"

"I couldn't tell you."

"Let Daeron know that I'm on my way. Where exactly does he live?"

"On the Île aux Moines."

"The Île aux Moines?"

"The Île aux Moines. In Breton, it's called Izenah."

"Isn't that the island right next to the Île d'Arz—where Madame Laurent lives?"

"They used to be linked by a narrow embankment of land, but it sank into the sea in a storm surge. Don't you know the story?"

Daeron and Laurent didn't live far from one another as the crow flew. They were practically neighbors.

Riwal clearly took Dupin's being lost in thought as an invitation to keep talking.

"A rich sea captain's son fell in love with a penniless fisherman's daughter. Every night, they met in secret on the embankment. One day the boy asked for her hand in marriage. His father was against it. But the young woman came and sang seductive songs. Then the father asked the ocean for help. The devil sent a storm surge and the embankment was submerged beneath the rough waves."

Riwal didn't just know all the legends—the more obscure and dramatic the better, although strangely those frightened him—he recited them with theatrical zeal. And there were legends for practically every place—nothing in the Celtic world just existed as is, anything and everything had its own story; Dupin was convinced therefore that the Breton nature was the most poetic and epic of all. This was how Riwal's nickname at the commissariat, "the druid," had come about. This belied his athletic appearance and his very practical and technical skills and had been followed up by "the bard," which he seemed just as flattered by.

"The devil—or God. Nobody knows."

Dupin cringed. It was ridiculous.

"Nobody knows whether it was the devil or God?"

"They each had their reasons."

This was not the right situation for stories, neither for telling them nor listening to them. But somehow, Dupin had to admit, he was a little bit glad: as odd as it sounded, it did him good; it restored some lovely normality, it gave him comfort. As long as Riwal was telling stories, all was still right with the world. Besides, he had learned something. From time to time, Riwal's stories, and generally the most fantastical stories, contained surprisingly interesting tips.

"I'll—I'll drive to that island."

"The gulf area has a particularly high concentration of supernatural stories and beings, boss. It's always been that way. Fairies and dwarves with Herculean strength." Riwal remained emphatically matter-of-fact. "So it's no wonder it's full of menhirs, dolmen, and *cromlec'hs*. Izenah is too. Caesar's golden sarcophagus is underneath the Pen Hap, the most beautiful dolmen on the island. But they say," he hastened to add, "people are only interested in the huge amounts of gold."

"I . . ." Dupin truly had no idea how to respond to this. For many reasons. For one thing, he found it hilarious that Riwal mocked people's base material interests, while simply accepting the absurdity of the idea that Caesar's corpse might actually, of all places, be there. The strangeness of these kinds of stories was intrinsic to them, but this particular story was especially strange: even if the victory of the most daring of Gauls, the Veneti (who came from the gulf!), had been crucial for Caesar's career, why in the world should Caesar's body have been brought here? To the most profoundly rebellious province of the Roman empire—*finis terrae*? But there would be a compelling story for that too, to explain everything; he'd rather not ask. And gradually he was getting fed up with normality.

"They are only interested in the gold and the other precious treasures that lay hidden beneath the menhirs and dolmen. Guarded by all kinds of creatures. People should know that things always go wrong when somebody wants to get hold of those treasures. At the beginning of the nineteenth century, a goldsmith from Auray founded an officially registered company to open up the treasure trove on the gulf. Almost everyone involved lost their lives in mysterious ways."

Dupin again wasn't sure what Riwal was trying to suggest. Should they consider a legendary treasure as a motive in this case? Was this secret society still active today?

"The gulf has a particular aura. Especially Izenah. Be careful."

The inspector had phrased this final sentence as if he were giving a warning about venomous snakes or other dangerous animals.

Dupin gave up. He'd had enough. He needed to concentrate on the case again.

* * *

It was a stone's throw away, about three hundred meters. The journey from Port-Blanc to Port du Lério on the Île aux Moines took just four minutes on the white-and-blue boat, even at high tide, which Dupin was grateful for. The water shone like a small lake—which made him even more grateful—yet it looked and smelled like the sea. But mild, like everything in this tamed mini-Atlantic. It was luckily just a mini-crossing too, although the boat's diesel engine, with its ostentatious buzzing and vibrating, made it clear that it could take on the open Atlantic. And even the small, loud flock of seagulls that followed them left no doubt that, despite it all, this was an ocean they were on. His case last year on the Glénan archipelago had forced Dupin, who hated boats, to make multiple trips by boat, and he had sworn off boats for a long time.

Port-Blanc shone from the water, dazzlingly white and living up to its name. The ferries crossed every fifteen minutes and Dupin hadn't had to wait. He had parked his car right on the quay in Port-Blanc—that was the advantage of having an official police car. He left it right next to the ramp that jutted far out to sea so that boats could be launched even at low tide. Dupin loved that image, found only at the coast: a street running headlong into the sea.

The Île aux Moines was a car-free island. And Daeron's house was apparently not far from the harbor. The slightly hilly island was in fact in the shape of a cross, which is why the monks had chosen it in the ninth century and built a monastery on it.

Commissaire Rose had just called. She had finished the rest of the conversation with the two women, which had mainly been about the exact links between Le Sel and the Centre. Clearly the links were very close. Her report had been to the point, and indeed pointed: *I report and expect the same from you.* What was more significant was the information she passed on about the first, preliminary autopsy report; some of the blood tests hadn't come back yet. Lilou was still alive when she had been thrown into the gulf. Although she had most likely been unconscious. The injury to her temple "from a powerful blow using a blunt instrument" had been severe, "potentially fatal," and clearly ante-mortem, but from a medical point of view, she had drowned. There was no doubt about it. Otherwise the body showed no other fractures, wounds, or hematomas. Nothing, which was practically a miracle given the strong currents, the sharp rocks and stones. She had probably been swiftly caught by the main current and washed right out into the large Larmor-Baden bay, directly opposite Kerpenhir. So the reconstruction right now looked like this: the perpetrator—or perpetrators—went to her parents' house, knocked her out—still no sign of the murder weapon—got her into her car, drove the short distance to the Pointe de Kerpenhir, and threw her into the gulf there. The perpetrator then went back to their car, probably not far away. The exact time of the crime was difficult to pinpoint, as it always was with drowning. The forensics team hadn't found the laptop, or any traces of blood mark-ing the spot where the attack had taken place, which was a long shot anyway with this kind of injury. But no blood or fingerprints had been found in the car yet either, just two tiny pieces of dark red textile lint on the driver's seat that weren't pressed down into it and hadn't revealed anything yet. Rose and Dupin still suspected that the perpetrator had driven to Lilou's house in Sarzeau later to remove papers and documents. Absolutely everything from the last six weeks was missing; the forensics team had confirmed it, Rose having asked them to check especially. Although they had clues only for certain elements of this, Dupin thought it a plausible hypothesis for what had happened.

Crucially, Rose had also had everyone's alibis checked—anybody who had given one. Dupin smiled when he heard who had volunteered for this job. Kadeg. Naturally. Nobody could badger people so nastily and with such great pleasure. Dupin himself preferred giving him these kinds of jobs. Maxime Daeron's wife had confirmed the dinner. Kadeg was dissatisfied because it was "just" the wife, and so not an "independent" person. Two of Paul Daeron's guests confirmed the tastings until one in the morning, Madame Bourgiot's husband also confirmed a shared dinner and that his wife had gone to sleep with him at half past eleven.

Rose wanted to take Jaffrezic "to task" again next (even this phrase was said in a friendly way). At first the commissaires hadn't been able to agree where and when they would meet and how to proceed, but in the end they arranged to speak on the phone again later. Dupin had tried to reach Claire again, twice on the journey and once from the quay, but again he'd only been able to leave voicemails.

The boat was on its way to the quay in Port du Lério; they'd be there any moment. Dupin was eager to find out what it was Daeron wanted to share—apparently only with him—and he was also glad to be on his own for a little while. The third exquisite caramel sweet was in his mouth. Magnificent summer villas from the nineteenth century were visible in the equally magnificent woods—the Bois d'Amour—that began right by the quay, with discreet paths leading into the Wood of Love. Stone pines, tall pines, holm oaks. Dupin saw a bustling fleet of boats in one thick row along the quay, big sailing boats, small sailing boats, motorboats of all lengths, canoes in garish colors, the swift Zodiacs. Every one of them rocking ever so gently. The gulf was a sea of boats and Dupin was enjoying the view. A cobalt blue with hundreds of splashes of color—lazily dawdling in the midday heat. The island was dozing, relaxed and calm in the sun, everything seemed weightless, airy. The surreally immaculate blue of the sky of the last few days and weeks was still unmarked by haze. Without Breton-style exaggeration, this was the Mediterranean atmosphere par excellence. You could see palm trees, fig trees, eucalyptus trees, olive trees, camellias, mimosas, agaves, all that the Mediterranean had to offer, even the stunning lemon and orange trees that fascinated Dupin so much. The climate was—objectively!—not dissimilar to the Mediterranean climate. The gulf recorded 2,300 hours of sunshine a year, while Nice, for example, got only marginally more: 2,500 (Paris a measly 1,300!); and, this was spectacular: just 23.6 inches of precipitation a year. Nice had 30.2 inches (Paris a miserable 35.4 inches!). Vannes's average temperature in January was forty-eight degrees Fahrenheit, and in Nice it was forty-three degrees. Henri knew all the figures by heart, he regaled Dupin with them over and over again—and Dupin was always suitably amazed.

That's why wine grapes had long been cultivated at the small sea, right up until the sixties, for more than a millennium; in the middle ages Christian Brittany had grown grapes all the way up to the Channel coast and to the edge of Finistère, everywhere. Wine for the Eucharist, of course. Wines like the ones from the Loire, white wines that, when cooled right down, were some of Dupin's favorite whites and which Bretons considered "theirs": wines like Muscadet, Anjou, Saumur, Chinon, Sancerre, or even Quincy.

A minute later Dupin was standing at the end of the quay. The boat didn't even moor properly; it touched the jetty briefly, delivered its passengers onto the island, and shuttled straight back. "Welcome to Izenah, the Île aux Moines—the Pearl of the Gulf." There were large signs, small signs, directions to all kinds of things: restaurants, hotels, beaches, natural attractions—and of course also to—Dupin smirked, remembering Riwal's stories—the *"Cromlec'h des Kergonan"* as well as the *"Pen Hap Dolmen,"* Caesar's final resting place amidst all that gold, as Dupin now knew. Nolwenn would have been pleased with him—he knew what a *cromlec'h* was. He was a good pupil. And (unsurprisingly) the largest stone circle in France had been built here on the Île des Moines. With a radius of a hundred meters and twenty-seven stones each up to 1.8 meters tall and a mysterious focus of ritual. Before he arrived in Brittany, Dupin had, like every normal person, referred to everything from the Stone Age made of stone as a menhir—but the technical differentiation had been part of Nolwenn's very first Breton lessons. The menhir—a Breton word that the whole world used as a technical term—was just the most famous stone, the standing stone. A large, erect monolith. *Maen* meaning "stone" and *hir* meaning "long." Dupin would be able to rattle off the surprisingly straightforward wording till the end of his days. And also in the case of the "stone table" found all over the world, the Breton word was generally accepted, the "dol-men"—a structure made from large unhewn stone blocks that usually served as tombs. They were much more common than menhirs or *cromlec'hs* (and preferred as a tomb for fairies). Dupin liked the menhirs best (although his favorite baguette at his favorite bakery was called a *dolmen*). In the stories told since primeval times, the stone menhir giants were alive. Some made their way toward the sea on certain nights to slake their thirst or bathe—or performed dances to honor the dead when the moon was full. They grew like plants, were oracles or enchanted virgins, protected people like saints did: for example, you struck the "Roh-an-aod" with a hammer to get protection from the sea. To Dupin, the creepiest stories were the ones about menhirs having a tiny piece bitten off them by a dark creature every full moon—once it had swallowed up all of the menhir, the world would come to an end.

There were all three kinds on the little Île aux Moines: menhirs, *cromlec'hs,* and dolmen. Izenah must have been a real draw, even for Neolithic people. With good reason, Dupin thought. Although in all likelihood not as many people had visited back then as did in the holiday season nowadays. Now, at the beginning of September, there was just a smattering of tourists. Dupin liked this, the exhausted, relaxed atmosphere of the off-season.

He got his bearings, walked along the quay, and five minutes later he was standing outside Daeron's house, or more accurately: outside the entrance to Daeron's house. It turned out to be one of those wonderful villas he had seen from the boat, in the middle of a large estate lined with gorgeous trees and bushes. The villa was right by the sandy paradise beach, only separated from it by the elegant little street. Dupin had expected something completely different, more like Lilou Breval's parents' house. The money for this villa couldn't have come from the salt marshes.

A large wooden gate, the house number engraved on a tall granite stone next to it, no name, an aluminum doorbell. Dupin gave it a quick push and a moment later the gate slid open silently as if a ghost were operating it. He was expected.

Maxime Daeron was coming toward him along the pale gravel path. He was wearing the same clothes as in the salt marshes, but he no longer looked like the man Dupin had met that morning. He looked distraught. Utterly distraught. And he made no attempt to hide it.

"Come with me, we'll go into the garden. And have a seat there." He looked imploringly at Dupin, miserably. "I know Lilou trusted you. So I will too."

* * *

"So she's really dead?"

Even his voice sounded different from this morning. It cracked.

"Yes."

Dupin was keen to find out where this conversation was going. They had walked past the house and into the garden, which looked as splendid as expected. There was a large pool with dark granite all around it. And a vast terrace between the pool and the house.

"She was murdered." Daeron's sentence was somewhere between a question and a statement.

"That's our assumption."

"Lilou's neighbor called me. An old lady who liked Lilou very much. And Lilou liked her too. A close friend of her late mother's. She had known Lilou since she was a child. The police were at her house this morning too."

"Why did the neighbor call you, Monsieur Daeron?"

"We"—and here Daeron looked Dupin directly in the eye for the first time; he had avoided looking at him until now—"we were in a relationship. Lilou Breval and I. For the last year."

Dupin was speechless for a moment.

"A secret relationship. I'm married. Although things with my wife, they're . . ." He fell silent.

"And?" Dupin couldn't disguise an aggressive undertone.

"I ended the relationship. Ten days ago. It wasn't working anymore. Although that's not what I actually wanted. I mean I didn't want to end it. But I couldn't do it anymore. I couldn't manage it."

Dupin was still struggling with this information. "Go on."

"She was hysterical. It seriously upset her."

Daeron was visibly struggling to speak, but Dupin had to ignore that.

"And then what, Monsieur Daeron?"

Maxime Daeron looked at Dupin in confusion.

"After this meeting where you broke up—was there any contact after that?"

"We spoke on the phone twice. On the following two days. They were . . . very emotional phone calls."

Maxime Daeron was struggling to maintain his composure. He looked truly distraught.

"She thought I didn't love her. But that wasn't it. I didn't want her to think that. I didn't know what to do anymore. I . . . I didn't know whether I actually wanted to leave my wife."

So far it all sounded like a pretty trivial story. Like a cliché. And it didn't fit with the Lilou he knew. But he hadn't known her all that well. And—these things happened, no matter how clever someone was, or how strong. He knew that. Above all and even more crucially: ultimately, nobody else could understand what existed between two people, so nobody could judge. Or prejudge. Sometimes, not even the two lovers themselves could say exactly what things were like between them; this was only revealed during the breakup, in the different, conflicting, embittered versions of the "same" story, which were then projected back onto the past as irrefutable "truths." But in this case there was only one version. Daeron's.

"I called her again yesterday and we saw each other. Even though—"

"You did *what?*" Dupin leapt abruptly to his feet. "You saw Lilou yesterday evening? When?"

"We met up. Just for half an hour. But it wasn't a good idea. It only made everything worse. It was terrible. I know I didn't tell you the truth this morning. We had promised not to tell anyone about the relationship. I did have dinner with my wife, but then I went out again. I said I needed to work. And went to the house next door where I have my office. I left from there."

This news was unbelievable.

"When exactly? When were you with her?"

"I arrived around ten to eleven and then drove back about twenty past eleven, but I couldn't say to the exact minute." Maxime Daeron was obviously making an effort to give precise information. He was aware he was now the chief suspect based on these facts. "She had only just arrived at her parents' house herself when I got there. The neighbor can confirm to you that I left at twenty past eleven." Dupin could tell this was—unsurprisingly—extremely important to him. "Lilou walked me out to my car. The neighbor was outside with her dog. We said a quick hello. Lilou and I only ever met there. At her parents' house, that was our place. And the neighbor knew about us. She knows me. She never said anything to anyone."

She hadn't told the police anything either. Not this morning and not after the murder. She had stated only that she'd seen Lilou. Her loyalty had obviously run deep. And apparently she didn't suspect Daeron. Perhaps because she really had seen Daeron leaving. Which ultimately didn't mean a thing. Daeron would only have had to park his car in the patch of woodland a few hundred meters away and then walk back along the gulf. The fact that Maxime Daeron had voluntarily got in touch and was making these admissions meant equally little. Anything was possible. If the neighbor had seen him that night, it might have ended up coming out, despite her discretion—so he was better off coming clean as soon as possible. This applied whether his story was true and he really had driven straight home, or he was lying and he was the murderer. Even if that were the case, it was smart to tell this story now.

"Where were you and Lilou?"

"In the garden. Almost the entire time. I walked around a lot. Lilou was sitting down. She went into the kitchen a few times—you'll definitely find my fingerprints."

That might explain the prints they'd found.

"When did you get home?"

Dupin had begun to note down the details. Especially the timing.

"Ten past twelve. I drove quite slowly. My wife was already asleep. I was absolutely distraught. And I didn't even know anything about the events in my salt ponds at that point. I was in my office when an inspector called me ten minutes later. And told me there had been a shooting. I called my brother immediately and told him. About the shooting. Not about meeting Lilou."

"The inspector got through to you on the landline?"

"Yes."

"So you were in the house when you spoke to the inspector? In your office?"

"Yes."

That was crucial. They could check that.

"Did you see where Lilou Breval's car was?"

"Right in the driveway, round the side of the house. Where the main door is and where you get to the garden from."

So it hadn't been complicated to place Lilou in her own car, unconscious, and drive away. This fit with the hypothetical reconstruction of the evening.

"Did you get hold of your brother directly after the call from Inspector Chadron? So around twenty-five minutes past midnight?"

"Exactly. Then I went for a walk. I only went to bed at two thirty. And got up again at six."

Dupin had drawn up a meticulous list of the timings in his Clairefontaine. Lilou's house was a good forty-five minutes' drive away. Daeron had been back in La Roche-Bernard at twenty past twelve, in his office. He wouldn't have been able to manage it, not if he had been seen with Lilou alive at twenty past eleven. Even if he had come back to kill her straight after he said good-bye. He would not have been able to kill her, take the body to Pointe de Kerpenhir, and come back by the time of his verifiable presence in La Roche-Bernard. Let alone also drop into Lilou's house in Sarzeau and remove documents. But he could of course have done that just as easily later in the night.

"Is there a witness who saw you at home? Did your wife wake up?"

"No."

It didn't really matter. The phone calls were watertight. It wouldn't have been possible in the time leading up to the phone call—but of course it could all have happened afterward, after the calls, the whole operation: Maxime could have come home and then gone out again without any difficulty. To commit the murder. Including the detour to Lilou's house—which would probably have meant him coming back around three in the morning.

"And later that night, after half past midnight, you didn't do anything that would give you an alibi?" Dupin knew this was a ridiculous question.

Maxime Daeron looked helplessly at Dupin. He answered haltingly: "No. No. My wife was asleep, as I said."

They weren't going to make any progress on this point.

"What was going on with the barrels, Monsieur Daeron? What did Lilou Breval uncover?"

"I don't know anything about that."

It seemed as though he had been expecting this question to come up earlier.

"You were in a relationship with Lilou Breval, you're a *paludier*— and she didn't tell you anything about the suspicion she had?"

"No. She never told me anything about it—that she was on the trail of something controversial in Gwenn Rann or anything like that. And yes, I'm sure she would have told me while we were still— together. So it must have been something that only came out recently."

"Have another think. What was Lilou Breval interested in? It's very important."

"She was very interested in the changes, disputes, and conflicts in the White Land. Conflicts between the independents, the cooperative, the business group, and also the local authority and the region. She was interested in competition in the so-called global salt market."

"We know that already."

Dupin could see that Daeron had tears in his eyes. He was visibly struggling to keep it together. If everything he was saying were true, that would be all too understandable. And he must have been making a huge effort to stay composed this whole time. Daeron took a deep breath to muster his strength before answering.

"I think she had been planning another long article about it. The one from last year was on the general side. So the interviews were more about specific conflicts. That's how we got to know each other. Through her research, the interview. She also spoke to Monsieur Jaffrezic and Madame Laurent again in the last few months. I gathered that much but she never said when she actually wanted to write this article."

"What did she specifically want from Monsieur Jaffrezic and Madame Laurent?"

"I'm not quite sure."

"Tell me, in detail, about the disputes in the salt marshes. What do you know about them?"

Daeron took his time answering.

"The cooperative wants the independents, and Le Sel does too. Le Sel wants everyone. The group is making us all obscenely high offers. And it's plotting at the local authority."

"Could you be more specific, please?"

"They want the city and the region to end the subsidies so that they'll have easy pickings, or so they think, but it's a fantasy. Most of the *paludiers* would never sell. It's a passion, a vocation."

"What else?"

"Le Sel has applied for an extension to the salt marsh area. Around the outer edges of the existing pools. They want to increase the amounts of salt harvested by any means possible. They also want to cultivate more intensively, shorten the harvesting cycles through technical modifications to the salt marshes, like in their salt marshes in the Mediterranean. Install machines, especially automatic pumps and pumping systems so that they can cut down on the canals and the large reservoir pools. They want to cut down on *paludiers* and increase the yields. All of that. You know how it goes. It's the way of things."

Dupin had been struck by an unexpected indifference and resignation in Daeron's last few sentences. This didn't sound like the proud *paludier* of this morning. Daeron seemed to have noticed this.

"But they simply won't achieve it"—he took a deep breath—"they're doing it all wrong. Their only chance, even economically, is if the cottage industry of salt survives. That's the only way. A cottage industry whose produce comes at a cost. Because it's the best salt there is, the pure, natural sea. They use the same words as us, but they mean something completely different."

"And this extension, has this application been officially drawn up?"

"Yes, it was drawn up two years ago. There have already been dozens of consultations about it. We're working in a strictly regulated, priority nature reserve. It's impossible really. But who knows? The local authority might suddenly grant these kinds of applications after all. Miracles do happen." There was unadulterated cynicism in his words.

"Who do you mean when you say 'the local authority'? The mayor?"

Maxime Daeron looked at Dupin in surprise. "The mayor? No. Much more powerful than that: Madame Bourgiot. She's not just the director of the Centre, she's also the local and regional delegate for the Salt Land. The mayor has handed everything to do with the Gwenn Rann over to her. She is . . . ambitious."

Nobody had mentioned that Madame Bourgiot was so powerful. It hadn't been obvious either. Until now.

"And do you know of any serious disputes between specific people in relation to that?"

Maxime Daeron looked downcast. Dupin wasn't sure whether that was because of the question or the situation as a whole.

"No."

These were all relevant topics, extremely relevant topics, but Dupin suspected he wouldn't find out anything more of substance in this conversation. Either because Daeron really didn't know anything— or because he didn't want to talk about it.

"How are things in your salt marshes? Financially? How's business?"

The change of topic was abrupt. Dupin was fond of this approach.

"I . . ."—Maxime Daeron seemed briefly annoyed—"fine. It's going well. It's not easy, but it's going well. I'm managing."

"Le Sel made you an offer too, after all. What—"

"I'm not going to sell." He sounded adamant.

"You've rejected it?"

"I'm not going to sell."

"Did someone sabotage your harvest, Monsieur Daeron? Is someone harassing you?"

Daeron's downcast expression returned. "No."

"We spoke about it this morning, you brought it up as a possibility yourself."

"That was premature."

"Why did you call your brother?" Dupin blurted out, although he had been meaning to ask something else.

Daeron looked confused. "He's the co-owner of the salt marshes. I . . . We're very close. I wanted to let him know. And so he wanted to be there this morning too."

"Business is very good for your brother, it seems?"

"Saucisse Breizh."

"Saucisse Breizh—that's your brother?" Dupin blurted this out too, with an eagerness he instantly found embarrassing.

"My father founded it. It was a little local butcher's shop. When he died, my brother took over. And made a huge success of the company." There was pride in his voice as he said these last words.

Saucisse Breizh was one of the largest companies in Brittany. Every child had heard of it. Sausage, cured sausage, ham, paté, rillettes. Dupin knew the whole range inside out. The most delicious things. They may have been made in great quantities, but everything was manufactured using old-fashioned methods. Saucisse Breizh was flourishing. Dupin's stomach began to growl.

"I was the black sheep," said Maxime Daeron, the trace of a tense smile showing on his face. "Everyone else in my family is in pig-breeding. Butchery. Sausage-making."

Dupin rubbed the back of his head. "This house—does it belong to your brother?"

"Oh yes. As does the property in La Roche-Bernard. Where we live."

Suddenly Daeron looked utterly exhausted. It was visible in his face and his posture. This had been a long conversation. But this was the first conversation on this case where Dupin had felt relatively back on form again.

"It's terrible. I can't comprehend it. I—" Maxime Daeron broke off.

"Thank you so much—for your frankness, Monsieur Daeron. I assume you've told me everything you know."

"Yes." Daeron had an absent-minded look on his face.

"Get in touch if anything else occurs to you. Whatever's going on here, this is all a great tragedy."

Dupin shot to his feet. Daeron did the same.

"I'll find my own way out."

Dupin nodded to Daeron and turned to leave.

He was just a few steps away from the house when his mobile rang. Commissaire Rose. It was unbelievable. Was she having him watched? Had she planted a bugging device or a GPS transmitter on him? Her phone calls were perfectly timed.

* * *

Dupin had walked back to the harbor slowly with his mobile to his ear. There had been quite a lot to report on both sides. Especially from Dupin's side, of course. He had made every effort to pass on as many details as possible. Rose was much less surprised by Daeron's confession than Dupin had thought she would be, and than he himself had been. She quickly sent someone over to the neighbor's house again to check Daeron's statements—and especially, more fundamentally and more importantly, the credibility of the old woman. An enormous amount depended on her statement. And she had ordered the fingerprints found in Lilou's parents' house to be compared with Maxime Daeron's immediately.

Daeron's admission made him a suspect, of course. With impressive speed, Rose had reconstructed Daeron's evening chronologically. And she embarrassed Dupin, who had painstakingly gone through everything in his notebook again as he walked along. Just as he was getting ready to conclude that Daeron may not have been able to commit the murder before but could *obviously* have easily done it *after* the phone calls with Chadron and his brother, Rose finished her observations with the matter-of-fact remark that this possibility was "in all likelihood" ruled out, since Maxime Daeron would have had to throw Lilou into the gulf *before* 1:40 A.M. Because if it had happened later, the water flowing out would have carried her into the Atlantic and not into the small sea. Which the murderer would certainly have preferred, but apparently they hadn't been able to plan their crime based around high and low tides. They must have had to dispose of the body as quickly as possible, and the chances of success in the eddies and shallows of the passage weren't bad. Still, the rhythms of high and low tide were unshakable—specifically at the point in time when the bodies of water in the passage started to flow in the opposite direction. 1:40 A.M. was the key—it must have happened before then. And it was very unlikely Daeron could have managed that. Dupin then insisted that it was not "totally out of the question." He felt like a bit of a rookie, an amateur in Breton matters; Rose mildly noted that these were simply criminological factors that "never needed to be taken into account in Paris." Dupin thought Rose could in all fairness have pointed out the "1:40 A.M. is key" issue earlier with Bourgiot's alibi (who could absolutely have done it before quarter to one if her alibi—which had been backed up only by her husband—lapsed at eleven thirty).

Rose summarized how things stood on her end succinctly. Nothing of interest had been turned up in Breval's email inbox yet. The same went for the landlines. She seemed to have used her mobile almost all the time. The itemized phone records, which Dupin had high hopes for, were available. Riwal and two police officers from Rose's team were working through them right now in reverse order, beginning with the most recent calls. The same went for the small number of texts there were. They were trying to identify the people involved. With a particular focus on the last few days. Every detail of Maxime Daeron's statements about his phone calls with Lilou Breval was corroborated by the list. This reminded Dupin of something else he had wanted to ask Daeron but it had slipped his mind at some point: Why had Maxime Daeron called Lilou specifically last night and not before then? And why not leave it till today? Of course it might be a coincidence. But sometimes things that looked like coincidences were key. The short phone call last night with Maxime Daeron had been the last call on her phone—apart from the mysterious call this morning. That call to Dupin himself, which was still on his mind. On Wednesday of the previous week and the day before that, there hadn't been many calls. There were two calls to Orange's service hotline (astonishing: Dupin always needed to make a dozen calls before getting through to anyone at the service provider), to her neighbor and to her colleague from the *Ouest-France* on Tuesday. Two landline numbers and a mobile number that still couldn't be identified. The only other person Lilou had called—and this was interesting—was Jaffrezic. Three days ago. They had been connected for four minutes. Rose had wanted to see Jaffrezic again, but hadn't been able to get through to him. Now there was another significant reason to do so. He had spoken to Lilou Breval on the phone three days ago, and for Dupin too, this sent Jaffrezic straight to the top of the list of "people to speak to" this evening. Rose had instructed that he be "found urgently," no matter what. The second intriguing call, three minutes long, was a call to Madame Bourgiot, also on Monday, which was even odder because Madame Bourgiot hadn't mentioned this call earlier. Which made Bourgiot—and for once Rose and Dupin were agreed on this—a candidate for the top of the list. Dupin almost didn't care what order they had the conversations in this time, so they went with Rose's suggestion. Jaffrezic would be first.

When Dupin arrived at the quay he was almost dizzy, everything swaying again like this morning at the Pointe de Kerpenhir, as if the world was suddenly tipping backward and forward. This time he mainly put it down to the fact that it was almost six and he hadn't eaten anything but salted caramels since this morning. When he had arrived on the island, he had spotted a café on the small tree-lined hill across from the quay, and even from far away it looked marvelous. He would try to get a good coffee there and a bite to eat.

* * *

Le San Francisco was a wonderful place, Dupin had not been mistaken about that. The name alone was wonderful. A terrace right above the harbor between stone pine trees, small palm trees, hydrangea, an evergreen oak. And a real kiwi vine! A wide, two-story stone building that looked a hundred years old and was not kept up in the least, the paint flaking elegantly from the shutters. There were comfy wooden chairs with beige linen upholstery. A breathtaking view of the gulf, part of the monks' island visible across the way, slightly hilly like here, and farther east was the Île d'Arz. Narrow stripes of deep green—just a handful of tall pines and stone pines soaring majestically out of the dense copse of trees. And in between: the blue of the water lying still before him. A landscape out of a nineteenth-century painting.

Dupin sat down at a tiny table in the front row. It was quiet. The perfect spot. The Île aux Moines was growing on him. This was Brittany in the summertime. The "*douceur de vivre.*"

The coffee—served in small, plain glasses—was just right. Dupin had ordered his first while he was still standing, got it straightaway and drank it straightaway, and against his inclination, a little hastily; Rose was going to be in touch again very soon and she would definitely expect him to be on his way back, not in a café of all places. He had cast an eye on the menu, however. It looked delicious. And he needed to eat something. He was still dizzy. Surely it wouldn't take too long for the kitchen to send it out. Just something small. *Tartare de lieu jaune,* one of his favorite kinds of fish (the list of his "favorite fish" had grown to about fifteen over his years in Brittany), *tartine de rougets* (red mullet was absolutely amongst them), "buttered" with foie gras, as well as homemade lamb terrine with figs from the island. It all sounded fantastic. The shrill ringing of a mobile phone intruded on Dupin's culinary fantasies.

Nolwenn.

"Where are you, Monsieur le Commissaire?"

He didn't have any secrets from Nolwenn. "I'm sitting in Le San Francisco."

"Great. Get the lamb terrine with figs from the island, it's the right time for it." Without pausing she added, "I haven't found any criminal activity relating to salt. No reports about any illegality in its production or storage," she said, sounding bitterly disappointed, "or more generally in connection with any salt marshes. Nothing at all. I've done very thorough research. I've already told Inspector Riwal."

Dupin gestured to the waitress with his left hand as Nolwenn was speaking, and a moment later she was standing next to him, her right hand on her hip. She had a short, black braid and a narrow straw hat with a black ribbon that some people wore on the island. She smiled.

"The lamb terrine. And another coffee, please."

The lamb terrine would only need to be plated, after all.

"We're not thinking up any new ideas this way, Monsieur le Commissaire. We've got nothing—not in the Guérande and not in the other French salt marshes. Nowhere in Europe. It's strange."

"And nothing on these wide-necked barrels?"

"No."

"They must have contained something, I'm sure of it." Dupin had said this with emphasis.

"Great. You're on the lookout for signs. Sometimes, you really are like one of us!"

Dupin wasn't sure why these barrels were a "sign." What's more:

Nolwenn had never said this before, that he was "one of us," or at least that he "sometimes" was. Dupin wavered between a flash of pride and uncertainty: Did she feel he needed a boost? Did she think the case was in a hopeless enough state for that?

"You have a sensitivity to the world of signs. And that's the Breton people's way, they move through the world as though it were an enchanted forest. Behind everything and everyone there lies a hidden meaning, a secret. Charles Le Goffic says 'the visible world is nothing more than a web of symbols to a Breton.' And never forget: nothing is more real than what you can't see!"

Whenever Nolwenn quoted Charles Le Goffic, a revered Breton poet, it meant things were getting serious. Dupin recognized these words from Nolwenn's "Breton Lessons for Advanced Learners." The difference between these lessons and the ones for "Beginners" was that there was less concern for specific knowledge and more concern for basic, philosophical knowledge. It was about a particular attitude toward the world and life—*"une façon d'être au monde."* But clearly Dupin still didn't fully understand Nolwenn's words. The Breton relationship to reality was peculiar. Peculiar, but, as he had learned, convincing. It was not about what existed or what appeared at the average first glance—and this was true for a commissaire too, of course, or so he understood Nolwenn's allegory—but about what lay "behind" it. But this very thing, contrary to what you might think, didn't make reality less important; it wasn't devalued, and Bretons weren't daydreaming. On the contrary: it made reality—here again, exactly like for a commissaire—damned important. Reality was urgently needed. Nobody had anything else after all. It needed to be observed very carefully, every last detail, almost obsessively, and that went for detective work too. Because every little thing could be significant, especially anything that seemed insignificant.

"So is there any update on the chemical analyses of the pools?"

This was typical too. Nolwenn was straight back to real, practical matters.

"Nothing unusual so far. But some tests take longer. When it involves organic material."

If he had understood correctly.

"Let's speak later, Nolwenn."

Dupin didn't have much time. He hung up. The rustic lamb terrine with the aromatic figs from the island was already on the table in front of him. As was the espresso. It hadn't taken long and looked as good as he had hoped. He would eat and have a think while he did so. Think in peace for once. Following that surprising, extremely pertinent conversation with Maxime Daeron.

He cut off a piece of the fig, which was ripe but not too soft, picked up a piece of baguette, and used it to slice off a corner of the terrine. It tasted exquisite, the hearty meatiness combined with the fruity sweetness. He took a drink; he probably ought to have ordered water too, he hadn't drunk much since yesterday, and unlike in Paris, water wasn't automatically served in Brittany: *"L'eau c'est pour les vaches,"* water is for cows, was the Breton view.

Dupin was a long way off having concrete suspicions in this case. The preliminary basis for ideas, certainly. But these were vague too, if he were honest. He needed to activate his gray cells and think clearly. And for that he needed coffee, his brain didn't function without it, although many people thought he was just being eccentric. Dupin loved the short medical reports in the papers, the latest-studies-prove reports—more specifically, when the "latest studies" unearthed positive new insights into his habits and preferences. He stopped reading the other reports immediately—a lot of frivolous stuff was written, that was well known. It had been researched and proven countless times: coffee stimulated the metabolism in the brain, the brain's concentration, attention span, and memory capacity were significantly improved, the signs of fatigue eliminated. The scientific truth was this: caffeine was simply a miracle substance. The caffeine molecule has a similar chemical structure to the main substance in the brain's metabolism whose main task is to protect brain cells from critical overexertion. They do this by slowing down the transmission of information from one nerve cell to another. This was exactly what it felt like when Dupin had not had enough caffeine, and he was very glad to have this scientific explanation for it. The caffeine molecule cunningly simulated this substance, but without causing the slowing down! The nerve cells didn't get a signal for slower work; on the contrary: they kept working at top capacity! Not to mention the fact that regular coffee drinkers were much less likely to suffer from dementia, according to the studies—a particular relief to Dupin, because he struggled with his memory quite a lot. And the healing properties of caffeine had been documented in headaches, migraines, inflammation in the body, Type 2 diabetes, and fibrosis of the liver. There were very few other foods with such a phenomenal range of effects, apart from perhaps chocolate and red wine (Dupin loved gathering the reports about the "latest studies" on these ones too). It was purely medicinal.

Dupin had just taken another bite of the terrine when his mobile rang.

Commissaire Rose. Of course. With some reluctance, he answered.

"Jaffrezic's wife doesn't know where her husband is either. And neither does anybody in the cooperative. He was there all day and only left around half past five. His wife says he sometimes goes fishing and always has the rods in his car. We're checking if he's at his usual fishing spot. On the large beaches beyond Le Croisic. Ground fishing. Perch, gilthead, pollack." This sounded very professional and

Dupin was impressed despite himself. "He's not picking up his mobile. We're trying it at regular intervals."

Rose was speaking in solemn tones that reminded Dupin of when they hadn't been able to get through to Lilou the day before. He was starting to feel slightly uneasy too.

"If we don't find him soon, we'll put out a search for him."

Dupin knew this would be a huge measure to take. But there seemed to be a ruthless perpetrator at large.

"We'll see. Let's speak to Madame Bourgiot next instead. The forensics team has compared the fingerprints in Lilou's parents' house with Maxime Daeron's: they're his. So that explains that. There's nothing else to report."

"We need to know all of the applications that were filed with the local authority and the region in relation to the salt gardens over the last few years. Applications for subsidies, for extensions to the salt marshes"—Dupin had wanted to say this earlier—"and we need to know the plans that Le Sel has for the White Land. For expansions of the marshes, for acquisitions, for changes to the manufacturing. We need to know their business practices. And the cooperative's too."

"Inspector Chadron and another colleague have been at their offices for two hours and they're researching everything. They'll find whatever there is to find. Where are you, anyway?"

"I'm already on my way."

"Madame Bourgiot isn't free till eight. We're seeing her at the Centre. You should really get going."

Dupin looked at his watch. It was more or less impossible.

"Fine, eight o'clock. I'll be there."

He hung up.

He really ought to make a move. He took one last piece of terrine and the rest of the fig, stood up, rounded up the bill very generously, and left.

By the time he got to the quay, he was already annoyed he hadn't just taken the rest of the terrine with him, along with a piece of baguette. He hadn't eaten all that much. And why had she said "really get going"? He had explained he was already on his way, hadn't he?

* * *

Up until just before Vannes things had been moving quickly. The speed limit was seventy kilometers an hour and Dupin was driving at an average of a hundred and ten, without sirens, which he hated anyway. Then, beyond a blind bend, in a small wood, the traffic had come to a sudden stop. Out of nowhere. Dupin had just been in the middle of dialing Riwal's number when he saw the cars in front of him. He slammed on the brakes with squealing tires and came to a stop a hand's breadth away from the bumper of the car in front of him. Perhaps slightly less. Everything that had been on the front seat—the big map, the salted caramels, newspapers from the last few weeks—was now lying on the floor. Dupin had simply dropped his phone so that he could have both hands on the steering wheel, and it had slipped into the gap between the front seat and the hand brake. The car had been completely under control, yet he noticed his pulse was racing when he stopped. And he smelled the burning stench of overused brakes.

There hadn't been many cars in front of him, perhaps ten. There was an idyllic clearing to the right and left.

Two men and a woman were approaching him, visibly upset. He was used to this—and it was one of the reasons why he would usually never dream of driving around in an official police car. As soon as anything happened, no matter what it was—the most banal thing, puzzling little things—and a police car and police officer happened to be in the vicinity, you inevitably became involved. Dupin rolled down the window.

"Are you carrying a gun?"

The question was posed by a slight man, around sixty, his voice anxious and unpleasantly pushy.

"What is—"

"Skippy! It almost rammed us."

Behind Dupin, two more cars came to a stop with extreme brake maneuvers.

The second man was even more worked up. "On the radio they're saying he might be mentally ill. Aggressive."

"In Australia, an aggressive red kangaroo attacked a ninety-four-year-old pensioner while she was hanging out the washing. It leapt through the washing at her and knocked her down. Then it jumped on her. She was in the hospital for three weeks. Multiple fractures."

The woman told her story like it was important scientific knowledge.

"She hit him with a broom. Her dog was so frightened. The police drove it away with pepper spray."

The slight man looked hopefully at Dupin. "Are you carrying pepper spray on you?"

Dupin hadn't been able to say a word yet. And hadn't known what to say. For a moment he wondered whether he was being pranked by one of those television programs.

"You saw a kangaroo here?" was all that he managed to get out in the end.

"It hopped across the road. Straight across. There was nearly an accident. So dangerous."

The two men were speaking in unison now.

"I called the police right away. We didn't think you'd come so quickly."

"They said Skippy is on his way home."

"Skippy?" Dupin was still trying to get his own mental bearings.

"That's what it's called."

"Kangaroos have set places they always return to. It's been looking for a home. Apparently this is his route; the police said so on the phone. It's completely normal."

"It's only a year old."

This time the woman's voice sounded almost affectionate. Not the appropriate tone of voice for an aggressive red kangaroo.

"I . . . I'm not here because of the kangaroo."

There was profound confusion on all three of their faces. And the fear returned.

"You should get back into your cars. And keep the doors closed. The officers on duty will be here very soon."

All three looked relieved. At least they had a direct police order now.

"Yes. This is a very dangerous situation. Anything could happen."

The slight man was already walking toward his car, the other two hurrying after him.

Dupin wound the window up. He still hadn't fully absorbed what had just happened.

He started the engine, maneuvered his car out of its boxed-in position, turned around in one go, and stepped on the gas.

It took a while for him to fish his mobile out of the gap with one hand.

"Nolwenn?"

"Monsieur le Commissaire?"

"Are you familiar with Skippy?"

"Well, I did tell you about him yesterday."

"I . . ."

"The kangaroo that escaped from his enclosure near Arradon yesterday. They've been trying to catch him again but no luck so far. There are constant reports about it online, and on the radio. Along with the reports on the murder obviously. Bleu Breizh has set up a Kangaroo

Watch. For every confirmed sighting of the kangaroo, you get a crate of Britt Blonde."

This was unbelievable. Everything about it.

"It's got ideal living conditions at the gulf, comparable to its habitat in Australia."

With some effort, Dupin refrained from asking any more questions. It was too absurd. And he would have had a huge number of questions. For instance, how could it be that Breton and Australian habitats were so similar—but given it was correct to speak of the Breton Caribbean (the Glénan) or the Breton South Seas (the Île d'Houat), and there was a beach here called "Plage Tahiti," he let it go. There were many Brittanies, perhaps there was an Australian one too. And Dupin also thought it might be worth asking what the special link between the excellent Britt brewery and Australian marsupials was.

"Monsieur le Commissaire." Nolwenn's tone had changed. It was clear that the kangaroo topic was long since over and done with. "Maybe you're coming home like this so that you can call Claire in peace again."

Dupin tried to compose himself.

"I think so. I'll call her later. When I have more time."

Dupin almost said in his own defense that he had tried her again earlier without success. That he had left messages. But that would have sounded too much like he had a guilty conscience.

"So you should be back in Concarneau before midnight then. And it will still be her birthday. Apart from that: I think that all in all the Amiral would do you good this evening. After everything that's happened."

He hadn't given any thought to this evening yet. Or whether he would drive back at some point or stay here, but it sounded tempting: going back to Concarneau. Back home. To the Amiral. He would see.

The wise move would definitely be to stay here and get a hotel room. He was bound to finish late, he would be utterly exhausted. Nolwenn had sounded slightly mysterious. But maybe he was just imagining it.

"We'll see. Bye, Nolwenn."

Dupin hung up and dialed Riwal's number.

"Boss?"

"I want you to do something." Dupin hesitated. "Or ideally Kadeg, and ideally immediately." Kadeg was always showing off that he used to do rally driving back in the day, practically Paris-Dakar once (he claimed). "I want him to drive from La Roche-Bernard to Lilou's parents' house, park a few hundred meters beyond it in the direction of Pointe de Kerpenhir, simulate the murder and the removal of the body, then drive to Lilou Breval's house, wait about, let's say, five minutes, and then drive back to La Roche-Bernard. It would be best if he began and ended at Daeron's house. Tell him to time how long it takes when he really hurries."

This still bothered him.

"We'll get it done, boss. I'll let Inspector Chadron know too."

Rose seemed to have Kadeg and Riwal completely under her thumb, it was awful. They no longer did anything without reporting to her. He didn't like it one bit. Dupin wanted to protest but something else occurred to him. It would be better this way:

"Riwal—change of plan. Tell Kadeg to leave out the trip to Sarzeau in the simulation—Daeron could have done that later. After the calls that prove he was in La Roche-Bernard."

"All right. And one other thing, boss: the old woman in Kerpenhir who lives in the house next to Lilou Breval's parents seems very credible. They sent an officer from Locmariaquer out especially, someone who knows the area and the people there very well, and has known the neighbor herself for years. Besides, her and Daeron's statements match up on every detail."

That was important. Although Dupin had never really doubted this part of Daeron's testimony. But still.

"Fine."

"Also, since we're on the topic, I thought of something else." Riwal took a deep breath. "The treasures underneath the menhirs and dolmen are stored, according to legends and accounts, in mysterious blue vessels. Blue!"

Dupin hung up. That was enough absurdity. He threw his mobile onto the passenger seat and stepped on the gas.

A few minutes later, after a brief hesitation, he turned the radio on. Bleu Breizh.

* * *

At first glance, Madame Bourgiot was nowhere to be seen. Commissaire Rose was standing in the book corner of the Centre's boutique, holding a heavy book. Dupin walked in a long arc, along the long glass wall, between the high-tech display walls and the scenes built to showcase the history of salt. He approached Rose from one side. He wasn't sure if she had even noticed him. She seemed completely absorbed in the book. He could see the title now. *Salt of the Guérande—Top Chefs' Favorite Recipes*. Glossy photographs.

"Madame Bourgiot was meant to be here. We had arranged to meet. I've no idea where she is. No sign of Jaffrezic yet either."

Seeming surprisingly laidback, Commissaire Rose hadn't even looked up. Dupin was twenty minutes late.

"I . . . you know about the kangaroo of course, it . . ."

Rose looked at him for a moment.

"It crossed the road and . . ."

He broke off. Rose was already—pointedly—lost in reading a recipe: *poulet de Janzé en croûte de gros sel de Guérande*. She didn't seem in the least embarrassed—on the contrary. Her expression was one

Dupin recognized from their conversation with Jaffrezic in the co-operative, when she had suddenly talked casually about the delicious salt lamb. Dupin had eaten that kind of chicken from Janzé at Henri's once, the juiciest and most flavorsome chicken he'd had in his life, baked in pastry made from flour and *gros sel*.

"It's quick. Really simple."

Rose sounded like an expert. Dupin knew this was one of those things real chefs said that was only true for people like them. For lay-people it meant: you could try for years and you'd never succeed.

"We're waiting."

Rose's words, something of a non sequitur, sounded like an order, as if everyone could do whatever they wanted until Madame Bourgiot arrived. By rights they ought to have had a few things to discuss. Rose turned the page, and even this was done perfectly calmly—and now she became absorbed by the *pommes "Pont Neuf" à la fleur de sel et piment d'Espelette*, Touquet potatoes cut into little sticks, roasted in *fleur de sel* and Espelette pepper. They had been Dupin's favorite food as a child, and he had always called the potato wedges—modeled on the massive buttresses on the Pont Neuf in Paris—"fat fries," and his bourgeois mother had been horrified every time. But that's really what they were: fat fries.

Walking around aimlessly, Dupin suddenly found himself in the middle of the Iron Age. In the "experience room," amongst the first Celts. One of them was standing right next to him, life-size and made of wax, while another knelt behind him. The figures showed how they produced salt here in the Guérande using a special fire method. A few meters away, four Romans were bending down. Dupin realized that salt production in the third century, unlike thousands of years before that, was already starting to look like salt marshes. He walked in a zigzag—six hundred years in a matter of steps—past the Caro-lingians, and was now standing in front of four monks from the

Landévennec commune, who had given salt production, through pains-taking scientific studies, its final, or in other words, its current look. Unchanged for a thousand years. Even the design of the tools used today harked back to those days. "An open-air factory," read the display board.

Next to the monks was a map of Europe. Dupin loved maps. It was remarkable: for hundreds of years, major trade routes across the whole continent were determined by the salt from the Guérande, from the starting point of a tiny little town that had been phenomenally rich for half a millennium. It wasn't just about a seasoning or the fact that humans need salt to survive—for centuries it was the only known way to preserve food, until the invention of the can at the beginning of the nineteenth century.

Dupin took a step closer to the display board. A few times today a thought—a rather vague one—had crossed his mind, and he now found it illustrated here to some extent. The monks had often used the large pools for different purposes at the same time. Not just as water reservoirs. For farming shellfish, for instance, and fish (to this day, he learned, sole, perch, and eels swam in the reservoir pools). It was an intriguing idea: perhaps this case was about the salt pools and not about salt at all. Were the salt pools possibly used for something else? But if so—what? Unfortunately, Dupin didn't have the faintest idea what this other thing might be.

The sound of Rose's mobile ringing wrenched Dupin away from his thoughts. With elegant speed, she put the book down and answered the call.

"Yes? . . . Hmmm. I want you to ask his wife, friends, and colleagues where else he likes to go fishing. Get a few more police officers on it. It's important . . . Yes, sounds good . . . Bye." She hung up.

"Jaffrezic isn't at his usual spot," she said.

She sounded very serious again. What did that mean? Had Jaffrezic disappeared? Of course it could be that the events they were dealing with—which had revealed themselves so far through the shooting and Lilou's murder—were still ongoing. Or were even getting worse. Had Jaffrezic made a run for it? Was he in danger? Or was he simply fishing at a different spot from usual?

"And still," Rose continued, "no sign of Madame Bourgiot. Maybe the two of them are miles away, together."

It hadn't sounded like a joke.

"We'll keep waiting." Rose sounded laidback again as she said this; it was only the somewhat delayed coda that was sharp: "For a few more minutes."

At first Dupin thought she intended to turn her attention to the cookbook again. Instead, she came over to him, walking swiftly past and toward the last display board as if she were looking for something specific.

Dupin followed her.

BLOODY SALT, was emblazoned across the board in menacing black letters. Various things were discussed. The *gabelle*, the crude salt tax imposed by French kings, which naturally gave rise to huge numbers of smugglers. Even more scandalously: in the Middle Ages Brittany was by no means part of France, so Bretons had legally bought salt untaxed and then sold it again in France—which counted as smuggling and, if you were unarmed, you were sentenced to the galleys but if you were armed you were sentenced to death immediately. A terrifying prospect that led to violent protests, and many people in the Guérande and Le Croisic lost their lives when the protests were crushed (in the course of the revolution, the people had done away with the salt tax—"free salt" had been the slogan. "Free salt for free citizens," that kind of thing always made Dupin feel sentimental). The display board also recounted the adventurous tales of famous smugglers.

"This is interesting."

Rose must have been reading twice as quickly as he was; it looked like she was scanning the lines.

"Major salt thefts—and even more interestingly: huge plots. Intrigue and love."

Dupin was standing next to her. The board was about a "War of the *Paludiers*" in the sixteenth century in which several "clans" apparently pulled no punches in the fight for white gold. It specifically mentioned "sabotage and devastation." And as with Romeo and Juliet, there was an impossible love—and subsequently the downfall of a dynasty. Salt involved a lot of money, lots and lots of money. A lot of money was always a surefire breeding ground for crime.

"It's a pity there are no other details about the sabotage." Rose sounded disappointed.

The Salt Land hadn't been a peaceful place back then either. Even then it had been the setting for various conflicting interests, substantial financial interests. The setting for cunning and treachery—for criminality. Dupin discovered something odd: two salt traders had been punished for breeding "monstrous creatures" in the pools, for instance gigantic sole (two meters long?!) and crosses between mussels and crabs—which was too much even for Dupin's very active imagination.

* * *

"Sorry. I was with the mayor. We've got so many things to discuss."

Madame Bourgiot's words did not sound like an apology. As she came toward them now, self-confident and challenging, she no longer had much in common with the Madame Bourgiot they knew from their first conversation. Commissaires Rose and Dupin were still standing at the "Bloody Salt" exhibit.

"For starters, we hope that in spite of the . . . incidents, everything carries on as normal in the White Land. The shops, the tourism. And," she hastened to add, "of course, the most important thing, the *paludiers'* harvests. The salt must not in any way be linked to the incidents."

It wasn't clear what Madame Bourgiot meant by this. Could the police please abandon all investigation so that no damage is done? The head of the Centre made no move to invite them into the conference room where they had been sitting that afternoon. The Centre was empty; even the employee who had still been there just now had obviously left.

"There's still no solid evidence that all of this is specifically related to the salt and the White Land after all."

"Oh, you think so?"

Rose's retort was sharp and a tenth of a second quicker than Dupin's: "What are they related to then, Madame Bourgiot—these 'incidents'?"

"I assumed that finding out was precisely what your job was, Monsieur le Commissaire. Mine is to promote the White Land. To ensure no damage is done. That—"

"You spoke to Lilou Breval on Monday of this week. For three minutes. Are you aware that you have perverted the course of justice in a murder inquiry by not telling us about that? And that because of this you are among the chief suspects?"

Rose sounded all the more threatening because of how coolly and matter-of-factly she spoke.

Judging by the expression on her face, Madame Bourgiot wasn't unfazed by this—but she composed herself again quickly.

"If there had been anything relevant in that phone call, I would naturally have told you about it," she said, trying to play it down.

"What exactly was your conversation about?" Dupin asked brusquely. "What did Lilou Breval want from you?"

He was not in the mood for clichés and these irritating verbal skirmishes.

"She asked me about the use of barrels in salt manufacturing here in the Guérande. We spoke in depth with Madame Laurent about the blue barrels this afternoon. I told Lilou Breval what I've told you: that I don't know anything about blue barrels, apart from the fact the cooperative—"

"What else did she want from you?"

"Just that. The blue barrels stuff. It wasn't a long phone call, as you know. I wasn't aware it would help you progress in your investigation to know that she was interested in blue barrels—seeing as you told us exactly that."

A good comeback. She went on. "She asked whether it was possible to speed up the manufacture of salt with chemical additives. An odd question. She herself couldn't give me more detail on what she was driving at."

Lilou Breval was concerned—although they'd already known this—about what they were also concerned about: What could have been in the barrels? On Monday evening it seemed she still didn't have a clue, and the same went for Tuesday evening during the phone call with Dupin. Perhaps even up to her death?

"Have you spoken to anyone about Madame Breval's interest in the barrels?"

This was important. Perhaps that alone had set off the chain of events.

"No. I forgot about it immediately. It wasn't significant."

"You didn't speak to anyone about it?"

"No."

"If you're behind it all, Madame Bourgiot, then Lilou inadvertently warned you—and provoked her own death."

Commissaire Rose had phrased this as a simple working hypothesis. Madame Bourgiot held her gaze, impassive. "That's true. But it's ludicrous. You know that."

"Now that we're learning things you were keeping quiet about, what else is there?"

Rose's gaze wandered around the room.

"Nothing at all. Lilou Breval, as I mentioned, spoke to me in more depth a year ago, here in the Centre. After that we spoke briefly a few times. About various things, a handful of questions. I do the public relations work too, after all. It's standard procedure."

She hadn't told them about these brief phone calls this afternoon either. Admittedly it had been more of a conversation with Madame Laurent than with Madame Bourgiot. Still. On a murder case, you at least mentioned something like that for the record.

"How often did these 'brief calls' happen this year?" Rose snorted.

"Four or five times."

"What did you talk about?"

"Things she thought were coming to a head. As she was of course free to think."

"What do you mean by 'coming to a head'?" Dupin pricked up his ears.

"She suspected there was a drama to the competitive environment here in the White Land, although that's very far from the truth."

"More specifically?"

"The different parties' various interests. The independents, the—"

"Wasn't it something more specific?"

They knew of this interest of Lilou's, that wasn't new. But in such general terms, it didn't help them make any progress. And Dupin was less and less convinced her interest had anything to do with the core of the case at all. They were still just groping around in the dark far too much.

"She had very vague questions, who had what plans to take over whom—those kinds of things. Lilou Breval's suspicion was very unspecific."

"Really?" Rose said harshly.

Madame Bourgiot gave a barely audible groan. "She wanted to know, for instance, whom Le Sel had made takeover bids to, which we in the Centre wouldn't know. And whether Le Sel wanted to introduce a pump system, if they've filed an application. But she also had questions about the cooperative. How strong it had become in recent years. Since Jaffrezic became the head of it. She wanted to know what role the Centre du Sel actually played—she said that it was for another major article about the Gwenn Rann, about the business and economic aspects of it this time. But none of that came up in the conversation on Monday."

"Has Le Sel filed an application for the construction of a pump system?"

"Yes, they have. Six months ago."

"And?"

"It is being discussed."

"And the expansion of the salt marshes—right into the nature reserve? We know you're a powerful person in the White Land. You could make the expansions to the manufacturing area possible."

"That's also still to be decided in the conventional way. That's out of my hands; it's a matter of politics. The procedure for these kinds of applications is fully and transparently regulated."

This was all futile. And much too haphazard. Dupin was getting impatient. They wouldn't get anywhere like this.

"Have there been any more results from the tests in the salt marshes yet? It's crucial for us. I've already told you that the institute is terrorizing us. Madame Cordier is determined to stop everything here. Production and sales. She's adamant. I won't allow it," Madame Bourgiot said.

There was something unintentionally comical in the way she complained about a ruthless person in a ruthless way.

Rose was just about to answer when her mobile rang.

"Yes?" She stepped aside. It was clear Rose was listening carefully, not saying a word herself. It was some time before she uttered a "great."

She hung up a moment later and turned back to them. "As soon as the tests turn up anything relevant, you'll hear about it, Madame Bourgiot."

Visibly relieved, she added in Dupin's direction: "Monsieur Jaffrezic is fishing on the Loire this evening. Not by the sea as usual. With an old friend. He's very well."

Madame Bourgiot looked at Rose with undisguised irritation. Then she said with emphasis: "I will do everything to keep the . . . incidents here in check as much as possible by whatever means available to me. The Centre has been under my leadership for four years now. So far it's been a success story. And I'm not about to let that change."

There was no doubt she was serious. And she was an intelligent person; she must have known that this ruthless vow—especially the vow to be ruthless—couldn't have won her any favors with police investigating a murder. But she obviously didn't give a damn. Dupin would have loved to know why she had been so nervous this afternoon, at the beginning of their conversation.

"That's it for this evening, Madame Bourgiot. For now." Rose managed to make an unambiguous threat out of these clichéd words.

She turned around, walked calmly back to the book corner, picked up the cookbook again briefly—clearly to memorize the title—and then headed for the door.

Dupin followed her, lost in thought.

* * *

Rose was leaning with her back against her car. Her hands in her pockets. The small police Peugeot right next to it was exactly half the length of her Renault. If that. At the other end of the dusty parking lot there was a chic new dark green Range Rover. That must have been Bourgiot's car.

Rose looked, for the very first time, worn out; but her clothes still looked like she'd just put them on. Toward the sea the sky was tranquil, a delicate pink working its way through mysterious shades and into a bright, vivid watercolor blue that got darker and darker the higher it went. The first stars would be out soon. The sky melded seamlessly into outer space this evening.

"I wouldn't put anything past her."

Rose's gaze wandered vaguely in the direction of the Centre as she spoke. After a small pause, she added: "Or any of the others, for that matter. Nobody is saying anything. Nobody."

Dupin leaned his back against his car, opposite hers: "So we now can turn to Monsieur Jaffrezic."

Rose smiled vaguely. "Madame Laurent is hosting a dinner in Vannes this evening. She's welcoming guests from the Île de Noirmoutier. *Paludiers*. We're expected tomorrow morning."

"They cultivate salt on the Île de Noirmoutier too?"

"Yes, but on a much smaller plot of land."

"Does Le Sel have a finger in that pie?"

"Not yet, as far as we know. But I'm having that looked into."

"Where are we seeing Jaffrezic? How long does it take him to get back from the Loire?"

"Inspector Chadron will let him know to expect us tomorrow morning too."

"Tomorrow morning?" Dupin had assumed it would definitely be this evening.

"We've booked you and your inspectors a room. In Le Grand Large. At this point, we all need to get some sleep."

Dupin had only just gotten used to the idea that Commissaire Rose survived without any food or sleep.

"I—"

"That's it for today. Nobody else is available. We have to marshal our thoughts. I'm driving home now."

This was not Dupin's way of doing things. Just calling it a day now. They needed to make progress. Apart from the conversation with Jaffrezic, all day he had wanted to be in Daeron's salt marsh by himself, although he didn't know *what* exactly it was he wanted there. Above all, he had wanted to take another look at Lilou's house. But perhaps Rose's idea wasn't that ridiculous. Perhaps he shouldn't do any more this evening. Today had been never-ending. His shoulder had also—for the first time since this afternoon—started to hurt badly; he would need to take another pill. Above all, his stomach was making it unmistakably clear that he finally needed to eat something. Something proper. And despite all of the medical benefits of coffee, his stomachache wouldn't be improved by any more caffeine.

And most important of all: this way he would actually be able to call Claire back on her birthday in peace and quiet. And tell her in more detail why he just couldn't come today. And also how sad that made him. And this was all during such an important phase of their relationship too. Right now, they should have been sitting together in La Palette. Right now.

"Fine."

He would be able to have a quick word with Riwal and Kadeg, in any case. In the restaurant of Le Grand Large. The sole, he thought—today he'd have the sole he'd wanted yesterday evening. That was something.

"Good night, Commissaire. Try to get some sleep." Rose's words sounded friendly, but like an order at the same time.

* * *

Ten minutes later Dupin was standing in front of Le Grand Large. He had let Riwal know over the phone and asked the inspector to reserve a quiet spot in the restaurant; Riwal had asked twice whether he wouldn't prefer to just go to Concarneau, he'd also be able to change his clothes that way. "Which would definitely be nice." Riwal had asked it in an oddly persistent and considerate way. Then he had reported on Kadeg's test drive. The simulation. Kadeg had just called from La Roche-Bernard. The number was 2:35. It had taken Kadeg two hours and thirty-five minutes. Dupin did some calculations. At night there would be virtually nobody on the road. But it wouldn't be possible in under two hours and fifteen or twenty minutes. So what did that mean? Maxime Daeron could very possibly have managed it. So at least they knew that for sure now. Riwal had of course already brought Rose "up to speed."

Dupin locked his car.

Like this morning, the tide was out. He walked to the unpaved edge of the quay. There was a sheer drop of three or four meters. Just as they had earlier, the boats lay patiently on the sea floor, weakly lit by yellow lights from the village that didn't reach far and faded quickly in the clear night. A little farther out into the lagoon, where there must have been some water still, there were two bright lights visible, presumably light buoys. Or boats. They were dancing silently back and forth. Even farther out, where the salt marshes must have been, there was a large, deep, black hole. Nothing, nothing was visible, as if everything had been swallowed up. The night loomed above the sea. A dark presence.

Dupin noticed how drained he felt. But at the same time he felt uneasy, deep down inside. Tingly, like quicksilver, a crazy feeling. If he were honest he was suddenly not in any mood to speak again. To anyone. Somehow none of this had been a good idea. And the journey to Concarneau wouldn't take all that long. And what's more: Nolwenn had said he should come back.

He turned round, walked to his car, and got in. He leaned his head back and closed his eyes for a moment. Then he smiled. A liberating smile. He started up the engine and drove away.

* * *

It was a quarter past eleven. Dupin parked his car as close to the Amiral as possible; the big parking lot right by the harbor was empty. He just had to cross the street and he'd be saved. And best of all: at home. Back on home turf. It had been a tedious journey, but he had got through it without any issues, taking the dual carriageway the whole way. There hadn't been any more Skippy sightings. He had listened to Bleu Breizh the whole trip, although he'd kept the volume low.

He had let Riwal and Nolwenn know he wouldn't be staying in Le Croisic. They were both in total agreement with his decision. Riwal and Kadeg were sitting in the restaurant, and by the sound of things, they had already started dinner. It had been a demanding day for them too.

Dupin climbed carefully out of the small car. A real breeze greeted him, wonderful. It smelled like the free, open sea here. It did him good.

The tall arched windows of the Amiral, where he usually began and ended his day—an unshakable and relished ritual—were still brightly lit. Dupin was relieved. The elegant, wide, white building from the nineteenth century with the red awning and the wooden shutters stood in the surreal film-studio light of warm, yellowish streetlamps.

The lights stayed red, they always did that at this spot, he had never known them to do anything different. But he had never seen anyone waiting at the lights. Moments later he was opening the heavy door.

His usual spot was taken. He almost let out a frustrated sigh, but at the last minute he held back.

He thought he was hallucinating. It wouldn't have surprised him, in his condition. But no, his eyes weren't deceiving him. In his favorite chair sat—Claire. Unmistakably. And on the table in front of her lay a hefty package wrapped in colorful paper. There was also a bottle of champagne and an enormous plate of langoustines.

Claire saw him immediately. Her chestnut brown eyes shone warmly. Then she stood up, sweeping away strands of her shoulder-length dark blond hair. She looked embarrassed. He was not dreaming. It was Claire. Claire, in all her reserved beauty, so unique to the women of Normandy. He had once shown a photo of her in the commissariat. Riwal had then begun an homage to Normandy women, who had been considered the most beautiful in France for centuries and often won the Miss France contests. Dupin had cringed outwardly, but deep down he had been glowing with pride.

"I . . . I'm here."

Unbelievable. It was unbelievable.

She had come to visit him on her own birthday. And this after the disappointment that nothing had come of their long-planned evening in Paris. And despite his miserably stammered words this morning. Now he understood why Nolwenn and Riwal had wanted to make sure he drove back to Concarneau this evening.

"Bon anniversaire, mon amour."

He hugged her. Kissed her. And looked at her again, still somewhat lost for words, and as if he had to make sure she was really there.

Paul Girard came out of the kitchen to say hello.

"I've put together a little birthday menu." He winked at them. "After the langoustines from Guilvinec, there will be sea bass flambéed with *pastis marin*, and a Chenin blanc to go with it. And for dessert, a *gâteau aux crêpes*."

That was a full-blown celebration of a birthday menu. Dupin didn't often have the sea bass—it was usually the *entrecôte*—but it was exquisite, the delicate, aromatic flavor, the tender, white flesh, the scent of the flambéed Breton aniseed spirit (they didn't need the south for that either). He knew that Girard swore by the langoustines from Guilvinec. And rightly so, because they were the very best. But the absolute highlight was the crepe cake: a dozen sweet crepes stacked one on top of the other with a delicious *crème pâtissière* in between the layers, thick and made from milk, egg yolk, and vanilla—a specialty that Girard only served for his "very best friends'" birthdays.

Dupin was touched.

Claire held out a glass of champagne to him. "To us."

"To your birthday. To you."

They clinked glasses and took a sip.

"How's it coming along? The case, I mean."

"Tonight, there is no case."

Dupin surprised himself with this statement. But it had been the correct answer. He saw it in Claire's smile. And he seriously meant it.

"You'll catch the perpetrator tomorrow," she said, and smiled again. "Thanks for the present. I'm going to unwrap it right away."

He knew Claire couldn't stand wrapped presents for a second longer than necessary. Nolwenn must have brought the package; she must have arranged absolutely everything, the whole operation, Claire's journey, this food, everything. The package had been sitting in his office for a few days now. Dupin had been in Valérie Le Roux's atelier, at the far end of the large quay. A terrific artist who made and painted the most beautiful Atlantic pottery: drinking bowls, cups, mugs, plates, and dishes in patterns and colors of the sea. Claire herself had once shown him an article in the *Maison Côte Ouest* about Valérie Le

Roux. He had chosen two large plates, two small plates, and two drinking bowls, one with a bright red crab and one with a bright blue fish.

"For Paris. For us, morning and evening."

"They're wonderful."

She sounded truly happy.

Dupin was still not entirely sure if he was still dreaming. But it didn't matter.

The Third Day

It was cooler. Not dramatically so, but enough for there to be a chill in the air this morning. For the first time in a long while. It must have happened sometime between one in the morning—when he and Claire left the Amiral—and shortly before six in the morning, because when they walked home along the quay after dark it had still been a "tropical" night, a term the local papers were very fond of using. By ten to six, with the very first blue light of dawn in the east, they had already left Dupin's apartment and Dupin had brought Claire to the train station. She would be in Paris by eleven and in the hospital by half past. They hadn't slept much, but Dupin felt more refreshed than he had in weeks. Since the moment he had walked into the Amiral and seen Claire, he hadn't felt the graze wound again. And it wasn't just the pain he had forgotten—he had even forgotten the case. It was nothing more than a dark phantom, far away. Claire hadn't asked anything else about it and Dupin had been glad. They had been surreal hours, truly like being in a dream.

Dupin walked straight from the train station to the car park—the Amiral was still closed, as were the other cafés—and then drove back up the dual carriageway the way he had come the evening before. He made a strategically important stop in Névez, at the pretty market square he liked so much, in the marvelous Maison Le Quern, with its lovely proprietor. It was just opening and—having learned his lesson the day before—he stocked up on four *tartines* and two coffees as supplies for the day. Of the *tartines*, only half made it to the Guérande (he kept the two smoked duck breast and Roquefort ones and ate the others, the ones with brie, walnuts, and grape mustard, on the journey). The Maison Le Quern, with its masterful entrecôte and homemade, crispy chips, was on his list of best places for *steak-frites*. A very important list, of course.

Dupin turned on Bleu Breizh again. A kangaroo expert from the Zoo de Vincennes in Paris was on this morning, giving listeners "basic information" about their "new neighbor" and answering questions. Lots of questions. The difference between real kangaroos and rat kangaroos—which weren't really kangaroos at all—was a fundamental zoological one, according to the expert. The relief amongst listeners generally had been enormous when they found out Skippy was a real kangaroo. The local councillor and the mayor of Arran had made the decision yesterday not to "hunt" it, since it really was a red kangaroo and almost six feet tall and weighed 192 pounds (not a rufous hare-wallaby; that was misreported), but so far it had not shown any signs of aggression. And apparently it was a strict vegetarian, and "primarily active at dusk and nighttime." It probably spent most of the day in the shade, but sometimes Skippy, and this was an odd habit, could be seen sunbathing. The expert found it plausible that Skippy might find a "permanent home" in the Breton fauna—in short: Skippy would become a free Breton. Today, unlike yesterday, most of the listeners were already referring to Skippy as "our kangaroo." By far the funniest story was the apparently apocryphal one about how the kangaroo got its name in the first place. James Cook, the first European ever to see one, supposedly asked the aborigines what the animal was called and they answered, "I don't understand," in their language: *"Gang oo rou."* Cook, the butt of the joke, then presented the "kangaroo" to the world. This story—one that was fundamentally illustrative for people—reminded Dupin of his first weeks in Brittany.

It was half past seven. It wasn't just the air, but also the light, that was colder than it had been recently, a milky white. Hazy. As though billions of matte particles were floating in the air. Nolwenn called this a "pale daybreak"—sometime before noon it disappeared, only seldom did it linger any longer. It was really an autumn phenomenon, not a summer one.

Without thinking about it, Dupin parked his car in the exact same place he had left it the night before last. When it all started. But this time he had thought to bring a second magazine.

Everything was of course still sealed off. Two of the police officers from Rose's team were standing on the path to Daeron's salt marsh. Dupin greeted them briefly, one of them looking blatantly skeptical, the other nodding neutrally.

As he'd driven there, the case had returned to Dupin's consciousness more and more with every kilometer he traveled eastward, and Dupin kept coming back to the issue that had been on his mind from the outset: What were the barrels all about? If the barrels had had something inside them, no matter what it was, then it was probably still in the salt marshes, although they hadn't found anything in the tests so far. Tests on the water, the ground, the sediment, the settling salt crystals. Dupin reached the hut that had been his salvation. And his prison. He felt a little lost for a moment. Then he stepped onto one of the narrow clay dams that ran through the harvest pools, following it, taking a turn onto another dam that led to the outermost pool before coming to a stop. It all looked different in this milky white light that robbed the world of its color, even here where the colors were in such abundance and intensity, including the sky. Everything was bathed in a strange coldness. A theatrical coldness. And strangely it also robbed the world of its smell, as if the billions of droplets absorbed everything.

Dupin looked around, letting his gaze wander. It was a baffling labyrinth. As far as the eye could see. The entire landscape. It was impossible to say where Daeron's salt marsh began or ended. The extremely precise, pedantic right angles and the intertwined reservoir pools and canals intermingled in apparent chaos. Dupin walked along another dam toward the bigger pools. The clay of the dams had significant cracks here and there, consequences of the long, dry, hot spell. The water flowed around dozens of bends and forks, sometimes sharp bends, sometimes gentle. No sluice gates anywhere. As a young boy, building dams and diverting water—in streams, rivers, lakes, by the sea—had been one of his favorite pastimes. Dupin would lose himself in it completely. One of his most vivid memories of his father was an image from the holidays, in a little village on the river Doubs in the Jura. The river in the water-rich region had hundreds of little tributaries and brooks of all sizes. The narrow brook that ran through the middle of the garden of their holiday home flowed in a torrent in the spring. On a warm May day, he and his father dammed it at a particular point to form a deep pool at least a meter deep. A small pond. From there, they had built the most complex new outflows in crazy loops and mad pathways. His mother scolded them because they were both soaked to the skin and muddy. They hadn't even noticed. To this day, Dupin couldn't help changing the course of a tideway when he saw it draining on a beach. Best of all, he liked to make it flow all over the place in crazy new routes.

Dupin walked back to the harvest pool the water drained into. He had suddenly had an idea. The pool's watercourse was clearly visible. He smirked. He would simply follow it. In the opposite direction. See how it flowed and hence see Daeron's entire salt marsh—it would be the only way to get a complete overview of it. He walked along the dams carefully to make sure he didn't slip off. The pools varied in size, shape, and depth. The four pools beyond the harvest pool were even bigger. They were followed by smaller, symmetrical ones. Nine of them. Dupin counted them as he walked. Even the clay, dark in itself, seemed pale in this light, the water milky. Now the tapering dam suddenly brought him to the other side of the harvest pool, where there were another nine symmetrical pools. He had to look carefully to detect the leisurely flow of the water. Dupin stubbornly followed it: every bend, every sluice gate.

He had been walking for a good ten minutes. To his right was a long reservoir pool nestled right up against the many medium-sized pools, significantly deeper, at least a hundred meters long and mis-shapen. The water was dark green. Tall, faded grasses grew all the way round it. He would surely be reaching the flow to this reservoir pool any moment, Dupin thought. From there, there was just the canal to the sea. He had learned that much. He continued on, following the channel with the water flowing through it. Dazzled by the sun, still low in the sky, he had to shield his eyes with one hand. The channel drained parallel with the large reservoir pool. On and on. And still parallel. For the length of the whole pool. Dupin turned right at the end of the pool to follow it round to its shorter side. After perhaps sixty meters the channel turned again—not to the right as he expected, in the direction of the large reservoir pool, but to the left. And then left again: into another, much darker-looking reservoir pool. Totally unexpectedly. A large pool in the shape of an enormous teardrop. A long-legged silver bird was standing at the edge, looking like he was inspecting Dupin.

Dupin felt an unease rising up inside him. This pool with the dark green water—perhaps three hundred meters away from Daeron's harvest pools as the crow flies—was *not* the reservoir pool that supplied Daeron's salt marsh. Even if it had looked that way at first. It was odd.

Dupin walked to the second long side of the pool. There was a bigger canal here, with an inflow you could follow toward the lagoon, securely sealed off with a wooden sluice gate. Dupin was walking faster and faster, and soon he was back on the side he had started on. This was crazy: the large reservoir pool was, apart from the drainage canal, totally cut off. It was definitely not connected to any salt marsh. Something wasn't right here. What kind of pool was this? Dupin paced round it one more time, his eyes riveted on the water this time. He stopped and crouched down. Trying to focus on the ground. There was nothing out of the ordinary visible. Not to the naked eye. But that didn't mean anything. The water was perhaps slightly cloudier than in the other pools. The samples taken so far came from different pools in the Daeron salt marsh that were all connected to each other anyway. But perhaps it was this specific pool—perfectly hidden in this labyrinth—that they needed to look into. They needed to take samples from here.

Dupin straightened up, pulling his phone out of his pants pocket along with his Clairefontaine. To his surprise, he saw four bars of reception. Two evenings ago, one would have been enough for him. But as Riwal would say at this point, he was actually a few hundred meters away from the hut, and it was daytime, the tide was in a different phase, as was the sun, the moon—whatever.

He needed an expert. Dupin thought for a moment and then dialed the number for the food chemist. Madame Cordier. She hadn't been all that cooperative, but that didn't matter now. Her voicemail kicked in. After a brief hesitation, he dialed Rose's number.

"Where are you? I've called you several times." Rose was furious. "The hotel said you didn't—"

"I need a chemist team in the salt marshes. Right now. I'm standing here."

"I can't hear you very well. You're standing . . . there?"

Rose's voice reached Dupin loud and clear. Her anger had given way to criminological curiosity.

"I can hear you very well," Dupin said slowly, and enunciating clearly. "I'm in Daeron's salt marsh. There's a large pool here that isn't linked to the rest of the salt marsh. It's about three hundred meters from Daeron's harvest pool."

There was a short pause, perhaps because the commissaire was struggling with how to respond.

"You're investigating in Daeron's salt marsh on your own? I'm sending the team. And I'll be there soon too." She hung up.

Dupin brooded. He leafed through his notebook, found what he was looking for, and dialed Bourgiot's number. He was walking aimlessly along the dam as he did so.

"Hello?"

Dupin could hear a rustling now, alternating between loud and quiet.

"Madame Bourgiot. I'm in Maxime Daeron's salt marsh—on the edge of the salt marshes."

"What can I do for you, Monsieur le Commissaire?"

It sounded sarcastic. He didn't care.

"There's a reservoir pool here that's totally isolated. Very large. It looks like it's Daeron's reservoir pool—but it's not, it's not connected to his pools. Or to any of the others."

Bourgiot was silent. Perhaps she needed to work out how to act.

"You haven't done your research," she said coldly. "It's a blind pool. There are a few of them."

"Whom does it belong to?"

"Daeron or Jaffrezic perhaps, but not necessarily."

Her voice was accompanied by variable rustling.

"Or Le Sel. I couldn't tell you. I—"

"Le Sel? I thought the neighboring salt marshes belonged to Monsieur Jaffrezic and the cooperative?"

"Over toward the lagoon there are some salt marshes belonging to Le Sel. I believe two of the large reservoir pools reach from there almost as far as Daeron's plot. And the blind pool. Maybe the blind pool doesn't belong to anyone at all. That can happen, and it's not all that uncommon"—there was undisguised distaste in her tone—"for pools that used to belong to specific salt marshes to become isolated over the course of centuries for one reason or another."

"Where would you have to go to get as close as possible to the blind pool by car?"

There was quite a long pause.

"I couldn't say."

"Is there anything unusual about this pool—this blind pool, I mean? Do you know of anything?"

"No. What would be wrong with the pool? Has something happened? Is there news, do you know—"

Dupin hung up, then dialed Riwal's number.

"Good morning, boss."

"Riwal—you need to get hold of a full scale map of the salt marshes. One to twenty-five thousand. Or even more precise. And an aerial photograph. And Kadeg is to get an exact map of the salt marshes from the land registry office. I want to know exactly who owns what land, which salt marshes, which pools."

"Are you in Daeron's salt marsh? Hello?"

Dupin had hung up so abruptly, he hadn't even heard the question.

* * *

He had walked quite a long way during the phone calls. A few times he had crossed some of the larger canals, lined with tall, thorny bushes. What he now saw in front of him were harvest pools again. They were recognizable from their little harvest platforms. Daeron's hut was long since out of view. The wide earthen dams between the salt marshes, overgrown with grass, seemed even higher in this section.

For a moment he was confused. The whole salt-flat world felt alien all of a sudden. A few steps farther on, two dams suddenly gave way to reveal a view of the lagoon, which Dupin appeared to have gotten closer to than he had expected. He could see extensive, dazzlingly white sand banks, turquoise water running in deep channels between the sandbars. Beyond lay Le Croisic. A faint, cheerful streak. Riwal and Kadeg were there. With a telescope you could have seen Le Grand Large. The sun was quite high in the sky, there was a strong aroma in the air, the unmistakable scent of the sea here: salt, iodine, seaweed, and algae. It was incredible.

Dupin suddenly stopped. He had heard a noise. He didn't move. A heavy, dull sound coming from diagonally behind him. Not far away. A high earth wall blocked his view. Instinctively, he turned around, ducking slightly and placing his right hand on his gun. He clasped it tightly. When he realized what he'd done, he tried to relax his fingers slightly.

He took one of the narrower footbridges that led directly toward the place he'd heard the noise coming from. It must have come from just over the earthen wall. He looked for a gap and found it ten meters farther on. Nimbly and silently, he approached it. He stood still for a moment and then stepped through, his hand firmly on his gun.

The other person had seen him first.

"Ah. Monsieur le Commissaire. On the trail of the perpetrator, deep in the salt?"

Jaffrezic. Hammer in hand. He was standing in front of an upside-down, bright yellow, rectangular wheelbarrow.

"They've been built in the exact same way for the last twelve hundred years, wooden down to the very last piece. We use them to transport the salt through the salt marshes—and this bloody specimen here seems like it's literally twelve hundred years old."

Jaffrezic was hammering a wooden bolt on the wheel.

"I had warned you about walking through the salt marshes at night or early in the morning. We talked about the dwarves. But not about the dreadful gigantic fox, the white woman, and the dragon," he said, then burst out laughing. "Fire-breathing monsters hide here, and a girl or woman with a pure soul has to be sacrificed to them once a year. Then they keep quiet, leave the swamp to us salt farmers, and we can go about our work in peace."

He laughed again. Dupin was speechless. He had not been expecting Jaffrezic or yet more fantastical myths.

"Maybe you're one of those Christian dragon killers? A Parisian commissaire in Brittany."

Dupin was aware this was not meant as flattery, because he knew a slew of Breton dragon-conqueror myths. The Christian knights were really figures of fun. In the myths the poor native heathens—and even the greatest heroes amongst them—each fought in vain for hundreds of years against the most gruesome of all dragons until—in a sign from God—a Christian knight came along and casually ordered the dragons to jump off a cliff and drown. Which the monsters then obediently did on the spot—so powerful was the Christian word and so simple was the moral.

"But if that's the case, then you've come too late this time, Monsieur le Commissaire. You haven't been able to save the virgin."

Jaffrezic's face changed as he spoke, and he looked troubled. The events of recent days seemed to have taken their toll on him too.

Dupin wanted to get back to the real world finally. He composed himself. "What did Lilou Breval want from you when she called you on Monday afternoon?"

Jaffrezic looked at Dupin, clearly at a loss. Dupin wasn't sure why.

"The commissaire just asked me the same thing. Is everyone investigating separately now? Parallel investigations, an interesting approach."

"Commissaire Rose?"

"She left ten minutes ago. She got a call suddenly. Apparently it was important."

This was outrageous. Dupin remembered Rose's inquisitorial tone. And he had almost felt guilty about going it alone!

"In any case. The journalist was here once about a year ago. It was about a big article." There was emotion in Jaffrezic's voice.

"But what did she want on Monday?"

"Most of the information in the article came from me. I can send you—"

"Monsieur Jaffrezic, please . . ."

"She wanted to know if I knew anything about some kind of barrel. Blue barrels! And what they might be about. I told her about *sel moulin*. And that there are no other blue barrels apart from those ones. Just like I told you."

"Did she say anything about her suspicions or hint at anything?"

"No."

If Jaffrezic was behind all of this, Lilou would have unwittingly been warning him. Just like Madame Bourgiot.

"Did she say that she had seen the barrels somewhere herself?"

"No. Not a word."

"And you didn't tell anyone about Lilou's question?"

"Why would I? It's all nonsense. Much as that journalist was very nice." His voice had grown hard. Like it had yesterday morning on the same subject.

"We know about the blind pool on the edge of Maxime Daeron's salt marsh, Monsieur Jaffrezic."

Dupin just had to give it a go. If the entire squad turned up at the pool any moment now, the rumor would go round anyway about the police showing a particular interest in the pool.

"What do you mean?" Jaffrezic's pupils darted rapidly back and forth.

"We've found the pool. The one it was all poured into. Our chemists have already begun testing it."

Dupin scrutinized Jaffrezic. It was a moment before Jaffrezic started to snort with laughter. "This is getting more and more ridiculous. I don't have the faintest idea what you're talking about."

"Is that your pool?"

"I have no idea which one you mean."

Dupin made a vague gesture. "The one next to your salt marsh over there, next to Maxime Daeron's."

"Ah. I think there are a few around there. But none of them are mine. I'd know."

"It's two or three hundred meters from Maxime Daeron's hut. To the north."

"Then I definitely don't know it. I can't see any of Daeron's land next to my salt marsh anyway. And my salt marsh is, as you know, to the southwest of Daeron's. It's quite far away."

Even Dupin knew by now that in the labyrinthine chaos of the salt gardens, saying one salt marsh was "next to" another one meant nothing at all. He had to admit it was plausible that Jaffrezic had never seen the pool before.

"Who owns it then?"

"Ask at the land registry office. Probably nobody. And therefore the local authority own it."

"Doesn't it belong to Maxime Daeron—or Le Sel?"

"As I say: I really don't know."

Dupin ran a hand through his hair. His mobile rang. Rose. He took a few steps to one side and picked up.

"Where are you? I'm standing at the blind pool. The two chemists should be here any moment."

"And I'm where you just were. I'm speaking to Monsieur Jaffrezic."

"The first time I called you was at your hotel at half past six. I was told you'd had to go back to Concarneau last night after all. I thought it would be irresponsible to arrange the investigation based on travel plans you'd kept from me."

Dupin was still wondering what to say when Rose changed the topic.

"We might have something. Here in the pool. Something interesting."

"I'll be right with you."

Dupin hung up.

"I've got to go."

"Has the dragon been spotted? Well, good luck then—wind and sun permitting . . . The closest cliffs are on the Côte Sauvage beyond Le Croisic."

Dupin made for the gap in the earthen wall and vanished, only to reappear moments later. Jaffrezic must have expected this, as he was grinning at him. "Take a sharp left after the wall, walk along the large *etier* for a few hundred meters until you reach a very large hut on your right. Turn left and you'll come to a little path that you'll recognize. And then keep going to Daeron's salt marsh."

Dupin nodded gratefully—and tensely—and vanished for good.

* * *

It looked strange. It was only dimly visible in the cloudy water—Dupin hadn't noticed it before. But the sun was a bit higher in the sky now and was falling on the water at a different angle. About four meters from the edge of the pool there was a low wooden structure. Forty centimeters tall, he estimated, half the height of the water level. It reminded him a little of oyster and mussel beds. It looked as though, and this was still difficult to make out, a net was stretched over it. A greenish color. Dupin had walked around the long reservoir pool again. The structure under the water was huge, taking up at least a quarter of the pool.

He was standing in front of Rose again now and she had finally stopped speaking on the phone. Only one of the chemists was on the scene, kneeling next to an enormous aluminum suitcase.

"A water sample is already on its way to the laboratory. They're going to do a few preliminary tests here."

Rose was tense. The same way Dupin had seen her yesterday after the news that the body had been found.

"What is that structure?" Dupin asked, annoyed that he hadn't seen it earlier.

"We're going to take a look at it as soon as we confirm the water isn't contaminated."

"Do they have structures like this in the salt marshes? Are they, or something similar, used in the salt-extraction process—in the large reservoir pools?"

"No. They're not used anywhere."

Dupin walked on a few meters. "The monks used to use some of the pools for other purposes too. For mussel farming, for example. Or fish farming."

Rose looked curiously at Dupin. She was interested. Dupin's mind went back to the display board again (he had wisely left out the "monstrous creatures"). This was probably not a case of clandestine mussel or perch farming, but still.

"They used the pool for things that have nothing to do with salt."

His instinct told him that this was a possible starting point. Perhaps the only one. Although it meant they were starting again from scratch—because it was not at all clear what might be going on here.

"That would explain why we haven't got anywhere with all things salt."

Rose still hadn't said a word. But her face showed she agreed.

"If there's a net stretched over it, then there must be something underneath the net—something that the net is meant to keep in. Let's concentrate on the pool and its secrets." She was right.

Dupin turned to the chemist. "Have you found any reason yet not to get into the pool?"

"No. But as you say: not *yet*. I would wait."

Dupin was struck more by the undertone than the expert's explicit recommendation.

He ran a hand through his hair. If it had been up to him, he would simply have got into the pool. He would have liked to get a good look at the structure. To see if there was anything to be found under the net—and if so, what that was.

"Your inspectors are bright," Rose said appreciatively, raising her eyebrows. "We've got the maps and information. If you want to get as close to this reservoir pool as possible by car, you're actually better off parking at Daeron's salt marsh. That's the shortest route if you want to transport anything fairly heavy here."

"And who owns the pool?"

Rose seemed to want to let the suspense build.

"It used to belong to one Mathieu Pélicard. He was the last registered owner."

Dupin looked confused.

"The registration dates back to 1889. At his death, there were apparently no heirs and it was not passed on to anyone. That means that at some point it became the property of the local authority. These salt marshes were laid out differently at the time; it was a part of a salt marsh that doesn't even exist anymore, your inspectors have found old maps too."

"The local authority—so Madame Bourgiot, to some extent."

"Yes."

This was interesting.

"Which might mean something, but then again it might not. The pool is just sitting here fallow. It would obviously be easiest for the *paludiers* on either side to approach the pool without being noticed. Especially for Daeron."

"If you were planning something criminal, would you—"

Dupin was interrupted by Rose's mobile, which seemed to be set on a much higher volume than yesterday. She answered it.

"Yes?" Rose listened intently.

Dupin could immediately tell something wasn't right. Something was not right at all.

She kept listening for what felt like forever. Only then did she speak.

"We'll be right there . . . Yes . . . Tell everyone to leave the area right now. Everyone. Nobody goes in there. Apart from the forensics team."

Rose hung up, closed her eyes briefly, and then looked piercingly at Dupin:

"Maxime Daeron. Damn it. He was found ten minutes ago by a housekeeper. In the house on the Île aux Moines. Two island police officers are on the scene. He's in a kind of garage where he had been building a boat. It's looking like suicide. One shot, to the right temple."

Dupin stood as though rooted to the spot. "Crap."

Surely this wasn't happening. What the hell was going on here?

Rose was already hurrying away, her phone to her ear.

Dupin turned to the chemist, who was looking expectantly at him: "Let us know as soon as it's safe to get into the pool. I'll send an inspector."

A moment later, Dupin was also walking swiftly away, making for Daeron's salt marsh, his own mobile to his ear.

"Riwal—where are you?"

"Almost at the car, still in Guérande, we're—"

"I need Kadeg. Tell him to come to the salt marshes immediately, to the large reservoir pool at the far end of Daeron's salt marsh. There's a man standing there—one of the forensic chemists. Kadeg is to get into the pool as soon as the chemist says it's not dangerous and look at the wooden structure that was installed in there. In painstaking detail. See if there's something underneath the net. I want to know everything—maybe someone could help him."

"All right, boss."

"Daeron is dead."

"Maxime?"

This technically correct follow-up question sounded macabre in such official tones.

"Yes. By the looks of things, it was probably suicide."

"I'd be wary of that."

Dupin almost laughed, this sentence sounded so odd. But he knew what Riwal meant.

"I . . . yes. We'll look at it very carefully. I'm driving to the gulf. Speak to you later."

* * *

It was a gruesome scene. A young policewoman greeted the two commissaires at the gate and led them straight to the extension, which had been built as a garage at some point but was now a workshop. A large one, at that. Professionally fitted out, it looked like a carpentry workshop. In the middle was a boat made from dark wood, clearly a sailing boat, and Dupin estimated it was more than four meters long. Still in the process of being built, rough around the edges, but largely finished. A laborious task; it must have taken years. The floor of the room was lined with cork, the walls were whitewashed, and workbenches and cupboards on two sides lined the walls right up to the ceiling. There was just one large window onto the garden.

The blood had sprayed up as far as the ceiling. A lurid painting.

Daeron was in the bow. On his right temple was a wound clotted with blood. His head was half tilted to the left, the exit wound from the bullet not visible from this angle. His legs were crossed strangely. His left arm rested at a sharp angle, his right arm and open right hand outstretched. The gun was about five centimeters from the fingers of his right hand, having shifted slightly, but not much. A huge amount of blood must have pumped out—there was a massive pool of it that had long since seeped into the as-yet-untreated wood.

Rose had been outside for a few minutes—having taken a quick look at everything—making phone calls, Dupin assumed. She was just coming back in and making her way toward the pathologist, a gaunt, older man with delicate features who seemed on the ball. He was standing near the boat, slightly hunched. Dupin was right beside him.

"What can you say about the time of death?" Rose asked.

"He's wearing the exact same clothes as when I visited him yesterday," Dupin murmured. "It could have happened in the evening or nighttime."

His memory was laughably bad sometimes, but it worked excellently well when it came to frivolous or ridiculous things. (Until the end of his days, for example, he would be able to recite all the chemical formulae from his schooldays, CO_2 assimilation, photosynthesis . . .)

"That fits with my preliminary examinations." Surprisingly, the pathologist didn't sound offended. Before now, Dupin had known nothing but chronically ill-tempered representatives of the pathologist species. "I think he died between eleven P.M. and two A.M."

"At this point, do you see any clues indicating anything but suicide?" Rose asked expertly. "We've got to be as certain as possible." Of course all kinds of thoughts had crossed Dupin's mind on the way there. There were perpetrators who tried to make murders look like suicides. But according to what they knew so far—not much, admittedly—it could just as easily be a tragedy. The unbearable loss of his lover. Or else he had been caught up in the case in some way and it had all gotten out of hand. And although the timing would have been very tight, they couldn't rule out him driving back to Lilou's parents' house during the night and killing his lover. Because she knew something she wasn't meant to know. Anything was possible.

"I'm assuming suicide for the moment," the pathologist said, his brow furrowed. "If it wasn't suicide, the perpetrator did an incredible job, he avoided any apparent mistakes. The deceased isn't holding the gun in his hand; most perpetrators get that wrong. The position of the body"—he seemed to be trying to use his hands to emphasize everything he was explaining—"the way he's lying there, that's totally plausible. And the pattern of injuries is typical, just a single shot, the gun placed directly on bare skin. We call that a 'contact shot,' with a typical wound. The gunpowder residue beneath the skin on his hand is clearly visible, the vague outline of part of the muzzle imprint from the barrel can even be picked out above the entry wound. There are also traces of blood and fibers on the gun and on the deceased's hand. A very coherent scene."

He took a step backward, his eyes fixed firmly on the dead man. Dupin was impressed by the short man with his firm, clear voice who, unusually for his profession, phrased things in a way that was easy to follow.

"I'd suggest we take him away soon, and I'll reconstruct the vital reactions in the lab so that we can see if he was still alive when the shot was fired. Apart from the gunshot wound, I haven't found any other wounds or injuries yet."

"Fine, take him away," Rose said offhandedly, looking lost in thought.

"I don't need to tell you this, of course, but nevertheless: we will never have absolute certainty. It could just be perfectly staged. But luckily that's your job, not mine." The pathologist's face relaxed for the first time.

The head of the three-person forensics team, a tall, smart-looking bald man (who was also surprisingly pleasant), joined them now.

"So far we've not found any trace evidence on the boat from anyone but Maxime Daeron. Or anywhere else in the room, for that matter. Just some traces on the door, on the door handle. We were able to check them easily. They came from the housekeeper who found Daeron."

"She has already been interviewed thoroughly. She has an airtight alibi and nothing important to say," Rose added.

"And the gun?" Dupin was particularly interested in this.

"P 239 Scorpion, one of the newer SIG Sauer 9mm guns, eight shots per magazine. RUAG bullets. With a short, compact silencer. Whether it's the same gun as the night before last, we'll have to see. The caliber and bullets are very common, they don't mean anything. And the gun is extremely new. A fashionable gun." That afterthought was full of professional condescension.

While Rose had been outside, Dupin had taken a good look at everything. He had paced slowly up and down the room. This "careful looking" was one of his few genuine guiding principles (if someone asked him and he thought hard, there were actually a few more, he realized to his astonishment—and there he was, the man who always denied having a method). Nothing unusual had caught his eye.

There was nothing else for him to see or do here. And the final results from the examination would take some time to come through.

"I'm getting out of here," he said quietly. Rose was only half listening, if she was listening at all, that is. She had her mobile back up to her ear. Dupin had noticed in the last few days there was an advantage to the unusual "joint investigation setup": here on Rose's "turf," she was inevitably saddled with the official paperwork.

Already at the door, he was in the garden within moments and there he saw the bench, the chairs, the table where he and Daeron had sat yesterday. He stopped. This was a terribly tragic story, whatever lay behind it.

Suddenly, as if out of nowhere, Inspector Chadron and Rose appeared next to him.

"We need the phone records, landline and mobile. Internet activity, emails. I want to know everything." Rose rattled expertly through these orders. "Get the house turned upside down, Chadron. We'll need more backup from Auray and Vannes. And do the house in La Roche-Bernard too. His little business. He had his office in La Roche-Bernard if I understand correctly. Check if he left any clues behind. A farewell letter, a note. I want all the neighbors questioned, on whether they noticed anything out of the ordinary last night. Question everyone who comes in and out of this house. The gardener, the pool-cleaning people. Find out who his friends were, talk to them. We've got to reconstruct Maxime Daeron's whole day. The last few days. Whom did he speak to and when." She turned to Dupin now. "I've informed Maxime Daeron's wife. We ought to speak to her as soon as possible. The housekeeper called Paul Daeron and he set off immediately."

Dupin wanted to say something, but Rose was quicker. "And your Inspector Riwal is to ask where everyone in the White Land spent their evening yesterday."

"Inspector Kadeg says," Chadron spoke neutrally as usual, "that the chemist has given the green light for the examination of the pool, but only if the person wears a protective suit. There are certain contaminants he can only rule out bit by bit, especially organic ones."

"Your inspector is planning to inspect the pool?"

Dupin had forgotten to mention this. On the ferry from Port-Blanc and during the short walk here, they had exchanged information on a few things—especially about their "separately" conducted conversations with Jaffrezic, whom Rose seemed to trust less and less—but not this.

"I—"

"Things are getting drastic. We should each carry out, and order to be carried out, everything we deem important. Everything. Every one of us."

Dupin couldn't tell if she was being serious. Or cuttingly sarcastic.

"Your inspector should definitely inspect the pool. We've got some protective suits. Chadron, let him know."

Without waiting for a response from Dupin, Chadron walked away and took out her phone.

"Let go of me, I'm his brother. This is my house. I want to go to him." Paul Daeron had clearly come through the garden, passing the house on the right. A police officer was trying to stop him.

"It's okay," Rose said, and then turned to Paul Daeron: "Come with me. The pathologist and the forensic team are still working."

"Thank you," Paul Daeron said softly, a mute horror etched across his face.

Rose walked toward the door to the extension with Paul Daeron following behind.

* * *

Paul Daeron stood next to his brother's body for a few minutes, rigid and silent. The corpse was almost at eye level. He pressed his lips together. A few times he covered his eyes with his right hand, his index finger on his forehead, his eyelids shut tight for moments at a time. Then he turned away and left the workshop on unsteady legs. Rose and Dupin were watching him discreetly. Paul Daeron looked devastated. But they didn't know who in this whole saga might be good at acting.

"You're bound to have questions," Paul Daeron said, once Rose and Dupin had followed him outdoors. Without waiting for an answer, he made for the set of furniture on the terrace.

"It's horrific." This sounded eerie. Angry and utterly despairing, dumbfounded. "The death of Lilou Breval was awful for my brother. We spoke on the phone a few times yesterday. I knew about the relationship," he said slowly, speaking in a soft monotone. "I can't say how serious it truly was for my brother, how deep the emotions went. But the murder—her death—affected him deeply. My brother was not good at matters of the heart. Never has been. He wasn't good at marriage either."

Dupin was stunned at how much Paul Daeron was telling them all of a sudden. He had been tight-lipped the day before. But in extreme situations people often acted differently. Daeron had sat down at the large wooden table while Dupin and Rose sat on the opposite side. They were surrounded on all sides by mimosas, a large crooked cactus to the right, which Dupin had taken a dislike to yesterday. He had never been fond of cacti.

"You suspect," Dupin said gently, "that the loss of Lilou was the reason for your brother's suicide?"

The answer came without hesitation. "I couldn't say. Perhaps. I've been thinking about it in the car. I would never have thought it.

I mean, that he would be capable of suicide. What do you think, what are your suspicions? Was he—was my brother caught up in something?"

"What could he have been caught up in?" Dupin was still speaking in a friendly way.

Daeron looked confused. "I don't know."

"We can't say anything yet, Monsieur Daeron," Rose said with unmistakable emphasis, "but we will find out. No matter how complex it gets or how long it takes. We will find out."

"Are you aware of your brother having any other . . . extramarital relationships?"

Dupin had to admit his question sounded somewhat strange in this situation.

He looked at them with sadness in his eyes. "I promised him I'd keep all his secrets, but . . ." He broke off for a moment, then continued more quietly, "There were one or two other women. Over the last few years. Not before then. He wasn't a womanizer, not the type to have affairs all the time." He raised his head and looked at them. "Ségolène Laurent. He had an affair with her before Lilou Breval; it didn't go on very long, I don't think. Nobody knows about that one either. Also . . ."

Both commissaires were briefly perplexed, then both interrupted Paul Daeron at the same time.

"Madame Laurent?"

"Yes. But as I mentioned—it didn't last long."

"When did it end?"

Dupin had been quicker.

"I couldn't say. It must have ended a while before the affair with Lilou Breval began. Just over a year ago, maybe."

"How did it end?"

"I wouldn't know, Monsieur le Commissaire. My brother—he plunged headlong into things, he'd be enthusiastic, obsessed, not on a whim or in a fickle way. He always took it seriously. But then somehow nothing would come of these things. It was the same in his love life. Nothing ever came of anything. I never understood why." Daeron's voice had lost the last of its strength. "He always tried so hard. Wanted it so much. He wanted to find his place in life."

"Do you know of any disagreements with Madame Laurent?" Rose intervened.

"No. But there could have been some."

"What did you know about the affair with Lilou Breval?"

"Just that it existed."

"He didn't tell you anything else? Anything at all?"

"No."

"What other affairs did you know about?"

"There was also an artist, but that was three years ago. In La Roche-Bernard. A painter. That's the only other one I know about."

Dupin had taken out his notepad. "Was he still in touch with the painter?"

"I don't think so. I don't know."

This was shocking news. Madame Laurent, the powerful, go-getting head of the conglomerate, and Maxime Daeron, the independent *paludier*.

"And his wife? Your brother told Commissaire Dupin yesterday that she didn't know anything about Lilou Breval—what about the others?"

"I don't know how much she really knew. I'm not sure. She's an intelligent woman. She's been away so much since she got that amazing job. I know that Maxime loved Annie, I think he's always loved her. I . . . . I don't know."

Dupin took over again. "It sounds very complicated, your brother's life. His marriage."

"Annie is away for half the month. They . . . they wanted children, but it didn't work out. Then she pursued her career in tourism. She's a wonderful woman," Paul Daeron said mechanically.

"Was there any conflict between Lilou and your brother? Before their relationship ended, I mean."

"I wouldn't know."

"Do you know of any other disputes, conflicts, or disagreements involving your brother? In his private life, work life, or in the salt marshes?"

"I don't know anything about that either."

"Or was there anyone who wished your brother ill? Have you reflected again about the incident in your brother's salt marsh? Whether it might have been sabotage after all, and who might be behind something like that? You can see how serious this is."

Paul Daeron looked at Dupin in obvious confusion. "You're insinuating there's a possibility that—that it wasn't suicide at all?" His deep agitation was written across his face.

"We're not insinuating anything. But we have only just begun investigating."

"He avoided conflict. I don't think my brother was caught up in anything . . . criminal." Daeron's tone of voice was difficult to interpret.

"I don't know much about the day-to-day running of his business. He didn't say much about it, he didn't like to do that." There was something inscrutable in Daeron's eyes. "But I understood that. I wanted him to be able to do everything the way he wanted to do it. I gave him the money he needed to do it. Nothing more. He started out by himself, with almost no capital, with a loan, but that was nowhere near enough, he nearly went out of business, so I helped him. The salt industry is tough, but he loved it. He had big ideas, good ideas, I could tell the ideas were always good." Daeron hesitated as if he wanted to say something else, but left it at that.

"And was he beginning to lose interest in salt?"

Rose had phrased this just as if it had been Dupin's own deduction. But Paul Daeron raised his eyebrows in surprise.

"I . . . I don't think so. No."

"Monsieur Daeron, do you know about the large blind pool right next to your brother's salt marsh? Have you heard of it—did your brother ever mention it, or anything to do with it?" Dupin spoke sharply. This time Paul Daeron looked downright speechless.

"No, I don't know of any blind pool. I don't have anything to do with the salt myself, you know, only when it comes to formal things. As a co-owner."

"When did you and your brother last speak?" Rose asked.

"Yesterday evening, around half past seven. I'd left Vannes and was on the way to my boat. It's in the Vilaine estuary, a quarter of an hour from La Roche-Bernard. A peaceful place. I told him he should come too. But he didn't want to. He was here on the island. He . . . he wanted"—his voice broke again—"he said he wanted to be alone."

"But he didn't say anything that might have worried you?"

"He seemed shattered, I told you that already. But—the idea that he might . . ." Daeron didn't finish his sentence.

"And what did you do on your boat?"

"I had arranged to meet a business associate of mine. We wanted to discuss something. But then he had to cancel. At the last minute. He didn't call till eight. I was on the boat by then."

"And then?"

"Then I drank a glass of wine on the boat. I was there for about an hour and then I went home."

"Who was this business associate?" Rose leaned back slightly, crossing one leg over the other.

"Thierry Du, a vegetable farmer. He supplies our herbs."

"When did you get home?"

Daeron clearly wasn't put out by Rose's meticulous questioning. Perhaps he was just too exhausted.

"Twenty past nine. I had a bite to eat with my wife and my daughter."

"Your family can attest to this?"

"Of course."

"Sorry to disturb you," said Inspector Chadron, who had appeared and was standing half-hidden behind a cactus. "Maxime Daeron's wife, Annie Daeron, has just arrived. She'd like to speak to you, Madame la Commissaire."

"I'm coming—thank you very much, Monsieur Daeron. This has been a huge shock for you, we know that." Rose stood up before she'd finished speaking. As did Dupin.

"Yes. It has been."

Paul Daeron remained seated. His scarcely audible words hung faintly in the air.

* * *

They had gone inside the house. Into the spacious but unpretentious living room. At first, the conversation had been very difficult. Dupin had been worried that Annie Daeron might collapse on a few occasions. She was absolutely distraught. She was shivering dreadfully, her breathing irregular, and crying nonstop. He wondered how she had even managed to make it here in the car by herself from La Roche-Bernard.

Annie Daeron was an attractive woman; dark slacks, a pale beige blouse, chin-length jet-black hair. She had sobbed out several questions in despair. He and Rose hadn't had much to say in response.

"We're only just starting to collect information, Madame Daeron. We want to know a few things from you that would be very important to us—but this is not the right time. It might be better if we spoke later." There was real sympathy in Rose's words, but also a police order.

"I . . . no. I can manage." She was summoning every ounce of her strength to compose herself, but her voice remained shaky.

"Was he that unhappy?" she sobbed again.

"Madame Daeron, you can't think like that. If it was suicide, it wasn't your fault! Under any circumstances!" Rose responded firmly.

"We lost each other at some point. I know that."

"You mustn't torture yourself like this. We need to concentrate on finding out what happened. When did you last see your husband?"

"The night before last."

"Not yesterday?"

"No. I left at six o'clock yesterday morning. I'm sure he was still sleeping. He has his own bedroom. And last night I didn't get back till one o'clock. I didn't know if he was there."

Tears ran down her cheeks.

"He's had his own bedroom for years. At first he only used it when he was working long hours and I had already gone to sleep. So he wouldn't disturb me. I thought . . ." Her voice faded away.

"You knew about the affair with Lilou Breval," Dupin said in a deliberately respectful tone. Annie Daeron didn't react, staring out the window as though uncertain, her head half lowered.

"Yes."

"Did he tell you?"

"He didn't say it directly. But he talked about her. I knew. And he was aware that I knew."

"You also knew that he drove to see her on Wednesday evening?"

"I thought he had."

"How did he seem to you that evening, before he left? During dinner?"

Annie Daeron looked Dupin directly in the eye for the first time.

"It was always hard to say what he was feeling. He had huge self-control. I . . . I"—her voice was failing again—"he . . . I didn't tell the inspector the truth yesterday. I . . ." She composed herself. "Maxime asked me to say we had eaten together. We didn't. He wasn't at home at all, before he . . . drove to see her. He—"

"Excuse me?" Rose cut in sharply.

"I'm sorry . . . I . . . He asked me to do it. He didn't want . . ." She didn't finish her sentence.

"So you . . ." Rose was clearly thinking feverishly. Dupin had to process what he had just heard too. This time he was quicker.

"When did he ask you to do that?"

"After the police called during the night. He came to me and said there had been a shooting in one of his salt marshes—that he didn't have anything to do with it, but that he didn't have an alibi either. I didn't question it, he said I had to do it for him." She looked solemnly first at Rose and then Dupin. "I know it was wrong. I thought, if I stick by him . . ."

"Where did you think he was?"

"I knew where he'd been, of course. I'm sure he was at the journalist's house. All evening."

"He wasn't."

Worry spread across Annie Daeron's face.

"How long was he at home for?"

This time she didn't seem to understand Dupin's question.

"When he came to see you in your room, how long did he stay?"

"Not long. Three minutes. Maybe five. He said he needed to get some air. And left."

"Why did you do it, why did you give him an alibi?" Rose's question resonated with rage.

Annie Daeron didn't look as though she would be able to answer. Dupin took up the thread. "So you didn't hear from your husband before half past one that night?"

This unexpected twist could mean anything. They needed to rethink everything.

"No."

"Your husband didn't get to Lilou Breval's house till just before eleven o'clock. That's the evidence your husband gave, and because of an eyewitness statement we know it must be true. Lilou Breval wasn't even home earlier than that."

"Maybe he was working late in the salt marshes."

"According to his own statement, he left the salt marshes at half past seven."

"Where did he go after that?"

It didn't look like an act. Annie Daeron seemed to be wondering this for the first time.

"At the moment, we're checking if the gun we found next to your husband is the same gun used to shoot at Commissaire Dupin in the salt marshes on Wednesday. Your husband said he didn't own any guns. Is that correct?"

"Yes, yes, that's true. Of course he didn't have any guns. This is all so horrific."

Annie Daeron looked lost. Kadeg had already checked into the gun question. There were no guns officially registered to Maxime Daeron, but sometimes guns got into people's hands through other means.

"So nobody knows what your husband was doing between around eight o'clock and eleven, before he really left for the gulf."

Annie Daeron's expression, practically pleading, made it clear she was incapable of answering.

Maxime Daeron could now—according to the new story—have been in the salt marshes himself after all. So perhaps he had been the assailant. Or one of the assailants. And it would also fit with the suicide—something had escalated badly, spun completely out of control. Whatever it was. Although something in Dupin balked at this.

They still knew too little. At least the ballistic analysis of the cartridges would soon shed some light on whether it was the same gun.

"We've got to ask you one more time what you were doing this time Wednesday evening. I hope you understand. And also where you were yesterday evening," Rose said very softly. Annie Daeron didn't look upset by this question at all. She seemed too distressed to realize she was now amongst the prime suspects in Lilou Breval's murder.

"On Wednesday evening I was at home and on the phone a lot, I had a long conversation with my best friend, Françoise Badouri. For at least an hour. From around eight till nine. I spoke briefly to my mother. And to one of my colleagues. And my friend again. But for longer. I can give you all their names."

"Did you speak on your landline?"

"Yes. I rang them all myself."

The phone records and people could be checked.

"When did your last conversation end?"

"Quarter to midnight, or maybe a little later."

If all of this was true, it couldn't have been her.

"And yesterday?"

"I was at an event in Audierne until eleven o'clock. Then I had to drive back and I wasn't home till one o'clock."

For some reason Dupin hadn't had Annie Daeron on his list before, not even yesterday. Although a wronged, jealous wife would obviously be plausible as a perpetrator.

"And your husband didn't say on the night of the crime what he thought might have happened in the salt marshes?"

"No."

It was clear she couldn't take anymore.

"I made it a point to call him yesterday morning to find out if he knew any more yet, but it wasn't to be. In the afternoon—I couldn't get through to him, in the evening . . ." She couldn't finish the sentence.

"You never heard anything about blue barrels?"

"No. A police officer already asked me about that yesterday."

"The situation has of course now changed tragically." Dupin was trying to phrase it delicately. "Was your husband caught up in something? Any activities in the salt gardens? Do you know about anything?"

"No. Nothing at all."

Dupin was positive that, based on what they knew so far, there was no question of her being the perpetrator, but oddly enough he couldn't be positive she was telling the truth. He dug deeper; they needed to get to the heart of the story at last.

"Was there anything unusual that he talked about or that you happened to find out? That seemed odd to you, as insignificant as it might seem?"

"No."

"Thank you, Madame Daeron. You've been really helpful," Rose said. She obviously didn't think Madame Daeron would have anything else useful to say. "You should rest. Perhaps even see your doctor. They might be able to prescribe you a sedative."

"I would like . . . to see my husband one more time. I can manage it now."

"Of course. I'll go with you. And then one of our colleagues will drive you home if you like. And someone else will drive your car."

"I"—she positively slumped—"thanks. Yes."

Annie Daeron stood up. Dupin was still worried that she would collapse.

"Your husband"—Commissaire Rose's voice was almost intimate—"ended his relationship with Lilou Breval two weeks ago."

Annie Daeron looked at her and at first it was hard to tell what her emotions were, but then gratitude spread across her face. She didn't answer.

Rose went on ahead, slowly. Annie Daeron followed her hesitatingly. Dupin let a few seconds pass before standing up.

He needed to think. To be alone. Get moving, walk a little. These were dramatic developments. In this ever more complex, ever darker and larger case. And he needed to make some calls. Five calls had come through during the conversation with Madame Daeron. Nolwenn, an unknown number, Riwal three times—he must have something important to report.

Dupin fell back inconspicuously. Rose and Annie Daeron were already a few meters ahead of him and making their way toward the extension. He hesitated briefly, then turned left into the garden. For the second time, Inspector Chadron materialized out of nowhere and stood in front of him.

"Where should I tell Commissaire Rose you're going?" Her tone was friendly, but definitely inquisitorial.

"I—" Dupin almost started stammering but he composed himself again. "Commissaire Rose has said it's important that everyone does all that's necessary without delay, so that we solve the case as swiftly as possible."

Chadron gave him a skeptical look. Dupin walked past her unperturbed.

"I was supposed to . . ."

"You can get me on my mobile."

Without awaiting any further response, he strode toward the front door.

His mood didn't lift until he was on the street again. He knew where he would be able to think properly. And he needed to go to the quay anyway.

* * *

"Voilà." With the same friendliness and incredible speed as yesterday, the young woman in the straw hat placed the espresso in front of him. She had greeted him as if he had been coming in for years, which he liked.

He was sitting in the same spot as yesterday, which was no coincidence. Dupin liked to turn things into rituals, and quite a few people affectionately made fun of him for it. Even Claire. Le San Francisco was wonderful again today, a happy corner of the earth, no doubt about it. It would be going on the list of "favorite places" he secretly kept; a very important, very personal list. He was sure Claire would love it too. Despite the chilling events of the morning, he kept thinking about her. She had come to see him—on her own birthday, it should have been the other way round—and he still thought it was wonderful.

He rummaged around for his mobile and got it out of his pocket with his left hand while drinking the still-hot coffee in small, expert mouthfuls with his right. He dialed Riwal's number.

"What have we got, Riwal?"

"Maxime Daeron wanted to sell his salt marshes to Le Sel nine months ago." Riwal sounded worked up.

"He wanted to what?"

"There's more, boss. It actually got as far as a meeting with a notary and a signed contract between himself and Madame Laurent. Then Maxime Daeron had the contract annulled. A few days later." Riwal left a meaningful pause. "Le Sel brought in a lawyer and was planning to sue him to comply with the contract. But then they suddenly dropped the suit. That was three months ago."

This was getting more and more baffling.

"Damn it, what does this all mean?"

"We'll find out, boss." Riwal's optimism was unshakable.

"Riwal, I'd like to know exactly what state Maxime Daeron's business was in. Get someone to look into it in forensic detail."

"No problem. And what do you think, was it suicide?" his inspector said in a deliberately brooding way.

"Everything points that way, Riwal."

"All the more reason to be suspicious."

"Really?"

"If this was a crime novel, you'd think: everything points toward suicide, so the readers should think it isn't suicide, because that would be too simple. But then for that very reason it actually is suicide, because that would be just as overly simple as if it wasn't one after all. But if someone were to think that up and if the crime novel was good, then there would—"

"I get it, Riwal. This is not a crime novel."

He hung up. Riwal's love of crime novels wasn't new, but for a while now Dupin felt it had been getting out of hand.

So was their case about business, takeovers, enormous plans, and financial hardship after all? Perhaps even that was just a part of the bigger story. Perhaps it was all linked in a way they just couldn't see yet.

Dupin's phone was almost still at his ear when it rang again. He glanced at the number.

Commissaire Rose.

"Yes?"

"Where are you?"

"I'm . . . investigating."

She hadn't known, apparently; but as he sat down just now he wondered if Chadron might have followed him, under orders, of course.

"Your colleague Kadeg has taken a look at the pool. Someone built a kind of underwater cage in it out of wood. It's big and flat, with a net over it as if they wanted to keep fish. But it was empty. Nothing inside, nothing at all, just a few traces of algae. Green algae. And no clues as to the person who built it."

This sounded mysterious. An underwater cage. He had seen green algae in some of the other, larger pools; it must get washed in with the seawater.

"And what's more: the chemist detected a noticeably high concentration of bacteria in the water. He can't yet say what the bacteria in question are. He says it looks like they might be '*destruens*.' Apparently the concentration is significant and could under no circumstances have developed through natural biological processes. There is something in that pool."

This last sentence sounded like something out of a horror film, even more so because it was so different from Rose's usual rational approach and her icy tones.

"Something was poured into that pool," Dupin said to himself more than her. This was big news.

He had been right. He had been right not to give up on the pool issue. And the barrels too.

"We're also having the pool where the four barrels were found investigated for this bacteria. We've sealed off all adjacent salt marshes. I will inform Madam Cordier just in case."

Dupin hadn't thought of that, but of course she was right. The state-appointed food chemist. They'd need to let her know. Although he didn't agree with it—just as he didn't agree with passing on any kind of information whatsoever during an investigation, on principle. A deeply ingrained quirk he passed off as his method whenever disputes arose, which was not that infrequently.

"Fine. Anything else?"

Rose didn't answer—perhaps he had been a bit abrupt. Dupin made an effort to create a particularly collaborative working environment with his next sentence:

"What I still have to report is that Maxime Daeron wanted to sell his salt marshes to Le Sel . . ."

"I'm up to speed. Your colleague couldn't get hold of you—and he then called Inspector Chadron."

"I . . ."

"I'm still a little tied up here. I assume we're agreed that we pay Madame Laurent a visit next. She has been in Lorient for work since this morning. She has been instructed," Rose spoke drily, "to drop everything immediately. So we're best off seeing her at her home. On the Île d'Arz. That's—"

"I know where it is."

"Where shall we meet?"

Dupin reflected. "On the ferry in a few minutes."

"Fine. See you then."

"Wait. What are *destruens*?"

"Microorganisms that decompose things—they break down organic material completely or partially. They're specific bacteria that decompose specific substances."

"Okay."

"At least that's how the chemist explained it to me. See you on the ferry."

Dupin stretched and looked at the sky. At last they had a real lead they could follow. A noticeably high, clearly unnatural concentration of bacteria. *Destruens*—if it were confirmed. Microorganisms that decomposed something very specific. But what? It was baffling. As was the odd wooden structure. What was the point of it?

Dupin signaled to the waitress and she came straight over. Rose's "I'm still a little tied up" meant he would be able to order another espresso. And perhaps another of the lamb terrines. It had been excellent the first time and he'd only been able to have a few miserable bites of it.

"Another coffee. And the lamb terrine with figs from the island."

"You'd like to try it again?"

She sounded upbeat and friendly. Dupin was only half listening. He was already lost in thought once more. The questions had multiplied with every new development and piece of news this morning. What did it mean that Maxime Daeron wanted to sell his salt marshes to Le Sel—and that he had kept it secret? And that he had told a lie about his whereabouts on Wednesday evening and made his wife do the same? That in theory he might have been involved in the activity in the salt marshes himself? That he had also had an affair with Ségolène Laurent? Above all, what did his death mean?

Rather absentmindedly, Dupin's gaze wandered about. The terrace was much fuller than yesterday, it was half past twelve—times of day took Dupin by surprise during a case, he lost all sense of objective time—and people were arriving for lunch.

His ringtone wrenched him away from his thoughts. He grumpily checked the number.

Nolwenn. Somewhat appeased, he answered it; he would have called her very soon anyway.

"Hard at work, Monsieur le Commissaire?"

"I . . . hard at work, yes."

"I'm up to speed. On the pool and its mysterious microorganisms too. Riwal is in touch regularly. And I'm keeping the prefect up to speed"—so that's what she had been driving at—"it's a special case for him too. So I think you should get in touch directly with him at least once, I'll take care of the rest."

Dupin's mood darkened.

The waitress came with a tray and laid everything out in front of him. He had completely forgotten about the prefect, as if he didn't even exist. As if he had never existed. Unbelievable. So much was different on this case.

"Will do, Nolwenn, will do."

"Préfet Edouard Trottet is always perfectly well informed. Commissaire Rose seems to be on top of everything at once. Préfet Locmariaquer doesn't want to be behind, I reckon. He said you shouldn't let Trottet's commissaire intimidate you, she is notoriously ambitious."

Dupin wasn't letting himself be intimidated.

"She's very good. It's a tricky case, Nolwenn. A tough case. She's doing an excellent job of investigating it."

He surprised himself with his instinct to defend Rose. He felt an odd sense of solidarity all of a sudden.

"I want to go to Lilou's house again."

Dupin didn't know why he had thought of this now, of all times. It had crossed his mind a few times before.

"You know best—you'll definitely find the *point magique*, Monsieur le Commissaire. You'll see."

It had been meant as encouragement, but Dupin had no idea what it actually meant.

"We were in Huelgoat at the weekend, my husband and I. Do you know it?"

Dupin had never been to Huelgoat. All he knew about it was that it was quite far inland.

"We were staying with Aunt Ewen, a very elderly aunt of mine. Ninety-eight. But looks sixty. She still harvests her own apples and distills them."

Dupin had never heard of Aunt Ewen before. But he had heard a lot about other members of the family. Nolwenn's mother alone had eight siblings, her father three, and Nolwenn five. It was a real clan.

"My husband had something to do in the village next to Aunt Ewen's. It's a little, let's say, complicated. He . . ."

"And there's a *point magique* there?"

"In the enchanted rocky 'high forest' of Huelgoat, in the 'Huelgoat Chaos,' there has been a one-hundred-thirty-ton monolith since time immemorial, known as the famous *roche tremblante* or 'trembling rock.' You can set it moving by just pressing it with your finger—if you can find the right spot. The 'magic point.'"

Dupin understood the allegory. It was a beautiful image. But he had other matters on his mind.

"I also wanted to . . . thank you for last night, Nolwenn. That was wonderful."

"Yes, it was important," she replied, and carried right on in her usual professional tone: "Inspector Kadeg sent me a shot of the wooden structure in the pool and I've done some research. The wood and the design match what they usually use in mussel and oyster farming, but its construction is different. I haven't found one like it yet."

Dupin was momentarily distracted. Commissaire Rose had just walked past Le San Francisco, making straight for the quay where the ferries came in and left from again. She must have set off immediately after their phone call after all. And, although he couldn't have sworn to it, it looked like she had waved to him as she passed by. Rose couldn't possibly have spotted him here by chance. From a hundred meters away, above the harbor, amongst the trees and shrubbery and all the other customers. Either she had been looking for him—or she had known where he was.

"All right, Nolwenn, yeah. I'll be in touch later."

Without giving it a second thought, he leapt up, got out some money, and placed it on the small plate. As he turned away he cast one last mournful look at the terrine—this time he hadn't even had a single bite.

* * *

It was odd. Dupin hadn't met Rose on the ferry. It had just come in when he got to the quay, covered in sweat. She hadn't been there. There were just a handful of noon's weary ferry passengers on board;

it was impossible that he just hadn't seen her. Had that not been Rose earlier? Did he just imagine it? He hadn't been able to reach her by phone, either, the line was permanently busy and he had been put through to Chadron. Madame Laurent, he learned this way, had "let it be known" through her secretary that she would be home at 3 P.M. "but no earlier." If he drove quickly, it would take him half an hour to get to Lilou's house.

After the short crossing, Dupin walked to his car, hitting his head again hard—he had really developed a great way of getting into the car recently—and drove away, cursing loudly. Only the latest Skippy coverage on Blue Breizh had been able to lift his mood somewhat. The kangaroo had, to universal disappointment, not been sighted so far today—more specifically: on close inspection, the photos people had taken with their mobiles while on the move and emailed in to the radio station were, without exception, of other animals. Or rather, parts of other animals. No kangaroos. The presenter patiently provided exact descriptions of the images: animals and parts of animals—ears, paws, a snout, fur—in the forest, in the undergrowth, behind trees, from far away, out of focus and blurry. Three times, if the presenter wasn't mistaken, the dogs were quite large, one was a horse, one a fox. Or badger. It was like with UFOs—the images were unfortunately always out of focus. Dupin had been in awe of the presenter, who stayed perfectly calm while ruling out photo after photo—"No, no crate of Britt for you, I'm sorry. Maybe next time."

Dupin had looked at clearings to the right and left once or twice himself, ones that seemed perfectly suited for a kangaroo to sunbathe in.

He had passed Sarzeau and it wasn't much farther to Lilou's house; he would be there very soon. There was a turn-off on the left for St. Gildas, the famous abbey. Dupin had seen the sign the night before last. And it had slipped his mind. Once she had learned the location of his "transfer," his mother had, without comment, sent him a copy of a letter by a learned medieval philosopher called Abaelard from Notre-Dame who, like Dupin, had been banished to Brittany from Paris, albeit for different reasons (the monk had seduced and married a schoolgirl). Dupin had been very upset by the story. "I live in a barbaric land whose language is incomprehensible and disgusting to me; I have dealings only with savages; I'm obliged to take my walks on the unpleasant shores of a churning sea . . . Every day I am exposed to new dangers." Following these comments, one danger did become real: the other monks tried to poison Abaelard—which Dupin completely understood now. In his first years in Brittany it had been the other way round—he had understood Abaelard, to some extent at least. Abaelard escaped at the last moment via a secret passageway. Dupin couldn't believe it himself sometimes, things had turned out so differently for him. His "Bretonization" was far advanced; he was approaching his five-year service anniversary, Nolwenn was keeping a keen eye on it. She thought, much to his chagrin, that a party would be appropriate.

Dupin parked his Peugeot 106 on the small, secluded sandy path right in front of Lilou's house. The abandoned, forlorn house of a dead person.

Two police officers were standing a few meters away from the house, apparently deep in a lively conversation, and they greeted the unannounced, unfamiliar commissaire politely but with some surprise. Dupin was in no doubt that Rose had briefed them and they would report to her immediately. Especially since he had asked them for police-issue rubber gloves.

Dupin had no idea why he had wanted to come back here this whole time. It was just a feeling. And it wouldn't go away. This was part of *his* way of investigating.

He took the path through the garden and entered the house via the patio door. His eyes gradually adjusted to the semidarkness. There was always something haunting about dead people's houses. And this was worse than usual. This was Lilou's house. Images from the evening he had visited came to mind. He shut his eyes for a moment. He had really liked her. He was finding this difficult. But now—right now he needed to find her murderer.

He slipped on the tight gloves as a precaution and went over to the large wooden table. The one with the books and foreign magazines that he and Rose had taken a quick look at the day before yesterday. The forensic team had given the whole house another thorough going over the day before. They had found some more of Lilou's working documents in drawers and also on the ground-floor table, but nothing of any relevance at all, nothing that might relate to salt or the salt marshes—which was the only aspect they had been interested in at that stage.

Dupin walked slowly once around the table and then carefully pushed some of the closest piles of paper aside. Almost exactly in the middle of the table, covered in magazines, there was a folder. Dupin eased it out carefully. A thick folder with a jumble of papers inside. Like on the desk upstairs. "National Food Consumption." A printout of a set of food statistics, 103 pages, with lots of underlining. And in the middle of it, a folded scrap of newspaper. Dupin opened it. *"La Crêpe: elle ne connaît pas la crise!"*—"The crepe: It's a stranger to crisis!"—by Lilou Breval. Dupin remembered the great patriotic crepe article from last year. He couldn't help smiling. That had been typical of Lilou. A passionate plea on behalf of the Breton specialty. The defiantly proud sentence was splashed across this edition of the *Ouest-France* in enormous lettering. Not only was the crepe a stranger to crisis, it actually became more powerful during crisis. Of course. And rightly so. The consumption of crepes had risen by an impressive 27 percent in France. And in Europe as a whole by at least 12 percent. The crepe was making the world more Breton, bit by bit. And Lilou Breval was making it the flavor of the month: delicious, sophisticated, endless varieties, locally produced and locally consumed, environmentally friendly, healthy and yet unbeatably cheap, a food for everybody, it was classless, egalitarian through and through: a delicacy for all. Dupin was reminded briefly of Nolwenn, who had been happy at the time that the terminology was correct and that there hadn't been references to the "galette." In southern Finistère they called the galettes of the North crepes. *Crêpes au blé noir,* with buckwheat flour. Dupin worked through the underlined sections—salt was also a national food, after all. But the only statistics underlined related to the crepe and its ingredients: eggs, milk, and flour. One thing he hadn't known was that the crepe, according to legend, came from the Guérande. A sad little princess lost her appetite one day and began to starve—a resourceful chef hit upon the idea of producing a food that you could toss in the pan—she enjoyed the spectacle, ate, and was saved!

Dupin jumped when his mobile rang.

Commissaire Rose.

He answered with some reluctance. "Yes?"

"Where are you." Rose hadn't made any effort to use intonation to make the question an actual question. Surely someone had told her where he was. She continued right on: "The gun found next to Maxime Daeron is the same gun that was used to shoot at you."

It was an extremely precise sentence. With sensational content.

"Unregistered, of course. A small SIG Sauer Scorpion."

Maxime Daeron, the man who had spoken so calmly to them about the shooting just a few hours later the following morning, was very likely the shooter! That's how it looked, anyway.

"And," Rose went on, "there's another bit of news: a young man from the boat rental company in Port-Blanc has given a statement saying he suspects one of his canoes was borrowed during the night by some 'prankster.'"

"And what does that mean?"

Dupin couldn't make sense of what Rose was telling him.

"If Maxime Daeron didn't commit suicide, somebody must have got to the island. And then away from it again. So long as there isn't another unexpected strand to this story and the perpetrator lived on the island. Of our suspects in the Salt Land, *none* of them took the ferry yesterday. I've had photos of them all shown to both the women from the ferry."

"Anything else?"

"The young man gets the boats ready for the night every evening. Mainly, that means he has to drain out the water that has collected in the plastic boats during the day. Then he turns them over to stop any rain getting in." She left a small, dramatic pause. "One of the boats was the wrong way up this morning and not in the place where he left it yesterday. Most important, there was some water in the boat this morning that shouldn't have been there. He rules out forgetting to empty the boat. The canoes are directly opposite the beach that borders Daeron's house. It's about two hundred meters as the crow flies."

"Why . . . why did anyone speak to him in the first place?"

It was a stupid question. But Dupin hadn't been aware how much Rose still seemed to be preoccupied with clarifying whether Maxime Daeron's death might be something other than suicide—especially when the theory of suicide seemed to be gaining more and more ground. But Rose was, purely from a criminological point of view, correct. And especially in the case at hand.

Rose passed smoothly over Dupin's question and drew a definitive line under this point: "We'll keep investigating. See if we find anything else. It may really have been nothing more than some prankster. At the moment it doesn't mean a thing."

Dupin wasn't sure how relevant this information was. It might be immensely relevant. Or it could be purely coincidental.

"You left very suddenly just now, Monsieur le Commissaire. You seem to like disappearing."

It was unbelievable. She was the one who had disappeared, walking right past him and waving, then being nowhere to be found at the quay. Not even reachable on the phone. Dupin's instinct told him it would be better to swallow any retorts along these lines.

"See you very soon at Madame Laurent's, on time. Chadron let you know, didn't she? And I'd like to speak to Madame Bourgiot again. She's expecting us later."

That was a definite order.

"Why Bourgiot again?" Dupin would have prioritized other things at this stage.

Rose didn't respond to his question at all.

"Perhaps we should invite the food chemist to the interview with Bourgiot. We'll really need to think carefully about how we deal with the bacteria. What precautions need to be taken. Potentially. We may have more results by then."

"Good." Dupin was half convinced.

"And if you get going in good time, you won't need to be a daredevil and go over the speed limit the whole time," she said, again very friendly. "You've been caught speeding seven times in the last forty hours by our radar unit."

This topped it all. Not least because Rose herself drove a whole lot more dangerously than he did. And all of his trips had been on police business. Since the number of mobile radar units in Brittany had been doubled in a great regional "traffic calming operation," Dupin had—admittedly also while not on cases—been getting caught in speed traps even more regularly.

"I"—this time he would contradict her, vehemently and firmly—"hello?—Hello?"

Rose had hung up.

Dupin stood motionless for a moment or two. Then he shook his head, murmured, "Take it easy, take it easy," shook his head again, stuffed his mobile into his pants pocket, and set about looking through the other papers in the folder. The next thing he came across was an article about the massive renovation of "Vinci" airport near Nantes and the protests against it. The resistance movement called itself "Opération Asterix" and used the slogan *"Veni, vidi et pas Vinci"*—Lilou had staunchly defended them. *"Résistance!,"* a Breton mantra. He remembered seeing lots of the little protest placards in the salt marshes with crossed-out images of planes landing.

In a clear plastic pocket there were articles from the *Télégramme* and the *Ouest-France* about the demonstration by thirty pig breeders in a supermarket in Quimper. Articles by her colleagues. Two pages of handwritten notes by Lilou. Key words. "Very important campaign." Dupin skimmed the page. There was a large photo of the supermarket campaign. Dupin took a closer look. At first he wasn't sure, but then he was. Paul Daeron was there. He had a microphone in his hand. Paul Daeron was quoted twice. He was, Dupin read, the vice president of the ADSEA, the Association Départementale des Syndicats d'Exploitants Agricoles, vice president of the pig section of the ADSEA, and first president of the FDPP, Fédération des Producteurs Porcines. Dupin couldn't help smiling; the Breton love of clubs, organizations, and societies was notorious. Paul Daeron had spoken out in favor of the rigorous principle of the *appellation d'origine contrôlée* for meat, like they had for wines, champagnes, and so on. This could be relevant—although Dupin had to admit he didn't have a clue how. He looked for an article by Lilou. The one where all this research had ended up. He found nothing.

Dupin got out his Clairefontaine and noted down the headlines along with a few key words for each one. In his mind, he went over everything they had looked through the night before last. They needed to find the story that lay behind it all. The subject, basically. It must be related to bacteria too, to "*destruens*" somehow. This was all just groping around in the dark. But Dupin was a vigorous champion of "groping around." He had never, although some people thought it old-fashioned, found a more precise or above all a more effective criminalistic method. There was always something to find somewhere. You just had to look carefully. Rummage. Everywhere. Over and over again. Even though he couldn't see anything at the moment; that was the part of poking around that Dupin found difficult—nothing could be forced or commanded. Nothing new occurred to him on the topics and key words in his notebook. But perhaps it was right under their noses and they just weren't seeing it. He had been in that exact situation before. In the Gauguin painting case, the key to it all had literally been hanging right in front of him, in a room he had been into dozens of times.

Dupin put everything back into the folder and then put the folder back exactly where it had been at the bottom of the pile. In Lilou's filing system. A system that would never make sense to anyone again. He left the table and walked across the room.

Based on their theory—still the most likely one they had—the murderer had been here too, on the night of the crime, although the forensics team hadn't found anything to that effect yet. Not in this house or in Lilou's parents' house, apart from Maxime Daeron's fingerprints, and not in her car either. The documents from the last six weeks hadn't turned up anywhere. The murderer wanted to stop them finding out what Lilou had been working on.

Dupin had reached the stairs. He was uncertain for a moment, but then went up the stairs. And into Lilou's bedroom. The whitewashed walls were—he hadn't really taken this in the night before last—full of photographs of all sizes. Impressive photographs, Dupin thought, mostly black and white, all landscapes, and he reckoned they were all by the same photographer. They were like landscapes from odd dreams, but without provoking any feelings of unease. You immediately longed to lose yourself in them. Clearly Breton landscapes, although he didn't know the places, or didn't recognize them. As if they were painted. Clearly a passion of Lilou's. Two intimidating towers of books stood next to the bed. Dupin went into the room next door, the room that consisted almost entirely of the large desk. He stopped at the nearest corner of the desk. He didn't need to go through this pile again. They had already done that very thoroughly. He couldn't help smiling— underneath a few books, the page about the "thirty-six dead wild boar" peeped out. The long article about the green algae.

Recalling Lilou's work like this was lovely, awe-inspiring—and very sad at the same time. She had always been standing up for something, a passionate campaigner with unshakable convictions. And quirks. And strong dislikes.

Dupin turned away, left the room, and walked back down the stairs slowly. He hadn't found anything. But he was still glad he'd come back.

A minute later he left the house the way he had come, back out through the door to the patio and from there into the garden. This visit had been a kind of farewell.

He stood in the wonderful enchanted garden. Directly opposite the patio was a narrow garden gate he had never noticed before. He went over to the gate and opened it. He stepped out onto a small granite ledge. At high tide the water would flow directly beneath it. At low tide, as now, with the water slowly draining away, you could climb down a few stones like they were steps. An amazing place. A sweeping view of the spellbinding gulf. The gate had opened easily and smoothly. It had been used frequently. Lilou must have come here often. Perhaps this had been her favorite spot, here on the rocks.

He looked at his watch. He'd need to get going soon.

* * *

Dupin walked along the sandy floor of the small sea. It was more of a trudge really; the sand was coarse, hard, watery, and full of mussel shells. The water was coming in slowly. It smelled instantly of the sea, of the refined miniature sea. He walked as far as the waterline, two or three hundred meters away. And there he stopped, looking around. The sun was beating down. Dazzling. There was something nebulous bothering him, going round and round his head. It wasn't even a concrete thought; more of an undefined connection, a vague link between things. A kind of inkling. He was familiar with this. That crucial split second when something took root unannounced. When he was standing at the desk upstairs and going through Lilou's topics in his mind, he hadn't been able to grasp this vague thing. And he still couldn't. But the feeling that he had had something important within his reach for a moment was strong.

Two men were coming toward him along the waterline—he hadn't noticed them at first—both wearing dark beige outdoor wear, one lanky, the other stocky.

"Are you a member of the 'Listen to the Birdsong' campaign? Have you seen the common shelducks and little egrets over there? Beautiful specimens, hundreds of them! Hundreds!"

The second man, Stocky, nodded eagerly. He had binoculars round his neck too—almost down to his knees—and carried a backpack. "And the herring gulls!"

The first man, Lanky, took over again. "Masses of saltwort and sea lavender. What's your specialty?"

"I . . . no, I'm not in 'Listen to the Birdsong.'" Dupin was almost so careless as to ask what that was, but he resisted at the last moment.

"You don't have any equipment either! Surely you're a scientist. You're taking part in the famous ornithological Wetlands International meet-up. This is quite something! You must be a real expert," the Stocky man said very respectfully.

"I . . . no. I'm investigating"—Dupin hesitated—"a murder case." The moment he uttered this, he knew it had been an extremely stupid idea to answer the man seriously.

The two birdwatchers looked at each other for a few moments— almost speechless and clearly worried about the psychological integrity of this strange man in the mud flats—and probably decided it was for the best to ignore his odd interjection.

"Almost two-thirds of the gulf is exposed at low tide, revealing gigantic sand-mud-flat expanses like this one here. You're in one of the richest bird zones on the Atlantic coast."

Their missionary zeal had been sparked. The tall man didn't stop now: "The mixture of sand, mud, and silt here encourages the development of grasses and algae where thousands of animals nest, up to four thousand per cubic meter, you've got to imagine it, shrimp, venus clams, larvae, snails, heaps of worms." Dupin automatically cast a mistrustful look at the ground in front of him. "A legendary pantry for a whole host of resident birds. And also for the migratory birds. Siberian wild geese, diving ducks, eiders, terns, spoonbills, they love this microclimate."

Dupin was not well versed in all things ornithological. Not well versed and not gifted. Nolwenn, Riwal, and even Henri had tried to teach him at least the basics, but in vain.

This situation was absurd. Dupin would bid them farewell with a fairly friendly *au revoir*. He really needed to get going.

"You even see little penguins here at the gulf sometimes. Not often though."

"Penguins?" Dupin blurted out.

Penguins were his favorite birds, perhaps because he had always felt a kind of affinity with them, also because of his very sturdy build.

Penguins looked portly and stiff at first and in fact not very dynamic if you saw them waddling. But once they were in their element, water, they were incredibly agile, quick as lightning and highly skilled.

"They actually live in colonies on the Sept-Îles in Northern Brittany, but now and again you see a few specimens here."

Dupin was stunned. But then again, Australian marsupials seemed to have found their natural habitat in Brittany, so why not penguins too?

The two ornithologists were pleasantly surprised that the strange man in the mud flats was now showing such a special interest all of a sudden.

"It belongs to the family of plover species that occur exclusively in the northern hemisphere. Auks. The size of geese. A diving seabird with legs set far back on its body so that it has a more or less upright posture when it's on land. Its morphological appearance resembles that of the penguin from the southern hemisphere. Unlike penguins, most auks have retained the ability to fly."

The second man chimed in. "The only flightless species from this family, the great auk, died out in prehistoric times," he declaimed dramatically, the emphasis placed on the "died" to great effect.

"I . . . thanks. I've got to go now. *Au revoir*." Dupin turned away with a vague wave.

"There actually has been a murder here, by the way, the media have been reporting it since yesterday. You should be careful with your jokes. And give bird-watching a go sometime—it's relaxing and it sets the soul free."

Dupin heard these words behind him very clearly and decided to ignore them.

They weren't really penguins after all. But in a way they were, if Dupin had understood correctly. But this information was enough to put the Sept-Îles on his list of places to make an excursion to. But now, now he would concentrate on the case again.

JEAN-LUC BANNALEC

Three minutes later, Dupin was standing by his car. He looked at his watch. He really needed to hurry. As he carefully got into his car—by now he had a technique that worked well for his shoulder—he saw to his dismay how dirty his shoes were from the mud and algae. At least his pants had stayed clean today.

* * *

"Why did you keep quiet about Maxime Daeron wanting to sell his salt marsh to you? And also about the fact there was a preliminary agreement already in place and that you almost sued him when he wanted to annul it? And that this happened shortly after the end of an affair between you? Which, I suspect, Maxime Daeron ended, not you."

Rose seemed to have taken the gloves off as far as Madame Laurent was concerned.

Dupin had almost been on time; he had caught the ferry in Port-Blanc. Rose was pacing up and down outside Madame Laurent's house, talking on the phone, when he got there.

"Business activities of that kind are absolutely confidential, especially if the seller requests discretion—why would I have mentioned it? And of course our legal department tackles things that are counter to our interests where the legal assessment is clear. That has absolutely nothing to do with me personally."

This was the same Madame Laurent whom they knew from yesterday. But it was remarkable that even in the face of what they now knew and were asking—and Rose's even tougher approach—she remained totally unfazed. She was wearing a colorful silk tunic with a clunky Hermès necklace around her neck and was sitting low in her black leather chair. Ostentatiously relaxed. Dupin and Rose were sitting in the two other chairs, diagonally opposite her. Everything in this large, long bungalow was intended to look sophisticated, tastefully sophisticated, but not sterile. Exposed oak parquet flooring with discreet, expensive rugs here and there on it. Arranged perfectly and hence, in Dupin's opinion, appalling.

"And of course I won't say a word about my private relationships. Not even now. That is no concern of the police."

"Your former lover is dead. A death that in all likelihood is related to the murder of Lilou Breval and the attack on Commissaire Dupin. It's very much the police's concern."

"Only a judge can order me to say anything about it. You know that. And to do that, you'd need to have me arrested first and file legal proceedings."

"Here's what we'll do, Madame Laurent: we will ascertain grounds for suspicion as quickly as possible and take you to my commissariat for questioning." Rose smiled that pretty smile of hers, and it could not have been more diabolical. "Then we'll see about the rest."

"How did the conversations about selling the salt marshes arise?" Dupin's voice was deliberately quiet.

Madame Laurent turned straight to him. And smiled herself. Sweetly. "At least they still have manners in Paris." She seemed to think briefly. For some reason she decided to answer this question, maybe purely to demonstrate her unpredictability. "Maxime came to me, requesting absolute confidentiality. Last October or November was the first time."

"And?" Dupin pressed.

"And what?"

"Why did he want to sell?"

"That was none of my business."

"You don't know?"

"No."

"How much money was involved?"

"I won't tell you that."

"Why did Maxime Daeron suddenly want to dissolve the contract? And back away from the sale?"

"That was none of my business either. And do you know how many deals fail to go through at the last minute? It's not that uncommon."

"You already had a signed preliminary agreement."

"Exactly. That's why Le Sel didn't want to just accept it. That's standard procedure too."

"And why did you then drop the lawsuit?"

"We decided the disadvantages would have outweighed the advantages for us. The frenzied coverage. Some people would have had a field day."

This was remarkably cynical. Yet Dupin managed to remain largely calm. "Did his brother know about the sale?"

"I couldn't say. And that's got nothing to do with me."

"I don't believe a word you say, Madame Laurent. Not a single word," Rose spoke up.

Dupin had to admit that he hadn't got very far with her either. "And we're going to prove it," she said.

"All right then, *bonne chance!*"

Rose tried another line of attack: "Where were you yesterday evening?"

"You mean when the tragic suicide of Maxime Daeron took place?"

"Which doesn't seem to have upset you in the slightest."

"I didn't know this was meant to be a forum for emotional outbursts."

"So where were you?"

"Here, in my paradise. As I am nearly every evening." She looked out into the garden, taking her time. "And alone again. In fact I can't stand having other people here."

She ran a hand through her hair with showy nonchalance. Dupin hadn't really been following this last battle of words. The vague link between ideas he'd briefly had in Lilou's house suddenly crossed his mind again.

"We know about the blind pool." Commissaire Rose returned to her aggressive style. "Right next to one of your salt marshes. About the microorganisms. Very soon we will also know what their exact purpose is. Tell us about that."

For the very first time, Madame Laurent looked rattled, albeit momentarily.

"Are we going to start talking about those blue barrels yet again? I have no idea which pool or what microorganisms you mean. This really does seem to be a rather mysterious case."

Dupin's mind drifted off again. He couldn't help it. This wasn't the first time. An idea had formed from the vague scraps of thought in his head. It sounded insane but—and this was one of the most important lessons of police work—that didn't matter.

"The barrels are in your—"

"I think we're done here," Dupin said, and stood up.

He turned around and walked toward the door, without waiting for a response or saying good-bye. He could still hear Rose saying something but couldn't make out what it was.

He went into the garden, and walked down the long, dazzlingly white gravel path with the stylish white enameled floor lamps that towered up into the sky at regular intervals. He went as far as the large driveway, where an Audi the color of anthracite was parked.

He opened the small wooden gate and was standing on the little island path.

It was just under ten minutes from here to the island's long ferry quay at Cale de Bélure. The position of the bungalow was captivating, there was less than fifty meters of rugged meadowland between it and the waterline, as well as a long stretch of sandy beach, one of the many beaches on the quiet, sleepy island. The idyllic path to the harbor ran alongside the water—just like elsewhere on the wildly overgrown, flat island full of hydrangeas, camellias, and small patches of woodland, you could always see the raging gulf everywhere. Dupin liked this fleet-footed sister island to the Île aux Moines; it wasn't responsible for its arrogant resident.

As he closed the gate, Dupin saw Rose on the gravel path. She must have left Madame Laurent right after he had.

"What was that about?" Rose came aggressively close to him. Her right hand in the pocket of her jacket, her thumb outside, the pose he knew so well by now. She looked him right in the eye for a few seconds, without blinking. Fierce scrutiny.

"I need to speak to the chemist. Right away."

This was no time for beating about the bush. Surprisingly, Rose went along with it.

"0 24 07 67 24—Didier Goal."

Dupin punched in the number that Rose clearly knew by heart.

He would have liked to make the call in private. Especially because his vague idea was still precisely that right now: vague. But that didn't matter now. So Rose would be there.

It only rang once. "Hello?"

A friendly female voice.

"Commissaire Georges Dupin—is Monsieur Goal there?"

"I take it this course of action has been agreed on with Commissaire Rose?"

"I . . . she's standing right next to me."

There was a brief silence and Dupin could literally hear the friendly voice considering checking this. She didn't.

"He'll be back in a few minutes. He just left the room. I'm his assistant."

"I'll call back."

"Please do."

Dupin hung up.

"Let's go, then we can make the ferry at quarter to," Rose said, and turned around. She headed straight for the harbor, her phone already pressed to her ear.

* * *

The fifteen-minute journey between the Île d'Arz and Port-Blanc—which, Dupin found to his dismay, involved a trip on a small boat—passed close by the Île aux Moines, along with a series of other sleepy islands with a handful of rather tall pines and stone pines poking upward and magnificent houses scattered across them. People said the little sea was most beautiful from the water (Dupin thought this unbearable rubbish—from Le San Francisco, for instance, it was all just as beautiful).

Rose had been on the phone constantly—a good half-dozen phone calls—but she had stayed close to him the whole time, even at the harbor. The chemist's line was permanently busy.

Dupin had taken up a position in the bow of the *Albatros*. The boat had just cast off with low-pitched vibrations and buzzing from the diesel engine. He waited for it to be a little quieter and dialed again.

This time the line was free. A man's voice answered.

"Hello?"

"Monsieur Goal? Commissaire Dupin."

"My colleague said you wanted to speak to me. We're still in the midst of testing. It's proving to be quite complex. We're trying to identify the microorganisms."

Rose had deftly come even closer to Dupin. Very close indeed. Their cheeks were almost touching now.

"Has the question of *destruens* been confirmed?"

"We're sure about that, yes. Clearly heterotrophic bacteria."

Dupin hesitated. But only for a second. "Can these kinds of microorganisms be used for special purposes? In a very targeted way?"

Dupin was now holding the phone in a way that meant Rose didn't need to get any closer to listen in.

"Of course. There are endless numbers of purposes."

"Traces of green algae were found in the pool, weren't they?"

Rose's facial expression changed suddenly, her eyes narrowing.

"As far as I know, yes. But you should ask the forensics team that, they documented everything."

"Could you use certain microorganisms," Dupin said slowly, cautiously, "specifically so as to decompose green algae? Is that conceivable?"

"By green algae you must mean the *ulva armoricana* and *ulva rotundata*. The ones from the '*marrées vertes*'?"

"Yes." Dupin had never heard of the ulvas, but he did mean the algae from the "*marrées vertes*." The huge masses of green algae that washed up whenever the "green tide" came in.

"Absolutely. I'm not aware of these microorganisms being used specifically for this algae before. But generally speaking, for a long time, microorganisms have been used to combat algae and also some micro green algae species. You can get various 'algae-killer' products on the market. In any hardware store. Particularly microorganisms that fight slime algae and thread algae. For a pool or aquarium. Of course it's theoretically possible for the ulva species too. You'd apply the microorganisms extensively in the large bays affected, as necessary, and perhaps even systematically prevent algae from forming."

There was quite a long pause. Two motorboats were driving past their ferry and it was loud.

"Hello, are you still there?"

"I'm still here."

Dupin's thoughts were racing, his mind working at a feverish pace. Was this the key to it all? He had slight goose bumps. The green algae had snagged his attention a few times. They had turned up again and again, especially today. A vague connection had formed in his thoughts: the blue barrels that must have contained something; the idea that it wasn't about the salt itself at all, that the pool had been used for something else; the discovery of the strange blind pool and of the *destruens*, including the issue of what they decomposed; finally, the remains of half-dissolved green algae they had seen in the pool—and above all, Lilou's article about the thirty-six dead wild boar.

"How complicated would that be—developing microorganisms like this?"

"Very complicated indeed. *Ulva armoricana* and *ulva rotundata* are of course much larger and more complex organisms than slime algae in pools. The thing that would make it very laborious and tricky would be the field testing. It might not be that difficult to develop a formula in the lab. But it would have to be perfectly safe. You'd need to observe it over the course of years and prove it thoroughly."

"How would you go about doing that?"

"You'd need to select which microorganisms would be involved. Various different ones, maybe. Or breed them from scratch, perhaps through genetic modification—but that might not even be necessary. It would be a form of adulteration. It would require a wealth of biochemical knowledge, a laboratory, and even possible studies in vivo, but it's all achievable, *theoretically*."

The chemist continued, describing everything else in a very professional way. He was completely absorbed by the scientific and practical achievability of this.

"Would a pool like that in the salt marshes be a suitable place for an attempt?"

"Absolutely. They would have near-perfect conditions. A large amount of seawater, constant replenishment as required, but absolute isolation, sun, wind, and therefore realistic conditions. That would be much more conclusive than some laboratory test. You'd have to build pools like that if they didn't already exist. But"—Goal's voice changed now, he sounded alarmed all of a sudden—"never in the heart of a food manufacturing system, of course. That would be extremely dangerous."

"Why?"

"Well, unsurprisingly the use of microorganisms can result in unforeseen circumstances. In the worst-case scenario, it could lead to toxic effects, primary or secondary, that could occur due to bioreactions in the ecosystem. And we haven't even touched on the variants of genetically modified species; that would be even more dangerous! But the adulterated microorganisms could unintentionally contaminate everything too. Depending on what kind they were. Just imagine it! In the middle of the salt! It would be criminal to do something like that in the salt marshes. Laboratories would only get the permission for open-air tests under very strict regulations, and only under full supervision by state institutions, all of which is why it would be very difficult to do something like this. Private companies wouldn't go near it." It was as though by voicing them, Goal's forceful remarks could ward off the possibility that someone had in fact hit upon this kind of plan in the middle of the salt marshes.

"Could you examine the microorganisms from the pool for this, Monsieur Goal?"

"You're considering the possibility that this is what we're dealing with in the pool? Really? Do you know what that would mean?"

"I consider it likely."

"We—we'll get to work. It will take a few hours."

"Thank you, Monsieur Goal. You've been very helpful."

Dupin hung up without waiting for a response.

For a moment the two commissaires stood next to each other in silence, elbows propped on the railing.

"The wooden structure with the net"—Dupin's mind was still trying to fit everything together—"would have been to keep the algae down, underneath the water. So that nobody would stumble across it. There must have been significant amounts of it. For a realistic experiment. And it must all have happened at night, when the salt marshes are deserted. You're completely alone. Perfect."

There was another long pause. This time it was Rose who ended it.

"Do you know the astronomical costs to the region caused by the impact of constant deposits of green algae? It's estimated at one point five million euro at this stage. The majority of that is for the laborious cleanup of the beaches, taking away and disposing of the algae—we're talking about thousands of cubic meters of algae being collected every year. And those aren't the only damages and consequences. Some damage, like the harm done to tourism, can hardly be calculated," she said pensively, staring at the wash of the sea over the ferry's bow. "The interest in a means of destroying or preventing algae would be absolutely enormous. It would be worth millions. And green algae doesn't just affect Brittany. This is a substantial motive."

Dupin was aware of these figures. At the end of August there had been overly detailed articles about them everywhere. The district council in Rennes took stock annually, officially reporting on the costs of green algae in the current year. People didn't realize the magnitude of it all. Every single beach needed to be cleaned immediately if green algae washed up, some were simply sealed off; if the algae lay on the ground in the sun, it could become dangerous instantly if toxic gases were released during the decomposing process. They had begun to build extra-large incinerators for the disposal of algae.

"Whoever it was," Rose said darkly, "they must have known the penalties they could face, what an enormous risk they were taking. Not only would their livelihood be destroyed, they would be going to jail for many years. That being said, the profits would be phenomenal."

Dupin ran a hand roughly through his hair.

This must be it. The story around which everything revolved. He would have smiled if it hadn't been so serious: if this was true—if it was really about green algae—then it was a very Breton story. And it was a big story that explained why so much ruthlessness was at work. A lot of money, big deals, and, if an experiment like this were discovered in the salt marshes, drastic consequences and penalties.

"*Monstrous creatures*—it's like it said on the board in the exhibition. Someone has bred some kind of monster organism in a salt pool," Rose said solemnly. She hadn't intended this as a joke. "So we have a solid hypothesis. Impressively deduced, Monsieur le Commissaire," she said, sounding sincere. "It would be a perfect motive. Now we need the perpetrator. We've got to go back to the drawing board with new assumptions."

It was true. The state of the investigation had changed dramatically. There was a lot to discuss, a lot to do. And yes, they needed to go back to the drawing board. But Dupin usually did that in a very different way: he walked around the area, through woods, by rivers, across beaches, sat on benches, stood by the sea, whatever—but always by himself.

Rose looked at her watch, took out her mobile, and vanished toward the stern of the ferry. They were just passing by the harbor at the Île aux Moines; they would be in Port-Blanc very soon.

Dupin had stayed standing in the bow. What was coming to light here was an insane story.

Rose came back soon afterward, the phone to her ear, and Dupin assumed it was Inspector Chadron.

Suddenly the ferry tacked hard to portside. For some reason the captain's steering was taking them in a huge swerve. A moment later Dupin could see that they were heading straight for the Île aux Moines.

Rose hung up and came to stand next to him. "We need to talk. Madame Bourgiot can wait. Inspector Chadron has already let her know. I've asked the captain to drop us off in Port du Lério. I've got to eat."

Dupin couldn't believe his ears.

* * *

Five minutes later they were sitting in Le San Francisco in the same place Dupin had sat at lunchtime (oddly enough, Rose had gone in first and made straight for his exact spot).

"I've given orders for Daeron's houses, office, and salt marshes to be carefully searched again. In light of the new developments. Along with his computer, mobile, all personal documents, bank records. And we've got to speak to his wife again. If this is about the green algae repellent, and he was involved, there will be traces. Of some kind. You need money, you need the raw biological materials, you need to buy them, store them, transport them, and use them. All of that leaves traces behind."

Dupin had only been half listening; he was still trying to reorganize everything in his mind. But of course it was true: they had to focus on Daeron. It all fit.

"Perhaps he wasn't acting alone. The whole thing would be a huge undertaking. And someone must have had access to biological and biochemical knowledge, at least to basic knowledge, even if you might be able to buy these substances freely. We need to know who, and fast."

"Ah, Sylvaine. *Bonjour*," the friendly young waitress greeted Rose warmly.

"Two espressos, please, Nadine."

Dupin couldn't get his head round this; Rose must come here a lot.

JEAN-LUC BANNALEC

"Two of the *tartare de lieu jaune,* with lime," Rose ordered en passant, without deigning to look at Dupin once. "You're already familiar with the lamb terrine."

How could Rose know about that? Dupin was too baffled to respond.

"And two glasses of *Chenin blanc.*"

It hadn't been a question.

Dupin pulled himself together.

"If the microorganisms were systematically adulterated and cultivated," he said, taking out his Clairefontaine, "a laboratory would be necessary."

They had a lot to do. The laboratory issue might be another starting point.

"A makeshift lab at least." It sounded as though Rose was thinking out loud. Dupin was familiar with this. "A secret lab. In one of the huts maybe, or in the warehouses."

"Maybe the substances were only mixed together in the pools. And that might not be that complicated."

They really didn't know what level of professional knowledge they were dealing with.

"It could definitely have happened in a real lab. There's enough at stake. Directly and indirectly."

Dupin didn't understand. Rose must have noticed.

"There are a good half-dozen private food institutes in the White Land, if not more, with dozens of employees."

Dupin hadn't known that.

"Every *paludier,* the independents, the cooperatives, and also Le Sel, they need to work with a food institute. There are strict requirements in place. There are plenty of private ones in every region: small, medium, and large. These in turn are controlled by state institutions. Food safety is its own industry."

"I see," murmured Dupin.

"Maxime Daeron will definitely have collaborated closely with a laboratory. The same goes for the cooperatives. Larger firms even have their own institutes or departments, Paul Daeron and his pigs might too. No doubt he works with a food institute. And a large lab at that—as does Le Sel, of course."

The service was swift as always, the waitress coming over with a large tray and putting everything on the table. Dupin picked up the coffee immediately, that was his priority.

"Bon appétit." Rose smiled. "The *lieu jaune* was caught here in the gulf earlier today and the filet was diced by hand. The zested lime comes from the trees near the dolmens where Julius Caesar was laid to rest." She gave him a nod of encouragement, then continued abruptly with her deductions: "Maxime Daeron could have had access to a lab through various avenues. We at least have enough grounds for suspicion to examine the lab that he worked with directly."

"We should look into whether there have been private initiatives or even applications in the last year for permission to research and test a green algae repellent legally."

"It would be taken into official state custody immediately—a major biochemical weapon." Rose elegantly ate a large forkful of tartare and calmly took a mouthful of wine. Dupin himself felt a little self-conscious. But then he reached for his misted-up glass too, and he could smell the subtle fragrance of orange blossom, delicate and smooth.

"Somehow Lilou Breval found out about the whole thing," Dupin said, and took a small sip. "The mysterious blue barrels. And I blundered into it all the evening before yesterday." He finished the rest of his glass in one go.

"And another thing: the most plausible explanation is that she found out from Daeron. The 'algae project' must have been very time-consuming."

Rose's final sentence was vague. There was a short pause, which Dupin used to help himself to a large forkful of the exquisite tartare and refreshing lime.

Rose leaned back: "One person did not do all of this, not a chance."

Dupin agreed.

"The profits would be immense." Rose sounded almost impressed. "Immense. If it actually worked, could be used in situ, and didn't have any relevant ecological side effects, there's no doubt there'd be a line of interested parties around the world. The repellent could then potentially be licensed. We should—"

The unmistakable ring of Rose's mobile interrupted them. She picked up without hesitation.

"*Bonjour*, Madame Cordier?"

Rose took the phone away from her ear, pressed the speakerphone function, put it on the table in front of her, and picked up her fork again.

"We've got to talk."

"Great. Let's talk. Quarter past five, Centre du Sel. We'll be expecting you."

"I've just been officially informed by the forensic laboratory that we are dealing with a significant population of certain unusual bacteria in a large reservoir pool. I take it this was suspected for some time. You ought to have reported it immediately."

This was said in that harsh tone of Cordier's that they had known since their first conversation.

Rose ate the last piece of her *lieu jaune* with complete equanimity. She made no move to respond.

"I'm going to speak to Paris at once. I don't know if it's clear to you that this incident falls into the most serious category. We'll be ordering a full-scale shutdown of the salt marshes. The entire manufacturing process. Until we are certain beyond doubt about what is going on here."

"Fine."

There was a pause that revealed Madame Cordier had expected a different response.

"You're aware that you are duty-bound to share all of your suspicions with me."

"Call the forensic chemist, I hereby give you permission to do so." Dupin listened in amusement.

"I've already done that; he didn't want to make any further comments to me and directed me to you."

"If we think it appropriate to express a suspicion, we shall do so."

"We're going to take a look at the pool ourselves, and carry out our own analysis," Cordier said.

"You will take a look at the pool when we think you ought to look at the pool. Precisely then and no earlier. See you for the official meeting at five fifteen. In the Centre du Sel. *Au revoir*, Madame Cordier."

Rose hung up. She turned to Dupin. "We've got to get going. We don't want to rush again."

Her face was impassive. Dupin quickly ate another mouthful. This time he didn't want to leave anything on the plate.

"We should bring our inspectors up to speed on the way." Rose had already stood up. "They mustn't lose any time investigating everything that might be relevant in light of this new information. They need to examine any links to the laboratories very carefully—who works with whom, what exactly the laboratories do. And after the interviews at the Centre du Sel we should all sit down together. All five of us."

There was almost a hint of emotion in this last sentence. She sounded unusually collaborative, which made Dupin instinctively skeptical, although it was admittedly a good idea in principle. It was a question of extensive, systematic investigation now, a lot of information to be assembled. And Dupin hadn't seen much of Riwal and Kadeg on this case, although they had been in touch on the phone regularly.

"We should also—"

Rose was interrupted by her phone again.

"Yes?"

Once again, Dupin couldn't make out anything, other than the fact it was a man's voice. At first, Rose listened for a while.

"Otherwise no indications of anything out of the ordinary? . . . All right, Docteur. Thanks for the information. So it's all up to us now."

She hung up a moment later. They had already left Le San Francisco and walked down the steps to the harbor.

"I'd like to know if there's any update on Maxime Daeron's autopsy. A tiny smudge of gunpowder residue was identified on the right index finger. The finger Maxime Daeron used to pull the trigger. A small space on the side of his finger is almost clean, which is only visible under a microscope. That could mean," Rose hesitated for a moment, "for instance, that another finger was on top of Daeron's. But the pathologist thinks this is not completely reliable and it can sometimes happen naturally. They've completed the blood tests and found no sign of any anesthesia. Although of course there are now some that can't be detected later. We probably shouldn't expect any more significant results from the autopsy."

They were standing on the quay. The boat would be docking very soon; it was only a few meters away and both of the blond women from the ferry were standing in the bow holding ropes.

As they boarded the ferry, Dupin started to make some calls. He was on the phone for the whole short boat trip to Port-Blanc, on the way to his car, and most of the car journey. He spoke to Riwal and Kadeg, Nolwenn—who reminded him firmly about the prefect—and he called the chemist twice but there was no answer.

Dupin brought Riwal and Kadeg up to speed and delegated the new tasks. He also told them they should be ready and waiting at the Centre du Sel.

His inspectors had looked into the financial state of Maxime Daeron's salt business and his private accounts. He had been earning next to nothing over the course of many years. He barely owned anything either; the two houses and the car belonged to his brother or his wife.

The radio was on from time to time, Bleu Breizh. Skippy was fine. Two crates of Britt beer had gone to two lucky amateur photographers and this time there was no doubt that Skippy had been sighted, in the same area as before; his new home was clearly somewhere nearby. This time there was also coverage of Skippy's past, before he had ended up in the Breton zoo; he had been born, hard as it was to believe, on "Kangaroo Island," an island off the south coast of Australia. And, this was the crucial thing for Dupin, something the expert mentioned only in passing: Kangaroo Island was an island where kangaroos and penguins mixed naturally! Unbelievable, Skippy had lived on his island side by side with real penguins.

Dupin spotted Rose immediately when he drove into the large parking lot at the Centre du Sel. They had set out at the same time and Dupin had not been driving slowly by any means. He would love to know how many speed trap photos Rose had been in recently.

She was standing next to her car, just to the right, in one of the first parking spaces. Dupin parked his Peugeot opposite.

"Inspector Chadron tells me Monsieur Goal, the chemist, wants to speak to you."

"I tried to get through to him twice, but no luck."

Rose shrugged. "Let's call him. Madame Cordier is waiting in the conference room. Madame Bourgiot is in her office. We're going to see them separately."

Dupin hesitated for a moment. By "Let's call him," Rose meant here and now. He took out his mobile.

Rose came very close, just as she had done on the ferry earlier. This time, Dupin turned on the speakerphone.

"*Bonjour*, Monsieur Goal, Commissaire Dupin here."

"I was in the lab when you called," Goal said solemnly. "We've run a series of specific tests based on your hunch. By which I mean, we've run tests to see if these microorganisms could exhibit specific traits that dissolve green algae in vivo. We tried it with small samples of *ulva armoricana*. Positive." Goal seemed surprised himself.

"You mean you can confirm that these microorganisms really can destroy green algae?"

"I said that they *could exhibit traits* to achieve this. Of course we haven't done thorough testing yet. But yes, they have the capacity for it, by the looks of things."

They were right. This was it. Incredible.

"I want to mention again just how risky microorganisms like this are. Having said that, we haven't been able to identify toxic effects yet, and based on our preliminary knowledge there is no danger of dispersal via wind or precipitation. It seems they need to be re-created every time and don't independently reproduce in weak salt solutions. But it's still to be determined what other chemical and biological effects they will display." Goal sounded anxious. "It's criminal. Highly criminal. The food safety inspectors will want to close all of the salt marshes. Préfet Trottet was instructed by Paris to allow the food safety authorities to carry out their own analyses in the pool. They've already taken samples. The boss is so aggressive—she's calling me every fifteen minutes."

"We're seeing her in a few minutes and we'll speak to her. The important thing is, Monsieur Goal: we would like to keep the specific capabilities of these microorganisms to ourselves for now."

"We can't possibly do that, Monsieur le Commissaire—" There was an audible sigh. "—but okay. It's your responsibility."

"Absolutely. You're acting strictly on my orders."

Dupin didn't see the need to divulge everything straightaway. The perpetrator—the perpetrators—still had no idea that the police knew the secret of the pool. They might be able to use this to their advantage in the investigation.

"Do you think the entire White Land needs to be sealed off, Monsieur Goal?"

Rose had come even closer to Dupin, speaking loudly over him into his phone.

"I don't know the exact regulations"—Goal was speaking unnecessarily loudly now too—"but based on my expertise I would only close the adjacent salt marshes for now and have them examined very soon. Along with the entire harvest from those salt marshes. Check if there has been any kind of contamination. But as I said: food safety regulations are stricter than our regulations."

"Get in touch as soon as there's any news, no matter what it is." Dupin hung up.

Rose moved away again and summarized: "All right. That's as much certainty as we'll get for now. This is it, our big story. We've got it. And now we'll find out who thought it up and did everything they could to keep it hidden."

A short time later they walked into the glass conference room from earlier. Madame Cordier was standing in the corner opposite the door, a sheaf of papers in her hand. Today her T-shirt was white with a large black copyright symbol; the jeans looked like the same ones from yesterday. A cold, arrogant gaze and bright red lips again, pressed together.

"You are duty-bound to inform me in full about everything, without keeping anything back, if it could be of relevance to food safety. We have taken our own samples, but that will take some time. Do you know what microorganisms are involved? The ministry's department of food safety is waiting for me to report to them. And everything depends on this. They are ready to take action immediately."

She made no move to sit down. Neither did Rose or Dupin.

"Madame Cordier, have there been complaints in the White Land in the last year? Anything unusual in your checks?" Rose sounded perfectly relaxed. Almost cheerful.

"No. Nothing at all."

"You monitor the salt producers and also the other food institutes that work in Gwenn Rann, is that correct?"

"Precisely."

"How often do your own checks take place?"

"Once a week." Celine Cordier folded her arms over the copyright symbol on her T-shirt.

"And the ones for the three salt marshes around this pool?"

"We take samples from all salt pools once a week."

"Do you carry out the analyses yourself?"

"Five employees do, under my direction. I'm going to ask you again, officially: What microorganisms are in the samples from the pool?"

"That is subject to police confidentiality. Our chemist will tell you what precautions he considers advisable."

Cordier unfolded her arms again. "So you *don't* know what strain is involved. That's all the more cause for concern!"

Objectively speaking, Madame Cordier's persistence was understandable.

"That alone would allow us to evaluate the situation. And then carry out the appropriate measures. So the only option left to me is to have all of the salt marshes shut down."

"Madame Cordier, where were you on Wednesday evening? What were you doing between half past eight and two in the morning?"

Madame Cordier kept her composure. "This is ludicrous," she said, shaking her head.

"Well?"

"I was in the institute until around half past eight. I left earlier than usual on Wednesday. I went home briefly and then out to a party. I was there till at least half past one without leaving the party for a single moment." She smiled sweetly. "It was a really fun evening."

"And where is your institute? And your home? Where was the party?"

"The institute is in Vannes. I live in Pen Lan. That's where the party was too. In the Domaine de Rochevilaine, an excellent restaurant. The local sports club was celebrating the fiftieth anniversary of its founding."

"And in the institute, at home, and at the party was there always someone who will be able to confirm your testimony to our inspectors?"

"The institute is big. But most of my colleagues leave earlier than I do. So I can't guarantee it. I live alone, but lots of people saw me at the party. Like I said, it was a really fun evening."

"Great, our inspectors will be in touch. Have we got anything else to discuss?"

Madame Cordier smiled again, coldly this time. "Well, I'm going to pass on my urgent recommendations to the ministry. And inform Madame Bourgiot right away."

"That will have to wait a little at least. Madame Bourgiot has an appointment with us first."

Celine Cordier got up expressionlessly, walked past Rose and Dupin, and left the room without another word.

"Where is Pen Lan?" Dupin had never heard of the place.

"At the mouth of the Vilaine. The northern side. Between the gulf and the Guérande. It's very pretty. Let's not keep Madame Bourgiot waiting any longer."

Dupin had never seen the Vilaine before, but everyone raved about it. It was a large Breton river steeped in history and part of an extensive web of waterways Nolwenn talked about a lot. She described gentle valleys, isolated, enchanted scenery, lock-keepers who sold vegetables they'd grown themselves, a paradise for houseboats.

Rose slipped gracefully through the door and turned left. Dupin followed her.

Apart from Madame Bourgiot's office, the Centre didn't have a second floor, just this one room. A steep, transparent staircase led up to it. The office was made almost entirely of glass too, which made it seem spacious, with sharp corners and edges like crystals, but best of all was the fantastic view. This elevation of just a few meters was enough to give a panoramic view of the flat Gwenn Rann area, across the bizarre, beautiful scenery of the salt gardens, the bright, pale green floodplains, across the turquoise lagoons as far as Kervalet, Batz-sur-Mer, and Le Croisic with its huge, angular church. Dupin was impressed.

"Madame Cordier is going to recommend to the ministry that all the salt marshes be shut down. She's going to come to you any moment now, Madame Bourgiot."

This was, after a brief formal greeting, Rose's cunning starting point, delivered matter-of-factly. Dupin still had no idea what the commissaire was hoping for from this conversation, which left him with a lurking anxiety. Madame Bourgiot was wearing a stylish teal suit today. She came across as flustered. Tense. Like when they had first met. They had already seen how erratic and unpredictable her behavior could be.

"That would be a catastrophe! That's why I spoke to the ministry in Paris myself. We've got to avoid it at all costs. Or are there any updates? Developments that mean it's actually necessary?"

The head of the Centre was sitting in an expensive but uncomfortable-looking designer chair, which, like almost all of the furniture in the room, was made of milky white plexiglass. Dupin's and Rose's chairs on the other side of the narrow desk were made of the same stuff and were difficult even to sit on. Rose had—no doubt deliberately—allowed a short pause to develop, and Dupin used it.

"We can't comment on that, Madame Bourgiot, but you could tell us what professional training you've done."

This was what he was really interested in. The constant verbal battle of wills was annoying him.

"What training I've done?" Her bafflement seemed genuine.

"Exactly."

"I'm a qualified agricultural scientist. École Normale Supérieure in Paris."

"So I assume you've taken some biology and chemistry?"

It was a few moments before Madame Bourgiot answered. Dupin glanced at Rose. She seemed quite amused.

"We did some biology and chemistry now and again, of course. And I was good at it. How is that relevant?"

The connections and the reasons why people in the White Land had biological or chemical knowledge were multiplying. And becoming more and more plausible.

"We like to build up a full picture."

Dupin sounded a little glum. If they were going to find out anything at all in this conversation—and Rose had been determined to have it—then it would probably only be if they approached it in a radical way. If they were to bring everything out into the open, trying to face the facts head on—an escalation. And then they would wait to see what happened.

"We . . ."

He was interrupted by Rose's mobile. She glanced quickly at the display and swiftly answered.

"Chadron? . . . I see. Wait a moment." She stood up and was at the door in just a few strides. This seemed important. "Madame Clothilde?"

As she asked this question, Rose vanished through the door, only to reappear a few seconds later and make a signal to Dupin to follow her. This was apparently truly important.

Rose walked through the "experience room," still talking, and stopped in front of the "Bloody Salt" display.

"And she really couldn't tell if it was a man or a woman? . . . And this was around eleven forty-five? . . . Fine . . . Thanks, Chadron. The team is to keep going with its inquiries. Maybe someone else was out and about on the street at the time."

She hung up and slipped the mobile into her jacket pocket. Then slowly she stretched her upper body, rested her hands on her sides, and tilted her head slightly.

"We've sent some police officers to the island to make enquiries. Madame Clothilde is a legendary old woman on the Île aux Moines. She's ninety-two. Everyone on the island knows her. Her house is near the harbor and she drives one of those tiny electric cars, like a golf cart. In fact she's *not* allowed to drive it anymore. She only does two routes, they've been the same for decades. One is to her best friend's house at the other end of the island. She always stays till it gets late." Dupin didn't have the faintest idea where she was going with this. "She has a big old dog and a cat who always go with her. There's a blind spot at the entrance to her plot of land when you're going in or out. So she always drives as far as the corner, counts to five, and drives on—"

"She does *what?*" Dupin had simply blurted it out. It was bizarre—this whole story. And Rose, it seemed to him, was only giving him so much detail so that she could think it through as she did so. "What's this really about? Tell me."

"She counts to five and drives onto the road without being able to see anything. As I mentioned, the cart is tiny. She, the dog, and the cat use up the small amount of air very quickly, and once they're underway, the windows fog up. If it gets too bad, she stops and opens the doors for a few minutes." Rose paused. She was clearly taking what she said very seriously.

"During one of these stops, she saw someone pulling a canoe up the beach directly in front of Maxime Daeron's house at around eleven forty-five."

Dupin's eyes widened. He understood immediately.

"She couldn't quite make out the person. She couldn't even say if it was a man or a woman. But somebody landed there in a canoe, she's sure of that."

Dupin ran a hand through his hair. This was awful news. While in theory it was possible that someone had just nicked a canoe last night for a little adventure and paddled from Port-Blanc to the Île aux Moines, to the Plage de Kerscot—the likelihood that this should happen to take place on the *exact* night of the crime, *exactly* at the possible time of the crime, and on the *exact* beach where the crime scene was, was not high.

"The canoe found with water in it this morning was examined straight after the young man reported it—there were no fingerprints on it. Nothing."

"Is this Madame Clothilde still all there? I mean . . ."

"Sound as a bell! Every morning at breakfast she reads the entire *Télégramme* and can then retell you every single article, in detail, in order, sometimes word for word. In the afternoons she sits in Le San Francisco and discusses it."

Dupin rubbed the back of his head.

"This is no coincidence. Maxime Daeron was murdered. Someone staged his suicide with impressive skill and extreme cold-bloodedness."

Commissaire Rose's words hung in the air between them for a while. No, this was no coincidence. So—it was another significant twist in this case.

Dupin was trying to rethink the case, or rather, one of the many strands of the story. "Maybe someone just planted the gun on him to frame him for the shooting too, as well as being involved in the algae project. The perpetrator was hoping we might eventually think the most plausible explanation was that he was also Lilou Breval's murderer."

"Or Maxime really was involved in some way. But not by himself. We're pretty sure we're dealing with more than one perpetrator, on the algae project at least."

It was dizzying. New configurations were constantly forming at top speed, one after another.

"Crap."

They did in fact—in all likelihood—have a second murder on their hands. More specifically, a callous second murder. They had almost been deceived. Almost.

Rose didn't even hear Dupin's exclamation. She was heading for the steps and Dupin was following behind. To his surprise, however, she stopped at the door to Bourgiot's office. She gave him a look that was hard to interpret but there was something conspiratorial about it.

The two commissaires went in together. Madame Bourgiot looked at them calmly, not showing any signs of annoyance.

"A few more questions, Madame Bourgiot. Where were you yesterday evening and last night? And please list all of the people who can testify to this effect." Rose had adopted her friendly, neutral tone. Strikingly focused.

Madame Bourgiot answered with perfect poise: "Should I infer from your question that you're no longer proceeding on the assumption of suicide?"

"If you could just answer the question, please."

Madame Bourgiot leaned back in her chair. "When I have no work commitments, I eat, as you already know, with my husband. As I did yesterday. In the garden. He came in around eight. I came in around half past. We sat there till midnight. Maybe even slightly later."

"Apart from your husband, can anyone else confirm this? Did you make any calls?"

"No. Just my husband. Two calls."

"From your landline?"

"From my mobile."

"Please have another think about Wednesday night, the same thing goes: Does anyone or anything occur to you, apart from your husband, who could prove that you were really at home? Before two o'clock in the morning?"

"No. I've already told you so." Madame Bourgiot could not be ruffled.

"We'll have another in-depth conversation with your husband then." Rose's words were an undisguised threat.

Of course Bourgiot may have done just that, spent a pleasant evening with her husband, but that was the problem with these kinds of alibis, and they'd already seen that on this case once before.

"It would be fatal. Another murder would be fatal for the Salt Land. All hell is breaking loose."

Bourgiot's despairing words sounded like a surrender. A realization of her own powerlessness.

"What do you mean by that?"

Madame Bourgiot looked right at Rose, but her eyes were blank. "Nothing."

Dupin was lost in thought about this new development. If Daeron had been murdered too, they were dealing with a very different kind of perpetrator than they anticipated at the outset. So on Wednesday evening a dramatic situation of some kind didn't just escalate dramatically—someone was acting in a systematic way. Daeron—perhaps implicated, perhaps a victim?—had been *disposed of.* Motives for murder come in all shapes and sizes: manifold human dramas, injuries, tragic passions, greed, revenge—the "heated emotions" as difficult as they are to identify from the outside sometimes. And there are cold-blooded perpetrators, calculating and ruthless, who would walk over dead bodies for their own ends. They pursue their interests in a twisted, rational way; victims are for them consequences they took in their stride in order to reach a goal. There are people without consciences. Dupin had come to know them.

"Where does your husband work?"

Dupin had no idea what Rose was driving at now.

"He works at the local council too."

"What does he do there?"

"He's the head of the water office."

Dupin pricked up his ears.

"The water office?"

"Yes, they're responsible for the drinking water supply—clarifying facilities, the pipe system, all of that."

"Here in the Guérande?"

"Yes, for the whole peninsula."

"Thanks for speaking to us, Madame Bourgiot." There was no trace of friendliness in Rose's voice now. This was an abrupt end to the conversation.

Shortly afterward the commissaires left the glass office.

Madame Bourgiot remained seated. It would have been impossible to say what was going through her mind.

* * *

The three inspectors were waiting in the dusty parking lot in front of the Centre du Sel. In the golden sunshine of early evening, Riwal and Chadron were chatting animatedly while Kadeg, standing a little apart from them, looked into the distance, grumpy and sulking.

"Along here."

Without further explanation, Rose made straight for a lane next to one of the large salt silos and they walked right down to the end of it. This was where some designated nature trails began, narrow and unpaved. Two signs showed the way—SHORT LOOP (20 MINS) and LONGER LOOP (60 MINS). Rose turned onto the "longer loop" path, which led sharply to the left. They were on the edge of the salt marshes. On the right-hand side were the vast salt gardens, a world of their own. But in front of them a different, completely unexpected landscape opened up. An almost jungle-like wood, thick, wild, low-hanging willows where a canal began, flowing straight as an arrow and disappearing far into the distance. Probably reaching as far as the enchanted Black Land, the Parc de Brière, a vast landscape of turf, moorland, and water, full of canals and lagoons that Dupin had driven through with Henri last year on the way back from Le Croisic. Where the canal began, there was a wooden footbridge out of a picture book, old and overgrown with pale moss. Tethered to this were three jet-black rowing boats with green seats.

In the shadow of the huge willows was a wooden picnic table with benches on either side. Rose, who was clearly familiar with all of this, was almost there already. Grasses grew along the canal in all kinds of green and yellow shades. The scenery was idyllic. Lavishly bathed in a mild, golden light.

"Someone must have drugged Maxime Daeron, perhaps even in the garage. They placed the body in the position in which the shot was fired. Then guided his finger."

Commissaire Rose, who seemed to take no notice of the fairy-tale landscape, had unceremoniously sat down during this concise report. The three inspectors followed suit, as did Dupin. A picnic party. This conversation in this idyll. There was something strange about it all. But at least they wouldn't be disturbed here.

"That would explain the smudge of gunpowder residue too." Unsurprisingly, an eager Kadeg was the first to respond. But he was right. It must have been more or less how Rose described it. If it wasn't suicide. And Dupin was convinced of that by now. Rose added: "It was perfectly staged. The plan might just have easily come off."

"You've got to insert yourself into the perspective and psyche of the perpetrator. As if you were writing a crime novel. That's how the experts do it."

Everyone looked at Riwal for a moment, who noticed their glances. It infuriated Dupin. The prefecture had made a big fuss of launching a qualification program for inspectors. Riwal had started his course two months ago, "The Perpetrator's Psychology—An Indispensable Criminological Tool." Kadeg's course was coming up in October—and in fact it gave Dupin even more cause for concern: "Decipher the Body's Signals—How the Limbic System Betrays the Perpetrator."

"It's all possible," Rose continued on systematically and calmly, "at least as far as Daeron and the gun go. It might be his, it might not. And if it is, there would still be any number of explanations. We don't even know for sure that Maxime Daeron was in the salt marshes on Wednesday night. All we know is that he lied about being with his wife."

"If the perpetrator did drug Daeron, he must have got his hands on one of those new kinds of anesthetics. Depending on what it was, that might not have been at all straightforward." Kadeg had rattled this off like a particularly nerdy schoolboy.

"We're assuming the perpetrator has access to biochemical knowledge anyway. That could include medical knowledge too. The perpetrator themselves or one of their associates. Access to knowledge and a laboratory. Then it would be a piece of cake," Riwal concluded matter-of-factly.

"So who has access to what knowledge exactly? And access to

which laboratories via what links? What do we know?" This still seemed to Dupin like a solid starting point.

"I've done extensive research into the three women on that point," Kadeg said. "I'll start with Madame Laurent. She's a trained biologist."

"Madame Laurent is a biologist?"

This hadn't really been a proper question from Dupin, more of a cry of surprise. Even though it was close to her profession, of course, he had never thought of it before. He took out his notebook and began to take notes. Kadeg didn't let himself be distracted in the slightest.

"She studied in Bordeaux. A native of Rennes. But she has never worked as a biologist, not even at Le Sel. She has been involved in management from the beginning. Le Sel has several of its own food laboratories, and also one in Vannes, but we haven't established any particular link between her and this laboratory as of yet. She also has an uncle who is a third-generation *paludier* in the Guérande." Kadeg was reading aloud from a piece of paper and intoning every sentence as though it were the critical accomplishment of long, demanding study. "Madame Cordier has a degree in food chemistry which is its own course at the Université Paris Sud. She specialized in food law and got a degree in it at the age of just twenty-three. She comes from Guérande town and is head of the department at the state institute in Vannes. Apparently she may become the overall head of the institute soon." Kadeg left an artful pause, as though he were preparing for the climax of his speech. "Madame Bourgiot is an agricultural scientist; she also studied in Paris, which usually includes courses in biology and chemistry. We don't know of any direct link between Madame Bourgiot or the Centre du Sel and a laboratory. After a brief time off, she came directly to the Centre after graduating. She's from round here too, from a little village between Le Croisic and Saint-Nazaire."

"Brilliant. All the suspects are getting even more suspect."

Dupin placed one hand on the back of his neck. In fact, all of this wasn't that remarkable: anyone who worked here, who was involved in salt, had in all likelihood pursued these kinds of career paths.

Two huge birds suddenly flew just above their heads. Dupin practically ducked. They landed by the canal at a spot where the bank was flat. They had remarkably long legs. No one else seemed to pay them any notice.

Chadron took over now. "Monsieur Jaffrezic has no apparent, specific link to chemistry or biology. He didn't study them or have any training in them. He came here from Paris at the end of the seventies. A hippie. He—"

"A hippie?" Dupin was gobsmacked, but then again, why shouldn't Jaffrezic be a hippie?

"In the seventies lots of dropouts came to the White Land searching for a life in harmony with nature, something original, contemplation," Rose said respectfully. "With their idealism they made a huge contribution to the survival and rebuilding of the salt gardens. At the beginning there was of course some serious conflict with the long-established *paludiers*."

"How old is Jaffrezic?"

"Sixty-three." Chadron took over once more.

"Sixty-three?"

The whole harmony and contemplation thing seemed to have worked; Dupin would have put Jaffrezic in his early fifties, around ten years younger than he was.

Chadron ignored Dupin's response and continued. "The cooperative works with one particular laboratory. *Nourriture sécure*. Has done for the last fifteen years. All professional communications are conducted through an employee of the cooperative, but of course Jaffrezic and the director know each other well. Very well, apparently. They're friends, in fact. We . . ."

"Friends who go fishing together sometimes?" Dupin nearly jumped out of his seat.

"We're checking whether it was him who went fishing with Jaffrezic last night. We'll know that soon."

Chadron was good. Riwal gave her an appreciative look; Kadeg looked sulkily at her.

"Paul Daeron's company built its own small-scale laboratory five years ago. Which is normal for a business of its type and size."

"Where is the laboratory?"

"At company headquarters."

When they came across the algae, Dupin had thought, with a certain investigatory euphoria, that he finally had reliable evidence that would drastically reduce the pool of suspects. But Rose had been right, it didn't help to reduce it much. Basically not at all. It was moot. Dupin was muttering, his gaze sweeping along the endless canal.

"We've got to—"

Rose's mobile rang. She looked at the screen and stood up immediately. "Just a moment."

She took a few steps and stopped directly beneath the willows with the low-hanging branches so that she was no longer visible. She seemed to be speaking very softly. Not a word was audible.

There was total silence at the picnic table. Dupin's gaze couldn't help roaming back to the two large birds. They were still there, and apparently on the hunt. One had just spotted something, perhaps a poor frog. Quick as a flash, its beak swooped down. Dupin liked frogs. He had always enjoyed playing with them as a child.

"We've got to move on. So, the alibis." Rose's voice tore Dupin away from his thoughts. Her phone call had been short and apparently she didn't intend to share anything about it. On the contrary, her expression was bullish, as though someone else had interrupted this important discussion. "What about Madame Cordier? Initially we didn't even pay attention to her. What about her Wednesday evening, the party?"

"I've already spoken to three witnesses. There were over a hundred guests in total, it was a large party. She was definitely there. From around ten until quarter past one at least." Kadeg hesitated after his report, as though he wanted to add something more. But he didn't.

"Great. In theory, it's possible she was involved in the shooting, purely from the point of view of timing, just about." Rose raised her eyebrows slightly. "Question Cordier again about yesterday evening. Commissaire Dupin and I didn't do that in our interview just now."

"I'll speak to her." Kadeg loved those jobs.

"And what about the others? Quickly please!" Rose was impatient, which Dupin fully understood.

"Madame Laurent: no alibi for either of the two evenings." Kadeg switched into his staccato reporting style. "Madame Cordier: we've just had her; the director of the Centre du Sel, Madame Bourgiot: dinner in the garden with her husband on Wednesday evening from eight thirty till midnight . . ."

"And yesterday too. Or so she says."

"We're checking that." Kadeg yawned.

"We know about Monsieur Jaffrezic's evening excursion yesterday." Chadron took over again. The inspectors were well attuned to each other by now. "On Wednesday he left the salt marshes at quarter past eight with his colleagues and then went for a 'bite to eat' with two *paludiers* he's friends with in Le Croisic. From half past ten he was at a Fest-Noz in Pornichet. Also with the two *paludiers*. Until after midnight. They both confirmed everything to us. Paul Daeron was still at a meeting in the early evening, again in Vannes, like the evening before, and we checked all of that. Then, as you know, he says he went out on his boat, which we have not found a witness to yet, and then went home. His wife and daughter confirmed that they ate together around half past nine. And they went to sleep around half past ten."

"He doesn't actually have an alibi for the relevant time. He could have got up again without anyone noticing."

"Right," Rose said drily. "I've spoken to the chemist again. They'll have needed a lab, however makeshift; they had to buy bacterial solutions; they had to select the bacteria through laborious processes; set up new trials all the time; buy nutrient solutions for targeted reproduction of the microorganisms to have enough for a field test of this size; they needed to transport large quantities of algae here; they then had to look at the results and water samples in the laboratory. Last but not least, they'll have needed money for all of this, as well as time. And if it wasn't the work of one individual, they would have been communicating with each other. There must have been phone calls, texts, e-mails, meetings."

"Without specific grounds for suspicion, we can't request data on any of these people," Kadeg added eagerly. "We haven't found anything suspicious on Maxime Daeron yet. Nothing. And his wife couldn't give us anything either."

"I've put someone on that," Rose continued, as though Kadeg hadn't said anything, "contacting the laboratories that deal in specific microorganisms. No progress so far—I've just received the first preliminary report, but perhaps we'll have some luck. But if they weren't very unusual microorganisms, just the kind you can buy in any garden center, it won't be much use."

Dupin was feeling more and more restless. Maybe it was because of the unfamiliar situation. He had never in his whole police career thought things over with so many colleagues—he usually had to force himself just to go to regular meetings with his two inspectors during a case.

"There are twelve cultural clubs and associations in the White Land relating to the Guérande and salt. The most famous one is Les Amis de Guérande. It focuses on the cultural heritage of salt." It was unclear how Riwal's remarks were relevant, which was something that happened now and again. Dupin sighed. Riwal continued: "There are also professional societies. Special interest groups, economic associations, professional organizations, I think there are at least ten."

Understandably, nobody reacted to what Riwal had said.

Dupin couldn't take it anymore. He stood up.

Riwal went on, "Each of our suspects belongs to several of these associations at the same time. In varying combinations. In some cases they founded them themselves. Jaffrezic and Bourgiot, for example, founded a club for the ecological protection of the salt marshes, and they're the presidents of it. It's got over two hundred members at this stage. Last year Maxime Daeron was elected treasurer. The club is very active."

Riwal had phrased this last sentence in the same way as the one before, thoughtfully but strangely nonchalant. This time all of the heads whipped round to look at him, which he didn't even seem to notice. They all stared at him.

"I took a look at it when I was in the town hall. And here in the Centre," he added almost apologetically.

"Maxime Daeron, Bourgiot, and Jaffrezic?"

Dupin was standing next to the table. It sounded nothing short of insane. But . . . this could be it. Precisely this. By chance. Riwal's idea of researching the clubs and societies to see who was meeting whom was pure brilliance.

"A club like that could potentially be the perfect cover for the algae project." Rose had grasped the significance immediately. "It's hard to imagine a better smoke screen."

Riwal leafed through the notebook lying open on the table in front of him, which was full to bursting. "There are any number of combinations of our six suspects. All six are active in the two large professional organizations. Apart from Jaffrezic, oddly. Laurent and Jaffrezic are members of the Society for the Promotion of the Marketing of Sel Breton. That's probably the most powerful society. Just as an example: Maxime Daeron, Madame Laurent, and Madame Cordier are registered in a subgroup of the Fédération Saliculture Guérandaise with an emphasis on flora and fauna."

Everyone looked at Riwal again, who spoke more firmly than he had before—with some pride too—but now looked confused at the disappointment on everyone else's faces.

"So it's not watertight evidence then," Kadeg noted triumphantly. "This way, it could be anyone anyway."

That was true—but it was a possible lead. A theory of how everything might have begun. Where people had met and how.

"I want to have everyone's current memberships collated in a clear list." Dupin was still standing next to the table, his right hand on the back of his head.

"It's already available."

Riwal had done a huge amount of work. He slid the notebook across to Dupin. Rose stood up, positioning herself next to Dupin, and began to study the list with him.

It was painstakingly laid out, in tiny writing, six pages of it, all of the clubs and societies on the left and all of the suspects who were members of them on the right. In fact there was nearly every combination. It was enough to drive you mad.

"Do we know the aims of the clubs and societies—what each of them focuses on?" For Dupin at least, only a few of the societies' names made it clear.

"In nearly every case, I know—"

Riwal was interrupted by Rose's ringtone. But unlike before, she took just a small step to one side before she answered. "*Bonj—*"

Rose faltered in the middle of the word. And stayed motionless on the spot so that Dupin and the three inspectors instantly paused. She pressed the mobile to her ear and didn't say a word. For what felt like forever. Then: "Of course." She tried to speak calmly but she sounded very agitated.

Then she listened again.

"No—Monsieur Daeron, wait—we're coming right now, where are . . . hello?—Hello, Monsieur Daeron? Hello?"

She waited, listening hard, for another nerve-shredding length of time. Then all of a sudden she took the phone away from her ear.

"Paul Daeron. He said he wants to talk to us immediately. And that we should come to him. That he wants to—" She hesitated for a moment. "—tell us the *whole* story." Rose seemed extremely worried and wasn't trying to hide it. "He was just about to say where he is right now—but then something happened. I could hear loud noises, like a struggle, he shouted something I couldn't understand, then the call got cut off. It was from a private number."

Chadron, Kadeg, and Riwal had jumped to their feet.

"We've got to find out where Paul Daeron is as soon as possible." Dupin peeled away and ran toward the bridge. He paused, looking at the canal with the perplexing greenish water. The surface was absolutely still. A swarm of black birds flew unhurriedly over the canal without making a sound. It was all infinitely peaceful.

"Shit."

He said this at the top of his voice. They would have heard it loud and clear at the table.

* * *

"Yes, exactly, we're looking for Monsieur Daeron. And it's very urgent."

Paul had done what they'd been afraid of: he had failed to call back. Rose, Dupin, and their inspectors had hurried to the parking lot at the Centre in the meantime. They were standing, somewhat scattered, near their cars, each of them with a phone to their ear. Dupin had Paul Daeron's secretary on the other end of the line.

"An hour and a half ago he was on a phone call that was much longer than his usual ones, Monsieur le Commissaire, and then he said he had to go. He told me he wanted to be alone for a while. He . . . he seemed shaken."

The secretary seemed at least as shaken, if not more so, now that the police were calling.

"Should I be doing something? Surely you don't think something awful has happened, do you? After the thing with his brother . . ."

Dupin thought about it for a moment. "Did he make the call or receive it?"

"I don't know."

"What phone was he on?"

"For once, it was his mobile." The secretary was getting more and more nervous. "Not that I heard anything, the connecting door is well insulated. But I would have seen a call on the landline on my screen. You know, Monsieur Daeron doesn't get on well with mobiles at all, he's always complaining, he says he has never even—"

"Give me the number."

"One moment. I never use it. It's 0 67 83 76 56."

"Is that his personal mobile?"

"Yes. Director Daeron doesn't have a work mobile. It's one of those prepaid phones. I don't think he uses it much."

"Do you have any of the relevant documents? We need the number from the SIM card."

"No." The secretary sounded guilty.

"Do you know when he bought it?"

"No."

Fantastic. Without the ID number from the SIM card they wouldn't get anywhere at all. No traffic data, nothing.

"And you didn't happen to, without meaning to, of course, hear a word or two of the phone call?"

"Oh no, not a chance."

Dupin didn't believe her. "This is extremely important. It would be so helpful to Monsieur Daeron."

"No, I genuinely don't know anything." This time it was almost a sob.

"One of my colleagues will be in touch about his landlines. And you don't have any idea where Monsieur Daeron has gone either?"

"No. Unfortunately not. He didn't say anything. But he never tells me what he does in his personal life. He's very discreet. You've got the addresses of the houses in La Roche-Bernard and on the Île aux Moines, don't you?"

"Yes. I take it he left in his car?"

"Yes."

"Thank you very much."

Dupin almost hung up. But he added one more time: "And you really can't think of what he might have meant by wanting to be 'alone for a while'?"

"He says that sometimes. But no more than that. As I say, he never gets personal."

"Thank you." Dupin hung up.

"Well?" Rose was standing right next to him. He summarized briefly.

"I've got a bad feeling about this," she said without any emotion. With that quiet composure that Dupin knew.

Rose signaled to all three inspectors and they quickly clustered around her. Only Kadeg was still on the phone, but he hung up quickly.

"Chadron, make sure we try to locate Daeron's mobile. That's the main thing. Then we need to know where each of our suspects is right now! What they're doing. Whether they're by themselves. Call them and pay them each a visit, send someone from the local police force on ahead if that's quicker." Rose was speaking rapidly. "Laurent, Bourgiot, Jaffrezic. And Cordier. Each of you take on one of the four. We've got to be fast."

This was laborious but exactly the right thing to do. Taking the risk of committing themselves to these four people. They needed to act. Paul Daeron was probably in extreme danger. Although he himself was likely to be involved in what had happened.

"A car is already on its way to Daeron's house in La Roche-Bernard. It'll be there soon," Chadron said.

"We'll take Laurent," Rose said, glancing at Dupin. Dupin would have chosen Madame Laurent too—he would only have wished to have a crack at her by himself.

"I'll go after Bourgiot." Kadeg already had his phone to his ear.

"I'll take Jaffrezic." Riwal had his phone in his hand. "We've also just got the message that the old friend he went fishing with wasn't the head of the laboratory. They don't usually go fishing together."

At least this didn't make Jaffrezic even more suspect.

"I'll deal with Cordier," Chadron announced grimly.

"I want—" Rose paused a moment. "—someone to take Maxime Daeron's wife too. Just to be on the safe side."

Everyone looked at Rose in some surprise.

"I'll do that too," Chadron said firmly.

"Off you go then. I've got to keep my mobile free in case Daeron makes contact again. You can reach me via radio."

She glanced at Dupin. "Let's take my car." Rose already had the car keys in her hand. "I'm driving."

Dupin rolled his eyes.

* * *

Madame Laurent's colleague sounded capable and friendly. "She was in the office until half past three. Then she left."

They couldn't get through to Ségolène Laurent on her mobile or at home.

"And you really don't know where she was going?"

Dupin's voice was strained. He had turned on the speakerphone so that Rose could listen too. He kept his right hand firmly on the handle above the door during every one of the many bends in the road. He would never have thought it possible, but Rose managed to drive down the narrow streets toward the gulf even more recklessly than she had done over the last two days. This time at least it was with the sirens and flashing lights on, but that wasn't making speaking or listening any easier.

"No. She doesn't have any more meetings today. She's off on a trip to Avignon tomorrow. When she's in the office and not away, she always leaves around this time on a Friday."

"What kind of trip is it?"

"It's to the salt marshes in the Rhône delta."

"When did she plan the trip?"

"Just this morning. She goes on spontaneous business trips now and then."

"Was she on the phone before she left?"

"I suppose so. She's constantly on the phone when she's in the office."

"Did she seem different in any way? Did anything about her strike you as odd?"

"She seemed normal. She told me to have a good weekend, she was friendly." The employee was unflappable. She didn't even seem particularly worried that a police commissaire was asking all these questions.

"Who might know where she is right now?"

"I don't know, sadly. Her best friend perhaps, Madame Sinon, the head of Le Gall, the big milk products manufacturer. Madame Laurent is often out. And when she's not, she's usually at home on the Île d'Arz. Perhaps she's swimming right now, she enjoys that."

"We need the numbers that Madame Laurent dialed in the last few hours from her landline. Could you look these up and call me back immediately?"

There was a pause before the employee responded. "These are important police matters, you said?"

"Very important."

"Call me back." She seemed to want to hang up.

"Wait—you don't happen to know if Madame Laurent was in touch with a Monsieur Paul Daeron, do you? In the last few days."

"Oh yes. Of course. He's a client of Madame Laurent's. Saucisse Breizh gets salt from Le Sel."

"What?" Dupin exclaimed.

"His firm buys salt from Le Sel to make sausages. They speak on the phone occasionally, and meet up too. Madame Laurent thinks it's important to see her bigger clients face-to-face on a regular basis, she takes it very seriously. I don't know anything about the last few days—there was no meeting scheduled, anyway. But you're better off asking Madame Laurent yourself."

"We'll do that. Is it a work mobile that Madame Laurent uses?"

"Oh yes. She uses it a lot."

"Do you know of another, personal mobile? A prepaid mobile?"

For the first time the employee seemed uncertain. "No. And I think it's very unlikely."

"So if you wouldn't mind having a look for those numbers?"

"I'm on it."

Dupin hung up.

It was remarkable. They were discovering more and more entanglements that nobody had mentioned before.

Rose sped hair-raisingly out of another very tight bend, making the car do a daredevil tilt. With this kind of driving they'd be there in half an hour. Rose had already sent two officers from Auray on ahead. Rose's radio came on. "Riwal here."

"Go ahead."

The commissaire only had one hand on the steering wheel now.

"Monsieur Jaffrezic is probably in one of his other salt marshes. Most likely by himself, according to statements from his colleagues. In the salt marsh where he has been these last few days, down below the blind pool. I'll be there any minute. I still haven't been able to get through to him."

"Okay."

"Riwal out."

Maybe they should have stayed in the Salt Land? Dupin suddenly felt uncertain. Had it been Paul Daeron who had wanted to meet someone—or had someone wanted to meet him? If Paul Daeron had suggested the meeting, then it was probably also him who had dictated the place. Rose had put out a search for Paul Daeron's car, a Citroën Crosser like his brother's, except in dark blue.

She still hadn't put down the radio when it came on again.

"Kadeg here."

"And?"

"Madame Bourgiot is in a salt marsh, it's probably a meeting about a new nature trail about salt, one of her colleagues says. It's not far from the open lagoon, out toward Le Croisic. Combined with bird-watching spots. It wasn't easy to find someone who knew that. I was only able to speak to Madame Bourgiot briefly, because the reception was so bad. We got cut off again immediately. It's possible she couldn't hear me. I'm almost there."

"So they're both in the salt marshes," Dupin said loudly.

There was a short pause. Kadeg didn't seem to know what to say. Dupin followed this thought through: "How far is the salt marsh Bourgiot is in from Jaffrezic's salt marsh on the edge of the blind pool?"

"I would say it's seven hundred meters as the crow flies."

Rose took over the conversation: "Tell Chadron to have a helicopter fly over the salt marshes and look for Daeron's car. And any of the suspects. The helicopter from Saint-Nazaire should be there in a few minutes."

"Understood. Kadeg over and out."

Dupin's mobile rang. Developments were coming thick and fast now. It was Madame Laurent's secretary.

"Yes?"

"The numbers."

"I'm listening."

Dupin let go of the handle and fumbled to get his notebook out. The secretary patiently began to pass on seven numbers, with the times of the calls and their durations, and whether they were "incoming" or "outgoing."

"That's it. Every call from the last few hours."

"Thank you very much."

Dupin hung up. None of the numbers meant anything to him. He would simply call them one after another. The radio came on again. Inspector Chadron.

"Paul Daeron's mobile cannot be located. It must be switched off. Or damaged. Some officers are at the house in La Roche-Bernard. No trace of him and no sign he's been there over the last few hours. We've spoken to his wife again. She's very worried, but she doesn't know where her husband might be. We haven't been able to get Cordier on the phone yet. After her conversation with you, she spoke to Madame Bourgiot, very briefly, and left the Centre. Her institute is closed on a

Friday afternoon. At this time of day, we couldn't get through to anyone there. I'm driving to her house in Pen Lan right now. Two local officers are already there. Her car isn't outside the door and it doesn't look like she's in."

"And Maxime Daeron's wife?"

"She's got a meeting in Vannes until four o'clock. She told a colleague she was going to do a bit of shopping afterward. We haven't got through to her directly yet."

"All right, Chadron."

Rose hung up the radio again, stepping hard on the gas at the start of a long straight stretch—Skippy would have no chance—and for once placed her other hand on the wheel, Dupin noted with some relief.

He was on the fourth number. One of the ones Madame Laurent had called. The first three, who had all called her, had been unremarkable business contacts.

"*Meubles et terrasses, Bonjour.*"

Dupin hung up. The next call—also placed by Madame Laurent herself—was a restaurant. Marée des Oiseaux. Madame Laurent had made a reservation for next Monday for three people.

"The best restaurant in the area. There's a very young chef there and he's going to be one of the big names. His fennel and sea bream in a salt crust is pure poetry."

Without a pause, as if she hadn't just said this, Rose was right back on topic. "We've got to get hold of this prepaid mobile. It might have been a clever way for them to communicate. It's possible each of the people involved had a prepaid mobile. It doesn't get more anonymous than that."

Dupin didn't answer. On the sixth number, an answering machine came on, but there was no name. The seventh was another restaurant. In Marseilles this time, for tomorrow evening. For three people. The business trip. No other names were noted on the reservation.

Rose went on: "He was going to talk. Paul Daeron wanted to tell us everything. Perhaps he himself is implicated and wanted to turn himself in. Get everything out into the open. And he told somebody this, another of the people involved. Maybe he wanted to meet up with this person."

This sounded plausible. Logically plausible, psychologically plausible. That might be what had happened.

"Or he's innocent," Rose concluded, "and learned something, uncovered what happened."

This was plausible too.

"We will find the *point magique* very soon," Dupin said, surprising himself with this sentence—at least as much as he surprised Rose—and he couldn't help smiling to himself.

* * *

They were still fifteen minutes away from Port Arradon, which was a bit closer to the Île d'Arz than Port-Blanc. Rose had ordered a police boat to be waiting for them at the harbor there.

The inspectors had all been in touch again, and Rose had not put her right hand back on the wheel once.

Kadeg still hadn't seen Madame Bourgiot or got hold of her on the phone. His despair was audible; the locations in the salt marshes were still vague. He was now systematically combing the outermost salt marshes, next to the lagoon. Kadeg had been able to establish that the mobile reception in the area was unreliable.

Madame Bourgiot was—at least for now—not with Jaffrezic either. Riwal had arrived at his salt marsh and met Jaffrezic. Just like yesterday, he was by himself, and he was in the middle of doing some harvesting. *Fleur de sel.* He claimed to have been busy with the harvest all afternoon. Just him. Alone. And that he had neither seen nor spoken to Paul Daeron, not today, and not in the last few days either. Riwal hadn't found any indication that Madame Bourgiot had been there, and Jaffrezic dismissed the idea as absurd. But Riwal had begun a thorough examination of the salt marsh and the surrounding area nonetheless, especially the hut. During their radio conversation with Riwal, the helicopter was audible twice, and it was extremely loud. It hadn't found anything so far.

Finally, according to Chadron's update, Madame Cordier was still unavailable, both of her phone lines going straight to voicemail.

"What do you think?"

For a moment there was silence. Rose had spoken with a certain emphasis. She meant this question very seriously.

"I . . ."

The radio again.

"It's the team from Madame Laurent's house here."

Dupin didn't know these officers. There was a certain swash-buckling excitement from this particular officer, who sounded young. It was as though he had said: "SWAT team on the scene, ready to engage."

"I'm listening."

"We've just arrived"—the radio connection was crackling like mad—"there's an anthracite Audi A8 in the driveway. That's her car. We've rung the bell but nobody is opening the door."

"She drove home from the office." Dupin had accidentally butted in loudly, but Rose ignored him.

"Gain access to the house. Examine the property very carefully. And the surrounding area. She likes to go swimming. It's not far from the beach. There's sure to be a direct route from the garden."

"We don't have a judicial order. No search warrant." The "SWAT team member" had switched into a reedy little voice.

"You're going in there now. *Exigent circumstance.* You have a direct order from me, which you will obey immediately." Rose's unequivocal words and icy tone ruled out any further questions. "We'll be right there."

Rose put the radio back down.

They had just reached the edge of Port Arradon, and Rose had reduced her speed to seventy kilometers an hour for this residential area. Dupin was dimly aware of counting three red lights that hadn't tempted Rose to brake. They cut right across the little village to get to the quay where the police boat was waiting.

"You think it's Madame Laurent," Dupin said in a contemplative voice. "You think she's not just involved in the algae project, she's the murderer too."

"I . . ."

Dupin's mobile.

He saw a number that looked unfamiliar.

"It's Directeur Daeron's secretary again here," she said uncertainly.

"Yes, Madame?"

"I've looked at the numbers Monsieur Daeron called this afternoon from his landline. There were just three of them. The long conversation that got him so shaken up was on his mobile, shall I let you have the numbers in any—"

Rose's radio interrupted the secretary.

"Are you there? I've got something." Chadron's voice was almost shrill.

"Has something happened?" The secretary sounded frightened. Dupin had forgotten to end the call. He hung up.

It was clear Chadron was trying to contain her excitement. "I carried out your instruction from this afternoon and asked the traffic crime division for every recorded speeding incident from the stationary and mobile patrols between Wednesday evening and this afternoon. Two officers analyzed them." She was speaking remarkably quickly, hardly breathing. "They compared that with the registration plates of the cars belonging to everyone we're looking into." A seemingly natural pause developed. Dupin still hadn't fully grasped what Chadron was saying, coming as it did out of the blue like this. But it was dawning on him.

"A mobile radar unit on the D28 near Crac'h caught a black Renault Laguna with the registration GH 568 PP–44 on Wednesday evening at eleven forty. The snapshot is poor, but the technicians think they'll be able to improve the picture enough to make the person identifiable. The car was doing one hundred and forty-five kilometers an hour." Chadron took a deep breath and then ended her message by adding: "Crac'h is seven kilometers from Kerpenhir. From Lilou Breval's parents' home."

It was a split second before Dupin realized the monstrous enormity of this news.

That was it.

They had her.

Before he could reply, Rose had stepped on the brake with no warning—and without saying another word to Chadron. There was an almighty screeching and groaning. A terrible juddering. When she slammed on the brakes, Dupin was flung forward against his seatbelt and pangs of pain shot through his shoulder, which he hadn't felt much all day. The whole incident took four or five seconds. Then the car stopped. A scene out of a film. Just a few meters from the quay. The gulf lay before them. That breathtaking panorama. A family with two small children and a father carrying a bright yellow rubber boat turned around and looked at the car in concern.

"We've only got one shot. If it's not already too late. Where do we go?" asked Rose.

It wasn't Madame Laurent. She hadn't murdered Lilou Breval, anyway. And in all likelihood she hadn't murdered Maxime Daeron either. Dupin remembered the big Renault—at the salt marshes yesterday, where the barrels had been found. It was the same car that Rose drove, only in jet black. He knew who owned it.

This was a coup. A coup for Commissaire Rose, who again hadn't told him what she was up to—had shut him out again. But that was beside the point now. This time they had caught them—Rose was close earlier with the canoe and the old woman. It was a simple but admittedly brilliant idea. They had had all instances of speeding from the last few days looked into. Brittany was riddled with mobile radar machines these days. A brilliant idea, because in this case it wasn't just the investigators who had had to do a lot of driving. And what's more: they had needed to drive very fast.

"Where shall we go?" Rose said, tearing Dupin away from his thoughts. She was right: it was the one question they needed to think about right now. Everything else would come later.

"Where could they be? Daeron and Cordier?"

* * *

Rose turned the car around. And started driving—without the sirens and flashing lights this time—slowly back through the village toward the motorway. They would have to turn right or left there. Toward the gulf—or toward the salt marshes.

They didn't say a word. Their thoughts were racing. The tension was palpable. They had just one shot. If that.

"He wanted to be 'alone'—his boat." Dupin's words broke the tense silence. "Wherever Paul Daeron's boat is. Somewhere there. He said it was a 'peaceful place.' It's *his* place. That's where we need to go."

This was not the result of logical analysis. It was instinct, a mental deduction. A feeling. Rose looked at Dupin for a moment, perplexed.

He got out his notebook and hurriedly leafed through it. He had noted it down, he was sure of it.

He found it on a page covered in scribbles. "The Vilaine estuary. His boat is in the Vilaine estuary. He mentioned Vannes and La Roche-Bernard and he thought it was about fifteen minutes away."

Rose's eyes flashed. "That would be almost exactly midway between Pen Lan and La Roche-Bernard. Where Paul Daeron and Madame Cordier live. Between the Salt Land and the gulf. Not far from here."

"Is there a harbor there?"

"No," Rose said softly, "that's the long northern side of the Vilaine estuary. Lots of rocky patches, meadows, big cornfields, hedgerows, heather, a few dolmens. It's all quite peaceful. Desolate. You need to know exactly where you want to go." Suddenly her expression changed. "At the Pointe du Moustoir, almost right in the estuary, where it starts to get hilly, there's a handful of buoys with boats attached. Far out into the river. There are also buoys on the two or three beaches off it."

Dupin didn't know the area. Rose fell silent for a few moments. Then she stretched, turned her head to the left, to the right, and stepped on the gas. The car actually jolted forward.

"We'll be there in fifteen minutes." She reached for the radio. "Chadron, can you hear me?"

"I'm listening."

"Send units to the northern side of the Vilaine estuary right away. To the beaches where the boats are in summer. Tell them to look for a dark blue Citroën Crosser and the black Renault Laguna. And for Paul Daeron's sailing boat. We'll be there very soon. We're driving to Pointe du Moustoir."

"Should I come? With Riwal and Kadeg?"

"No. But let them know. Keep investigating where you are. We still don't know everyone who was involved. I don't want any more surprises. They might not even be there. We're taking a chance."

This was important: they didn't know everyone who was involved. Who they were, and how many of them there were. But one person was clear. In all likelihood, the murderer of Lilou Breval. There was no two ways about it. Céline Cordier had stated she was at the party in Pen Lan on Wednesday evening. From around ten until half past one in the morning. The entire time, never once leaving the party. She had unquestionably been seen there at ten o'clock and at quarter to one; they had witnesses. But in between those two times she had been recorded fifty-seven kilometers away from the party, driving at an extremely high speed. And that was at twenty to midnight. Just seven kilometers away from the scene of the crime—the scene where Lilou was murdered at around the right time. There was only one conclusion to be drawn. Dupin had no doubts about it. It was her.

* * *

Dupin had a scale map in his lap. Between Pen Lan and the end of the huge Vilaine estuary, there were seven little roads that led to the sea, all of them branching into even smaller paths. They had just left the Route Nationale and now drove past Billiers and straight down to the river. Taking a right for the Pointe du Moustoir. Just five kilometers away. The street forked yet again at the end. There would probably be a few unpaved paths. A few hamlets.

He and Rose hadn't exchanged a single word. And strangely, the mobile and radio had stayed silent.

This was a risk. They were staking everything on this.

The road ran between fields of corn. It was at most a meter wider than the car and it was doggedly straight. Dupin happened to look at the speedometer: 150 kilometers an hour. They had just left a dense patch of forest. He put the map in the backseat without even trying to fold it.

Commissaire Rose slowed down. Dupin sat up straight and instinctively grabbed his gun. They were coming to a turnoff. Rose turned right. An even narrower street. Gently sloping. A slight bend. All of a sudden they saw the bright greenish-silver river. Right now, between high and low tides, it was a real river—not a fjord—a river with broad strips of sand and silt on either bank. The road led right down to the river, with fields of corn still on the left-hand side. On the opposite side were the first of the boats, tethered to the typical colorful buoys.

"The boats are on the southern bank here. This isn't it."

Rose reached for the radio. "Chadron, can you hear me?"

"I'm listening."

"Are there boats on the northern bank at Pointe du Moustoir too? We've come from Billiers."

"A little farther into the estuary, just below Kerdavid, there are three little dead ends that go down to the river."

Rose hung up the radio again and said, "Chadron is a sailor."

This street led away from the river. Small woods, shrubbery, and hilly ground blocked their view now. Rose slowed the car down noticeably. Dupin saw why. To the right was a turnoff for an unpaved path. That must be one of the three dead ends that Chadron had meant.

Again it was a game of pure chance.

"The middle one." Rose stepped on the gas, only to brake abruptly again a hundred meters later and take a turnoff to the right onto a path that looked just like the first one, lined on either side with crooked oaks and dense, tall gorse bushes. The path wound its way down to the river. At least she was driving more slowly now.

A moment later Rose stopped the car. They couldn't go any farther. The path ended at some big hawthorn bushes, the river shimmering through them. Along with several boats. Boats on their side of the river.

There was no sign of a Citroën Crosser or a Renault Laguna.

They got out without saying anything. In one deft movement, Rose took off her jacket and threw it on the driver's seat. Her SIG Sauer was clearly visible now. Dupin headed for the small footpath among the bushes and trees that led down to the water. Rose followed him.

They reached the bank a few minutes later. There was a slight bend in the river at this point.

There were fifteen boats here, Dupin estimated. Upstream and downstream, scattered at large intervals over a distance of at least a kilometer. Motorboats, a few real motor yachts and sailing boats.

Upstream, about thirty or forty meters away, they saw a stream that meandered down the hillside, widening by a few meters before reaching the estuary. Somewhere beyond that must be the other path leading down from the street to the Vilaine. The third one.

On the riverbank in front of them were five small hard plastic dinghies for ferrying people over to the ships. Not a soul in sight. It was perfectly silent. Not even the gently flowing water was audible.

"It's best if we split up. I'll go downstream, you go upstream. Maybe it was the first path after all—or the third one." Rose's brow furrowed. "Or they're not here at all."

She pulled a second radio out of her trouser pocket: "Here, this is for you."

Dupin took it and turned round. He moved off, not running but moving at a swift pace, his right hand on his gun. His focused gaze swept back and forth between the boats on the river and the dense shrubbery on the left.

He was approaching the mouth of the stream that ended at the Vilaine. Suddenly he saw something dark and metallic shimmering in the shrubbery beyond the estuary. Indistinct. He walked to the water-line. It was easier to make out from here.

Yes. Something dark blue. The roof of a car. That could be it. Without thinking about it, he undid his holster and took out his gun. He kept on walking as he did so, right into the stream, which was deeper than he had anticipated. He was wading through it.

"Commissaire Rose, can you hear me?"

"I'm listening."

"I think I've found the Crosser. The third path on the other side of the stream goes right down to the Vilaine. That's where it is."

"I'll be right with you."

Dupin had reached the other bank of the stream. He set off to the left, keeping close to the undergrowth, gun at the ready.

It was definitely the dark blue Citroën Crosser that belonged to Paul Daeron. Dupin kept going, ducking down instinctively. To the left, a narrow footpath led down to the river, similar to the one where they had parked.

There was nobody here either. Nothing unusual. Dupin turned onto the path. Behind the Crosser there was a second car, so close it was almost touching the bumper of the Citroën. A jet-black car. A Renault Laguna. Registration plate GH 568 PP–44.

They had been right.

Paul Daeron and Céline Cordier were here.

Dupin approached, his gun still at the ready. Suddenly there came the sound of footsteps, muffled but unmistakable. Behind him. With an expert leap, he ducked into the bushes, turning in the air, gun at the ready.

Rose. It was Rose. She was coming up the small path with her gun drawn and her face set. Dupin hadn't counted on her getting to him so quickly. He could tell from her wet trousers that she had taken the direct route through the stream too. She didn't seem to take any notice of the gun trained on her. Dupin didn't lower it till she was practically standing in front of him.

"Where could they be?"

This wasn't really a question.

Rose looked briefly and carefully at one car after the other. There was nothing of interest there. She tried the doors. Both cars were locked.

"There's something over there."

In the long grass part of the way up the path, something flashed. Dupin happened to see it out of the corner of his eye. A few meters away. It was catching the light. He went over.

It was a mobile. A basic, small mobile.

Dupin picked it up. It was switched off.

He turned it on and scrolled through the recent calls. He recognized the first number straightaway: Rose's. Before that were ten other calls, the same number each time, also a mobile number. There was only one other call listed, from 7:24 yesterday. It all fit. Rose was standing next to him now.

"Paul Daeron's prepaid mobile."

What had gone on here?

"Paul Daeron called me from here. That was the phone call earlier. Cordier must have disturbed him. And it must have ended in a struggle."

They searched the stony ground for clues. There was nothing out of the ordinary. No signs of a struggle.

"Let's take a look at the boats as well as we can from shore. I've requested a police boat. The closest harbor is in Pen Lan so it'll take a while. We've got to find out where Paul Daeron's boat is and what kind of boat it is. We can't get hold of his wife right now."

"We should split up again." Dupin could feel how tense he was.

"Farther up there toward the street, there was a small footpath off on the left. Parallel to the Vilaine. There should be a better view from up there."

"I'll walk along the river." Dupin had already set off. "Upstream."

As before, he kept close to the undergrowth. A wild hedgerow, denser and denser bushes, and some knotty oaks stretched almost all the way down as far as the riverbed. It was about another three hundred meters to the very first boats. There was a bend in the river, gentle at first but then a sharp curve.

Suddenly Dupin saw a small green dinghy a little farther upstream, not far from the bank. And as far as he could make out, there was a person there too. It was impossible to say whether it was a man or a woman. He couldn't understand why he was only seeing the boat now.

"Commissaire Rose?"

She came on immediately. Dupin had lowered his voice, so much so that she could barely hear him. "I'm listening."

"I see a green dinghy near the first boats. On our side of the bank. It's blocked by trees in a few places."

"How many people?"

"One, as far as I can tell."

The boat was getting closer and closer to the bank.

"Has the person seen you?"

"I don't know."

"I'll see if I can follow the boat from here."

Dupin walked some way along the exposed patch of muddy, sandy riverbed, although he ran the risk of being spotted. He had to follow the boat. He couldn't lose sight of it. He was getting closer and closer to the shore.

Nothing. He couldn't see it anymore. It had vanished somewhere along the bank, behind trees and shrubs. His radio came on. It was Rose.

"Can you hear me?"

"Perfectly."

"I've got a good view from up here. I don't see a dinghy. But I've just been told what kind of boat Daeron owns. A sailboat. Twelve point eight meters. A Bénéteau. I can just about make out the second boat up ahead. It's a large sailboat, that could be it."

Dupin had stopped and was looking down the river. He could make out a tall mast. Almost thirteen meters was an impressive length. He counted another seven boats in front of it. Three sailboats; they looked smaller. One sailboat was almost directly in front of him, also a Bénéteau. But definitely not 12.8 meters long.

Dupin walked on, closer to the undergrowth on the bank.

Suddenly, out of nowhere, there was a hissing sound. A high-pitched, metallic hiss. A clear sound. The last time he'd heard it was forty-eight hours ago. In the salt marshes two evenings before. A gunshot.

A second one followed immediately. A silencer, just like the day before yesterday. His instinct told him it came from up ahead and to the left. But from quite far away. Dupin fired straight in the direction he suspected the shooter was. Three times. Then he threw himself into the bushes. In an instant, he was squatting down and no longer visible, although his assailant would still know his whereabouts. Dupin held the radio in his left hand and whispered into it. His voice sounded strained.

"I'm being shot at. The shooter is between around fifty and a hundred meters ahead of me, upstream, a little farther away from the bank, I think."

The answer came just as softly. "I'm moving forward. Parallel to the river."

What was going on here? Cordier and Daeron must be in the area, and one of them had shot at him. Probably Cordier. But where was Daeron? Was he under her control?

Dupin walked cautiously onward, through the thick shrubbery close to the bank. One leap and he would be on the bottom of the riverbed.

He put the radio in his pants pocket and looked for some big stones. He found two. He threw the first one underhand as far as he could with the reduced swing. He threw it a few meters to the left and toward the street. He didn't get lucky until the second stone, but the sound wasn't all that loud. He seemed to have hit a tree. Nothing happened.

He took the radio out of his pocket again and whispered, "Throw a few stones. Away from the river."

"Okay."

Dupin kept going. Then he paused.

The radio came on again.

"Boss?"

Unmistakably Riwal.

"Quiet, Riwal, I can't talk right now, *I'm being shot at*," Dupin whispered.

"They've identified the speed trap photo, clearly Madame Cordier. And she was also a competitive shooter when she was a student in Paris. But we haven't found any registered guns. Still, you should be careful, she knows what she's doing."

"Thanks, Riwal!" Dupin almost burst out laughing.

The high-pitched metallic hiss came again. But it seemed to be heading in a different direction. The shot wasn't meant for him.

Another hiss. Then silence again.

Dupin stopped, motionless. A loud gunshot cracked. A SIG Sauer without a silencer. Rose.

The seconds went past. Lengthened. Nothing happened. He assumed nobody had been hit.

If Rose walked down diagonally toward the river now, she probably wouldn't be far from him. He was unsure whether to move. Cordier could be somewhere to the side by now.

"Hello? Hello? I'm here."

The loud call echoed across to him from the water from one of the boats. Not far away. It must have been Paul Daeron, although Dupin couldn't identify the voice.

Dupin was trying to peek through the bushes. His radio came on again, muffled.

"Cordier must be exactly halfway between us. Daeron appears to be unharmed," Rose whispered.

"Cordier must know that backup will be here soon. In fact, the only option she has left is to flee."

He did think Cordier fully capable of another attack, but only if she could be sure her chances of success were realistic. Not as some dramatic showdown. She wasn't desperate. She wouldn't want to die in one final epic battle. The way she had acted during this case had a clear—albeit ruthless and brutal—logic. She wouldn't see the point of dying here. It wasn't clear how far she might get, but she could certainly get out of this situation, she'd be able to figure that much out. The terrain was absolutely vast.

"This is the police. Give yourself up, Madame Cordier." Rose's voice was loud and aggressive. "Put down your weapon and come out with your hands up."

Dupin thought it over briefly, but decided to remain hidden. Even Rose herself had to be speaking from her hiding place right now.

"We will not hesitate to shoot. It's over—you're out of options."

Again, no response. Nothing. For the first few minutes, images from Wednesday evening had raced through Dupin's head. Images from when he was standing in the pool, then in the hut. The powerlessness, the helplessness, and yes, even the humiliation. Someone had shot him; it had been close. His profound, burning rage returned.

It wasn't going to happen to him again. He wouldn't allow himself to be cornered again.

The radio came on.

"I can see a green dinghy just a few meters away from the bank. It should almost be where you are. It's probably the one from earlier. But it looks empty."

"Could be a distraction technique. Or a trap. And she wants us to reveal ourselves." Dupin was less than half a meter from the riverbed.

Suddenly he could see the small green dinghy too. Just four or five meters away. It was drifting in the current. Moving more quickly than he would have expected. He couldn't see anyone either.

The hard plastic boats weren't long, but they were quite deep. A slim woman could be lying flat on the bottom inside it.

Yes, it could be a trap.

But he would take the risk.

As quick as a flash, he stood up halfway, enough to be able to get a look into the boat.

Empty. It was empty. The only thing in it was half a plastic bottle for bailing out water.

Dupin took cover again immediately. He needed to think. Think hard.

If Cordier had been watching all of this, and there must have been some point to the maneuver, then she must know where he was now. He picked up the radio. "The boat's empty."

"She just wanted to know where we are. Get a handle on the whole situation. She wants to escape. We can't see anything when we're hiding."

This was true. But if they gave up their cover and Cordier was in a good position, they would be offering her some easy targets.

Suddenly it hit Dupin. Something had occurred to him. Maybe it was crazy—but this could be it. Cordier was sophisticated. It would be a clever move. He thought she was capable of it. And if he was right—then he needed to act immediately. Even if acting would be highly risky. He wouldn't wait helplessly again. Not this time.

"Give me covering fire. Right on the bank. Try to stay reasonably well hidden. Now!"

"What are you planning to do?"

Dupin had already dropped the radio.

With one huge leap he jumped out of the undergrowth and onto the hard sand of the riverbed. He went straight into a sprint, his gun in his right hand. Everything was happening at top speed.

His sprint ended in line with the dinghy and he ran into the water. It was up to his knees, and then, visible through the milky water, the water suddenly got deeper. The channel.

The green plastic boat was about three meters away from him. The SIG Sauer was trained firmly on the empty boat.

"Madame Cordier," Dupin said loudly, his voice deep, penetrating, firm, "drop the gun immediately."

He stared at the empty boat. "I'm going to shoot. The bullets will penetrate through the plastic. Three, two . . ."

Before he could count "one," something black flew through the air from behind the boat and made a loud splash as it hit the water. A pistol.

Every possible course of action was pointless. Cordier knew it. She had no cover and couldn't see Dupin. And he would have opened fire. Without hesitation. She had known that too.

It was over.

A moment later, he saw two hands grasp the back wall of the boat.

"That's good. Maneuver the boat onto land."

It had been a brilliant idea. Cordier was not in the boat—she was behind it. In the water. She must have got into the river by the thicket in front of them, setting the dinghy she had used earlier expertly into the current. Swimming, invisible to Dupin and Rose. If her plan had worked, she would have let herself drift farther down the river and would have got away.

Dupin was still standing in the same position, his gun trained on the place where her head had to be behind the wall of the boat. But now the boat was moving unmistakably in the direction of the bank. Two or three seconds later, Dupin grabbed it. He held it fast.

"Come on." His tone was harsh.

Céline Cordier appeared round the left-hand side of the boat.

She stood up slowly. Totally self-assured. The water was up to her waist. With provocatively measured steps, she walked to the bank. Her white T-shirt and jeans were covered in greenish mud. Still not saying a word. A clear, determined look in her amber eyes. Dupin let go of the boat, keeping the gun still firmly trained on her.

"That's it, Madame Cordier. That's how this ends."

She looked at him. Frankly. Fearlessly. Calmly. For a moment their gazes locked.

"How did you find out? How did you end up here?" Her voice was clear too, firm, determined. No drama. She was genuinely interested.

"That's unimportant. All that counts is that we're here."

Dupin heard footsteps behind him. He didn't turn around. A moment later Rose appeared, her gun already back in the holster on her belt. But her handcuffs were open.

"I'm arresting you for the murder of Lilou Breval—and for the suspected murder of Maxime Daeron. And for the attempted murder of Commissaire Georges Dupin." Rose was standing right in front of her.

Cordier held her arms out without being asked. Rose put the handcuffs on in just a few deft movements. Her gaze met Cordier's briefly. Dupin saw a flicker in Rose's eyes.

Then Rose turned toward the river. "Monsieur Paul Daeron—this is Commissaire Rose from the Commissariat de Police Guérande.

Come out of your hiding place. A police boat will be here any moment and will bring you over to us."

It took a moment for a head to appear abruptly above the railing of a motorboat twenty meters upstream, much closer than Dupin had thought it would be. The head was followed by the rest of Paul Daeron. He made a hand signal to show he had understood everything.

The radio handset came on. "We're with you, Commissaire. There's a team in every dead end."

Excellent. Good timing.

"Arrest successful. Everything is secure."

"Good. We'll come to you. Over."

Rose stashed the radio away in her pants pocket.

Four police officers came running toward them from the small path next to the stream.

Madame Cordier made no move to say anything. She looked around, calm; defiantly calm. And superior.

Dupin had so many questions. Questions only she could answer. But he felt extremely reluctant to ask her. He knew asking her would give her some satisfaction. And she knew she mustn't say anything, not one word.

The police officers came running over to them.

"Take her away. To the commissariat. I'll question her there. She's going to want to speak to her lawyer."

There was a smile on Cordier's face. Just a hint of one, but Rose must have noticed it. She paused for a moment. Looking Madame Cordier right in the eye. Penetratingly. Then, out of nowhere, a smile spread across Commissaire Rose's face. A frank smile. A smile of victory that wasn't even particularly meant for Madame Cordier. How must she have felt. It didn't get more brutal than that.

"Do you know why murderers do it all? They think they'll get away with it. But they don't get away with it. *You* didn't."

Rose's voice could not have been icier. Without pathos or aggression. It was a sentence that restored order. And made Madame Cordier into nothing more than an exemplary aberration. An eradicated aberration. Dupin understood these words. Profoundly. Deep down inside.

The police boat had now come level with where they were on the river. The captain had seen them and was standing on deck with a megaphone. He was in the process of mooring by the motorboat Daeron was hiding on.

"We'll bring him over to you now."

Dupin walked a few steps along the waterline. He took a deep breath. He closed his eyes, held his breath for a few seconds, breathed out hard, and opened his eyes again. He half turned and saw four police officers surround Madame Cordier and head for the small path where the cars were parked.

* * *

A dinghy brought Paul Daeron across and then went straight back to its mothership. The captain asked whether they still needed him—but everything was done. The police boat, majestic and gleaming in the evening sunlight, was already turning around.

They were alone with Paul Daeron.

They would go to their car soon too. Paul Daeron was stooped, his gaze vacant as he stared at the silty ground. The sun was coloring the river a metallic orange. The silence was absolute.

"It's all my fault. I made a terrible mistake. Lots of terrible mistakes."

He looked utterly exhausted. Broken. Even worse than this morning. This was no pretense. This was familiar to Dupin, the moment when people began to talk. Finally needed to talk.

"Maxime had this . . . this disastrous idea. With Céline Cordier.

Yes, maybe it was their joint idea really. I don't know. I wasn't involved at that stage. A green algae repellent. It was intended to be used in the affected areas. They both sat on one of those committees where algae kept on coming up." Riwal's theory had been correct. "At first it was just a vague idea to my brother, I think. Completely and utterly insane. Céline Cordier said it was doable. Then they got more and more caught up in it. Maxime saw it as the chance of a lifetime. And that there were millions to be made. It was his chance to turn everything around. He was so naïve. At some point he came to me, as always. He asked me for money. He openly told me why he needed it. He told me everything. I said no. I . . . I tried to talk him out of it. I told him it was illegal. But . . ." He broke off for a second, breathing shallowly. "But I didn't do anything. And Céline Cordier was fanatical from the beginning. She never considered going to a research laboratory with it, she always said they'd just steal the idea. And that it would take years to get a license—if they ever did get one—and that she didn't believe in it. She knew the procedures, knew how things worked. I should have realized then how ruthless she was. At some point it became clear to me that she would stop at nothing, but by then it was too late. She could be convincing. Very convincing. She tried to explain everything to me in forensic detail. But I said no. Then my brother decided he wanted to sell his salt marshes to Le Sel. To get his hands on some money. They needed money. Quite a lot of it. Céline Cordier didn't have much, but she invested all she had." Daeron wasn't easy to understand, he was speaking so softly and monotonously. "Then I gave Maxime ninety thousand euro because I didn't want him to sell the salt marshes. That was crazy. I never believed their plan would be successful. I made a terrible mistake. I should have ended it immediately. Céline Cordier wanted me to be in on it. So that I would be putting everything I had at stake too. Everything, everything. I should have seen then how far she would go. But how . . . Who could know that everything would get out of hand like this? She pressed ahead with everything. Organized it all with military precision. Maxime soon didn't have a role anymore. She . . . could only think about her own profit. Not about anything or anyone else. And she thinks that's her right. Her God-given right. Maxime was a sidekick. Still, I . . . I was even more naïve than Maxime, much worse, unforgivably so, I should have—"

Daeron broke off again. He turned toward the river and looked at the sluggish but ever-flowing dark green water. Only now did Dupin notice the usual river smell, the brackish water.

"Maxime . . . I always wanted to do things right, and I did it all wrong. Somehow he could never get his act together. Not that he didn't try. He always tried. Again and again. He was serious about it. But he never saw it through." Paul raised his voice slightly. "He always threw it away. His whole life. He always seemed like such a strong character, but that was deceptive. Everything he tried, it failed, every time. And then, then he'd come to me. Always. To me. And I never said anything. I always sorted things out for him. I just wanted him to have a good life."

It all sounded awful. Unfathomably horrible. Maxime Daeron had seemed so confident. This was a harrowing tale, Dupin felt. And, as sincere as his elder brother sounded—the "successful brother," who had achieved everything—it didn't take away from how awful it was. It must have been brutal for Maxime Daeron. And tragic. Besides: nothing could free Paul Daeron of his responsibility after the fact; he was aware of that himself. He had *not* acted when he heard what Cordier and his brother had planned—he had even got involved in a highly illegal project. He went along with it, enabling everything that had ended up so horrendously for his brother.

"It was the same in his professional life as his personal life. His marriage. It all fell apart."

"How far had you actually got with the algae repellent?" Dupin had had enough of the fateful brothers' tale.

"It was as good as ready. Céline Cordier wanted to complete the final testing by the end of the summer. She said she was already in serious talks with several firms outside France. About selling it. The finished formula—its illegal origins wouldn't be clear from looking at it. The companies could then get the license themselves, register the patent, and produce it completely legally."

"How did Lilou Breval come to stand in your way? What happened the evening before last?"

Daeron's gaze was still fixed on the water, which was getting more and more intensely orange by the minute.

"She found out something from a phone call between my brother and Céline Cordier. Something vague. But enough that it was clear to her that something underhanded was going on. She picked up something about the barrels they used to get the microorganisms to the salt marshes. The microorganisms and also the algae. She brought it up with my brother. He denied everything. She didn't believe him. They argued." He looked at Dupin for the very first time, with an expression of profound resignation. "Everything he told you about it is true—as is everything I told you in our conversation this morning." He turned back to the water. "Lilou Breval then tried to find out more under her own steam. She failed, but she didn't let up. On Tuesday she took my brother to task again and threatened to go to the police. I think she was worried about him. That he had got caught up in something. That's when I told him he had to end the project. Maxime panicked. He called Céline Cordier and told her about Lilou Breval's threat."

Paul Daeron stopped. At first Dupin thought it was just a brief pause. But Paul Daeron remained silent and motionless.

"And then? Go on," Dupin said brusquely. He realized he had been feeling more and more on edge as Daeron spoke. He didn't care.

Rose kept her eyes fixed on Paul Daeron the entire time, and it was impossible to tell what she was thinking. She hadn't said a word yet. She seemed to want to leave it up to Dupin.

"My brother would never have done anything to Lilou Breval, never. Céline Cordier was furious. They were going to suspend testing for the time being. She and my brother drove to the salt marshes on Wednesday evening. They were going to dispose of all the evidence, including the barrels at the pool. And drain the water out. Everything. Then," he hesitated for a moment and turned back to Dupin, "then you arrived. Maxime didn't even know that Céline Cordier had a gun. She just opened fire. He told me everything later that night."

"It was always that blind pool"—this was a practical inquiry from Rose—"the experiments were only ever carried out there?"

"Yes. Only there."

Dupin wanted to return to the crux of the story.

"Did—" He hesitated uncertainly. "Did your brother know that Céline Cordier was going to drive over to Lilou Breval's?"

"No. It never even crossed his mind. She told him she was going to a party. To have an alibi for the evening. And that he needed one too. He found out about Lilou's death the next day, from the radio. And collapsed. When we met you that morning, we still didn't know anything. We thought all that had happened was that shooting in the salt marshes."

This was plausible, of course. But it would all be difficult to reconstruct. They would listen to what Cordier had to say. If she said anything.

"He called me late that night. After he had been to Lilou Breval's house. He was out of his mind. He told her everything that night. And said that they had called off the experiment. That he was done with it. That he had made a terrible mistake."

"But Cordier didn't know anything about that, did she? That he was at Lilou's?"

"She suspected it. Or at least that he was going to tell Lilou something."

"And you? What did you say that night? What needed to be done following the shooting? You were involved in the whole thing, after all."

Paul Daeron seemed close to a total breakdown. "Everything got out of hand, horrendously out of hand."

"Go on. Why did your brother not react when he heard about Lilou Breval's death—why didn't you? Why didn't the two of you end it all there? Turn yourselves in? You must both have suspected that it was Céline Cordier."

Dupin was getting more and more enraged. Perhaps unfairly.

"It was awful, you know." Paul Daeron's face hardened, his voice lost all its strength. "Our entire existence was suddenly at stake. Everything would have been destroyed. My life. Everything I'd worked for. My company. My wife and daughter's lives would have been ruined too. The lives of people who had nothing to do with any of it. I thought . . ." He spoke flatly. "I . . . I was a coward. It was only this afternoon that I found the courage to do what I should have done on Wednesday night. Rather than waiting till after . . . after the . . . the death of my brother."

"What were you planning to do? Why did you want to meet Madame Cordier?"

"I wanted to confront her and defend myself. I called her this afternoon. She threatened to blame it all on me because I donated the money. She said she had destroyed everything and that nobody would find anything at her home. She said she had an idea, and that we should have a quick chat before I did something I'd regret, that we should meet up. That it could all still work out okay."

"Didn't you think that a meeting with her might be dangerous? In such a secluded place? You knew she was a murderer."

"I didn't care. I had to speak to her. End everything face-to-face. Here, on my turf."

Dupin understood. Besides, on its face, it would be rather stupid of Cordier to commit another murder. The chances of there being some kind of clue leading to her would be even greater.

"And here? What happened here?"

"She was half an hour late. I almost drove off again. She tried to calm me down. She spoke about it as if we were having technical difficulties. She said that if neither of us talked, nobody would ever dream we were tangled up in it. Then at some point the police would hit a wall, and have to lay the blame for the algae project and the murder at Maxime's door—and that due to my brother's suicide they would file all of this away as a tragic love story at some point. And that, so long as we pulled ourselves together, we had every chance of getting away with it. She was as cold as ice. She said we should live as though none of it had happened."

It could all have worked out. It could have happened like that; Cordier's plan could really have come off.

"When I heard her saying that, I knew I finally needed to act." His voice broke again, but his next sentence sounded more certain and strong than any of his previous ones. "I knew I could never do that—that I could never live like that, as if it hadn't happened. I told her it was over. That it was all over. Irrevocably so. And that I had wanted to tell her so to her face myself." Paul Daeron balled his hands into fists. "I left her standing there, walked back to my car, and called you. Suddenly she was standing in front of me and wrenching the phone out of my hand. She was beside herself. We wrestled briefly but I was able to get away and throw myself into the undergrowth. I know every last stone around here. I ran down to the river. From my hiding place in the undergrowth I could see she had a gun. I managed to swim over to a boat up there by the thicket, I . . ." His voice failed. Paul Daeron stood frozen, silent tears running down his face.

Rose took a step closer to him. She spoke softly. "Your brother's death wasn't suicide."

Paul Daeron didn't react. It was as if he hadn't even heard what she had said. It was a bizarre scene. He closed his eyes. Still motionless.

So that was it. That was the story. The story as Paul Daeron had observed it. As distorted as that might be. There were still a lot of details missing—things that might never be known.

But even if the story was incomplete and not everything corresponded to the truth, that was—broadly speaking—what had happened. Maxime Daeron might have told a different story. And he too would have been totally sincere. He might not have been able to stand the story they had just heard. And even Céline Cordier would— if she talked—express her own "truth." It was always like this: the "complete" and "objective" story of a case was never told. Dupin was no stranger to this. During the reconstruction, the case became a ghost. As a reality, it disintegrated, falling apart into various subjective stories which, the more they were told, discussed, and even "confessed" to, had less and less to do with one another. But that didn't matter. For a moment, Dupin had seen the crux of it. And crucially: they had arrested the perpetrators. What came after that was not his job. He could have an impact so long as there was something to be investigated, and make sure to restore order. Make sure that at least some people didn't get away with their plan of just walking away.

"Let's go, Monsieur Daeron. I'm hereby arresting you for illegal business activity, several serious environmental offenses, and being an accessory to the murder of Lilou Breval. In the commissariat you will give your account again for the record, in chronological order, down to the last detail," Rose said, and waited until Paul Daeron slowly turned away from the water. The sun hung low on the horizon, a yellow bar shimmered at them over the gleaming orange of the river. Around the sun, the horizon was a menacing fire, and only gradually, far up in the sky, did it drift into a blue that became more and more delicate. And there, faint and far away, the first stars were visible.

* * *

They had already passed the town boundaries of Guérande. Rose had driven only slightly more slowly than she had on the way there. Paul sat next to her, without handcuffs, while Dupin sat in the back. They hadn't exchanged a word since they'd set off. Rose had made a few phone calls and barked various terse orders, including that the blind pool and the adjacent salt marshes would remain sealed off, that extensive biological and biochemical testing would now follow, in order to analyze the ramifications of the experiments very carefully. Dupin's mobile rang and rang, forlornly. He hadn't even looked at the incoming numbers. He was—alone on the backseat—oddly absent; he couldn't even have said that he was truly thinking. Or what about.

They were just at the rotary on the main street, at the turnoff to the salt marshes. Rose was driving toward the commissariat building that Dupin hadn't even been to once over the past two days. Céline Cordier would be in one of the interrogation rooms there by now. There were dozens of important things to be done. But not by him.

"Commissaire Rose—could you let me out here, please? I . . ."

Dupin didn't finish the sentence. Rose tried to meet his gaze in the rearview mirror for a moment. And—he wasn't sure if he was imagining this—she smiled briefly. As though she had been expecting this and was in complete agreement.

Instead of answering, she eased off on the gas and pulled to the right-hand side.

"Your car is parked at the Centre." Dupin would have had to

think hard about that. His car had been parked in so many different places during this case. "Should I ask someone to drive you there?"

"I'll call my inspectors."

Paul Daeron didn't even seem to be aware of their conversation.

Dupin opened the door and got out.

"Speak soon." There was a definite smile on Rose's face now.

"Speak soon."

Dupin slammed the door shut. Commissaire Rose drove off moments later. He had no idea what she meant by "speak soon"—or what he'd meant when he said it back.

Dupin walked back to the turnoff for the Route des Marais.

He had arrived here around this time the evening before yesterday. Dupin took his mobile out of his pocket. Before the connection even established, he saw a sign. The same sign they had seen at the picnic area: LONG LOOP with the addition CENTRE DU SEL (20 MIN).

Dupin only hesitated for a few seconds. Before putting his mobile away again.

He followed the path that led to the "long loop." At first he walked past a few houses, across a field. Then, strangely quickly, without warning, the path went straight into the salt marshes. Into that crazy, wonderful world, that bizarre shadowy kingdom with its dwarves, fairies, white virgins, and dragons. Where the whole story had begun. The sun had just disappeared beyond the horizon. For the first time in weeks, clouds appeared. Out of nowhere. Thick, sharp-edged, cotton-wool clouds were arranged at regular intervals like battalions marching past. The rays from the sun that had just gone down were still making their way toward them. Even in the west, the sky may now have been dark blue again and the orange stripes above the horizon very narrow, but around their edges, the clouds seemed to have absorbed every single shade of the spectacular phenomenon: lilac, pink, magenta, violet, orange. Their huge forms still shone bright white. They were eerily reflected in the salt marshes' tangle of metallic blue pools, seeming to shine of their own accord. They looked like mystical mirrors of the sky. To the right, close to the path, there was a group of tall white pyramids of salt. Twelve or maybe fifteen of them in a row. Like strange monuments, illuminated signs. And suddenly the beguiling smell was there again too. Dupin felt the taste of rich clay, salt, iodine, and violet in his mouth.

He didn't walk particularly quickly. He wasn't in any rush. Not anymore.

His mobile rang. Reluctantly, he checked the number. He knew he couldn't just go to ground; there were still a few things to do, and some of them would need to be done by him. When he saw the number he was glad. Very glad. Nolwenn.

"Bravo, Monsieur le Commissaire."

It was wonderful to hear her voice. It felt like there had never been any other case during his career in Brittany so far when he had spoken to her so little.

"Inspector Kadeg has brought me up to speed on everything."

Of course.

"On the main things at least. You can tell me the details. Come back from your excursion first, in your own time. Come back home." By her standards, Nolwenn was speaking with great emotion.

"You were right from the beginning. You were obsessed with the blue barrels! And that was it! The *point magique*! You had an idée fixe that nothing in the world could distract you from, you were stubborn—a real Breton!"

Dupin didn't quite know what to say. But this was definitely a compliment.

"And then you hunted them down!" The satisfaction in Nolwenn's voice was almost macabre.

"Commissaire Rose and I did. We did it together."

"I heard. Who would have thought it?!—However: *a bep liv, marc'h mat—a bep bro, tud vat.* There are good horses in every color, good people in every area. That's how it is."

She had said this cheerfully. Dupin wouldn't immediately have thought of a horse when he thought of Rose. But even this was meant as a huge compliment, he knew that.

There was a mysterious pause, which wasn't Nolwenn's style at all. There was never anything like this between them.

Then he realized what she wanted to say. "I've got to call him. I know."

"Whom do you have to call?" It was perfectly acted.

"The prefect."

"Oh no. You won't be able to speak to him. But he's aware the case is over, don't worry. And he has negotiated with Préfet Trottet that they won't appear in front of the press officially until tomorrow. He and Trottet are doing it together. You're aware of course: that big hundred-and-fifty-year celebration of the railway is on in Quimper this evening. He's the president of the Amis des Chemins de Fer. The big speech this evening. I'll be headed there myself soon."

Of course. It had been a hot topic for weeks. Dupin had even received a VIP invitation. Along with every other commissaire in Finistère. And lots of emails, daily in the last week, always ending with the firm wording: "You are expected." A hundred and fifty years ago this September, the railway line between the "metropolis" and the "province" had been launched with a fancy party. The very first train from Paris arrived into Quimper. At 8:20. After an endless seventeen-hour-and-twenty-minute journey. The newspapers had been full of articles and historic photographs for weeks. A dirty, small black steam engine was visible, a genuine art nouveau railway station: the perfect idyll of a model railway facility. But Dupin had learned that—unlike today—people hadn't felt euphoria back then; on the contrary. The "*karrigell an ankou*," the carriage of death, "a stupid black monster that gives off smoke"—an "intruder who purports to be a friend" the comments had read. Dupin had only understood it once he'd read what had been written by the then state secretary for the ministry of defense in a confidential memo about the project—which the papers were going to town on: "A railway line between France and Brittany will teach the Bretons French in ten years, it's more sustainable than the most skilled teachers we could send out there. This alone justifies the cost in the millions!" That had been the declared state aim: make Breton disappear. And not just the language—their entire cultural identity. The railway was to communicate the "ideas of civilization," or in other words: "civilize the barbarians." That sounded almost funny today, but it had been deadly serious. Only people who knew stories like this had a chance of understanding the Breton soul, the issues with the "central government," the deeply conflicted feelings toward Paris and toward what Paris represented. Of course it had turned out very differently from what the state secretary had anticipated. The Bretons had made the smoking black monster theirs and turned the tables. Dupin suspected that this was the secret reason for the scale of the celebrations today. That they had showed the world. Yet again.

"I'm so glad you were able to close the case in time. This way there's a better atmosphere. For the party." Nolwenn sounded serious again and Dupin laughed out loud.

"You've got to get going, Nolwenn. We'll . . . talk soon."

"Oh yes. The prefect is expecting your call tomorrow morning at seven o'clock. He also asked me to pass on a message: 'Well done, *mon Commissaire.*'"

It did him good to return to his everyday life with its rituals. Even the prefect's sayings, which usually made Dupin feel a white-hot rage, almost felt soothing. But perhaps that was just because he didn't need to speak to him in person today.

"I'll be in touch."

Dupin hung up.

He took a deep breath.

He dialed Riwal's number.

"Boss?"

"Where are you?"

"We're at the hotel. Inspector Kadeg and I. Commissaire Rose said we—"

"Go home, Riwal. You and Kadeg. They've got everything under control."

"Are you sure, boss?"

"I'm sure. That's an order. See you on Monday."

"You don't need us tomorrow either?"

"Tomorrow is Saturday. You wanted to go to the Glénan with your wife to go fishing. The September sea bream. Your boat."

Riwal and his wife had been given a used Bénéteau by their parents and parents-in-law for their wedding last year (7.8 meters!), and it meant the world to Riwal. He had remarked at the beginning of the week that it was the last weekend of the summer; he greeted this forecast with the same offhanded certainty with which he might say the sun would rise in the west tomorrow morning. As a fact.

"All right, boss. That was a tough case."

Riwal had phrased this second sentence in his typical fundamentally mysterious tone of voice. Dupin knew he wasn't expecting a reply.

* * *

It was only the conspicuous signs for the nature trail that prevented Dupin getting lost in the twilight and the tangled labyrinth of the salt marshes. Ten minutes later he had reached the Centre du Sel. He approached it from the place where the "small" and "large" loops forked. Off to the side was the picturesque picnic spot where they had had their discussion that afternoon. That already felt like days ago, not hours.

His car was in the parking lot. Right at the entrance. On Monday his dearly beloved XM would be back and—he was also pleased about this—it would be his last journey in the tiny Peugeot.

He walked toward the car. At first he wasn't sure. Someone was leaning against the door. Then he recognized her. The hands in the jacket pockets, the thumbs outside. Relaxed. Yet very serious.

She smiled at him.

"A walk in the evening air. Be careful—during the harvest, the aromas can bedazzle you. You have the craziest hallucinations. You see and dream the most fantastical things."

"Oh, yes."

Dupin would have liked to have a wittier answer ready.

"I tried to speak to Cordier for the first time. She's not saying anything. Her lawyer is on his way. We're searching her laboratory now. Her computer. Her mobile. We're going to find something."

Dupin had no doubt about that. Something had crossed his mind, something he ought to have asked Cordier at the river just now.

"Why did she call me from Lilou Breval's mobile? The morning after she killed her?"

"She probably wanted to know who Lilou had called, her last conversations—to find out whether she had really spoken to the police."

"Yes."

That sounded like a good explanation. He'd been thinking along these lines too. But strangely it didn't give him any comfort. With hindsight there was something sinister about the call. Something chilling.

"I wanted to bring you something. I was in Lilou's house again; my parents' house is very close by and that's where I'm staying to-night."

Dupin had thought so. Rose came from the gulf herself. That's why she knew everything and everyone here: Madame Clothilde, the women on the ferry, the waitress in Le San Francisco . . .

"I think you should have this." She drew a small notebook out of the right-hand pocket of her jacket and held it out to him. Without explanation.

He took it. Leafed through it.

It was a calendar. From the last year. With one dog-eared corner.

Dupin turned a few of the pages. Handwritten entries. Meetings and comments on the meetings that looked like they had been noted down afterward.

"The dog-ear was me. Look."

It was the twelfth of May: "8:00—Georges Dupin/At home." Next to that were a few hastily scribbled words. Very nice evening! A crazy one. Lovely. See often.

Lilou. It was Lilou's calendar. The entry for their meeting last year.

Dupin could feel goose bumps. Before he could even say anything, Rose turned around and walked to her car. She waited until she had the door open before looking back one last time.

"I've got to get back. They're waiting."

"Thanks." Dupin's voice was firm and clear.

The "thanks" was for the book. And for so much more besides.

"Thank you."

Dupin realized she had understood.

"We'll be seeing more of each other, Monsieur le Commissaire. Wind and sun permitting."

A moment later she was in the car and starting the engine. The Renault jolted forward and positively flew out of the parking lot.

* * *

Dupin switched on his engine and began to turn around.

Out of the corner of his eye he saw the young woman who had served him at the boutique counter yesterday in the Centre du Sel. She was by herself. The Centre was long since closed. It looked like she was rearranging the shop window, absorbed in her work.

In the middle of the reversing maneuver, Dupin stepped on the brake. It had occurred to him yesterday and it would have been inappropriate then. But now . . .

He stopped right outside the entrance. He got out and knocked on the glass panel in the door.

The young woman noticed him—without the slightest surprise, it seemed—and came toward him. She pressed a button next to the sliding door so that it instantly slid open without a sound.

"Yes?"

She was just as taciturn as yesterday.

"I'd like to buy something, please. In the shop."

He knew it sounded clumsy.

"Okay."

She turned around and went back to the window display.

Dupin walked straight into the boutique.

There were a lot of things displayed in not much space. His gaze wandered around. Right ahead and to the left was the salt. Dozens of kinds. Including one that had caught Dupin's eye yesterday: an assortment of three kinds of *fleur de sel*. *Fleur de sel à l'aneth et au citron* (for seafood and fish), *fleur de sel au piment d'Espelette* (for meat and poultry), and *fleur de sel nature* (for foie gras, grilled food, salad, vegetables). Excellent. And then three colorful little ceramic bowls. He would get these for Claire. He picked everything up and moved toward the cash register. The young woman seemed to have been watching him. They met there. He paid.

A short time later, the little old Peugeot was finally moving off. He left the Centre du Sel, the magic White Land, drove through the magnificent little town of Guérande one more time, crossed the Vilaine near La Roche-Bernard, and reached the gulf for the last time.

To the left of the Route Express, in the dying dark blue light from the west, he could see an offshoot of the little sea. A mysterious shimmering. That had been Lilou's home. Her gulf.

Dupin glanced quickly at the passenger seat. There it was—Lilou's little calendar. At some point he would drive to her house again. And sit on the large stone right by the water, in front of her enchanted garden. To reminisce and to think of her. From there, he'd go out looking for the little penguins; they must be somewhere round there.

Dupin had switched on the radio. Bleu Breizh. Skippy had been appointed an honorary citizen by the mayor of Arradon. And not only that: the wood that was Skippy's new home would soon officially be known as "L'Australie." The residents had made it known they wouldn't mind if the kangaroo were to eat a lettuce from their vegetable beds occasionally. One woman had even found out what Skippy most liked to eat—for the next planting season. The last sighting had been in the afternoon. At a clearing. Skippy had been seen sunbathing. Apparently. Things were looking good for Skippy.

Dupin ran a hand through his hair. He would be in Vannes soon. He'd be halfway there then. He could feel how exhausted he was. It was the absurd stress of the last few days.

* * *

Dupin parked the car in the big parking lot at the front of the harbor, by the Ville Close. Outside the Amiral, where he always parked.

He didn't go into the restaurant straightaway. He was hungry, but he wanted to stretch his legs a little first.

He walked slowly along the stone quay away from the parking lot. To the left was the sea, the bay with the Port de Plaisance, to the right were the vast squares and the row of old fishermen's houses behind. Everything was bathed in the warm yellow light of the streetlamps that made the harbor area look like a backdrop from some gorgeous old film at night. The sky had turned a blackish purple and bathed the sea in the same shade—here and there yellow buoys peeked up out of it. Now and again a buoy emerged fully. There was a chill in the air now. It wasn't cold, but it was very brisk. This wasn't a mild summer's evening anymore.

Dupin loved this walk. It was amongst his most important rituals, best taken early in the morning or at night, like now, no matter the season or weather. He walked on the shaky wooden planks and pontoons right onto the old town's island, fortified with enormous defensive walls, the impregnable Ville Close where the footbridge abruptly ended. Spotlights had been set in the brattices underneath the battlements, making the walls blaze dramatically. Like in a huge, sublime open-air theater; the fortress completed by the star builder to the sun king—Sébastian Le Prestre de Vauban—was very impressive. The light fell down the enormous stone walls the way tar had once done. Above, dozens of lamps installed close together traced out a bright line that could be seen even from out at sea, many kilometers away, a daring symbol.

Dupin walked along the footbridge at the harbor, through a group of boats of all shapes and sizes. The sailboats' gently swaying masts stretched boldly into the darkness. The little bells attached to the tops of the masts created an ethereal concert that filled the whole harbor area on summer nights. He could even hear it from his apartment round the corner when the door to the narrow terrace was open. He and his father had always played a game when they were at the seaside in the summer holidays. They looked for the most marvelous boats in the harbor and told each other where they would set sail for in them. What great journeys they'd make in them. The adventures to be had on them.

Dupin paused at the end of the footbridge. He folded his hands behind his head and tipped his head back briefly. He would go and eat something now. And call Claire. And perhaps Rose, to find out whether Céline had confessed. Dupin turned and looked at the lights of the town.

Suddenly a smile appeared on his face, spreading right across it. He'd had an idea. He dug out his phone and dialed.

It took a while. Then she answered.

"Claire?"

"Georges? I"—she sounded sleepy, worn out—"I'd already gone to bed, it was chaos in the hospital today. I'd so hoped you'd call at some point. How's your case going?"

"I just wanted to tell you I'm bringing brioche and croissants for breakfast."

"You're . . . what?"

"I'm taking the six o'clock train. You sleep in and I'll wake you with breakfast."

"Really?"

"Really. Now go back to sleep."

"Okay."

She was too tired to question anything.

"See you soon then, Georges."

"See you soon."

Dupin hung up.

It was a brilliant idea. And on Monday it would be fine for him to be back at eleven. He would book the table in La Palette for tomorrow evening. The table they should have had on Claire's birthday. And they'd go for a walk in the Jardin du Luxembourg. On the first autumn day of the year.

And now, now he would go into the Amiral. And eat the sole he had wanted to eat in Le Croisic. Fried to a golden brown in salted butter. Salt from the White Land, the finest in the world.

Everything was going to be all right.

Acknowledgments

My dear Don Rinaldo "Che," my dear Reinhold Joppich, thank you. Thank you very much. For everything.

TURN THE PAGE FOR A SNEAK PEEK AT
JEAN-LUC BANNALEC'S NEXT NOVEL

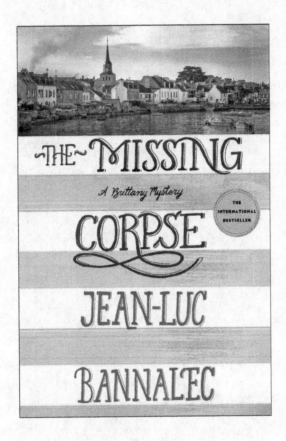

AVAILABLE APRIL 2019

TURN THE PAGE FOR A SNEAK PEEK AT
JEAN-LUC BANNALEC'S NEXT NOVEL

AVAILABLE APRIL 2019

The First Day

He was the biggest of the lot. He gave a loud cry. Brisk. Monosyllabic. His head craned arrogantly upward. The vigorous cry was to a buddy who peeped out from behind a rocky ledge and was now rushing over. It was cold, around zero degrees, and the air smelled of damp ice.

Commissaire Georges Dupin from the Commissariat de Police Concarneau was standing directly in front of him, not unimpressed. In spite of the fuss he was making, the figure opposite him really was imposing, and he was at least a meter tall.

A black head, piercing brown eyes, a black throat. Bright yellowish-orange patches on the back of his head. A long, elegant bill, dark on the top, a deep orange on the bottom. His chest a garish yellowish orange with radiant white below; his back shimmering from nape to tail, a silvery slate gray. Like the flippers. His feet and legs, on the other hand, were also jet-black. The king penguin was an exquisite spectacle: royal.

By this point, his buddy, who was a little shorter than him, had joined him. Dupin knew that individual penguins could reliably recognize each other by their voices.

Suddenly they both began to cry out in a curt, clipped way. Threatening cries. Unmistakable. For a moment Dupin had thought the cries were meant for him. But he was mistaken. Three of his favorite penguins were standing on the other side of the ledge in the snow-covered Arctic pavilion: gentoo penguins who, along with a group of southern rockhopper penguins, made up the largest penguin colony in Europe here in the Océanopolis in Brest. It was why Dupin, the penguin lover, made a detour here every few months, whenever he was near Brest. Today he was with Henri, who had become his best friend in his "new hometown," a fellow ex-Parisian who had found his great love and happiness at the End of the World more than two decades before. "Everything begins at the End of the World," was what people said: *"Tout commence au Finistère."* One of the Breton sayings that got straight to the heart of things: this was what people thought and felt here.

Commissaire Dupin was on his way to a police training seminar in Brest, which unfortunately was part of his "promotion," and on top of everything else, he still didn't know what exactly the promotion meant. Officially speaking, he was no longer the chief commissaire but the "supervising commissaire," although as far back as anyone could remember, there had only been one commissaire in the Commissariat de Police Concarneau anyway. A very modest commissariat, yet it was the only one in France that, according to a never-checked claim, had a panoramic view of the sea. And also of the old town in the large harbor with its enormous fortress walls. A very modest commissariat, but one whose "regional jurisdiction" had expanded bit by bit in recent years—with every retirement of a commissaire in the neighboring districts and the serious financial difficulties in the public budget. Dupin's promotion had almost coincided with his fifth anniversary of working in Brittany. During the "ceremonial" phone call, the prefect had murmured something about "not bad" and that it was "a reasonably good job" that Dupin was "putting in." That one "could certainly talk about some respectable joint investigative successes, in fact." On the first of March five years earlier, Dupin had reported for his first day at work in Brittany following his unceremonious "transfer" from the metropolis—increasingly outlandish tales were developing around the reasons for this transfer.

The topic of the current training course—it had been assigned to him personally as a "bonus" by the prefecture—was "Conducting Systematic and Systemic Conversations in Investigative Situations." Based on the latest results from academic psychological research, of course. Dupin was downright notorious for his unconventional, undoubtedly highly unpsychological conversations during investigations. They were anything but "systematic," or at least not in the usual sense.

But taking part in the course was obligatory and the promotion came with a not very generous but still attractive pay raise. So it was blackmail. This was why Dupin wouldn't have had any problem skipping the introductory meeting today, if only it hadn't fit so nicely with Henri's plans. He had to go to a meeting of restauranteurs near Brest.

The two kings were now waddling toward the three gentoos, at which the gentoos appeared to give each other signals with their flippers. They started to move a moment later and dived into the pool in one daring leap. At breakneck speed, doing crazy turns, but most importantly in a provocatively good mood, they scattered, each of them going in their own direction, before abruptly turning around, darting boldly just past each other, and then disappearing into the waterways to other pools. The little show had lasted less than five seconds. As soon as the birds who looked so clumsy on land—and who had lost their ability to fly over the course of their evolution—were in their element, they turned into by far the most skillful and swift buoyant bodies in the aquatic world. They could get up to speeds of forty kilometers an hour, Dupin knew, streamlined to perfection. They could dive for up to twenty-two minutes on a single breath, reaching up to five hundred meters deep. Dupin read everything there was to read about penguins, and he had these facts and figures at his fingertips. He was particularly impressed by the penguins' sense of direction: they used keen eyes and unrivaled mnemonics to memorize the details of an area many kilometers square under the ice sheet and on the seabed. At any given moment, they knew the location of their nearest hole to the surface—vital to their survival. As it was for a commissaire too, in a way. Just like the ability to maintain a constant body temperature of 30 degrees Celsius at a perceived temperature of a hellish minus 180, during howling storms, weeks of darkness, and without food, a thought that horrified Dupin.

Henri and Dupin had been trying unsuccessfully to keep their eyes fixed on the three gentoo penguins. They were just about to turn away when the three of them shot out of the water behind the two king penguins in one almighty leap. A moment later they were standing sure-footed on the icy ledge—like an operation out of a film. So the gentoo penguins' scattering had been far from random—they had been planning an ingenious operation. Penguins were unrivaled for teamwork.

The two king penguins looked visibly annoyed. For a moment, it seemed as though they were contemplating some aggression: they drew themselves up to their full heights, their bodies ostentatiously tense. The larger one let out a few harsh cries as they did so. But then, just as suddenly, the kings slipped into the water without any fuss, in an almost lazy way, then looked up again and finally swam away.

The ledge where the feedings took place now belonged to the three gentoo penguins.

"They know how it's done!" Dupin said, and smiled to himself.

"In the end, cleverness is strength." Henri laughed.

The penguin colony in Brittany was the largest in Europe, but there was something else much more spectacular than that: these were *French* penguins. They came from official French territory, the Îles Crozet, sub-antarctic islands. And, even more crucially: these islands were, in fact, a Breton archipelago! Due to being discovered by the naval officer Julien-Marie Crozet in the eighteenth century. He came from Morbihan, near the famous gulf. A Breton! These penguins—they were Bretons. Which also meant there was an authentically antarctic Brittany! It might sound

odd to Brittany-beginners—but Dupin had long since stopped being surprised. In recent years he had got to know the South Pacific Brittany, the
Caribbean one, the Mediterranean one, and even the Australian Brittany.
"There's no such thing as *La* Bretagne! There are many Brittanies!" was
one of his assistant Nolwenn's basic philosophies.

"Did you know that penguins can catapult themselves up to two
meters out of the water using explosive acceleration techniques? Weapons
engineers have copied it for firing torpedoes and—" Dupin's raptures
were interrupted by the high-pitched, monotonous beeping of his mobile.
He fished it out reluctantly. Nolwenn.

"Yes?"

"This is completely unacceptable, Monsieur le Commissaire! This will
not do!"

It was serious. That much was clear. Even though Dupin had rarely seen
it in all these years: his assistant—all-around wonder woman and generally calm and composed in even the diciest of situations—was very agitated. She took a deep breath. "The last lighthouse keeper in France is going
to leave his lighthouse in a few days! Then they'll all be controlled by
computer. And they won't be called *phares* anymore, they'll be Dirm-
NAMO!"

"Nolwenn, I—"

"An entire profession is disappearing. Over and done with. There will
be no more lighthouse keepers! Jean-Paul Eymond and Serge Andron
have lived in the lighthouse for thirty-five years, at a height of sixty-seven
and a half meters, enduring the harshest storms with waves where the
foam pounded over the dome so that all you could do was pray. How many
times did they repair the lighthouse in storms like that and risk their lives
to save others! Will the computer be repairing its own faulty cables in heavy
storms soon? The smashed glass?" She took another breath and continued.
"The lighthouse keepers—they are an important historical figure, Monsieur le Commissaire! As I say: this is completely unacceptable!"

As desperately sad as this news indeed seemed, Dupin wasn't sure what

Nolwenn actually expected him to do. That he intervene as a policeman? Arrest someone?

"A murder? Has something happened?" Henri spoke in a hushed voice, making an effort to be discreet, but still noticeably curious. Dupin's face had obviously reflected something of Nolwenn's emotional state or even just shown his bafflement. He played it down quickly with a soothing gesture.

"Are you already in the seminar center, Monsieur le Commissaire?" Nolwenn's voice had completely changed from one second to the next. Thoroughly unsentimental now, purely matter-of-fact. Dupin was used to this. The words "seminar center" conjured up images in his mind of flower-patterned plastic thermoses on brownish Formica tables, with dreadful, lukewarm water for coffee brewed hours before. He'd been under strict medical orders since last week to avoid coffee for a month anyway—and after that to "*drastically* reduce" his "excessive consumption of coffee," in the words of Docteur Garreg, his determined GP. Garreg had (once again) diagnosed an acute inflammation of the gastric mucous membrane—painful gastritis, Type C. And that's how it felt too: painful. But Garreg had not only diagnosed Dupin with gastritis, he had diagnosed more fundamentally a "serious medical caffeine addiction with prototypical symptoms." Which was ridiculous. And the caffeine ban was a nightmarish command for Dupin. It was capable, if he took it completely seriously, of throwing him into a severe crisis psychologically, and that crisis would be a great deal more severe than any nonexistent addiction symptoms. So he had privately agreed on one *petit café* in the morning, and on the rule that a small coffee wasn't a coffee.

"I . . . no, I'm—"

"I can hear the penguins." Nolwenn wasn't saying this ironically. He sometimes had the creeping suspicion she had tagged him with a GPS transmitter. He wouldn't have put it past her.

"Monsieur le Commissaire, the seminar begins in exactly three minutes."

"I know."

"Okay. Riwal still needs to speak to you. It's about the break-in at the bank last night."

"Is there any news?"

During the break-in at a bank branch in a tiny backwater, somebody had not only stolen the money from an ATM but the entire ATM. Which required heavy-duty equipment. And which, all things considered, did not sound like a good idea.

"He and Inspector Kadeg were at the bank earlier. They've just come back."

"Tell him I'll be in touch from the car straightaway."

"Have fun, Monsieur le Commissaire."

Nolwenn hung up. Henri was still looking inquiringly at him.

"Nothing important."

"I've got to go." Henri turned toward the exit.

"Yes, me too." Dupin followed his friend with considerable reluctance. But there was nothing for it. He would have to suffer through this seminar.

* * *

The water was coming from everywhere: from the side, from the right, from the left, from in front, from behind, obliquely from below—sometimes, and rather as if by chance, from above too. This rain was unique: you couldn't see droplets of rain; these were infinite numbers of infinitely thin threads, tentacles that worked their way into clothing, driven by fickle movements of the wind as it constantly changed direction. No clouds were even visible; the sky was a nebulous, dull gray material. A monotone block. And it hung very low. Which Dupin found depressing on principle and which practically never happened in Brittany—it would all go perfectly with the seminar center. On top of this, it smelled of rain; the whole world smelled of rain. Musty.

The thirty meters from the exit of the main building to the entrance kiosk where he and Henri were taking shelter had been enough to leave them literally soaked through to their underwear. In the past, in Paris, rain had simply been rain. It was here in Brittany that Dupin had first experienced what this was: *real* rain—the same was true of the clouds, sky, and light. And of all the elements. Of all the senses. He had learned to distinguish between all the types of rain, just like the Bretons did; like Eskimos with snow. Even worse than threads of rain was heavy, full-on drizzle—*le crachin*—which was even less visible and which you only really noticed once you were dripping wet within seconds. But the most important thing Dupin had learned was—an admittedly abstract realization on days like this—it rained far less than the persistent, mean preconception would have it. He had recently read in a Paris paper: "There are two seasons in Brittany—the short period of long rainfalls and the long period of short rainfalls"; all serious scientific statistics belied these kinds of defamatory claims. In southern Brittany, there was less annual precipitation than on the Côte d'Azur. But something else clinched it: Bretons didn't actually take any notice of rain—a sophisticated attitude, Dupin thought. Not because they were so used to rain, no, but for two significant reasons: it was, after all, *just* the weather, and some things were more important. Life, for example. People would never have dreamed of calling off one of the countless festivals here just because it was raining. What's more, Bretons were resistant to their very cores to having anything dictated to them from "outside." Whether it was centralized Parisian plans or simply the weather. That's how one of the Bretons' most beloved idioms had come about, with which they launched their attacks if other people complained about the rain: *"En Bretagne il ne pleut que sur les cons"*—"In Brittany it only rains on idiots." Going out the door during heavy rain without even noticing it had made it onto the legendary magazine *Bretons'* list of the ten unmistakable traits that mark out Bretons. Along with things like making a big fuss when butter is unsalted; within the first two minutes of meeting someone saying: "Shall we have a drink?"; or as soon as more than twenty people are together, getting Gwenn ha Du out of their pocket—the Breton flag—to make it into a Breton gathering.

Henri and Dupin had parked next to each other, in the first row at the front of the enormous parking lot. Right now, on an ordinary Tuesday at five in the evening in the week before Easter, it was practically deserted.

The loud, steady beeping sounded again.

"Brilliant."

Dupin took his phone out of his jeans pocket, the screen covered in streaks. Hopefully the device was waterproof; he went through at least two mobiles a year on average. This one was just a month old, the commissaire's first smartphone, a small revolution instigated by Nolwenn.

Dupin saw Riwal's number. Of course. But now wasn't a good time. They needed to get going.

"I don't want to be late, Georges," Henri said. He was getting ready for the second sprint of the day, about another twenty meters to the cars. "I have to put in my plea for Breton bacon. I'm absolutely dying to get it through. Nothing else has so much flavor! Especially the bacon from Terre et Paille in Bossulan."

It really didn't make any sense to wait and see if the squalls would die down.

Dupin let his phone ring. The call would be forwarded to Nolwenn. Henri's words had made his mouth water despite the circumstances. Henri's meeting was about the annual ceremonial vote on which foods or dishes would be the theme of this year's "Semaine du Goût," or "Week of Flavor." For a week, four or five foods were celebrated in schools, nurseries, cafeterias, and also restaurants. An homage to the sheer endless sensuous treasures of France.

"Everything starts with bacon!" Clearly Henri still had time to go into raptures. "Brown the bacon in salted butter in a large casserole dish and gently caramelize it with some wild honey: for a Friko Kaol, a Breton cassoulet, the bacon is the most important ingredient—along with smoked sausages, potatoes, onions, and kale from Lorient—hmmm, my instinct tells me I'll have several good ideas."

"I'll be interested in every single one."

The piercing, monotonous beeping again. Another call from Riwal. Dupin hesitated. Maybe he should answer after all.

"Stop by again soon," Henri said, and dashed out into the deluge. "*Salut*, Georges!"

"See you then, Henri!" called Dupin, his phone already at his ear. "This is not a good time, Riwal. We—"

"It's about the break-in at the bank. They've—"

"We'll talk later, Riwal."

"They've accidentally stolen the banking terminal, not the ATM!"

"What?"

"You know how the two machines look the same, you get money at one of them, and at the other you do your banking. There are still no clues to the whereabouts of the perpetrators."

"They've . . . stolen the printer that gives out account statements?"

"It's not just a printer, you—"

"Absurd."

"For example, you can make transfers or—"

"We'll talk about it tomorrow."

"Okay, I just wanted you to know, I—"

There was a loud thud audible on the other end of the line, like a door being flung open with some force, and Riwal abruptly broke off mid-sentence.

For a moment nothing happened, then Dupin could hear a voice, extremely clearly. A commanding tone. Kadeg, his other inspector.

"Hang up immediately. We've got to inform the commissaire straightaway. This instant. It's an emergency." Dupin could hear Kadeg perfectly: "We've got a corpse! Covered in blood. Not far from the Belon, in the grass next to a small parking lot. At the tip of the Pointe de Penquernéo. If you walk along the river from Port Belon to the estuary nearby, via the upper footpath that leads to Rosbras, there's a large field and from the right—" Kadeg's military style had given way to his equally typical long-winded, overly detailed style.

"What?" cried Dupin. "Riwal, what's going on?"

"Kadeg has just rushed in and reported that—"

"Hang up!" Kadeg seemed to be standing directly next to Riwal now and yelling into the handset at the top of his lungs.

"Kadeg, this *is* the boss!" Riwal desperately defended himself. "The boss is already on the line!"

"Riwal, give me Kadeg," Dupin ordered.

A moment later, the other inspector was on the phone.

"Monsieur le Commissaire? Is that you?"

"Who else, Kadeg? What's happened?"

"A man, he's currently—"

"Who is the man? What do we know?"

"Nothing. We don't know anything yet. The call has just come in from a colleague in Riec-sur-Bélon. An old woman was out walking her dog and saw a man lying there in an odd position, not moving. She says there was blood. She got to a restaurant as quickly as she could because it was closer than her house and she called from there. La Coquille, it's—"

"I know La Coquille."

Kadeg let an unnecessary pause develop.

"And?"

"Nothing. That's all we know. Two of our colleagues from Riec are already on their way; they ought to be there in a few minutes."

"I . . . fine. I want a report immediately. I'll leave right now and I'll be there in forty-five minutes. I'll see you both there—you and Riwal. Call me as soon as you know more."

"Will do, Monsieur le Commissaire."

"And tell Nolwenn to send me the exact details of this parking lot where the body is straightaway."

"As I say, up on the cliffs, if—"

Dupin hung up and stood there motionless for a moment.

"Shit."